Let it Be

Let it Be

Irene Chain-Kalinowski

BookWhirl Publishing
PO Box 9031, Green Bay
WI 54308-9031, USA
www.bookwhirl.com

Ordering Information:
Quantity sales. Special discounts are available on quantity purchases by corporations, associations, and others. For details, contact the publisher at the address above.

Printed in the United States of America

Library of Congress Cataloging-in-Publication Data: 2013952356

ISBN-13:   Hardcover   978-1-61856-379-8
             Softcover   978-1-61856-375-0
             Pdf   978-1-61856-376-7
             ePub   978-1-61856-377-4
             Kindle   978-1-61856-378-1

Rev. date: 10/23/2013

Disclaimer
This publication is designed to provide accurate and personal experience information in regard to the subject matter covered. It is sold with the understanding that the author, contributors, publisher are not engaged in rendering counseling or other professional services. If counseling advice or other expert assistance is required, the services of a competent professional person should be sought out.

Dedication

I dedicate this book to all the women who did not find their Prince Charming and for those who did marry Prince Charming, to both you men and women who have loved and lost love and to those who lost love and have found love, and of course to those who have yet to find out what love is. Especially to all the women who have yet to find freedom. You see it is quite true that fairy tales do exist for a great majority; as a matter of fact we have all lived a fairy tale existence in some way or another. Even if only for a few sporadic moments, throughout our lives, we all have stories to share.

It is not until we get old and look back on the lives we have led that we catch up with our old school friends, the people that have entered our lives for whatever reason, and family members and together begin to paint the colors of our past and reflect upon the most unpredictable journey of our lives. I don't think that anyone has moved through life without some kind of heartache. Let It Be is a story of just how life is so unpredictable and how we have loved, lost love, found love, and journeyed into the unknown. How we see the world for what it is and how it is possible to hold on to those memories; how sometimes we need to move on and when we do just that we manage to forgive and use our experiences to bring joy into the lives of others. With a heart as big as the ocean, we can give hope and optimism so our friends can learn to swim in it; and by doing that we can all become the fairy tale.

Chapter One

JANET AND JOHN were simply two kids brought up in a small coal mining town in Yorkshire. They were brother and sister. They were born just fifteen months apart to a normal working-class family. John was the first boy in the family, you would have thought he was destined to be a king as boys took precedence over girls, heaven only knows why. The day Janet was born her mother cried wishing for a second boy. And if you are reading this book and have yet to have children, be careful what you wish for . . .

Janet would follow John everywhere—she would climb trees behind him, she would play soccer with Johnny and his mates on the street and on the playing fields at the nearby parks. She could be so annoying, and sometimes Johnny would find it hard to breathe because Janet adored her big brother so much she would find it hard to let him out of her sight. Johnny would often yell, "Mother, will you please tell her she can't come with me today?" Then as soon as he looked toward his sister's large brown eyes and saw her fluttering black eyelashes, he heard her say, "Oh please, oh please let me come with you." His spoken words would melt away like a piece of butter on a hot potato and when melted would turn to mush. He would take her by the arm and she would join in with his adventures.

It was 1963. When John was around eight years old he decided to pitch up a tent in the backyard—his first ever campout; and although Janet didn't invite herself to spend the night in the tent with the boys, she spent the whole night peeping out of her window listening to the boy's gossip, songs, and laughter. In her room would stand an old record player and playing was a 45-rpm record that she borrowed from her older sisters; and the song playing in the bedroom which blared out of the window was The Beatles' "I Want to Hold Your Hand." Janet had a hairbrush in her hand close to her mouth—the only microphone she could find. "And when I touch you I feel happy inside . . . ." She so much wanted to be having fun with the boys, and despite being seven years old, she knew her brother needed some space, for a few hours at least.

At the crack of dawn, she rushed down to the kitchen and cooked up a breakfast of baked beans and toast then ran out to the tent saying, "Wake up, boys, breakfast is here! Rise and shine!" There was a huge hustle in the small tent, which collapsed as the boys were startled and they were scrambling around in their boxer shorts at the unexpected wake up call. As much as Johnny could have metaphorically killed her, his friend yelled out, "Let it be," and with that he took a deep breath and forgave his sister for crashing his party. They soon re-erected the tent and Janet had joined in the party, a game of cribbage. John had taught his sister how to play cards, and Janet knew how she became to be so good at math in school. At the age of seven, Janet seemed to clearly show how smart and how full of wit she could be. As soon as Janet placed down her five cards, she said, "Fifteen for two, another fifteen for four. Add a pair that makes six and one for the jack makes seven." She would blurt out before the boys had even glanced at their cards.

There wasn't much else to do in 1963; television did not accommodate many programs for children. Janet and John were fortunate to have a television in their home as many of their friends could not afford one at that time. They used to socialize with kids in the local area as very few families owned a motorcar, and they walked to school or relied on public transport. The television showed *Bill and Ben the Flowerpot Men*, *The Horse Named Mr. Ed*, *The Lone Ranger and Tonto with Roy Rodgers*, and *Tom and Jerry*. Actually the kids at that time were so used to occupying themselves you rarely ever saw them sitting in front of the television. They were much happier playing outdoors with the kids on the street. You might argue that kids actually were much happier in that era. They didn't have a lot but they knew how to create their own fun.

Winter snow was very heavy; John's father had made a sledge for them to take to the local park. Janet would jump on the sledge and Johnny would proudly pull his sister along the snow-ridden roads to the local park where they would sledge down the hills and hurl snowballs at one another.

They were inseparable and their brother-sister friendship was not an issue until they became teenagers. As Johnny's testosterone levels begin to rise, he needed to be the macho man at school. He certainly did not want his baby sister clinging to his arm anymore.

John's big break came when he headed to a larger comprehensive school. Janet was twelve months behind him. Janet spent the last year at primary school away from Johnny. He was twelve and she was eleven; she just had to find other interests in her life. She just needed to keep herself very busy, that way she would not feel the emptiness in her heart because when alone she missed those magical moments she used to spend with her brother. She knew Johnny must find his own way in the world, and she just had to learn to let it be. She knew they would never stop loving one another. Their life was just beginning and they each had their own fast lane to follow. Janet knew they would always meet up at some roundabout. They were undoubtedly reaching the crossroads of their life.

The last of the pre-teenage years proved to be quite a challenge for Janet. The only friend she had was her brother; she knew she was different and she had never encountered conversations with the young girls her age. She had never conversed with girls before. She actually looked forward to going to her new school where she could join her brother. She thought it not to be beneficial to start friendships at her current school when she would no longer be with her classmates. She turned to her family and decided that all she needed to do was to spend time with them. Janet's parents were always busy building and renovating homes as well as her father was a coal miner. They had been Polish refugees and settled after the war and they were given the hardest of jobs. They taught Janet that nothing in life comes for free, and they certainly demonstrated how hard you must work to accomplish your dreams. Janet spent the last two years helping her mother clean boarding homes for the refugees who were finding it hard to settle in a new country. Every Thursday was cleaning day and Janet used to go to the boardinghouse with her mother. Janet will never forget the smell and the stench of the alcohol and smoke-ridden rooms. Neither could she understand the irresponsibility where the burns from cigarettes had left large holes in the carpets. Pictures of families that had been long lost during the war were sitting on the glass and bottle cluttered bedside tables. That was the moment she had labeled them as "pigs." How unclean these men were. Yet when she actually met and conversed with these older gentlemen they were well educated and had many stories to tell, they were just very lost as English was not their first language and they could not find work.

Janet's father would help give them odd jobs to do despite their reduced income that they would exchange for work. They would help paint the house for reduced rent. Janet so much wanted to learn about the stories from these older people. They were from a country where her parents came from and where her sisters came from. A land she had only heard of. "I wonder where I would be right now if there had been no war in Europe." She looked around the room with the empty bottles of alcohol and stained sheets. "Certainly not doing this job." Then she thought how heartless she was making judgments on how something looked. An old gentleman was sitting in his armchair and reached out his arms to Janet. "Come and sit with me." Janet was rather shy; she looked at her mother who then took Janet by the hand and introduced her, "This is Gregory, he is a wonderful man and has many stories to tell you. Sit with him for a while and I am sure you will learn something." Gregory talked about life in the villages of Poland, how they were raised on a farm and how they worked very hard and celebrated life. "We were poor but we were very happy." He went to his closet and pulled out a very old accordion. "Come let me teach you something." He played a Polish polka. The music was so full of life that the messed up room Janet was sitting in was completely beautiful. "Music is the soul and you need to appreciate it," he said with a beautiful warm smile.

Janet so much looked forward to her Thursday visits that she wanted to do something for Gregory; and she knew she would need to make some pocket money, so she used her skills. Actually she was born in the Year of the Monkey and for you that are not familiar with the Chinese horoscopes, monkeys are intelligent and hyperactive with a sense of humor. They are practical, curious, mischievous, observant, introvert, and kind. This monkey had to do something to give back to Gregory, so she used her mischievous skills. Firstly, Johnny her brother had become quite lazy when it came to homework and cleaning his room, so Janet approached him and offered to help. "For two pounds I will clean your room and for another two pounds I will help with your homework, and if I do your homework, it dœsn't mean that you'll flunk your exams and upset mother, okay?" Johnny could not refuse. Janet offered to babysit for her sisters and make another two pounds. Then she visited her grandmother who said, "Here is five pounds but don't tell your parents." Then she visited her mother who also said, "Here is five pounds but don't tell your father." And finally, she visited her father who told her, "Here is five pounds and don't tell your mother." Janet smiled. "Gosh, how many secrets do adults keep?" She knew exactly what she was going to do with her pocket money; she used the money to buy new bedsheets, table lamps, and pictures for Gregory.

Slowly week by week she added something to Gregory's room hopefully without her mother noticing. The room was so bright and cheerful and Gregory had an adopted daughter. Janet lit up his life and he had opened Janet's perception of the world. The polkas continued and with that came Janet's confidence with dance, music, and a new understanding for life.

Janet was so inspired with the music that she sat on her father's knees. "Why don't we join the Polish community and go dancing?" she asked. "It is so boring just sitting around at people's homes and what we need is community life." And with that her father agreed to take her to the Polish community house. Every weekend was taken meeting other families. The accordion music filled the hall. The music was playing so loud and so beautifully, Janet's father started to dance with her "Wow, I didn't know how beautifully you dance," she whispered in his ear. For those magical moments she felt like a bride and a first dance with her father. "We always used to dance on the farms in Poland. The war was very harsh and we forgot how to enjoy life again. And now you, my daughter, have inspired me!" He spent every weekend teaching his daughter how to dance. "You don't need to learn steps, you need to feel the music in your soul and then the movements become so natural," he said. "You need to dance like you are floating on air."

That year passed by very quickly, and it was time to join her brother at secondary school. A new uniform and a new chapter to her life was about to unfold. Janet went shopping with her parents to buy the new uniforms. This was 1967. It was the fashion era of Mary Quant and the 1960s fashion of the miniskirt, and with that came the death of stockings and the introduction of pantyhose, pinafore dresses, and knit fabrics. There was a choice of the pinafore grey tunic or the grey skirt with a white shirt and red and grey striped tie. Janet's mother looked at the price tags in the shops and knew that the costs were out of her league, so she opted to use her Polish talents and make Janet's school clothes. Janet was about to learn the art of needlework and the mother and daughter confrontations around fashion. Her mother wanted Janet to wear skirts to just below the knee so as not to entice the boys at her new school, but Janet so much wanted to wear the miniskirt and show off her shapely legs.

"Mother, will you stop being so old-fashioned and prudish with my clothes, I want to show off my legs." Janet's mother clenched her teeth with a pin between her lips and said, "I grew up with young boys and I just don't trust them, I will sew your skirt and it will stop at the knees." Janet did not want to hurt her mother's feelings and she chose to wear the knee-high skirt.

It was her first day at a new school. She was equipped with her down-to-the-knees skirt, pantyhose, a brown satchel, and—wait for it, Janet's eyes were quite weak—she was dressed with large brown-rimmed health service glasses. Her long fine hair was parted down the middle. She actually felt quite smart until she arrived at school. The girls in the class were well equipped with miniskirts, dyed bleached hair, and brightly colored satchels.

Janet knew that she must have been hiding from the fashion world. Suddenly she felt like she wanted to hide in the back row. She felt like a nerd. She walked into the playground and found an empty bench. She became an onlooker while the other girls in the class who were dressed for a fashion parade grouped together in a faraway corner. "What is she wearing and look at those glasses! Eyeball! Eyeball!" They shouted at her. Janet just wanted to run away. She closed her eyes and put herself into a space where polka music and dance flowed around in her head; she just needed to hold on to her own happy space. "Let it be," she whispered to herself. "You'll get through it like Gregory got through the war," she told herself. Janet's welcome into the world of young women gave her a first taste of school ground cruelty and egotistical young women.

Janet opened her eyes and across the playground was her brother Johnny, grouped with his friends. She ran over to him and gave him a hug. Johnny had become the school's macho star. He pushed her away saying, "Go away, little sis, not right now." She felt so totally rejected that she ran to the nearest restrooms, threw down her satchel, sat down with her hands over her face, and cried till the tears were endless. She hated everyone and she hated her new school. "How could growing up be so cruel?" she asked herself. She walked over to the bathroom mirror; her brown rimmed glasses magnified her red eyes. "I feel so horribly empty, and my stomach aches." She felt a wet patch on her skirt, rubbed it and there was a smudge of blood on her finger. "What the . . ."

With that came a voice from behind saying, "I think you'll need one of these!" Janet turned around and there was this young girl with jet-black hair bobbed and parted down the middle waving an oblong shaped piece of cotton. "No one warned me either," she said. Janet looked at this young girl as if she was a little loopy. "It's called a period." The girl handed over the cotton pad. "Go to the loo, and put this down there."

"It won't flush away," Janet replied.

"No, not down the toilet, silly. Down in your pants to catch the red drips."

Janet did exactly what she was told. She came out of the toilet with her hands over the back of her skirt covering the red patch. "Hi, my name is Maggs and I'm from Scotland. We moved down here last week." Maggs pulled a grey scarf out of her bag. "This always comes in handy." She took the scarf and wrapped it around Janet's minute waist. Janet felt so relieved, and she had found a new friend with an accent, and a scarf that covered her accidental patch. "Here's my address. Come around and we will catch up after school." Maggs had invited Janet to her home. The girls' homes were on the same road just thirty houses away on the small terraced street. Janet could never understand why it was called a street when actually it was a very steep hill that seemed to take forever to reach the top.

<h1 style="text-align:center">Chapter Two</h1>

MAGGS AND JANET were inseparable for the next four years. Janet used to visit Maggs home most evenings; she loved the Scottish culture and hospitality. Maggs' mother used to enjoy a little tipple at the weekends and although the girls never touched a drop, they used to join in the family evenings in front of the dartboard. Janet learned how to throw the darts and she will never forget her first attempt—she landed the dart through a picture of Edinburgh Castle. That was about a yard away from the dartboard.

Maggs had an older sister who was courting at the time. June and her boyfriend would join in the games—a round of cricket on the dartboard. It was a game where teams played batting and fielding. They would have to knock out one another by hitting the numbers around the board. It was always a double to start and trying to hit a double could take most of the evening. They would then gather round the table as a family and play cards. Janet taught them how to play cribbage and Maggs and her mother taught Janet how to play gin rummy. At the end of the evening, June and her young man would smooch together on the couch listening to the latest hits of The Beatles. It was 1970 and "Let It Be" headed the charts. That became Janet's favorite song, as she remembered that they were the words her brother used to shout whenever she annoyed him. "Hey Jude" was Maggs's favorite and sometimes the girls would mimic singing both songs at the same time. They had a competition as to who could sing the loudest. They found a bottle of cider behind the couch and, as teenagers would do, they drank one glass that was enough to sing so loud that Maggs's mother came hustling down the stairs in her tartan nightgown. Her head had tight rollers that were covered by a red scarf. "I'll take that, ladies." She instantly grabbed the bottle of cider and whisked it away to a place where the girls could do no harm. "Time for bed you two!" Maggs's mother ushered them upstairs.

At the age of fourteen the girls were invited to Scotland to meet Maggs's grandmother. A small coal mining town called Cowdenbeath in Fife. That is all Janet needed to know. She went home to find her father's road map plotted a pencil mark on the town. She plotted down the nearby places such as Perth and Kinross, the Ochil Hills, Edinburgh, Dunfermline, and St. Andrews. Janet was excited as if was to be her first time on a train. It was Easter, and Maggs had prepared Janet for the Easter egg roll down the hills of Scotland. The girls spent a whole week painting eggs.

Janet had saved her pocket money and the girls decided to do a last minute shopping. There were not many stores to choose from at that time, both girls were from a working-class family and where better to buy affordable clothes than C&A. Denim jeans, acrylic machine knitted jumpers, hot pants, and maxi coats; not forgetting the patent leather laced shoes with a high square heel. Their bags were packed and they were ready to go. The girls were dressed in blue hot pants, panty hose, jumpers, and their rust-colored maxi coats. Janet's father had taken them to the train station. He made sure the girls were on the train and they set off on their journey to Scotland. The girls sat face to face parted by a small table on the train. Janet couldn't help but notice the reflection of her face in the window. Her long brown fine hair looked very straggly, and how she hated her fine hair which parted from the middle of her forehead and seemed to make her face much larger and rounder. She couldn't help but notice the teenage acne sitting on her forehead. Inwardly she did not like what she was looking at. How she had wanted curls and blond hair. "You are so vain," Maggs pointed out. "You are very beautiful and you don't realize it. You need to stop being so sensitive because your sensitivity will kill you." Janet smiled and turned away from the window. She put her head against it and slept for most of the journey.

They eventually arrived at their destination and they were to wait in the coffee shop at the station until her aunt came to collect them. They found a very small corner in the coffee shop it was very dull and clouded with smoke. Almost everyone in the coffee shop clenched the local newspaper holding a cigarette. Janet leaned back in her chair and with that her maxi coat opened and her long shapely legs could not be missed. A young man across from the next table dropped his cigarette and turned around to look at what Janet was showing off. "Nice legs, shame about the knees!" Janet's face flushed red. She jumped up and covered her legs, grasped her handbag and left the cafe. Maggs followed directly behind her. "Why are you so sensitive about everything? You have to learn to stand up for yourself. You have to learn to appreciate yourself, you have to let it be!"

The girls spent four days in Scotland and Janet never wore her hot pants again. That night they walked to the town center and stopped by the local fish and chips shop. There were two young men in the queue for fish and chips. Both were wearing flared corduroy trousers that folded over the tips of their muddy shoes. Their snug-fitting Shetland sweaters boasted the tail ends of their checkered shirts which were hanging down to below the hips. They couldn't get close enough to the two girls who were strangers in town. "You first, ladies." The boys ushered the girls forward to the counter. Maggs didn't ask Janet what she wanted. She thought she would surprise her. "Wait outside and I'll bring a surprise." That she did. She handed the tray of what looked like fish and chips to Janet. Janet took a large bite. "This is amazing, I was expecting fish."

"It's haggis made from sheep's intestines," Maggs explained. Maggs was expecting Janet to throw a tantrum or something but Janet said, "We have a dish in Poland that's made from pig's blood and buckwheat. I love that and this is just as tasty."

At that time the boys had also left the chip shop. The girls were leaning against the wall and the boys decided to join them. "I'm Billy and this is Jimmy." Janet tried to hold on to her sense of humor, but she couldn't help but blurt out, "And what other names would you expect to find in Scotland?" Maggs gave Janet a prod. "Will you stop doing that?" she whispered in Janet's ear. Billy had the hots for Maggs, and Jimmy and Janet were kind of thrust together. They invited the girls to the Easter Egg Rolling on the Ochil Hills on Easter Sunday. "Of course we will be there," Maggs was definitely into Billy.

They arranged to meet at the chip shop the next evening. They spent the time walking and chatting about school and subjects and the latest music. Janet found the conversation to be boring, so she decided to talk about dancing the polka and the stories that Gregory had shared with her. "Wow, you are amazing and you know so much." Jimmy then took Janet by the hand. This was certainly not what she had expected and for the first time this monkey felt very shy. Her brother and her mother's words echoed around her head.

Be careful with the boys and don't bring back any trouble.

Janet knew she would be too scared to do that.

The girls were excited and they dressed in their denims and thick jumpers. "To the hills, to the hills." Maggs and Janet headed off to the hills on a loaned pair of push bikes. The Easter eggs were well packed in the rear baskets. They had no trouble coasting down the country roads. The boys were waiting at the foot of the hill. The foursome set off for what should have been a long hike up the hills. Janet was mesmerized by the blankets of purple heather on the hillside. What she did not expect was the blistery cold winds of Scotland. They had stopped halfway and Jimmy put his arms around her to shield her from the wind. They advanced a few hundred yards. "Here's the spot. Let's have the eggs then," Jimmy pointed to the basket. They divided the colored eggs between them and hurled them down the hill. "On, on," Maggs called as they followed the eggs down the hill. Maggs was the first to reach the winning egg. "I win!" yelled Maggs as she reached the egg that had rolled the farthest, there wasn't much of the egg left as it had crashed against the rocks.

"How do you know that it's yours?" Janet asked. "There is no paint left on it."

"Oh, I never lose," Maggs laughed as she replied.

"Cheat, cheat, how we love a cheat." Billy remarked. The wind was howling by this time. The boys took the opportunity to snug up to the girls. Jimmy turned to Janet her pulled her close to him. "Close your eyes," he said. "I have a surprise for you." And with that he pulled her closer and kissed her. On her first kiss, she did not move. *I should be flying and I feel numb and cold,* were her thoughts as Jimmy let go and looked at Janet hoping for her to say it was wonderful. Janet licked her lips, they were dribbling wet. She pulled out her handkerchief and wiped her mouth.

"That was surprisingly wet," she said.

"I can do better," Jimmy replied, and with that he pulled her even closer and gave her a Scottish snog. Janet felt warmer as his body snug to hers but she felt really unmoved and certainly it was not the Cinderella kiss she had seen at the movies. However, she would never forget the first kiss. She was thirteen and she would remember Scotland, the eggs, Jimmy, and the wet kiss for the rest of her life.

The girls had returned to Yorkshire they really had a great time. Janet got over her pity about the knees escapade and returned to wearing her hot pants. She was becoming an ardent follower of fashion and would spend the weekends at C&A looking at the new arrivals in the store. Janet knew Maggs loved music, and this time she spent her pocket money buying Maggs a present for her fifteenth birthday. Janet decided to surprise Maggs, so she arranged to meet Maggs by the old playing fields at the local park. That is where they used to go walking and where they would watch the boys play soccer at the weekends. Janet had packed a small cake in a box with some candles. She carried another box with the surprise birthday present in it.

"What on earth are you going to do with two boxes?" Maggs asked.

"One stops me from falling over, I need to keep a life's balance," Janet replied. They walked to the end of the field where the boys were in the midst of a soccer game. "Why is it most soccer players have bandy-shaped legs?" Janet asked

"That's easy," Maggs replied. "They have to be bent so they can bend the ball into the net."

"Ha-ha very funny," Janet laughed.

"Here we are, time for lunch," Janet said. She opened the small case and placed a blanket on the ground. The girls sat down to start their picnic. "Now close your eyes," Janet said to Maggs. Maggs then rolled her eyes and said with a somewhat distrustful grin, "Why, you are not going to kiss me I hope."

"Don't be silly, I'm still recovering from my wet episode in Scotland, you know Jimmy, anyway I don't kiss girls, so please close your eyes." Janet insisted that Maggs should close her eyes. Maggs closed her eyes and Janet placed the other box in Maggs's hands. "Open this."

Maggs fumbled with the box, opened her eyes and there was a tape recorder. "It's the latest." Janet was so pleased with her gift and Maggs was so excited with her new present. "Now press this button and play it," Janet said as she turned up the volume. Rod Stewart's voice echoed across the playing fields singing "Maggie May." The boys across the field had stopped for a break. "Oh no, put a bloody plug over it!" yelled a tall young man who ran over to see if he could turn down the volume. Maggs was delighted with her present and loved the sound of Rod's husky voice, but then she became absorbed by the good-looking young man trying to turn down the music.

"Excuse me, it happens to be a song about me, my name, and it is my birthday you bum!" Maggs pushed the young man onto the ground and fell on top of him, and the tape recorder landed on his forehead. Rod's husky voice slurred as the tape snapped. "I am so so sorry," Maggs grabbed a cold bottle of water from the picnic box and threw it over his head. She then grabbed the blanket and tried drying his forehead.

"Will you please stop attacking me?" The young man was very annoyed. Maggs was mesmerized by this hunk of a man with his mouse brown colored hair and the largest of blue eyes and his long brown fluttering eyelashes. He was perfect and she was smitten by him. "Now that you have finished beating me my name is Paul, I know who you are as you live three doors away from my house. I know your sister—she is getting married to a friend of mine. I will be at the wedding in two weeks' time and hope to see you there. Happy birthday, by the way." With that he ran off to rejoin his soccer game. For two weekends Janet had to accompany Maggs down to the soccer field so she could get close to the boy next door. Maggs would get up at 6:00 a.m. and watch him take his bike to work; he worked at the nearby coal mines. She was besotted by him. Two weeks passed by very quickly. Maggs and Janet were to be bridesmaids at her sister's wedding. They were looking forward to Maggs's sister's big day. Maggs had chosen the dresses, royal blue halter neck dresses, with a high banded waistline and A-line skirts that reached to the floor.

The wedding was as normal a wedding could be, the girls looked stunning with their long hair in a Scottish bun with side ringlets skimming their cheeks. Both girls had colored their hair black. They looked like sisters except Janet had large brown eyes and Maggs had large blue eyes.

The girls were dancing most of the evening. Janet was showing off her waltzes. She wasn't very good at the modern dancing as she needed a partner to dance with. The music filled the hall. Janet always had an ear for music, and most importantly she would listen to the words. "Why do they play 'I Will Survive' at weddings when the couples just got married. They are not supposed to be walking out of the door." She had been allowed a couple glasses of champagne which was clearly bringing her wit out of the closet. "You are so funny at times," Maggs replied. They were very happy Chubby Checker was playing "Let's Twist Again." Maggs was showing Janet how to do the twist and afterward the bride and groom danced to "Third Finger Left Hand." Then as they left for the honeymoon, the bride's flowers were tossed into the air. Maggs pushed Janet to one side and grabbed the flowers. "They are mine and it's my turn." Janet could not understand what Maggs was thinking about. Paul had noticed Maggs vault into the air and he came to join in the flower landing celebrations. Maggs would not leave his side; they just seemed to get together. They did have the same eye color. They danced and they danced. Janet was happy talking to other guests; she had been mingling and socializing with just about everyone. Paul had danced with Maggs for most of the evening but he didn't want to leave Janet out of the party so he asked her for a dance. Paul had a waltz with Janet. Janet was talking to Paul about how well suited she thought he and Maggs were and she was hoping that he and Maggs would stay together. They talked about her brother Johnny who was a friend of Paul's. "I was one of the boys in the tent of your backyard, where you killed us playing cards way back when you were much smaller. How beautiful you have grown and that wicked sense of humor has become even wicked!" Janet knew exactly what he was saying. "I'd better get back to Maggs and don't worry I will take care of her," Paul reassured Janet. And with that he gave her a small peck of a kiss on the forehead and left to find Maggs.

Janet decided it was time for home so she left for the car park and she had called a cab. While waiting in the car park, she heard a stomping of feet coming from behind her. Maggs had downed a couple of glasses of champagne. She looked very angry. Janet turned around and as soon as she did Maggs gave a right fisted punch to her left eye. "I saw you dancing with Paul! How dare you try to take him from me!" Janet fell to the ground and before she could say anything, Maggs was gone. Janet jumped into the cab and made her way home. The first thing she did was open the freezer cupboard, grab a piece of frozen steak, and slap that cold piece of meat over her eye. She went straight to bed. That night she had hardly slept and could not understand why her best friend had become so jealous of her for no reason. *Why did she get so jealous? I did nothing but wish Paul all the best, I told them they were suited.* The tears rolled down her face and she endured the heartache of losing a best friend about a boy.

Janet never saw Maggs again. Maggs married later that year. Maggs wanted a family and wanted to settle down. She wanted Paul and nothing was going to get in her way, even if it meant losing her best friend. Janet really had to get her head around what Maggs could have been thinking about, and she had to get over the heartache of losing a friend. She learned that she was dispensable and that good things don't last forever. Janet felt so alone and after the split and she vowed she would never do that to anyone. No boy or man would come in between a friendship. She was just beginning to learn about life, the meaning of friendship, and how jealousy can damage a relationship. "Why do people get jealous?" she asked herself. "I have yet to find out."

Janet was lying snug in her bed when she heard the door open. "Hi, you didn't make it for breakfast, so I popped in to see if you were okay." It was her father's voice. Janet sat up to greet her father and as she moved, she had forgotten about the right hook she had received to her left eye. "Why is there a dried piece of cow meat on your cupboard, and why dœs your eye look the same color as the piece of cow meat?" her father asked rather sarcastically. With that Janet burst into tears. Her father gave her a warm hug, and Janet told him everything that had happened in the car park after the wedding. "Goodness, you are so young and still have so much to learn. You have to *let it be.* You must remember that some people will come into your life for a reason, a season, or a lifetime. You met your season and I am your lifetime," he smiled and with that she knew she was so lucky that she had not only a father but he was her best friend.

Janet was in her final year at school and she was to decide what she wanted to do and where she wanted to be. That was a tough decision to make for a sixteen-year-old. She had absolutely no idea about what she wanted despite knowing what she did not want. Janet knew there was a shortage jobs in 1971. Many of her school classmates were going to college, and she was so undecided about what to do. She actually hated her last year at school and the breakup with her best friend did not help as she did not focus too well on her studies. She knew her father would support any decision that she would make. They had a trusting relationship—one that was very open. "Why don't you try applying for a job and if don't get one—or if you do get one and don't like it—you can always study. I will always support you. You need to find your own way and I know you will as you are smart and I have every confidence in you." And with that Janet decided to go job hunting.

Janet was more than well equipped to find some work. She was good-looking with an outgoing personality, she knew what her roles and responsibilities would be, and she had remembered the stories that she shared with Gregory. She was already supporting her father with paperwork as he had little comprehension of the English language. She was fluent in two languages—German, taught to her by her grandmother, and English of course. Her father did not want to teach her Polish. There were many reasons for that. He knew only too well that for Janet to survive in a very racist society, she would need to be 100percent British. Polish blood with a British accent. So to everyone she was just a likeable, outgoing Yorkshire lass and that's the way her father wanted her to be.

Janet had applied for her first job as an office junior working for a small company that sold pots and pans from Finland. It was a company that sold produce via a party plan. Women would host home parties and sell the products. To get to the interview took two bus rides; it was a very wet and windy day. Her hair was somewhat windswept when she arrived for the interview. She was dressed by her mother in a neat knee length corporate skirt, a tidy white shirt, and blue jacket. She was extremely nervous and so much wanted to show her parents that she could survive in the big world. She quickly took the brush out her bag and straightened her hair without the use of a mirror.

It wasn't really an interview as Janet was escorted around the warehouse and office by a rather grey-haired man who looked as though he'd just come out of the rain. "The job is yours. You will earn £6.00 per week." Janet took a deep breath in as she had made more money than that when she collected money from her parents, babysitting and helping her brother with homework. However it was her first job, and she knew there were a lot of job shortages at that time. She knew she had to start somewhere and it seemed as though this company couldn't wait to get her started; they had offered her the job and she took it.

Janet was so excited about her new job and couldn't wait to break the news to her parents. They celebrated with a good Polish-style meal, and her father gave her a small glass of Polish vodka. It was custom to celebrate that way and he thought she was old enough to drink socially and responsibly. He didn't need to remind her about the abuse of alcohol because he knew she had seen the results from the overuse of alcohol when she had been cleaning the rooms with her mother.

It was Janet's first day in the office and there was a simple orientation to the roles of being an office junior. She met a young woman just one year older who had been doing the job for one year; she was leaving to take up studies at a university. Janet was keen to get started. She could not help but notice how the office was so cluttered with papers and the desks appeared to be so untidy. She was introduced to everyone in the office. They made her feel extremely welcome. Her first job was to file all of the orders; she just filed hundreds of sheets of orders in alphabetical order. She couldn't possibly have forgotten her alphabet. That part was so tedious. Every morning for a week she would arrive at 9:00a.m. and file papers in the appropriate filing cabinets from A-Z. The drawers were bulging and overflowing with filed papers. The flimsy sheets of paper invoices were very crumpled because of how they had been crammed into the drawers. Janet still kept cramming the papers into the drawers because the company refused to buy any more filing cabinets.

Paula, the young woman who had shown her around was very kind to Janet. "There is a group playing at the Fiesta Club in Sheffield—The Four Tops. Would you like to come with me? My friend works there and I have two tickets, normally they cost an arm and a leg," Paula asked. Wow, this was her first big adventure into the nightlife. Realistically you needed to be eighteen to get entry into the clubs; Janet knew that there was nothing that a bit of makeup couldn't do to fix that. She knew she could use her monkey skills to persuade her father to let his daughter go to the ball.

Janet couldn't wait until the weekend. She knew she would have to look much older, so she returned to the C&A shop. On that shopping expedition she found a beautiful royal blue maxi dress with a sweetheart neckline that showed her cleavage. Her mother had loaned her a string of pearls. There was one thing that Janet was endowed with—it was her breasts and the pearls emphasized what she had. She had her father's permission. He trusted her and she promised to be a lady. He knew she was only sixteen but he remembered his own youth only too well and with him being so strict with Janet's older sisters. They were married and pregnant by the time they were seventeen.

On the evening of the performance, Janet's father drove his daughter and Paula to Sheffield. Janet looked so breathtaking. She was very shapely; she had all of her curves in the right places. "You look like a million dollars," he said and that was what her father feared about the most. He didn't want her to be catching trains and buses late at night. "Have a great night and I will be waiting here outside at 1:30a.m." Janet gave him a kiss on the cheek and with that she lifted her dress, and she felt like she was Cinderella going to the ball.

Janet ran up the concrete steps to the club, almost tripping on the hem of her skirt. "Careful!" Paula yelled as she grabbed a hold of Janet's dress and pulled her back. That just saved Janet from landing on her face. "Oh, I'm okay. On, on we need to dance." The entrance to the club was quite grand and they paid their 10p to hang their coats. Both girls looked stunning. "Watch out for those boys you two," smiled the lady handing out the coat tickets. "I don't think you'll be dancing by yourselves all night and that's for sure." The girls beamed with confidence and made their way to their seats. The entrance was on quite a high level and the rows of tables with small orange lamps descended down toward the dance floor level. The stage was huge and was lit with dazzling colored lights and glittery curtains. They found their seats one step above the dance floor. The waitress came to the tables taking orders for food and drinks. They were dressed in black miniskirts and white aprons. They were all very pretty and had such shapely legs. "Two glasses of Coke and two scampi and chips," Paula had ordered. The girls sat chatting as they were eyeing up the boys on the nearby tables. They men were sitting in groups around the tables. They were wearing cravat ties; they had huge wing-shaped collars on their jackets and their shirts. Their shirts were neatly tucked away behind large buckled belts that were strapped tight to their flared trousers. "Wow, what a choice!" Janet couldn't take her eyes away from the local talent. The waitress arrived with the two glasses of Coke and the food. Paula seemed to shuffle around in her bag. "It's all clear so pass me your Coke," Paula said to Janet as she pulled up a bottle of water out of her bag and poured some of it into the Coke. "Why are you diluting my Coke?" Janet asked. "Shush, be quiet or they will hear you, it is not water—taste it." Janet tasted it and she actually liked the taste. Paula had added a little vodka. "This will get us in the mood." Paula laughed and raised her glass. "Bottoms up," she said.

The DJ had started to play the music; the girls danced to just about every record. They would dance and sing the words out loud to the O'Jays' "Love Train."

"What they do, they smile in your face every time they want to take your place, the backstabbers." They would send their voices to the nearby group of girls. It just seemed so natural for girls to be competitive. Janet couldn't understand the competitiveness between girls as the young men outnumbered the young women by 2:1.

At ten in the evening, it was showtime with the Four Tops live on stage. Janet was mesmerized by their symmetrical and synchronized moves. They played many of their well-known hits "Reach Out I'll Be There,""I Can't Help Myself (Sugar Pie Honey Bunch),""It's the Same Old Song," and "River Deep Mountain High." They performed on that stage for an hour and a half. The girls danced most of the night. At the near end of the performance Paula jumped up from her seat saying, "Come with me." She took Janet by the hand and they headed backstage. The Four Tops were making their exit. "This is Denny, my best friend. She arranged for this, and by the way, happy birthday." Paula was leading Janet to the stage. "They are heading this way." Janet jumped up and down with excitement. Standing right in front of her was Levi, Lawrence, Duke, and Obie. The famous stars shook hands with Janet and Paula. Janet felt as if she was flying in the air. "I met somebody famous!" she exclaimed.

With that the girls left and it was time to meet their ride home. Janet had no interest in the young men that night, she was so mesmerized by the music and that she had celebrated her birthday shaking hands with famous people.

That year they visited the fiesta at least four times, and each time Paula took Janet behind the scenes where she shook hands with The Drifters, Ike and Tina Turner, and many more famous people. Janet remembered this as the most fun year of her life. "Life just couldn't get any better, could it?" Janet was so happy. She continued to go to work at the same small office; Paula had moved on to study in Nottingham. She made sure her friend had other friends and promised they would always keep in touch. The small office was becoming tedious for Janet. Paula had left and the girls would always pick faults with Janet. Janet would work late hours and she was promoted in her position to becoming a ledger clerk. There she learned accounting and how to balance the books and do some stocktaking in the warehouse. The other office girls envied the way Janet was so organized with her job. They would leave notes, ugly notes like, "You didn't add that up right, bitch!" Janet was not coping with the sensitive remarks. She arrived home late one evening, and her father was sitting in the lounge watching the latest news on the TV. "What is a matter with you, you look very depressed." Janet sat down in her father's arms ant talked about how cruel the girls had been in the office. "I really don't want to go tomorrow." Her father looked into her large brown eyes and said, "Well, don't go. I will call in sick for you. You need to *let it be*. You don't have to put up with that nonsense at all." That he did and the next day he brought home a newspaper, and he started to help his daughter hunt for jobs. This time it was a large steel company, another office. Janet called that office and they interviewed her the very next day. Her father had taken a day's holiday and he drove her to the interview. She was dressed for the occasion. It was a quick interview and she took the job—another nine-five position. Every morning she would start the day filing invoices, the only difference with this job was that she was not filing alphabetically; she was filing by numbers. She soon gained recognition in that company and was promoted to team leader within six months. Janet found the job to be so repetitive and tedious. She knew there would be more to life than filing papers and splitting invoices; she knew somebody had to do it, but she knew office work was not for her. There were a few girls working in the office; men were the main workforce in that office. She found it so much easier to relate to her male colleagues than the females in the office. She could converse easily with the men. After work she would meet with boys, she took up sports, and she was able to give them a good game of squash, badminton, and tennis. She would often go to the soccer games with them. She looked forward to every Saturday afternoon with her glass of sarsaparilla and a good game of soccer.

<h1 style="text-align:center">Chapter Three</h1>

THE FOLLOWING YEAR passed by very quickly. Janet had been promoted to office typist and had undertaken a typing course at the local college. There she met some new friends. They became very close for the next eighteen months.

It was her seventeenth birthday and her parents and family had booked a week away at the Seaside Resort in Lincolnshire. Janet thought she was going to spend her birthday alone. It was a Saturday night and she did not want to spend her birthday alone. She called her friends and she decided to meet them at the local pub in the city. They asked her to visit the dance hall across the road. The dance club was above the local cinema, and there was no bar. The girls met in the local pub. They used to mix a cider with a sherry—one of those and Janet could dance all night. They had two drinks in the pub and the crowds in the pub sang happy birthday to Janet. Janet felt very warm inside and she had a very happy, lively feeling thanks to the sherry. They left the pub and walked over to the dance hall. There were no dancing lessons here, but the guys used to teach the girls to dance. She had been to the bathroom to retouch her makeup, and there she had drunk a small Cherry-B to give her courage to dance so she could be the center of attention when she felt comfortable. On the way out she stumbled over, not from the drink but she had tripped over her long skirt. She always seemed to be falling to the ground. She needed to be rescued. She was just about to get off the ground when a someone's long arm reached out to her. She looked up and there was a gentleman much older than she was, by at least five years. His brown wavy hair fell below his shoulders. A caramel tweed Jacket and a pair of dark brown corduroy

33

flared trousers. He was very tall around 6 feet. She was tiny, around 5'2". "Do you want to dance?" he asked as he towered over her. Janet looked up at him. "As it is my birthday and I have nothing better to do then why not." It was a slow record; Michæl Jackson's "Got to Be There" was playing. He took Janet by the hand; she thought she was going to waltz and so held out her hands. "Oh no, that's old-fashioned. We do the smooch." He gently placed her hands on his shoulders and placed his arms around her shoulders and they smooched silently. Janet did not know what to say, but silence was just what was needed. He whispered in her ears, "My name is Dave by the way." He was so good-looking, and had the face of a man that was rough shaven—not the babyish boy look. She was dancing with a man. Dave had introduced his self as a school teacher. They actually dated for several months. No sex of course; she was from a good catholic family where girls don't have sex before they get married. David was very patient; he would meet her every weekend with beautiful red roses, cards, and gifts. He always wanted to make her happy. He was getting very serious about Janet, but she was afraid, she knew she did not want to marry or settle and she had no magical feelings about the romance. Her older sister was going through a very bad time with her marriage and Janet did not want to follow her footsteps. She knew she would have to break off from Dave. How she could do that without hurting him? How do you break a relationship without hurting someone? She remembered how hurt she felt when Maggs dumped her. She promised she would never hurt anyone. She spent a few weeks of sleepless nights wondering how she could not hurt Dave. She would practice talking to herself, trying to mimic the right moment to say how she felt. The problem was the right moment never came. And the weeks dragged along. She felt so guilty every time he brought her flowers, and she stopped holding him so tight. There came a time when he sensed there was something wrong.

Janet knew she was being very cowardice in her behavior. She would make excuses as to why they should not meet and then she would spend the whole night they did not meet thinking how hurtful she was being. She was not ready for commitment. He adored her and she had to let go somehow. She hated herself so much, and she had lost the sense of fun and laughter. She knew she was becoming a bore. Life was boring—the same dance every week, the same conversation, the same food. She had to do something. Dave was everything she knew her mother would have wished for her. He had a good profession; he was stable, and good looking. That wasn't enough for Janet. She knew she still had a life to lead and there were many things she still had to do. She was learning how difficult it was to confront someone. Then one night she made excuses not to see Dave. "I have to stay with Grandma, she is not well and she needs me." That was so untrue. Instead she opened her father's writing cabinet and pulled out his fine ink pen. She started to write "Dear Dave" but that was it. She had a total mind block; she could not express the way she truly felt. She poured a glass of her father's homemade apple wine. One glass and she started to cry—the teardrops fell upon the paper and slowly the words came together. First she wrote about all of the wonderful attributes Dave held: kindness, gentleness, and so on. Then came what must be the most used word in the dictionary.

But I am just not ready, I wanted to tell you so many times and I could not find the words. I did not want to hurt you, but I am going to hurt you and I know I must live with that. It is the wrong time for me and the right time for you. Right now I am hurting you—but it is better this way. I am so, so sorry, I want to tell you

I love you but I can't because I don't know what love is. I know it is out there and I know you love me but I just can't love you back. We have to *let it be.* I am so, so sorry. Janet.

And with that the teardrops smeared some of the ink. She read the letter three times and eventually folded it and placed it in an envelope. She did not go to the dance that weekend but she sent her brother with the letter. "Why do I feel so sick inside? He is the one that is heartbroken and yet my heart aches because I know I have broken his."

She spent two whole weeks at home and visiting her sisters. Baking cakes with her mother and learning to cook with her grandmother. She then picked up the courage to go to the dance hall. Dave was sitting alone in the corner. Janet did not go over; she mingled with her friends and danced with the other young men. She would jive to the music of T.Rex, dance the "Wooly Bully," and would try to show Dave she was getting on with her life. The truth was that it just didn't work. Dave had asked the DJ to play the Chi-Lites song "Have You Seen Her." It went something like this: *Oh, I see her face everywhere I go, on the street and even at the movie show, have you seen her.* Johnny, Janet's brother, had turned up to the dance and he noticed how stupid Janet was being. She had a few drinks and was flirting with everyone. That was not the sister he knew. He pulled her to one side and said, "You have to stop this nonsense. You are being cruel and that is just not you." He took her by the hand, pulled her over toward Dave, and sat her down next to him. "Now don't move until you sort it." He placed Dave's hand in hers, and walked away. Dave looked at Janet; she looked into his eyes and said, "I am so sorry." They both released the very same words at the very same time. Janet truly apologized, "I know someday you will find someone wonderful, more wonderful than me, and I will be more than happy to hear you have moved on. I want to always be your best friend, and we will always be good friends if you will let it happen." And with that Dave gave her a huge hug. He took her by the hand and they smooched for the last time. There was silence and at the end Dave gave her another hug and left the hall. She never saw Dave again. She was grateful that her brother had given her a little tough love, and she would always remember just how much he cared for her.

Dave did meet someone wonderful; Janet heard that he had married later that year. She was very disappointed that Dave decided not to continue the friendship, but she knew it was for the best and she learned to *let it be.*

Janet had resigned from her boring nine-five job in the office; she knew she was destined to do much more than file, type, and balance books. She hated the daily routine and rituals. She could predict what was going to happen every day for the whole eight hours. The job was a monotonous schedule of calendar events. She simply wanted a career where she could help people and make a difference. She knew she needed to move on and that she did. She had applied to start her nurse training, but she was too young. She was accepted to do six months in a pre-nursing course where she would have to take up extra studies at a technical college. She was looking forward to meeting new friends.

Janet returned home from school; she was tired as she had taken two bus rides home and walked a fair distance from her bus stop. She dashed in to the house through the back door and into the kitchen and said, "How I hate taking buses in this cold, wet, windy weather. I had a terrible day. I was taking care of this old man and I dropped his dentures in the toilet—how stupid was that? I wonder if I will ever get through this . . . Damn it, just damn it!" She threw down her bags. Her father moved to one side and standing in front of her was this young man; he was so tall around 6 feet, he had jet-black wavy hair that reached to his chin, and the deepest blue amethyst eyes. There was a dimple around his chin and he had the most amazing white smile. He was the son of a friend of Janet's father. Her father had been fixing a window for them. Janet felt so embarrassed; there was nowhere to hide, she could not take her eyes away from who was standing in front of her, and she felt she had been raised to the ceiling floating on air. "Right then," she said as she ran her finger through her hair and flicked her long hair backward. "Must dash—no time to stand around. . . Have to go . . ." And with that she walked away to her room. She threw herself backward over her bed. "Oh my god, I think I am going to marry him." She couldn't believe she had said those words. "What am I doing?" she started to talk to herself.

That evening she sat beside her desk and started to write her essays—the dreaded homework. She could not focus upon what she was trying to learn; she could only mirror the man she had seen earlier in the day. She turned to her record player and put on the music from *Calamity Jane* titled "It's Harry I'm Planning to Marry." She didn't like the name Harry but she wouldn't care what his name was. He was the one!

The next day she went to college and she made up an excuse for forgetting her homework; she couldn't possibly let on that it was because she had hit an emotional high over a man. The whole day she spent day dreaming about jet-black hair, blue eyes, and a Kirk Douglas dimple on his chin. The college bells chimed and it was time for morning tea. Janet packed her books and headed off to the cafeteria; wanting to beat the queues for food, she dashed down the corridor. Straight ahead of her the very same young man was standing against the cafeteria wall. This could not just be coincidence. "Fate, definitely fate," Janet uttered to herself. She could hardly turn away so she soldiered forward. "Hi again," she said as she looked him in the eyes and pushed past him to enter the cafeteria. She sat at the usual table with the girls from the prenursing course. Cadets, they were called. The girls were sitting trying to make plans for the weekend. There were so many nightclubs in the town, they were spoilt for choice. Janet hardly held their conversation; she just kept nodding her head as if she was a part of the girl's conversation. Her head had turned to the next table where the young man was seated. He was surrounded by his classmates. She tried to catch their conversations.

"He's the one!" one of the girls blurted. "I know," Janet answered, thinking that they had noticed the way she had been staring at the table. "He's the one that ditched Ally. They had been courting over a year. She is heartbroken." Ally had just started her nurse training; she left the cadets a month ago. Janet had only met Ally twice. She didn't care. "He's not taken then—not now!" Janet smiled. "Maybe it is just meant to be." She finished her morning tea and gathered her books together for the next class. She walked away past the young man at the next table. "See ya," she whispered over his ear. She couldn't believe that she just did that. She simply could not help herself.

She made the same journey to the cafeteria every day, for one week. The young man was always standing there waiting for her to pass by. For one week they passed by one another and she would repeat the words, "Hi again, you again, and see you." They always chose to sit at the same tables with the same group of friends.

On Friday, she made her usual trip to the cafeteria and the young man was standing there leaning against the wall. This time he suddenly jumped out and stood in front of her and blocked her entrance to the cafeteria. He towered tall over her. "Hi again," he said to her. He was wearing her favorite color: a royal blue shirt with the winged collar tied down by two very tiny studs. His Wrangler jeans clung to his perfectly shaped rear end. "Was there anything not perfect about this man?" she asked silently.

"I think we have been standing on the corner way too long and it is best that we meet. I'm Paul by the way and I know you are Janet. I am a friend of your brother's, I know all about you" Janet's knees just about gave away as he put his arm around her. "How about joining me for coffee? I have been wanting to meet you since the day I saw you at your home. You were very angry with the world and yet so funny with it. Your brother made me promise I would not date you, but I could not resist." How Janet suddenly hated her overprotective brother, and how good she felt walking into the cafeteria with Paul. This Paul did not belong to Maggs; this Paul was to be hers. This time they did not sit with their friends; they found a quiet little corner. "Your father is Polish and so is mine, so we are off to a good start, aren't we?" Paul took her hand and Janet nodded.

They had the usual first date banter about where do you work? What hobbies do you have? And what are you studying? Janet would tell the stories Gregory shared with her. "I so much want to travel," she said. "I had two office jobs and I hated the routine and boring tasks." Paul talked about how he got an apprenticeship in the rolling mills because his father worked there. He didn't really enjoy what he did, but it was a start and a trade. Janet talked about how she had worked in the offices for the same rolling mills and found them to be dull and boring. So she decided to become a nurse.

They met like this for the next six months and used to stop by the local town pub after college. Here she would meet his friends; they would play pool, darts, and cards. Janet spent a lot of time with the boys; her brother would join them. Janet just loved hanging around and she adored their clowning around. It seems she had found another camp to crash. It felt good because she was hanging around her big brother. Paul was fifteen months older than Janet. He loved music and when not working he would play DJ at the local nightclub. It was time to let the parents know that they were actually dating. They would spend alternate weekends at their parents' homes—separate rooms of course. One of the parents were keeping a close eye. "No hanky-panky before marriage," his father would say. They couldn't really escape anywhere and they were both on apprenticeships so they had little income. They used to cuddle arm in arm on the settee watching movies with the family. "Put her down, you'll smother her." Paul's father used to say. They would spend family caravan weekends away together every year. A lot of time was spent at the nightclub at weekends. Paul was the DJ and did a wonderful job; he played a lot of Motown music. He would get up and dance with the groups. Oddly enough Janet never had any jealousy when he would be dragged onto the floor by the girls. He loved it, he loved himself and his ego was irresistible. Janet didn't want to change any of that; he was his own person and she wanted to just be herself. They were kind of together as a couple but not really. Janet thought they would need some extra cash, so she took a job working behind the bar. He was good-looking and so was she—the difference was he knew it and she would not accept how pretty she was. Janet adapted to bar work very quickly and she was able to pull a good pint with a good head on it. They had many parties at the club, they worked hard; and when all the guests left, they would party until breakfast time. They would make their own music and dance the night away. Janet enjoyed her time working the bar; she was a wiz with figures and could add the cost of drinks quickly in her head—thanks to the cribbage her brother taught her. The year flew by and the couple managed to balance family and their social times together.

There was more freedom at Janet's home than at Paul's parents. Actually if the truth be known it was her father who enticed them to spend the night together. The first night she will always remember was when her father said, "Isn't it time you both went upstairs for a rest?" Janet was shocked but her father knew the relationship was going somewhere. He was wise because he knew it was getting to the more intense stage of the relationship as he called it. You would never mention *sex* in the house. This was the first time for Janet; she was somewhat shy and nervous. She never asked Paul about his sexual relationships as it wasn't the proper thing, and she would never hear her brother discuss his sexual encounters. No one ever did discuss them.

They didn't actually race upstairs to the bedroom, Paul actually took her hand; the old house had wooden stairs and boy, did they creak. The whole household knew they were making their way to the attic. Paul chose some music such as "Can't Get Enough of Your Love, Babe" and "You're My First, My Last, My Everything." Barry White was a good choice and Janet was just so into Barry White. She would mimic the words, "Can't get enough of your love" through her hairbrush. Paul loved her crazy dance.

Paul and Janet must have made love at least ten times that night; they had not slept. Janet could still feel the touch of his skin against hers the whole of the next day. It was as if there was a warm wave of air against her skin. It was then they spent most of the time at Janet's home. They just felt more comfortable there.

The couple had been dating for two years Janet had reached twenty. Somehow, somewhere at some time they decided they would marry after Janet's twenty-first birthday as soon as she had passed her state final exams. They told their parents and announced their engagement on Janet's twentieth birthday. Janet's father had hired the Polish community hall for the big event. They had so many friends between them. More than 220 people arrived at their party. Janet wore her long blue dress with the sweetheart neckline that she had worn for her very first visit to see the Four Tops a couple of years ago. It still fitted perfectly; as a matter of fact she was slimmer and even more beautiful.

They danced to both Polish and modern music. The presents arrived—so many engagement presents. She held her hand to her right eye hoping everyone would notice her ring. You actually would need a magnifying glass to see the stones. They didn't have much money and that was all Paul could afford at the time; she was so happy that she had a ring. It took two days to sort out the presents. Janet couldn't help but show off her blue sapphire ring. Paul and Janet hosted their party so well, everyone had a wonderful time. They were so busy entertaining everyone, they realized that they never danced together at all that evening; but they made up for it when they arrived home—they danced and made love the whole night. They truly were in love.

The couple worked shifts and spent less time together after their engagement. Paul would meet her in the morning and they would go for breakfast and devour strawberries and cream; they would catch up with what they had done during the week. Janet would be working shifts she was studying for her state finals and still managed to work behind the bar. The nights at the club were tiring as it became a popular venue and with that came the drunken customers. There were fights and the front door and not a weekend went by where someone had not thrown something through the glass doors or put a fist through them. Janet was getting tired of the nightlife but Paul was in his element—he loved being the center of attention. Despite all of this she passed her state finals and the wedding date was set. Janet was getting scared—was she doing the right thing? This was a commitment after all and there would be no turning back. Her responsibilities at work were growing; she had spent three months working in accident and emergency rooms taking care of intoxicated young men who had war wounds from the nightclub brawls. She knew that she didn't want to see Paul amongst them.

Janet's father had put some money to one side and he took the kids as he called them to a building plot that was to be next door to her older sister; he knew family would support the young couple. He had paid for half of the house to be built and it was reaching the final stages. This was his wedding gift. Janet knew there was definitely no turning back now as she could not disappoint her father. *Let it be, let it be, Mother Mary come to me, bring your words of wisdom* . . . She had changed the words around a little but she never gave up her optimism, and she knew just had to keep reminding herself that everything would be just fine. She took a deep breath. We are getting married and it will work.

Most of her friends would have taken twelve months to prepare for a wedding; Janet and Paul managed it in twelve weeks. There was a little discord about the church as Janet was of the Protestant faith and he was the Catholic faith. Janet didn't care and she knew no matter what church in England they'd marry there was grandeur of history and architecture. It was rare to find a church that did not fulfill its architectural and historical obligation and the surroundings would hold a natural aura. She knew the departed souls in the nearby graveyard would be watching over them. She had often walked through the churches and spent time reading the headstones on the centuries-old graves and admired the stone carvings and how every unique headstone represented the past lives of our predecessors. Janet chose the Catholic church. Her father was Catholic and her mother Protestant. She remembers only too well the challenges they faced in 1940 especially in Poland. Her father married in the register office in Poland to keep the peace but Grandmother kicked him out of the house and told him not to come back as the husband of her daughter until they had married in church. Yes, they had two wedding anniversaries. Janet certainly did not want to create a family feud, and she knew they shared the one God. She just could not understand what all of the fuss was about and she certainly did not want to create family wars.

There was no time to make and fit a wedding dress—it was to be off the shelf. She had visited the only department store in town, and after trying on all of the six dresses in the store, she made her choice. The fine lace embroidered bodice fell into a split V line from her neck. Not only did it complement the fine string of pearls that belonged to her grandmother, but it gave her femininity as the edged lace highlighted the cleavage of her breasts. She swirled around, the A line skirt swirled a full 360 degrees from below her high waistband. Although the dress was around two inches too long, there was no time to fix the hem so Janet bought a very high pair of stiletto white satin shœs with a small platform that raised her dress just above the ground. She had always been very practical, and she did not want to add any extra costs to her father's responsibility of paying for the wedding. She chose a tiara slightly raised and made from a fine silk webbed mesh trimmed with tiny pearls and white flowers. Her headdress was a fine net, trimmed with the finest link of daisies; it trailed about two meters behind her and fell to just above her string of pearls at the front. She had chosen a bouquet of fine silk flowers, the palest sapphire blue carnations with tiny pink roses, and white dahlias and a hint of green foliage. There was no one beside her to say, wow! She was the one who looked in the mirror and she knew just how beautiful she looked. She had decided to shop by herself. She always shopped by herself as she knew it would be something she liked and she could make a cut and dry decision of what actually suited her. She had tried shopping with her sisters previously, but their tastes were certainly not what she would choose for herself. She used to buy dresses influenced by everyone else's taste and would often return them to the shops the following day. "That is so much not me," she would often say as they tried to dress her in colors that did not suit her complexion.

The house they were to live in was completed six weeks before the wedding just in time to celebrate the Queen's silver jubilee street celebrations on June 6, 1977. It was situated in a small cul-de-sac with around twenty houses that boasted Georgian windows; with their small crossed windows, they were such a pain to clean despite looking very ornate. The couple had moved into the house prior to the wedding, so they could get to know their new neighbors and what a way to meet them with a street party. She would never forget the silver jubilee celebrations, the whole street congregated together. There were garlands of the Union Jack flags weaved from one house to another across the street. Door fronts boasted a Union Jack flag. There were posters "To the Queen to the Queen" and the guys had clubbed monies together and bought around eight kegs of beer. Every one boasted a pint pot bearing' a picture of the queen. Needless to say, they raised their glasses, "To the queen, to the queen," umpteen times that day. Hits from the '70s echœd along the streets. Street games such as sack races, three-legged races, tag, and local bands were playing live music. The party continued and friendships among the neighbors flourished. Everyone was there to support the new couple to the street. Janet and Paul were always popular, they knew how to entertain, and they loved to be entertained.

They mingled freely and easily among both the young and the old.

They lived together twelve weeks before the wedding. Both would take turns to make the evening meals, they wined and dined in the comforts of their own home during the week, and Paul would take the nightclub at weekends. She was more than happy for him to have the Friday night with his friends, and she would take the opportunity to keep her sister company next door. "Can you trust him with all those women around him?" her sister used to ask. "Of course I can," Janet replied. "There can't be a marriage without trust."

Living together was probably a good thing as Janet knew that there would be differences between them. Paul had been taken care of by his mother; he never had to wash his own clothes. There was always a laundry batch scattered over the chairs waiting for someone to do the big wash. There was the lack of clean up in the bathroom, shaving foam that had glued itself to the sink, and the old razorblades turning to rust. The cap never replaced on the toothpaste and so on. Sometimes they would fight over the smallest of things, and sometimes they would refuse to speak to one another for several days. Janet would find her father—he was her best friend. The couple had not spoken for two days because Janet left the cap off the toothpaste. "How can silly small things cause so much heartache?" Janet asked her father as he took her by the hand. "We have differences but you just have to work it out, if you have a difference you have to make up before going to bed at night. You must never carry your discords on to the next day, that is very unhealthy and most things can be sorted." With that Janet purchased a toothbrush and toothpaste holder, and every day she placed the toothpaste where it should be. She bought a bag for Paul's shaving stuff, and he routinely placed everything in its correct place. "See it's so easy and we can work it out always." She smiled at Paul and muttered the words "I love you."

He never heard her say that and he never said that to her. She thought they didn't need to be so sloppy about life and that they didn't need to keep repeating what was obvious. They were experiencing the realities of love and life.

Thursday before the wedding, Janet hired a bus and she had arranged to take forty of her friends and family to the Hofbrauhaus in Sheffield for her hen night. The girls met at the local pub around the corner from her house. Everyone wanted to shout her a free beer to put her into a partying mood. There was only so much she could drink and she never got stoned. Her father taught her how to enjoy a drink and enjoy life; he used to tell her that life was a series of memories and that they should be remembered. "If you go dancing you should remember the dance always. That is, you should never get so stoned so much that you don't remember your life."

Janet dressed in her flared trousers and halter neck top. She had visited the hairdresser in Rotherham; he was the famous Peter Bird and her father her treated to the hairstylist. Her long straight hair had been shaped and styled with the '70s perm. It was the fashion, and the natural flow and wave with highlights made her look older yet innocent as the curls softly swept her face.

"Let's party on!" her friends cried out. It was time to catch the bus; her friends were certainly in the party mood and they played the usual prewedding songs, "Going to the Chapel,""Sugar Pie Honey,""You're Sweet as a Honeybee." The bus was laden with BYO as it was too expensive to buy drinks from the bar; they simply couldn't afford it.

It was only twenty minutes by bus from Rotherham to Sheffield. They scrambled off the bus and made their way up to the steps of the Hofbrauhaus. The girls carried packages to dress up the bride to be and they had two long tables adjacent to the stage. The Hofbrauhaus boasted the colorful flags of Germany and its famous beers. They hung from the ceiling. The tables were long enough to seat twenty girls and they boasted strong wooden benches. It was only a few moments before the waitresses dressed in their yellow and green miniskirts, which were Bolero-shaped, and showed a white lace underskirt. The blouse was designed to perfection and they were definitely the "Boobie Girl" blouses that make the German beer festivals so famous; that is, they certainly showed their cleavage. The modern Anne Boleyn boobs as Janet called them and in their arms they carried at least eight steins. Janet was so happy with her chosen venue. It was a happy place and full of life, the umpa bands would lead the "EinProsit, EinProsit" and "UmpaPaUmpaPa Pa" certainly got the girls into the dancing spirits. Janet didn't need to drink because she was drunk with the atmosphere. The bandwagon of girls had shared presents which were all of brightly colored condoms, a chocolate-coated biscuit penis, and a veil. "My god, you girls are crazy!" Janet said as she raised her glass, and then they handed the chocolate-coated "middle leg" to Janet and raised their steins as she took the first bite. "I can't believe I'm doing this!" Janet's older sister accepted an offer to dance; Janet could not help but notice how happy she was. She had been married some eighteen years. This was an opportunity to be free. However, her daughter was so angry. "You love my dad, how can you flirt with someone else!" She pulled her mother off the dance floor. At that it was time for the girls to leave. That was a night that Janet accepted all dancing invitations as she knew it would be the "last fling" before commitment to marriage.

The girls scrambled onto the bus chanting the songs from the Hofbrauhaus. The bus left the club and once around the corner the girls pulled out the stein pots they had somewhat borrowed from the club to keep as souvenirs. They handed one to Janet signed by all of her friends, "Cheers." She knew she had some amazing friends and they vowed to always be there for one another.

Paul had moved back to his parents until after the wedding. The girls continued the party at the house until early hours of the morning. Janet made a point of entering her hen night in her diary. She clutched her diary and fell asleep listening to the words of The Beatles' "Let It Be."

Friday evening she went to the church and placed beautiful fresh flowers down the aisle of St. Benedict's Church. The church was built in 1842. It has such a peaceful aura. She could hear the floorboards creak under her feet as she walked down the aisle to place the flowers. She crept into the aisle seat and glanced around at the historical surroundings. It was as if a rainbow was shining through the glass-stained windows. On the north wall were the four square stained glass windows depicting incidents in the life of St. Bede. The stained glass colors of the monk and child were so still yet as alive as the light shone through them. To the right she could not help but stare at the royal blue colored stained windows in which Edward the Confessor was staring directly toward her. "And he will be truly looking over me tomorrow," she said. She began to say her small prayer, "Thank you father for giving me such a wonderful life, thank you to my wonderful parents and for my beautiful Paul. I promise to take care of him always." And with that she continued to place her flowers along the aisles.

Janet didn't sleep much that night; she spent a good few hours with her father. There were many questions running through her head, and she could open her heart to him. "I'm so scared," she said to him. With that her father pulled out a small shot of Polish vodka. She curled up on his knees on the armchair. "Come let's drink to your big day, everyone is a little afraid and no one knows what the future has in store," he said. Janet would remember the stories of Gregory and how the war had been unpredictable. "Yes, I am going to live every day and do good things and I will keep my promise." She fell asleep in her father's arms.

Janet woke up to a good smell of a well-cooked breakfast. Her parents had prepared for her; they sat around the breakfast table the same as they had done for many years and this was to be the last time she would celebrate breakfast with her father and her mother. She was the baby of the family and it was hard to let go. At 10:30a.m. the doorbell rang and Janet answered the door. There was a large bouquet of red roses and card as large of the breakfast table that boasted hearts and champagne glasses. She opened the card, *To my darling Janet and our lifelong journey together. Kiss kiss kiss, Paul.* Up to this day she wanted to hear the words I love you but they were not to be seen in the card. He had the most perfect writing; it was on a slant with the most perfect curves around the J for Janet. Janet quickly placed the card and flowers in the lounge. The bridesmaids had arrived and they needed to get to the hairdressers, appointments had been booked for 11:30 a.m. at Peter Bird's Hairdressing Salon. It was in the market place and noted to be the best in Rotherham at the time. The girls were in a hurry and there was this one woman holding up the queue. Peter had done a marvelous job sprucing up her hair. But the woman complained she did not look like the picture in the style book. The picture was of a young model in her twenties the woman was approaching sixty. Janet wanted to speed up the queue and the woman was waving the style book. Janet was getting impatient. Peter had been so polite. "He's a hairdresser, not a miracle worker, and he is certainly not a plastic surgeon!" Janet snatched the book from the woman and said, "You can only look like that when you are that age! So accept the crinkles and wrinkles as a good sign of maturity." With that, the woman moved on to pay her bill and stomped out of the salon. "Sorry, Peter, but she was getting on my nerves and she just needed to know the truth. Hope I haven't lost your customer," Janet said.

"Oh, I won't worry at all if she doesn't come back, but she comes religiously and had done for the last thirty years and I am sure she will be back next week—and all will be forgiven." Peter smiled. Peter had done a wonderful job with all hairstyles, so natural and so becoming. The girls had their hair in a bun style with side ringlets and the maid of honor had a Farah Fawcett look. Janet had soft curls whispering to her cheek. Her tiara sat amongst the curls as if had been designed for her.

They arrived home around 12:45 p.m. and Janet was dressed for her big day. By 1:30 p.m. she was ready to leave for the church. The doorbell rang. "Are we expecting anyone?" Janet asked as she opened the door, only to be greeted by a somewhat shocked young man.

"I'm from the electricity board and we need to read your meter," he grinned.

"Oh, not today," Janet was not very happy.

"Excuse me, madam, I have strict instructions from the company to read your meter. Do you have your last bill?" he asked refusing to move.

"You've got to be kidding," Janet replied. "Not now, go away."

"Sorry, ma'am, but I cannot leave or I will lose my job." He still refused to move from the door.

"Dad, we need the electricity bill!" she shouted into the house. Her father fumbled around as if to look for the bill and it was 1:50p.m. with a twenty-minute ride to the church.

Her father came back with two shots of vodka. "Well done, son." He shook the man's hand. "It's traditional for the bride to be late." Her father raised the glasses. "Of all the . . . I could pleasantly kill you." she said to her father. She hated to be late; she was never late—always early but never late.

She definitely needed the shot of vodka this time. She was so very excited and so very nervous, and she looked stunning. She had lost some weight with all running around over the last weeks in preparation for the wedding, and when she put on her shœs, her dress had lowered to touch the ground.

They arrived at the church by 2:15p.m. The bridesmaids arranged her veil so it trailed beautifully behind her. They played the wedding march and she walked forward proudly at the side of her father. Straight ahead there was a huge ladder in the middle of the aisle. Apparently the organist had locked herself out of the organ room so she had used the ladder. Janet and her father parted hands and moved around the ladder as gracefully as she could. The bridesmaids followed wearing their royal blue dresses and carrying baskets of white rose petals. She was so nervous she could only look forward toward Paul who was waiting for her at the front of the church. He was dressed in a black velvet suit with the widest of collars and a white silk shirt with a blue sapphire colored tie. With his jet-black hair and olive skin he looked a million dollars and the colors of his clothes brought out life to the stained glass windows. She knew the angels were looking down upon them. *I thank you for your guidance,* were the warm thoughts moving through her head as she looked up at the cross. This was the first time she had seen Paul wear a suit. He was irresistible. And she was in love.

The Catholic mass took almost two hours. They exchanged vows and placed on their rings. Janet's fingers had swollen and Paul had force the ring on her finger. The hymns followed. As it happened, the priest and the organist had had a little Irish whiskey that lunch time, so the music was rather slurred. "All Things Bright and Beautiful" sounded like an old 45-rmp record playing like "His Master's Voice" at 16-rmp.

The speeches followed the slurred song and they seemed to go on forever, then with a little Irish humor, the priest began his speech about the couple. "Here is Paul, a turner by trade and, wow I'm sure he's good at turning most things, there is Janet who runs around with hypodermics jabbing everyone." Everyone laughed and it was certainly a service to be remembered.

Signing of the register followed the speeches and the couple made their grand exit as husband and wife. Janet swirled and her lace veil swirled with her as it caught the light from the glass stained windows that created a rainbow effect. She felt a million dollars and as a bride should feel on her wedding day. It seemed as if they had posed for hundreds of photographs—the kiss, the garter, the best man, the family, the friends, the gardens, and so on.

After the photography shoot the couple hosted their reception, the usual speeches, and dances as any wedding. They had a mass of presents, and they danced till early hours of the morning. They were the last to leave.

They arrived home at 5:00 a.m.; it was just about sunrise. The house was wrapped with the jubilee street flags, bearing the Union Jack and colored red, white, and blue. Paul opened the front door and carried Janet over the threshold. The house was dark. There were no lights as all light bulbs had been removed, and decorations were hanging from every light shade. The boys had made banners saying "Start as you mean to go off, meet the boys at the pub on Sunday."

Confetti and rice filled the carpets. There was no bed in the house—it had been moved to the garage, and there was a big note saying "You will always remember your wedding night." In front of the fire there were two champagne glasses and a bottle of champagne with a dozen strawberries. "And may you remember your first breakfast," another note said. The couple were exhausted and crashed out on the carpet in front of the fireplace.

At 8:00 a.m., there was a clanging of bells and the neighbors brought in a cooked breakfast and a bottle of vodka, nothing like a greasy breakfast and a hair of the dog. That was one breakfast they never celebrated together; that was a breakfast they celebrated with the whole street. By twelve noon they were heading to Devon for their honeymoon with a good eight hours of driving. They had packed their bags two days before and were more than happy to get away for a few days. They shared the drive down to Devon so they could catch up on sleep. The drive was silent as one of them was always sleeping. Janet had chosen a small hotel she found advertised in the local rag—the Honeymoon Hotel in Devon. It was a price they could afford and the pictures of the rooms looked to be Georgian style English and very quaint. They arrived at the hotel around 11:30p.m. it was very dark. The hotel looked nothing like the pictures in the rag; it was Georgian style but needed a good coat of paint. There were about twenty steps to the front door and it was very dark. Paul took a cigarette lighter from his pocket so they could see where the steps started and ended. They found an old door knocker, and Paul gave a few hard knocks. The door opened, but there was no one there to greet them. They walked along the narrow hallway and turned to a door where a light was shining beneath the door. They opened the door and there was a very old man sitting by an organ playing music that seemed to come from outerspace. The old gentleman took his stick and pulled himself up from the organ seat; he handed the keys to Paul and said, "Up three flights of stairs and third door on the right." They followed the instructions. The two dragged their cases up the three flights of stairs and by the time they reached the top they were quite breathless. There was a large bang as they dropped their heavy cases at the doorway. Paul fumbled with the keys and opened the door. It was the height of summer but the room was very cold. The four poster bed with draping curtains certainly held the Georgian era.

Paul quickly opened the suit case and pulled out a bottle of champagne. "I think we deserve this," he said. He poured the champagne into the two crystal glasses that they had packed—a present from the bridesmaids. "I don't know about champagne, we need good vodka to warm up the blood." The room was very damp.

As they unpacked their bags Janet pulled out her satin negligee and with that came showers of rice and rice bubbles with colored confetti, not forgetting a colored packet of condoms. "I wonder who packed these!" she asked and they laughed as they were covered with confetti. Janet slipped to the bathroom while Paul continued to fight with the clothes and battle with the rice and confetti that was in every garment.

Janet brushed her hair and put on her pale pink satin negligee. She looked beautiful and the satin cloth flowed to the floor from the cleavage of her breasts. They were married now and despite having lived together, she felt like a nervous, blushing bride. The floor was like a carpet of snow as the rice had covered the carpet. Paul was sitting on the bed wearing he Calvin Klein royal blue boxers. His muscular body with his olive skin was totally irresistible. They raised their champagne glasses. "Here's to us and bugger the rest," he said looking at the bed of rice and confetti which covered the floor. They scrambled beneath the sheets and made love as if it was their first time. They certainly did not need any artificial heating that night.

They managed to rouse themselves by 9:00 a.m. and made it to the downstairs restaurant for breakfast. As they walked through the lobby they noticed a large notice board which boasted UFO sightings in Devon. There was a picture of a giraffe with a probable UFO above his head. The owner was very much into wanting to build a landing station for Martians. "Where would they see a giraffe in Devon? And no wonder the music was a little eerie last night." Janet laughed. "UFO's and Martians on our honeymoon, better we keep the bedroom window closed tonight. Don't want one landing on the bed, do we?" Paul loved Janet's wit.

They had the usual cooked English breakfast, which was devoured very quickly after the previous night's activities. Janet could not help but notice a young girl who was heavily pregnant sitting with her husband at the breakfast table; the onlookers were other honeymoon couples. "Shameful," the snide remarks echœd around the dining room. "As if getting pregnant and then married never occurred." Janet was furious. She had been bridesmaid at the age of fourteen and her sister was expecting at the time. Paul had noticed how Janet had been infuriated about the snobbery and disgust shown by the naïve onlookers. "Time to leave," Paul said as he took Janet by the hand and left the hotel for their trips around Devon. During the five days they had visited Dalwood, which was the most charming little village in the Devonshire countryside and it had a wonderful old thatched pub where they had a roast dinner and a good pint of local beer. They walked through the village and took photographs by the picturesque stone church that boasted gravestones that were centuries old. It was rather quaint.

"Shall we go in and tie the knot again?" Janet asked.

"Once is enough," Paul replied.

The couple returned to the hotel that evening and relaxed in the open antique freestanding bath in their bedroom. They toasted their health and more with a bottle of champagne. Paul had leaned backward to lie against Janet. He tilted his head backward and she poured the glass of champagne over it. "You should be pampering me," she said. With that, he turned around and he tipped his cold glass of champagne over Janet's head "It is 1977 and women are fighting for equal rights you know. You scratch my back and I'll scratch yours, honey, always." They both laughed and cuddled up snug to one another, and with that came more sex and more sex.

The next morning they devoured the same cooked breakfast. Janet still could not help but notice the young girl who was pregnant and how the onlookers continued to stare. "Let it be," Paul insisted. That morning they drove to Cockington; Janet could not get over the gorgeous, idyllic thatched village. Here she felt she was walking in ancient times, the village was so old that in 1086 it was mentioned in the doomsday book—Janet remembered that from her school history class. She used to come top of the class in history and she loved the costumes from the pre-fifteenth century, and while walking through the village she felt she was right there in that century at that time because everything around appeared to be the same as it was in the Tudor and medieval times. She could not help but notice how the sweet little stone cottages peered out at her from beneath the lush, thick thatched roof tops. She couldn't resist the temptation of devouring the fresh creamed scones which were topped with strawberries served in the tea rooms. She found a small haberdashery shop; she left Paul and did a little shopping. "Hope you didn't break the bank account," Paul said as she came out with a small package. He wanted to know what she had purchased. "You will see," she replied. She would always remember the lovingly preserved village of Cockington.

Paul had decided to surprise Janet while she had been shopping—he had treated her to a romantic drive around Cockington in a sedate horse-drawn carriage. The couple enjoyed the countryside and they enjoyed that togetherness feeling which was far away from the industrial town they had left behind in Rotherham. They enjoyed being present in Cockington so much that they returned the next few days to enjoy the delightful walks around the lakes and they were breath taken by the wildlife. They brought their own picnic where they shared the champagne, and they went rambling in the woods. "If I had a tent, I would camp here with you and we would watch the stars at night." Paul held her so tight she did not mind being breathless at all.

On the last morning at the hotel Janet and Paul went for their usual breakfast, and the young pregnant girl sat on the table opposite. Janet took a parcel to the young girl, "This is for your baby." The girl smiled and took the parcel. "By the way," Janet said in a loud voice, "Our daughter is at home, she is one year old and she was born before wedlock." Paul looked at Janet—that he did not expect. "And she is beautiful, isn't she darling?" she prompted Paul to nod his head. She felt so good as they left the room. "What are you like, and what am I going to do with you!" Paul loved the kindness and sincerity that his wife exhibited. And with that they left, the honeymoon was over and they set off on their long drive north to Yorkshire. Paul never knew what was in that package.

$$\textit{Chapter Four}$$

THE NEXT YEAR flew by and Paul was getting tired of his job and there were to be redundancies in the steel company. Janet had changed from nursing to midwifery; she was paid as a nurse to do her training. Her income was enough to cover the small mortgage; she knew Paul would do well in a white collar job—he was destined to manage and she thought he was too intellectual to continue to work on the shop floor. Paul had been offered a course on Industrial Management studies. Janet had no objection and he didn't really need to ask because she knew he had to find something he loved to do. This course was to study time and motion and she had already been familiar with that process in the health system. She was timed as to how long it took her to make a bed. Paul started his six months training and he passed with flying colors; she was so proud of him.

He arrived home one evening, she had set the table and prepared dinner, it was their first wedding anniversary. She had placed the two champagne glasses they had used on their honeymoon on the table; Paul had arrived with two dozen red roses. They had a beautiful dinner and they had just finished a toast to their future. "I have been invited to go to America and subcontract for an aircraft company in San Diego. California. It is really good pay and they pay for accommodation. We don't have to decide now but I want you to think about it."

Janet had never expected this so soon after they had been married; she threw herself back in the chair, her body felt like a stone weight. She knew that if she said no he would hold it against her for the rest of her life and if she said yes it would change things forever. She could not sleep that night. Paul tried so very hard to comfort her, she did not want to be hugged, she needed to think; and thinking was going nowhere because it was not going to change anything and she knew what the answer was, and that was an overseas adventure.

She did not need to wait until the morning to tell Paul what she had been thinking, she had been direct by saying, "If I say no, you will hold it against me for the rest of my life and you will regret it for the rest of your life, so I must say yes. It has taken me by surprise and I should be so excited for you, but I truly don't know how I will feel." She remembered her father wanted to buy a farm many years ago and her mother said no, and how he had held it against her mother for all of these years, how he regretted not buying that land, and how he never got over it. She did not want that to happen to her marriage because they needed to support one another. "You have to go and I have to support that choice." She knew this was going to change their lives forever.

"Wait there and don't move," she said as she went downstairs and returned with the two glasses of champagne that they had not finished earlier. She played some music and she began to sing, *And when the night is cloudy, there is still a light that shines on me, shine on until tomorrow, let it be . . . .* If Paul Lennon and John McCartney were sitting in front of her she would be saying your words saved my life.

"To the future and may the unknown bring happiness to both of us." They said as they drank the champagne. They made love till the early hours of the morning. "And who knows what tomorrow might bring," Janet toasted but Paul was sound asleep. Janet's unpredictable future was spinning around in her head. *Tomorrow, tomorrow, I love you tomorrow, it's only a day away.* She had recently been to the production of *Annie* released in 1977, and how Annie's words gave her hope for the future.

By mid-January 1979 Paul was given his papers and airline tickets; he was to fly to San Diego on the seventh of February. If he was going to go, it couldn't have been a better time as that winter had been quite harsh, the roads had been knee high in snow, and it was not unusual for them to leave the snowed under cars at home and walk to work. It was a good two-mile walk for both of them to the town center. He was not sorry to leave the snow and the cold behind. Janet drove him to the airport that day. She had purchased a leather satchel and Paul's name was embossed at the front. "Now you will never lose your papers," she said.

It was a quick cup of coffee at the airport as the four hour drive took six hours due to the heavy traffic on the M25. Heathrow was bustling with passengers and car parking was an issue; there was no baggage trolley to be found on their arrival. There were long queues at the ticket desks. "Where are your tickets?" she asked. He waved the blue Pan American airline tickets in her face.

He walked through the flight passenger doors. Tears strolled down her face, she was so afraid of the unknown and she was not looking forward to being alone. It was a long drive home to Rotherham and there was emptiness in her heart.

She received a phone call the next day to say he had arrived safely, and although it was winter, there he boasted the warmth of San Diego at 24ºC. He boasted of the studio apartment setting of Madrid suits; the Jacuzzi and the swimming pool were shaped like a three-quarter moon. He described the tall palm trees overlooking the apartments which were situated on El Cajon Boulevard, close to Howard Johnston's Inn. His new home was very close to the San Diego State University Art Gallery and Mission Basilica San Diego de Alcala. He described the local area attractions which included San Diego Zoo and Balboa

Park. There were six Brits working with him, and he had already dined with them.

She received letters twice a week. He was so excited, he enjoyed the work setting and it wasn't too long before he bought a Mustang. Janet had no idea what a mustang was other than *a horse.* Why would he want to buy a horse? He is living in the city. She remembered learning about the mustang from her school geography lessons. A mustang is a free-roaming horse of the North American west sometimes referred to as the wild horse. Yes, she could well relate the mustang to Paul's personality—free and wild. The end of the letters were the most important for her and they always ended with "love you" and "can't wait for you to join me and the gang." She responded, "Why did you buy a horse, dœs everyone take a horse to work in California?" She really had no idea; Paul creased up laughing when he received the letter and decided to send her picture of the rust colored car with a paper cutout.

The 1974 introduction of the Mustang II earned Ford Motor Trend Magazine's Car of the Year honours again and actually returned the car to more than a semblance of its 1964 predecessor in size, shape, and overall styling.

"What an ugly car," Janet remarked, "if that is supposed to be trendy I may as well be Dutch."

The letters continued to flow between the pair of them; Janet was working and studying hard for her final examinations at the end of March 1979. Paul had sent her a letter containing a ticket for a return flight to Los Angeles. She just wanted to be with him and he apparently missed her.

On April 15, 1979, Janet's bags were packed and she was to take the train to Heathrow. It was after Easter but there was thick snow in England. She was looking forward to seeing some of that Californian Sunshine that Paul had often described. She was hellish scared as she had never been on an airplane before, and the flight was ten hours to LA.

Catching the train to London was a mission. She had packed her bags to the brim and filled her case with many presents of clothing for Paul. The bag just scraped in at twenty-one kilograms when she had weighed it at home. She had strapped her case to a portable trolley with wheels, which seemed to tilt to either side, and take her with it. By the time she reached London there were multiple bruises on her legs caused by the impact of the suitcases. She was walking with a limp.

Her next ordeal was to descend the steep stairways at King's Cross station to the underground where she was to take a tube from the Piccadilly line to take the tube to Heathrow. The line had been extended to reach Heathrow in 1977. Two years previously she would have had to take a cab in the overcrowded polluted London roads.

She could not manage to hold her bags at the top of the escalators and they were so steep and not designed for baggage or the portable trolleys that carried her suitcase. The strap from her case caught in the side of the escalator and her case separated from the trolley and somersaulted down to the very bottom of the escalator. It was 5:00 a.m., thank goodness it was not peak hour for passenger traffic. "I haven't arrived there yet and this is so traumatic and exhausting. How can people want to do this every year?" She did not realize this was the start of her many ventures and that she would be balancing cases and cursing those escalators at King's Cross for many years to come.

The total distance from London to Los Angeles, California, is 5,454 miles. Flying in a northwesterly direction, the whole journey took approximately ten and a half hours. She was nervous the whole journey; she had seen the news just two weeks earlier where the Pan Am Flight 1736 Clipper Victor collided with a KLM 747 on the runway in Tenerife. It was the deadliest disaster in aviation history where a total of 583 people were killed. It was all over the front pages of every newspaper, and the TV news headlines. How could she not be nervous? Every time the plane hit some turbulence she would close her eyes and silently remember her favorite song "Let It Be." She knew she had to have faith. And what more to help her sleep but a good bottle of Californian wine.

Paul was waiting at the airport; she hardly recognized him—he was wearing a beige Stetson hat with a black band and a tight denim shirt with Levi's jeans that fits so snugly around his butt. She just couldn't wait to grab it either as they hugged or kissed one another. She had waited so long to hold him again, yet she couldn't find the words to say just, "How was the flight?" he asked.

"Long," she replied. She didn't dare say she spent half of it hanging on to her seat or that she had been so very afraid. "My entry through customs left a lot to be desired, they were so unfriendly and they asked how long I intended to stay. I was so nervous and it was a twenty-minute interrogation—as if I was going to stay permanently. And I told them I had no plans to stay forever, so California would be safe. Why do they think everyone wants to come to America? They were all too serious," she said. Paul laughed at that. "So where is the horse?" she asked. He knew she was talking about the car. He took over the responsibility for her bags. She sighed with relief as she had lugged them across London.

Janet sat in the passenger side of the mustang; the front seats were so low and she was so short that she could barely see out of the windows. It was midday and very hot. Paul turned on the air conditioning. "Wow, what crisp cool air, where dœs it come from?" Janet asked, He had explained the concept of air conditioning; this was very new to Janet as they never needed cooling down in the UK as it was always bloody cold most of the year back home and the only air system available was oil heaters or gas central heating. "My, we learn something new every day." she said.

Janet was expecting a scenic drive from Los Angeles to San Diego, it was about a 120-mile trip and took around two hours to drive southbound taking State Highway 5. It seemed rather strange sitting on the opposite side of the road as she was use to the left-hand drive in the UK. She couldn't help but notice the clear blue skies; that is about all she could see because the Mustang seats were really low and reclined. She took a note of the names of the exits that appeared overhead and to her left—Anaheim, Santa Anna, Irvine, San Clemente, Oceanside, and finally San Diego. It seemed rather strange sitting on the opposite side of the road; the roads were enormously wide and the grass was so dry, and California lacked the grand aged oak trees and greenery of England.

They arrived at the small condominium plaza. She could not get over the beautiful palm trees that surrounded the plaza, and when she saw the crystal clear water in the bluest swimming pool, she couldn't wait to go for a swim even though she was not confident at swimming. Paul helped her unpack; they had a tiny studio apartment with a brown and orange striped canvas couch that converted into their bed at night.

She had a shower and although very tired she took Paul by the arm and they walked around the corner to the local bar which was actually a restaurant/diner—Howard Johnston's. The waitresses bore short orange dresses and were wearing white shoes; they looked more like nurses than waitresses. They sat on the orange seats at the dinner table and ordered two ranch style steaks. The waitress leaned over. "How are you all today?" she asked. Janet could not help but notice the large orange badge which had "P PP" on a smiley face.

"What's P P P?" Janet asked the waitress.

"Oh, it is our logo, we are People Pleasing People!" The waitress smiled. "Is that to remind the customers to be polite or to remind you to be polite?" she asked. Paul gave her a nudge meaning "don't be rude," but Janet could not understand why people needed to be reminded that they have to please people when providing a service. "Don't they use any common sense?" she asked. Paul shook his head and said, "Now I know what I've been missing, that wicked sense of humor that has to analyze everything."

The waitress returned with this huge plate. "That's not a plate, that's a trough, and look there is almost a whole cow on it!" Janet exclaimed. Just looking at it made her feel overstuffed. "Is everything so large over here?" she asked.

After lunch they changed into their swimwear and made their way down to the poolside. Janet looked so lily white in her bikini, and Paul was already boasting a golden tan. "Good job, I'm not prejudiced about your dark skin." Paul smiled. "There you go again, you are so funny." He gave her a kiss on the cheek and with that he leapt into the swimming pool. Janet was so enjoying absorbing the Californian sun. She had her first taste of Budweiser beer by the poolside.

Paul had made plans for the week he had taken a week off. "Tomorrow we are going to Laguna Beach and then we have a trip to Disneyland. The company has hired Disneyland for the evening and is going to hold its annual celebrations there. We will be staying at the Anaheim Hotel overnight and we will visit Universal Studios. So once again you will need to pack a weekend bag, and don't sit in the sun too long because you will burn easily," he said. Janet was so excited and she felt so glad she had not stopped him coming to California. They spent a few hours that night in the Jacuzzi where she met the other Brits who were working with Paul and their wives. She made friends very easily and they loved her sense of humor. Paul and Janet were certainly entertainers and they were good at it.

The next day they set off back up State Highway 5 to Laguna Beach. They had parked at the top of a cliff and took many steps to walk down to the beach. Janet could not get over the green color of the sea and the blue skies, yet the cliffs looked so barren and dry with little—very little—greenery. They walked down into the cove and placed their picnic basket, blankets, and towels across the floor. There was another couple from Yorkshire who were about eight years older than Janet and Paul—Janice and Gordon. Taffy was the only single male in the group; he was around the same age as Paul. Taffy and Paul had become good friends. They spent the day soaking in the warm waters of the Pacific. Janet's lily white skin was turning to a beautiful Californian golden tan. As they left Laguna Beach for Anaheim it was around 4:30p.m. Janet will never forget the picturesque sunset scenery of the Pacific coast.

The group arrived in Anaheim around 6:30p.m. It was already dark. They had time to shower and change. They walked across the block to Disneyland. Janet just caught her breath as they entered the magical Disneyland. The castle at night looked so magnificent as if it were alive.

She felt like a child princess as soon as she walked the gates. Lights were flickering in the trees and the buildings were robust with colored lights. The bands of music were playing all of her favorite childhood songs and the old country music from the era of Mark Twain. The group had walked around for hours stopping off at the various waterholes; the pubs had real pints of Guinness in pint glass pots. The beer was pulled from the taps as if it was from Ireland. They always said that Guinness did not travel well as the taste is never the same, but Janet drank the creamy head and it sank like velvet. They jumped into the seats of Alice's Tea cups and they spun the table so fast that they were in another world. Paul pulled her tight toward him and they let the whole world spin around them. It didn't matter which ride or which part of this magical place they went, they were children again and just like children they played and had fun the whole night long. The firework display was spectacular as the skies filled with the same bright colors that sparked all around them from the buildings and trees; and when the colored sparks from the fireworks fell down from the skies toward them, the atmosphere pulled the couple together and they kissed beneath them. They had their fairy tale and they were in love. The night came to an end and as they walked toward the exit gate; Janet was still in her fantasy world and said, "Have you ever wondered what happens when Disneyland closes up for the night? Sleeping Beauty will take a nap, Mickey will have a hot chocolate before tucking into bed, and the ghosts of the haunted mansion will go into a deep sleep. Cinderella will make love to her prince, and so will we!" Paul looked back into her beautiful brown eyes and nodded, took her by the hand and they walked arm in arm across the block and they did make love all night.

Janet had felt this was a second honeymoon; she never wanted to leave it. The next day they visited Universal Studios, and in the audience arena was a special show to entertain the onlookers. Paul and Janet sat just three rows from the front. Out into the audience came Count Dracula and his bride and sought to pick out a vulnerable couple from the audience. Countess Dracula took Paul by the hand and led him on to the stage. Count Dracula had taken Janet by the hand and led her onto the other side of the stage. They were transformed into Dracula and the bride of Dracula; with the organ music playing, their seats swiveled around so they faced each other—microphones were placed in front of them. "My god, what an improvement!" they said to one another at the same time, and with that they howled with laughter. The audience laughed so loud and with that out came Lou Ferrigno dressed as the Incredible Hulk. This huge hunk of a green man took Janet in his arms and carried her through the audience. The two were so stunned; they could not believe that they had been chosen. And of course, Janet said, "I have met another famous person, wow!" Janet was having the time of her life.

They spent the next day lounging around the pool at Madrid Suites, and that evening they went to the local bar that Paul had found with Taffy, The Wranglers Roost. The bar was quite dark and had a small dance floor. There was a pool table and a small stage. Lanny Prewitt and his band were playing the country and western dances and the couples were dressed in Levi's jeans and checked shirts wearing Stetson hats and were dancing the American way. Taffy, Paul, and Janet took seats by the bar and a woman in her midthirties with beautiful long wavy black hair welcomed them.

"Well how are you all doing this evening?" she had said with a very warm smile.

"This is Randy, and she is not at all like that," Paul introduced them. Janet asked for a Bacardi and *Cooke* in her Yorkshire accent. "My, you Brits do talk kind of cute." She smiled and passed the Budweiser to the guys and the Bacardi to Janet, served in a long glass with ice and lemon with a serviette wrapped around the glass. "Wow that is so different than the hot Coke in the tiny glasses served in England," Janet said. She took a sip of her Bacardi and Coke through the straw. "What are they dancing to?" She had turned to the dance floor. The band was playing "Blue Moon" of Kentucky and the couples were doing a dance she had never seen before. "That's a cowboy polka, ma'am," the waitress answered.

With that, an older gentleman came to the bar and said, "Hi, I'm Andy, can I take this beautiful lady for a dance?" He looked over toward Paul. "Sure," Paul replied. And he took Janet's hand and passed it over to Andy.

"But I can't dance that," she said.

"Now is your chance to learn," Paul answered. How she loved the country music and before the end of the night she could do the cowboy polka, the country swing, and of course the waltz American style. Janet just loved to dance and thank goodness Gregory and her father had taught her to dance like she was dancing on air. Her steps came very natural. "My, you Brits can move," Andy commented. Paul and Taffy had moved to the pool table. Janet could have joined them but she preferred to dance to the music. Andy gave her his life story; he had been married five times and he also explained that Randy was into her fourth marriage. Janet found the stories very fascinating.

"Is everybody in America divorced?" she asked.

"Only the ones with any sense," he replied. Janet laughed

"Do you want to dance?" she asked.

"My privilege," he replied, and with that they danced to the country music for most of the night.

Paul and Taffy spent most of the night playing pool and enjoying the Budweiser beers. At the end of the night Janet walked arm in arm with the guys. They were all in a very happy mood.

That week flew by and Paul was to start back to work and Janet spent each of his work days lazing by the poolside, topping up her Californian tan. The expat wives were showing off their designer swimwear and their elegantly painted nails, reading the latest magazines and planning their next shopping trips. They were a lot older then Janet. She was only twenty-two years of age and the wives were in their midthirties. Janet enjoyed the time to relax and let the world go by with her music. She had barely had time to breathe in the UK due to her work and studies. She was waiting for the results of her examinations and every day she waited for a phone call from her family. She felt like she was still on a long holiday and sometimes wondered if she was dreaming all of this.

The following weekend they had decided to take a shopping trip to Tijuana, Mexico, where the international border crossing between San Ysidro, California, and Tijuana was only twenty miles south of downtown San Diego and she had been told that it was the world's busiest port of entry. Thousands of people cross that line every day. The M25 motorway in England was notorious for its traffic jams and that was nothing compared to the cars at this border crossing. Janet was completely aghast with the orchestral sounds from the tooting of horns and music blasting from the cars surrounding her in the multiple lanes—trucks, bikes, scooters, Cadillacs, Mustangs, and Camaros. All of which boasted the rust, blue, green, and red colored cars of the '70s and with the large engines the petrol, fumes were overwhelming.

"Thank goodness for the air con," she tried to mimic the American accent as she quickly wound up the windows of the car. She could not get used to the vastness of everything—the roads, the cars, and so on. It took them almost two hours to get through customs. The sign at the border greeted everyone "Bienvenidos a Tijuana" meaning "Welcome to Tijuana."

Andy, that guy she had met at the Wranglers Roost had told Janet that Tijuana was an ugly city, that it was a very poor and dirty city. She found it to be completely the opposite. Dusty, yes. Yes there was poverty and she couldn't help but slip a few dollars into a small boy's hand as they were selling packets of chewing gum. That small gesture brought a lot of young admirers tailing her from behind as they walked down the street; there must have been about twenty children behind wanting to sell chewing gum as the kids had echœd generous "Gringos" to their friends. Paul tried to shoo the kids away but Janet thought their laughter and cheeky mannerisms were quite exhilarating. "Don't be such a meanie!" she said to Paul. "They are such awesome kids."

"Maybe but your kindness will have every child in Tijuana trailing behind you and you will become the Pied Piper of Mexico," Paul answered. And she said, "Wouldn't it be wonderful," Janet replied. "I just adore children." Paul took her by the arms and raced her down the street so he wouldn't have to deal with his wife becoming the Pied Piper of Tijuana. Tijuana was alive with its bright colors, she loved the bright Aztec yellow sunflowers and the vivid colors of the woven Mexican blankets. She just wanted to take that entire color back to England. "My, how boring our homes are in England, with their pretty, pastel-flowered curtains. I want to make our home bright and happy." she said. She had bought lots of flowers which were made of wood and the brightly hand painted pottery that boasted centuries old designs. "They look so alive."

Janet did find the bartering quite challenging because she was not very good at it and she saw how poor some of these people were, she would have given the asking price. She left that to Paul, otherwise they would be returning back to San Diego penniless. "If I won the lottery, I would throw it in the air right here and let everyone enjoy every penny of it. And I would dance on the streets with the children and have fun. I would bring Disneyland to Tijuana." Paul didn't pay much attention to her fantasy world, and she did not care because she was on a youthful high and she was dancing on the streets of Tijuana.

The boys were very thirsty and they stopped off a Tijuana Tilly's—a cantina bar/restaurant. A cantina is a kind of neighborhood bar, it was nothing fancy. This visit found the three of them seated in a booth. They ordered a Corona beer which was served with a slice of lemon. Janet had a good look at the menu, and she ordered a tossed salad. It was too hot for a cooked meal. The boys ordered tacos and enchiladas. The waiter arrived with a large steel bowl on a trolley which was filled with lettuce. He added Mexican spices, cracked in two raw egg yolks, and literally tossed the salad with his hands. The boys looked with disgust, but Janet smiled and said, "Well that is certainly a tossed salad."

"Do not worry, madam, Rodrigo has been tossing salads here for the last ten years and he has not killed anyone yet." The second waiter had a beautiful Mexican smile that was so sincere. He passed a spoonful of salad to Janet. That was the best salad she had ever tasted. "It's delicious," she commented.

Tijuana Tilly's boasted a ceiling full of forty-five records hanging down and a multitude of ties. Anyone entering the Cantina wearing a tie left without one. The Mariachi Band came to the table dressed in their white suits and wearing sombreros. Janet noticed the small group of five men, singing, playing instruments, and moving from table to table. They wore white suits and wore hats (sombreros). One played a violin, another, a guitar, two lifted muted trumpets, and the smallest of them held tightly to his guitarrón, an oversized, bass version of the guitar. They were mariachis. They came to the booth table and began to sing "La Cucaracha." Janet loved the melody to this song and she could not stop singing the words. "What is a cucaracha?" Janet asked. One of the Mariachi said, "It is a song about a 'cockroach'" Janet took a look at her salad hoping not to find a cockroach in it

"Do not worry, señorita, the only cockroaches in the bar are the men," he said with a smile. "That's a very appropriate song to hear in a restaurant!" she said with a grin. "Oh, it is a love song and it is about a cockroach that dœs not have a foot, señorita." Janet loved the way he said *señorita.* "You need to be very jealous, darling, because I am in love with Mexico." With that she raised her bottle of Corona and said, "To Mexico and cheers." With that she placed $5.00 in his hat.

They stopped at many more cantinas and they became quite merry from the Mexican beers and the heat of the sun. The mariachis were in every cantina. On the way back to the car they stopped at a small stall and purchased two one-dollar guitars and a pair of castanets. The boys strummed the guitars and she played the castanets. She sang, *La cucaracha, La cucaracha.* A tourist passing by dropped $5.00 in her hat and with that the local sheriff took them by the hand and pointed to the overhead street sign. One of the signs warns all that immoral conduct will result in arrest. They were advised that they required a license to sing on the streets of Tijuana, and they were not Mexican so they were performing an illegal act. The sheriff confiscated their musical instruments. "Can you believe that we were almost arrested in Mexico?" she said as she still hummed the words to the song she would remember for the rest of her life; she would remember the tossed salad, and the cockroach song. Janet remembered reading a guide to Mexico on the aircraft and she noted that Tijuana boasted quite a culinary history. It is where Italian chef Alex Cardini tossed the very first Cæsar salad, where the clamato juice was first mixed, and where the national cocktail, the margarita, was created. She was yet to taste a margarita she knew there would be another reason to return to Mexico.

It was late and they needed to return to San Diego. They found their car parked on the side street. It seemed to be tilting to one side. Someone had removed two of the wheels. Paul and Taffy had to take a cab to a garage and buy two more wheels for the car. Janet waited for them in the nearby cantina, enjoying the Mexican music and atmosphere. As they drove through customs, they were given the last chance to buy the decorative Mexican goods. Their car boot was full of Mexican pottery, leather goods, blankets, flowers and so on.

Another week flew by and Janet was writing letters home to her family about their exciting times. Of course, she did not let her father know that they had a Sheriff incident in Tijuana. Weekday nights were spent at the Wranglers Roost and Janet began to master the country dances. Paul spent most of his time on the pool table with the boys from work as she called them. Wednesday night the Roost had a crazy hats night and there was to be a prize for the craziest hats. Taffy, Paul, and Janet decided to be different. They turned up wearing Mexican blankets, and sombreros. The crawled in to the club on their knees to look like very small Mexicans. Randy was working behind the bar and thought this was to be the best they had seen; the guys got a free drink and won the night. Randy introduced a new drink to Janet saying "Here, this will put you in the swing of things." It was creamy and tasted like a coffee milkshake; it was laced with Kahlua brandy, tequila, and fresh cream. With a good dollop of ice, it was better than a Baileys. "It's called a Dirty Mother. I make a drink dirty by adding something dark to something clear. For example, a Dirty Mexican is tequila with a bit of Kahlua. Perhaps say use dark rum instead of white for a mostly clear drink. I also add Kahlua to orange juice and it tastes really good but looks muddy," Randy explained. "Well that's a few dirty drinks I can add to my bar skills," Janet replied, and with that she raised her "dirty glass." The boys had dressed in blue and white soccer shorts and braces over their dark blue denim shirts and had exchanged their sombreros for straw cowboy hats they bought in Mexico. Janet wore a beautiful Hollywood deep pink satin dress with her halterneck tie and V shape front that showed of her Californian tanned cleavage. She had the string of pearls which came to life against her tanned skin. Her dress had a split from her midthigh to the floor. She looked like a Hollywood star and felt like a princess. That night Andy could not get a dance because Paul was boasting his wife to everyone.

By the end of the week Janet received a phone call from her family—she had passed her exams and she celebrated her future as a midwife. To celebrate, Paul decided to take her to Las Vegas. "Another honeymoon?" she asked as she was so excited. Diana Ross was to appear at Cæsars Palace and Paul had booked a night there. She had seen the movie *Mahogany* and she just loved the voice of Diana. Janet could not believe how she had seen so many amazing places in such a short time. It seemed she had jumped on board a never ending journey of happiness.

The road trip to Las Vegas took around eight hours; the wide, wide roads and the lack of greenery made Janet say, "Everything looked so orange." Paul was happy to be driving and he was not going to hand his precious Mustang over to Janet. This was something he did not want to share. As they drove north through the Mojave Desert, Janet noticed a white sign on a hilltop, "Calico."

"What's 'calico?'" Janet asked.

"Don't know, didn't a jester dress in calico, that is, the bright patches of color—it has something to do with patches of color, you know like the fur of a calico cat."

"Oh," replied Janet. She admired Paul for his knowledge, probably acquired by the number of crosswords he used to enjoy completing in his coffee breaks. "Shall we go and look at some color then?" They were ready for something to eat. With that Paul turned off the main highway and they drove down a very dusty road to take a look at Calico. They parked the car and walked up the main street. Calico was an old gold mining town. Calico was named as such because the overlooking mountains boasted a myriad of colors. The main street reminded Janet of the musical movie *Calamity Jane;* she could just imagine the Wells Fargo coach pulling up here. "Maybe we can find me a sarsaparilla," Janet tried to mimic the accent of Calamity. The couple found a bar where they had a cold beer and a steak. Unfortunately there was no sarsaparilla. They walked up and down the main street and then visited the places where they used to mine for gold. Janet could feel the presence of the old miners. "It feels ghostly," she said. They returned to their car and headed north on State Highway 15to Las Vegas; they still had more than two hours to drive.

Just before arriving at Las Vegas, Paul noticed a sign that boasted private air tours of the Grand Canyon. He knew it would be too vast and too large to drive with so little time; he pulled in at the private airfield and negotiated a price. Within twenty minutes they were in the small airplane. Paul was sitting at the front next to the pilot and Janet behind. They were in the air and they were totally taken aback by the myriad of colors displayed by the Grand Canyon rocks as Janet called them. "Wow, that is a *calico*," she said. The plane descended down into the Indian reservation and along the river. Paul was given an opportunity to take the flight with instructions of the pilot. It was very noisy and Janet could not hear herself speak, so this time she remained silent. *If my family could only see me now*, she thought. The flight took about an hour and as the plane veered from side to side and dipped down she felt quite nauseous. She did not let Paul see her weakness. When they returned to base, she stepped off the plane and she was swaying and feeling somewhat lightheaded. "Are you feeling okay?" Paul asked as he put his arm around her and suddenly she felt very stable.

They arrived at Las Vegas around sunset. It wasn't quite dark; she noticed the palm trees lining the main road and the "Welcome to Las Vegas" signs. Las Vegas looked so very barren. As they drove by the "Welcome to the fabulous Las Vegas, Nevada" sign, she had only then noticed that they were no longer in California. Ahead she saw the sign for the Frontier Casino which stood very high in the middle of the street. It boasted Joan Rivers and Bobby Vinton playing at one of the casinos. A few hundred yards behind was the Stardust Sign that seem to be lost in the desert haze. "Definitely dust," Janet remarked. "We just need to see the stars." Paul smiled as they drove down the main street. It was far from glitzy at that time of day. Paul drove toward Cæsars Palace where he had booked a room. Janet waited in the car. She could not believe the grand entry of Cæsars Palace, the driveway, and the fountains of water that reached into the sky. Paul came from the palace looking rather annoyed and he was rather irritable. "Sorry I have some bad news, I cannot cash a Californian check in Nevada. They won't accept it." Janet could see his disappointment. "What, no Diana? It dœsn't matter, you have just got to let it be." Janet kept her sense of humor and started to sing, *Do you know where you are going to, do you know what the night has in store for you, do you know . . . .* She had changed the words a little. "See, I can be Diana." Paul started to laugh, he drove the car twice around the driveway at the palace so Janet could enjoy the fountains and then they left to the main strip. There they found a small motel with rooms vacant. They pulled into the motel. Madrid Suites was a five-star motel in comparison to the dusty drab motel, but it was all they could afford so they checked in. The room was small and the sheets were dull. Janet flumped down on the bed and the bed moved as if she was floating on sea waves. It was a water bed. Paul turned on what he thought was the lamp and on the ceiling projected an X-rated movie. Janet put her hands over her face. "That is so immoral," she said. She was showing signs of her tribal influence of her Catholic father, and that was definitely a big *no*. Paul was amused and he was starting to be taken in by the movie. "No, I am not doing it to that." Then she put her hands over her face, but couldn't help but have an occasional peep through her fingers as to what was happening on the ceiling. She just did not like it. She jumped off the bed and took a shower, painted her face, and slipped into her bright yellow cotton dress. The dress was halter neck and that boasted her cleavage. The skirt was snug to below her knees with a split to her upper left thigh. Paul was too busy looking at the ceiling and did not notice how the dress showed off her femininity, especially her small waist and hips. That's when she turned off the switch and grabbed her bag saying, "Time to go and see the bright lights of Las Vegas." Paul was dressed in his Wrangler jeans and royal blue shirt; he put on his Stetson hat, and they set off walking down the main street of Vegas. Day had turned into night, but the strip had turned into day with the multitude of lights. They walked past the magnificent casinos—the Golden Nugget, the Horseshœ, and Stardust; and they stopped at the most breathtaking site of the Horseshœ which boasted seven miles of neon and twenty-eight thousand lightbulbs. The Golden Nugget offered 99¢ breakfasts all day so they spent the rest of the evening there and ate breakfast four times—that is all they could afford. They sat by the slots as they were given free Bloody Mary's while playing the gaming machines. Paul had a game of poker and Janet tried her luck at roulette; they did not win the jackpot, but they had the time of their lives.

They were walking back toward their motel; Janet had wandered in front of Paul. She would often go into her own world; she was so happy and started singing "MacArthur Park" as if she were Donna Summer.

I recall the yellow cotton dress
Foaming like a wave
On the ground around your knees
The birds, like tender babies in your hands
And the old men playing checkers by the trees

She did not notice a large black Cadillac crawling at the side of her exposed left thigh. A black-suited hand was waving a fistful of dollars at her. Janet turned around as the dollars swept her thigh. She turned around looking for Paul. "Paul darling!" she shouted and then looked at the driver and said, "So sorry you are too late and I am on my honeymoon." Paul took her by the arm and with that the Cadillac pulled away. "Poor man, but that could have been our ticket to see Diana," Janet remarked. Paul answered, "I get so worried about you. You could get into trouble here doing things like that with strangers." Janet was just too trustful. With that they left for the motel. They opened a bottle of bourbon and coke and let's say they spent a night on the ocean waves.

They were to drive back the next day; Paul left Janet by the poolside. He was concerned that they did not have enough petrol to get back to California. He went to the pawnshop and he sold the watch that Janet had bought him for their engagement. It was the only way they could get petrol for the car. He returned with a full tank of petrol. He made the excuse that he had lost the watch on the prior evening. Janet never knew where the watch was lost. Paul did know to make sure that when they next take a trip into a new state, he would not rely on his California checkbook when moving to another state.

Janet could not believe how quickly time was moving, it has been three weeks since she left her hometown in Yorkshire. She knew after the adventures in America that Paul would not want to return to England after his contract and that their whole life was about to change. Janet spent her last week lazing by the pool at Madrid Suites during the day and the evenings were spent at the Wranglers Roost.

Chapter Five

JANET WAS LAZING around the poolside and she overheard a conversation between a young woman and an older gentleman. The woman had fingernails that were spoon shaped, and the gentleman said he could help her. He was an endocrinologist that practiced with natural therapies. He had prescribed some pancreatic enzymes, adjusted her diet, and within a week her nails had returned to normal. Janet could not help but talk to the gentleman.

"How do you know so much and how positive are you that you can make a difference? Have you been doing your kind of work for a long time?" she asked.

"For twenty years," he replied.

"Well what can you fix?" she asked.

"Many, many ailments. You see if you support the body and its immune system to heal, it becomes what we call a healthy healing. People have much more energy when they are well. Modern diet makes people sicker. The sugar can kill you."

"Can you teach me?" Janet asked, "My name is Janet by the way, I am a nurse and a midwife—well only just a midwife."

"My, how you are so young, how old are you?" He shook her hand and continued, "My name is Bo. Meet me here tomorrow lunch time and I will show you what I mean." Janet met Bo by the poolside the next day at lunch time.

"I brought you some lunch." He had been to McDonald's and bought her a cheeseburger, chips, and a regular coke.

"Oh, but I have never eaten at McDonald's, my parents only gave me healthy food at home," she said.

"All the better," he replied, "I will be able to show you something." She had a bite of the burger, the bread tasted very sweet, and so did the coke. She ate the meal. Bo started to converse with her. "Food can affect people emotionally," he said. "The carbohydrate can put you on a high. That is why children become hyperactive and they have attention deficit disorders, it can actually lead to mischievous behavior and crime. That is, carbohydrate turns to sugar and creates high energy levels." Just as he finished speaking, Janet had an overwhelming tiredness and began to yawn. "Gosh I feel so sleepy, and down, I need to lie down. I don't have any energy."

"That is what I am trying to teach you. Your blood sugars are now out of balance, you should not feel sleepy after a meal, and food should energize you for the day. You should not have highs and lows." Janet was young but she was experiencing everything he was talking about. She continued to yawn. "You see the bread contains sugar, and it is carbohydrate, the meat has carbohydrate and additives and the potato chips and coke are pure sugar and if you continue a diet like that every day you will get diabetes. Your body needs to make insulin to break down the sugar, and it will get tired. The part of your body that produces insulin is your pancreas."

"I know that." Janet said. "I am a nurse and I have taken care of many people with diabetes, but no one ever explained that to me."

"They won't," Bo answered, "and people will not take notice until well after I am long gone. The pancreas is the most important gland of your body and if you don't take care of it you will get sick." Janet could not believe just how tired and sleepy she was. "Would you like to come to Ensenada with me tomorrow, I have a private clinic there and I will show you a different kind of healing." Janet trusted Bo and was excited. "I would love to. I will meet you here at 8:00 a.m.," she replied. With that she had to go upstairs and sleep. She was exhausted. Paul came home from work that evening. She needed to tell Paul about her intended trip. "You are so naive," he said. "A complete stranger wants to take you to Mexico, and you want to go, he might sell you over there." Janet was not buying into that, she was usually intuitive and this felt real. She invited Bo over and he met Paul. Once Paul had been introduced, he agreed that Janet may go to Mexico. Janet felt a little intimidated because she was old enough to make her own decisions; she might be young, but not stupid.

The next morning they drove to Ensenada, and Bo took her to his clinic. She was impressed as the clinic was not dusty or in a back street. There was a receptionist at the front desk. "Your first client is waiting." The receptionist pointed to a very old Indian gentleman. He had pure white hair, long and tied behind in a ponytail. His arm was in a sling. Bo invited the gentleman through into his clinic room, and there he undressed the bandage. There was a deep wound; it was about three inches deep and about two inches wide. It was a previous burn wound that refused to heal. He had been prescribed many antibiotics, but the wound refused to heal. Bo went to the cupboard and took a needle and syringe; he had first cleaned the wound with a small amount of hydrogen peroxide. The wound went kind of fizzy, that is to take away the dead skin. He then injected a fluid. "What is that?"

"That is adrenal cortex hormone, it comes from your kidneys. It will naturally get a blood supply into the area, and encourage the wound to heal."

"Why do you have to do this in Mexico?" Janet asked.

"That is because natural practices are not allowed in America. Many drugs are banned by the FDA. There are many good practitioners working in Mexico. Film stars come here for treatments. We give placental hormone extract to alleviate aging." Janet went to Ensenada twice a week for the next two weeks. She saw the burn wounds healed, and people with bowel disorders cured. She would never have known that some thirty years later this work would be practiced in America; adrenal cortex extract would be used to fight chronic fatigue. She never saw a film star but she had learned that there were many ways in which to heal people. She had three trips to Ensenada, and she started to read many books that Bo had loaned to her. She spent the two weeks reading the books by the poolside while topping up her Californian tan ready for her return to England where she had to return to her profession as a midwife. Paul didn't like the idea of Janet taking up witchcraft. "Don't be silly," she used to tell him. "It is really interesting."

Janet knew that Paul was settled in America and that his only way to stay there would be for her to take up nursing there, that she would have to sit the American exams as *British* nurses would not be accepted unless they passed American exams, and that midwives did not exist in the private health care system which was run by private obstetricians. She paid a visit to the local bookstore and she bought some nursing textbooks which were nurse and obstetric nurse combined. She managed to get some old papers from the previous exams, and she began to study. Her only failing was that British nurses were not psychiatric trained. She knew she would have to do a lot of work and make inquiries once she returned to England. She had recently completed her Midwifery studies and it looked like she would have to go back to school. There was yet another challenge ahead of her. She had discussed the options to try and help Paul get a Green Card. He was so happy, yet she felt empty as she wanted to be a midwife as her grandmother had been.

Leaving Paul behind was not easy; she knew she would miss him terribly, but there was no choice, her visitor's visa was about to expire and she would need a new one. She would have to leave the country to get that renewed. Paul drove her to LA and she returned on her Pan Am flight. The ten hours of flying went very quickly and she knew she would return in October, and she spend the whole flight reading the books that she had purchased. She needed to earn some extra money as she had to pay the mortgage as Paul's income kept him in the U.S. She returned to England on the seventh of April. Her bags were packed with Mexican pottery and presents that she had bought for her family. She battled the escalators at King's Cross as she had previously, except this time she managed to hang on to her suitcase. She took the train from London to Doncaster and her father collected her at the train station. She was so happy to see him and she was so excited to tell him about her travels that she blurted everything out in one hour. She was verbally rambling about her experience.

She had settled into her new job and spent a lot of time with her books; she could not find a course to study psychiatry, but she found a company that assisted British midwives to study for the American examinations. She couldn't wait to relay the news to Paul. Janet visited the nightclub in Rotherham where they used to work and she caught up with new friends to boast her Californian tan and experiences. Nothing had changed in her absence, not even the weather. It was wet windy and raining. Rotherham was very cloudy and the River Don was as muddy as ever with the industrial waste pollution. She stopped going to the night clubs because it seemed that without Paul she became vulnerable; the male testosterone levels saw her as being the lonely wife, and many wanted to take advantage of that. Rumors from friends to family started; if she was seen with one of Paul's friends, it was assumed she was having affairs, and that led to interrogation by Paul's family. How she hated the venomous gossip of who she thought were her friends.

Letters from Paul came every week telling her of the parties at the Wranglers Roost and how everyone asked how she was; Paul's letters were full of travel and excitement. Her letters were so monotonous such as paying the bills, getting the car fixed, shopping, and her new job. Despite the monotony of what she was doing the time moved quickly and it was time for her to return to California. She could not wait to absorb the Californian sunshine and visit the bars over there.

Paul collected her from LA in October and they returned to Madrid Suites. It wasn't the lustful greeting that she had expected. It was as if a good friend had turned up to meet her—a friend fulfilling a dutiful obligation of collecting her from the airport. He looked so brown with his Californian tan and she looked so lily white. She did not care as she was back in the Land of Opportunity—that's how Paul had described it in his letters. They arrived back at the apartment, and there was to be a dinner party that evening to welcome her. She crashed down and slept for the afternoon; she was exhausted. Paul had to return to work.

That evening they went to the apartment, Taffy was having a party; it seemed that their boss at work had them working lots of overtime as there was pressure to get the job done. There was a lot of discord around work. The boss's name was Tom. Taffy had bought a parrot; that parrot was learning to speak. They had a few tequilas that night, and suddenly the parrot was repeatedly saying, "Tom's a wanker, Tom's a wanker." Taffy gave the parrot the worm from the bottle of tequila and with that the intoxicated parrot hung upside down from its perch in the cage. Janet never forgot how the parrot was swinging upside down from its perch, with the worm swinging from its beak. "More tequila and you guys will be swinging upside down from the balcony." Janet was tired and she retired to the apartment, leaving the boys to finish the bottle of tequila. "Why do they have to get so pissed?" she said. She didn't like what she was experiencing but she had no choice.

Days would pass by and she would spend time by the poolside, painting her nails, waiting for the post to arrive every day at 1:00 p.m. She was getting bored, and she did not like the feeling of being a kept woman. She had given up her job and her independence. Bo had seen her by the pool and she took up going to Ensenada to the private clinic so she could learn more about holistic health. She spent a lot of time trying to understand psychiatry. She was to take the state exams in New York in February.

Paul had a long weekend and he and Taffy had hired a black Chevrolet. Paul told Janet that she was going for a long weekend trip to Tucson. Janet would do anything to get away from the party binges that were happening far too often. They set off early that morning. They had packed clothes into the car for a weekend and the car was large enough to sleep in. The trip was some 410 miles. It was a very long and boring drive along the dusty desert roads; they were well informed to fill their tanks with petrol every time they passed a gas station. There was a bar with a skeleton over the front. Inside was a pool table and the boys downed a Budweiser. Janet was so amused by the rocky horror state of the bar. They played pool and set off on their journey after refilling the tank with petrol. They had travelled for twenty minutes when behind them they saw the flashing lights of a state highway patrol car, no one had warned them of the extra presence of the state highway patrol, and thank goodness the boys only had one Budweiser. Paul pulled into the side of the road and the threesome were asked to put their hands on the dashboard and then the good-looking tanned policeman asked for ID. "Do you realize you were travelling 70 miles per hour and the limit is fifty-five?" he asked. They had not seen the signs anywhere and the motorways in England had a maximum speed limit of 70 miles per hour. It was rather scary. They were asked to step out of the car and sprawl with their legs wide and hand stretched over the top. Firstly the patrol officer did a quick body search on Taffy. Janet's sense of humor couldn't help herself. "You won't find much there," she said as the patrol officer searched below Taffy's belt. Next came the search on Paul. "I can vouch for that one," she said as she knew her husband was well-endowed with the correct equipment. She could see the officer was trying to grin and smile and yet be completely serious. Then came the search on Janet. "Before you start, I am totally clean and well equipped, *but* could we please have a photograph with your car, my father would be so happy to see an American officer doing his job as he thinks that there is no crime control in the States." She had that mischievous monkey grin and as he searched her she couldn't help but say, "Wow, there will be some lucky woman taking you out tonight!" Then the officer completed the paperwork and was very accommodating. They posed for photographs holding the speed gun with the car. Paul was given the opportunity to pay a fine or to go to traffic school for a day. Paul opted for traffic school as he thought this would be interesting. "Oh my goodness, nicked and nipped in Arizona, what a note for the diary. Thank you so much, Officer, have a good day and we will be sure to behave just like the posh bees do, you know in a bee hive."

Paul nudged Janet as if to say "that's enough of the British humor." With that, dawn was approaching and so was the sunset. They would never forget the brilliant red skies as the sun went down. They were not prepared for the cold of the desert. Taffy had parked the car and they slept the night with the heaters on. They woke in the morning and the milk had turned to ice, and the bacon was frozen. He wrapped the bacon in silver foil and placed it on the engine under the bonnet so it would thaw as they drove a little further. They stopped by the side of this enormous cactus plant. It seemed to reach upward to touch the skies. Goodness knows how old it was, but standing next to it, she felt like one of the little people from Gulliver's travels in Lilliput.

They arrived at Old Tucson which reminded her once again of the movies she had seen of the Wild West. The street had an old hotel and in it a bar where they took a cold beer. "Apparently they filmed *The Gambler* here," Taffy remarked. She could see herself snug next to Kenny Rogers and she didn't care whether or not it was that movie. She just wanted to slide into her own dream world. "Maybe *The Maverick* too?" she asked. Taffy and Paul smiled. There was a stunt show of the *Wild Wild West*. There was a gun fight from the rooftops; Janet walked and tripped up on a plank of wood and fell to her face. Paul picked her up. "Don't worry, folks, it's all part of the show," he said loudly to the tourists.

They then ventured to the site where there was a replica of Wyatt Earp and Doc Holliday from the Gunfight of the O.K. Coral. They mimicked a gunfight between them. Paul and Taffy put out their three fingers and aimed them at Janet saying, "Powpow!" Janet replied, "Better take up shooting lessons, missed, missed!" And with that they went to Boot Hill graveyard and looked at the old gravestones, there was an aura around them and the messages on the stones.

So much of the good and so much of the bad of early Tombstone lies buried here, and over the graves of both is growing the true crucifixion thorn. Janet began to read out the history, "Boot Hill Graveyard was laid out as a burial plot in 1878. Called the Tombstone Cemetery, it was the burial place for the town's first pioneers and was used as such until sometime around 1884 when the present plot was opened as a burial place. There had been many violent deaths here and buried in Tombstone were outlaws with their victims, suicides, and hangings—legal and otherwise—along with the hardy citizens and refined element of Tombstone's first days." Janet walked around the stones and was amused and yet taken aback by the messages on the stones.

Ewa Waters aged three months, scarlet fever

Billy Clanton Frank McLaury Tom McLaury: Murdered on the streets of Tombstone, 1881. Tragic results of the O.K. Corral Battle, which took place between the Earp Brothers with Doc Holliday and the cowboys. Three men were killed and three were wounded

In memory of Frank Bowles, born Aug. 5, 1828, died Aug. 26, 1880.

"As you pass by, remember that as you are, so once was I, and as I am, you soon will be. Remember me."

Lester Moore "Here lays Lester Moore, Four slugs from a .44, No Les, no more"

And finally Janet being the midwife could not help but feel for Mrs. Stump. Stump died in 1884 during childbirth from an overdose of chloroform given to her by the doctor. "Doctors bungle births too, It is a pity they did not add that to the stone" Janet remarked knowing that midwives were undermined by the medical profession. "And they thought midwives were incapable of managing birth". With that they continued to walk around the graveyard.

There were eleven rows of graves and each had its own story. "We just don't realize how lucky we are today, do we?" she said. For one brief moment she felt rather sad as she remembered the stories of World War 2 shared by Gregory and her parents. "We listen but we don't really understand and perhaps we never will." Janet had a few tears strolling down her face as she whispered to Paul who did not have her sympathetic heart. "Optimism is what we need, we need to soldier on optimism." Then she started to sing, *Always look on the bright side of life.* How she needed cheering up after Tombstone. She began to sing the words from her favorite song. *For though they may be parted. There is still a chance that they will see, there will be an answer, let it be.* And with that, Taffy remarked that Paul McCartney had bought a ranch near Tucson recently. He surprised Janet that he actually knew something about The Beatles. "Paul McCartney is the most famous Arizonan. Yes, he is a Brit. But he owns a ranch in Southern Arizona closer to Tucson than to Phœnix, he bought it for Linda you know." Taffy let his knowledge be known. "My, Taffy, I didn't think you knew anything much more than how the worms got to be in the bottom of the tequila bottle!" she remarked. Taffy answered, "First off, there are no worms in tequila. The worm is associated with Mezcal, the agave spirit hailing from the area around Oaxaca in southern Mexico. The worms are moth larvæ that live within the agave plant. It is also said that the worm absorbs the impurities in the spirit, thus improving the flavor. And still another story claims the adding of the worm was just a ploy to get gringos to drink Mezcal and add to the fun of the experience. In any case, the worm is quite harmless—but it is also great fun to introduce a new experience to someone who has never tried Mezcal! Like you, Janet, huh!"

"Okay, I get your point," Janet said as she pointed to the O.K. Corral. "Are you ready for a shoot-out?" She pointed three fingers at Taffy. "Pow, pow!"

"Come on you two, it's time to head off home." Paul did not join in the fun; it seemed as though he had his mind on other things. Janet was about to find out just what those other things were. She slept the whole ride back to San Diego. Janet was becoming her own person, a woman, and she was no longer walking behind the shadows of Paul.

Janet spent the next day resting by the poolside reading her books, lazing in the Californian sunshine. Bo joined her later in the day. They talked about life. Bo had been divorced, it had been quite traumatic. Bo put the hurt from his life into his work to help others. "You know sometimes we cannot change the direction of our life but we can change how we deal with everything God intended us to learn from it." He explained how he had been very sick lethargic and depressed. His wife just got fed up with trying to cope with his depression and she moved on. "I was so low, I almost topped myself. When tiredness and depression sets in you just get into a state and then you don't know you are in it. You just don't see how bad things are. I spent a whole year sulking after the divorce, I would lie in my room and not want to move," he said. Then the cleaning lady came to the house. She was from Mexico. "Why you like this, senior, it is no good for you." He explained how Melissa had swung open the windows, to let the light in. "You must always let the light shine on you and you need to use your pain to help others, you need to dance." Melissa had turned on some of Bo's music that day and she took him by the hand. "In Mexico, we dance." She played some Mariachi music. "I work here to pay for my son's health, he cannot breathe well and he is very sick and needs medication." Bo said that day his heart reached out to her. He had asked Melissa to bring her son to see him. "I cannot bring him over the border, I only have a work permit, and we are taking care of him in Mexico," she said. That day he had forgotten his own pain. He dressed and took Melissa to Mexico, and they went to see her son. He was only nine years old; he was extremely thin and had a very pale face. He spends the day with an oxygen mask. The boy was very sick, but the house was full of life and vibrant colors. Music played in the home. Bo had explained how Melissa used to dance and sing "Optimism, Optimism." Bo travelled to his clinic and took the herbs and medications to heal Melissa's son. He had spent six months visiting Melissa's home and he never forgot the hospitality. They had little money, but they gave him food, kindness, and optimism. Bo had fixed Melissa's son to health. Melissa still cleans his house. They are good friends. That's how Bo spent his life healing and helping others, and he told Janet the rewards of kindness and friendships were priceless. "Sometimes if you help someone the rewards may not come from that person, but if you live your life with an open and caring heart, then your life will be rewarded from the many other people that come into your life." Janet loved his words of wisdom and experience. She was too young to take onboard all of what he was trying to say. "You will learn in time, young one." Janet felt so uplifted with his stories. "One day I will be just as wise as you." She smiled at Bo and with that she went to collect the post. Her father wrote to her every week. This letter was truly informing her of her family and how well everyone was doing and that he was looking forward to seeing her very soon.

Paul had been working late nights, sometimes until 1:00 a.m. Janet had plenty to do with her studies. They went to eat at Howard Johnston's (HJ's). He just did not seem interested in Janet's stories. He just used to say, "I don't like you hanging around with that man Bo." Janet did not care; she was not going to give up on her only American friend. That night in HJ's a young waitress came over to serve coffee; she was petite and had beautiful long blond hair tied back. She was wearing the orange dress and white shoes; she had such a trim waist. She smiled—it was a smile you would have seen from Hollywood, the wide American smile with large white glistening teeth. She had beautiful blue eyes and a figure that would fit Farah Fawcett. "This is Shelly," Paul introduced her to Janet. "He is a friend of Taffy's."

Lucky Taffy. Janet thought. The American girls just loved the British accents of the boys. After dinner Paul invited Shelly to the table to sit with them; she was studying something to do with working as a secretary in the medical system. Janet offered to help Shelly with medical terminology for her studies. Every day after school Shelly would collect Janet and they would go to study. Shelly was very warm and she had an irresistible smile. She used to tease the boys. The boys invited Shelly to the Wranglers Roost but she was not able to go in because she was only eighteen and in America you need to be twenty-one to get into a bar. They were very strict on ID. The foursome used to meet at one another's house. They used to party and have fun together. Shelly would go out of her way to cook Mexican food. The girls would enjoy a couple of glasses of Californian wine and the boys would enjoy the American beers.

Janet thought it was good that Taffy had a date. She used to go to the bar with the boys at night but she would wait outside in the car park. How she must have hated being eighteen. Janet could only remember how she used to fake her ID and party at sixteen. Janet would spend the night dancing the cowboy polkas and country swings; she loved the music so much. Lanny had released a song "A Fistful of Avocados and a Bottle of Wine" and he had released an album titled "That Kind of Man." Janet bought the record for a keepsake and she couldn't get over how much he looked Like Kenny Rogers. Paul used to entertain himself on the pool table with the boys, Janet couldn't help but notice how he didn't seem to notice her any more, and he used to come over for an occasional dance. "Give me one of those Dirty

Mothers," Janet asked Randy at the bar. Janet explained how she was feeling to Randy, that Paul would not leave the pool table. Paul had joined Taffy to speak to Shelly outside the club. Randy took Janet to the pool table. "Listen, hun, there's one lesson in life—if you can't beat them, join them." Randy put the pool cue in Janet's hand and started to teach Janet how to "shoot pool." Randy had lined up the balls, and then she lined Janet's body with the ball and the pool cue. Randy was a pool hustler; she often played for money. Janet took to the game and just like the dancing, she was as good as the boys. She spent many nights at the bar shooting pool, she even won games. "Keep your eye on the ball Keep a straight line and knock them in, gal!" Randy often used to shout that from over the bar as Janet played her game. "Life is a game and you always need to be on top of the game," she used to tell Janet. Janet was well occupied and she never noticed how many times Paul used to escape outside to talk to Shelly. Taffy used to keep Janet occupied shooting pool. Andy would look over across the bar; he had lots of experience with relationships. He rescued her from the pool table and took her for a dance. "You know if you love someone it is like a bird, let it go, and if it loves you it will return. Try to clip the wings and it will hurt you forever," he whispered into Janet's ears but she did not want to hear, she was confused. She felt alone, and she began to lose her sparkling personality. She would ask Paul if everything was okay, she would hint that it wasn't good to be seeing so much of Shelly, and maybe they should go away for a few days. Paul told her not to be so silly and that she was imagining things. There the emotional abuse started. They did go somewhere, Paul took all four of them back to Disneyland, and Janet was hoping they would go alone. This time Disneyland was not the fairytale and Snow White was to fight for her prince. The four sat in Alice's Teacups and Taffy spun the wheel so fast. Shelly fell over toward Paul and Janet found herself hanging on to the back of the cup. "Slow down, Taffy." They came off the cup ride and Janet felt sick, not from the spinning effects of the ride but the stomach pains felt from heartache. They had visited the shops and were putting on sombreros. Janet took a quick look at the Kodak snapshots and she seemed to be hiding in the background—you could barely see she was in any photograph. They had stopped at a restaurant for something to eat. Shelly had moved to the side next to Paul. Janet decided this was war so she took a Reserved sign from the next table and she planted it exactly where she wanted Shelly to stay away from and that was on Paul's crotch. Shelly moved away from Paul and Janet sat beside him with a huge grin on her face.

They returned to the apartments, her days by the pool were lonely and she just did too much thinking. Shelly would arrive in her swimsuit, her long painted nails, and Hollywood body. It didn't matter what she was wearing, she looked stunning. Janet was feeling rejection and she would look at her reflection in the water; she used to compare herself with Shelly. She hated herself. Paul would make excuses of working longer nights and blamed the contract for that. She would be alone in the evenings with a cooked dinner and would eat it herself, alone. She would play Barbara Streisand.

> *Life is a moment in space*
> *When the dream is gone*
> *It's a lonelier place*
> *I kiss the morning good-bye*
> *But down inside you know*
> *We never know why*
> *The road is narrow and long*
> *When eyes meet eyes*

And the feeling is strong
I turn away from the wall
I stumble and fall
But I give you it all

Chorus:
I am a woman in love
And I do anything
To get you into my world
And hold you within
It's a right I defend
Over and over again
What do I do?

She finished the song and with that she drank a few glasses of Californian wine. She needed to sleep; she needed to forget what was happening. She was not looking forward to the next day.

She woke up the next morning to find Paul by her side but there was silence. "How was work yesterday?" she asked.

"Okay," he replied. "I will be home this evening and working late tomorrow." He did come home that evening, and they did make love. He was hiding something, and their lovemaking was short, quick, and unemotional.

December had arrived and they had decided to return to England; they were to surprise everyone. "Why don't you invite Shelly?" Janet asked. "It would be nice for her to see England." Janet used her monkey charms as she knew she was going to keep an eye on things. Maybe when he saw their beautiful home and family he might change his mind. They did return home that Christmas. They arrived Christmas eve at her father's house. They started singing carols at the front door. "No carol singers today, we've paid enough out, go away." The threesome continued to sing, *Good King Wenceslas last looked out on the feast of Stephen* With that, Janet's father opened the door and she was so happy to see his excited and smiling face.

Janet did some bureau work at the hospital to save money for their next trip back. Shelly was working on the in-laws. "My, she is just so wonderful, she makes the bed every morning." Janet felt sicker inside and she had no control. They spent Christmas day with Paul's family around the Christmas tree. *'Tis the season to be jolly . . . .* "What the hell is jolly about it?" Janet would ask herself. They sat around the room and exchanged presents, the first being from Paul's family to Janet. It was a scroll tube wrapped in blue ribbon. She opened it while everyone watched over her. She tipped it down and out fell a piece of lettuce and tomato.

"We have just the right diet for you." Paul's mother smiled. "Now, Paul, how is the Land of Golden Opportunities, you do plan to stay over there, don't you?" With that Janet left the room and ran upstairs to the bathroom—she vomited, her eyes filled with tears, and she looked in the mirror while hating her body; she hated them even more. They were so cruel and they had succeeded in making Janet feel ugly. Paul constantly reminded her to stop imagining things. "Can't you take a joke?" he said with a smile. "You are just too serious." Shelly laughed too. Janet could not forgive him for that mental cruelty.

She went to St. Bede's Church, the very place they married; she sat in the aisles, and this time the light was not shining through the church windows. She asked forgiveness for her jealousy. She didn't hear an answer. She found herself with the priest; she had opened her heart to him. She couldn't tell her family; she had to keep holding on to her own secrets.

She followed Paul to the nightclub for New Year; here roles were reversed, as Shelly's Yankee accent had captured the hearts of everyone and she was the center of attention. Janet did what she did best— she beat everyone on the pool table that night. No one noticed how beautiful she looked; all eyes were turning to Shelly. They would go shopping and Janet tried to continue as normal as possible. She had purchased a green corduroy dressing gown for Shelly to take back to the U.S. They left on January 4.

Janet could not return to America until February as she was to take the state board examinations; she was Paul's Green Card entry to the Land of Opportunity, but she knew he had found a Green Card in Shelly. Her heart was not into study. She was studying Erikson's Trust versus Mistrust Theory. And she came to the stage of fidelity. "Who am I, how do I fit in? Where am I going in life?" Erikson believed that if the parents allow the child to explore, they will conclude their own identity. However, if the parents continually push him/her to conform to their views, the teen will face identity confusion. Janet was certainly on a trail of exploration and she was certainly confused with her identity. She did not know who she was anymore.

Janet spent a lot of time with her father, though twenty-three, she would sit on his knees; he was her best friend. "You know when the world comes tumbling down, how do you build it back up again? The walls came down around Jericho and they rebuilt Jericho, I need to rebuild my life," she said as she told her father how she felt about the relationship, that she felt so insecure. "Baby, he came to me one week before he married you and he asked if he was doing the right thing. I told him, 'If you love her, marry her and if you don't, go join the army, go do anything but don't hurt my daughter.'" Her father said no more except that he would support her.

Paul's letters were not as frequent as they had been; he asked how the studies were doing and complained about the long hours at work—that was it. Janet just kept busy with work and studies.

Chapter Six

FEBRUARY CAME BY very quickly and she packed her bags to fly to the Big Apple. Her father took her to the train station. It was snowing. "Why do you always leave in the snow?" he asked. She was going to New York for one week and then returning home, to earn some extra money to cover the flight costs to the U.S. Once again she had packed her winter clothes and she found herself fighting with those steep escalators in King's Cross. The flight to New York took around seven hours. Janet was engrossed in her books. The books took half of her baggage allowance. They were heavy. She arrived at JFK early hours of the morning. She was greeted by the company who was arranging for her to take the examinations. It was freezing cold—thank goodness she was wearing her tanned fur coat. It had been her grandmother's, 1900style. It wrapped almost twice around her and was very snug. It was -5 degrees. Every time she exhaled air it formed a cloud of fog around her. The hotel was on the corner of thirty-ninth street, a few bus stops from where she was to take her examinations.

Janet was overwhelmed with the tall skyscraper buildings which reached the sky. It was extremely cold and the streets lacked sunshine. The company guide checked them into the hotel room situated on the twenty-seventh floor. Janet could feel her ears pop as they ascended the escalator. Once they had checked in and found their rooms they met in the hotel restaurant. Janet was the only European in the twenty-something group—most were from the Philippines and Malaysia. They were all trying so desperately hard to get a Green Card through nursing. Janet could not understand why she would have to resist examinations in a country where English was the first language and the USA and Britain were buddies. American nurses could come to the UK, but the Brits weren't good enough for America. "What the hell am I doing here?" she asked herself.

The route for the examination rooms were set; they were to either catch a bus or tube and they were advised to arrive early. The examination would be set over two days. Janet did not like the feel of New York. Police sirens were sounding every few minutes. They were told to be very careful and watch their bags at all times, preferably not to carry valuables with them. "Be wary of the subway system, it is not safe. You could call it our 'Jekyll and Hyde' period of the New York subway system where crime was abysmal. It has the filthiest trains, the craziest graffiti, the noisiest wheels, and the weirdest passengers, so only travel on the subway during the day—*never at night.* You may not read the signage because of the graffiti so here are your subway maps!"

Janet felt like she was a schoolchild all over again, but she knew the woman was being serious, and she knew she just had to be safe. Janet continued to study that night; she started to read about Erikson's Intimacy and Isolation Stage between the ages of twenty-four to thirty-four. According to Erikson, this would be the time to decide whether to marry or not. "Intimacy—none." She couldn't take Paul from her mind. "Isolation—never! I have too many friends and a great family," she said to herself.

The next morning she dressed to go for a coffee before getting on the bus. She stopped in at a coffee shop because it was freezing cold; her fingers were numb after standing outside for ten minutes. She would have a coffee, go out for the bus, the bus was late, she would freeze, and she would take another coffee. The guy at the coffee shop was scratching his head. "Just how many coffees?" he asked. She must have had at least four coffees; her heart was pounding from all of the caffeine. She decided to give up on the bus trip and go to the underground. It was 8:00 a.m. and jam-packed with people. It was filthy and graffiti was all over the trains, the walls and the signs—paper cups were lying everywhere. The stands in the Rotherham football grounds were cleaner after a Saturday game. She did not like New York, and she had not seen any of it. She arrived at the hall where she was to take the exams; it was lined with more than sixty desks, and sitting behind them were the Green Card hopefuls as she called them. "They must be desperate to want to stay here," she talked to herself. The hall was quiet, the bell rang and they started to complete their multiple choice questions. There were security guards walking up and down the aisles between the desks. They were in uniforms and were wearing guns! Police sirens echœd around the room every few minutes. It was so loud and noisy. She couldn't focus as she would have done; she sailed through the medical, surgical, and obstetric papers. She lost the plot when it came to psychiatry. She could not turn away from the thoughts of Paul. She was trying to move her psychology into his head and nothing was working. She had completed the papers but she knew in her hearts she was not going to pass those exams and she was not going to be the one that provides a Green Card for Paul. She needed to do something for herself, she needed to find out the truths and she needed to do it there and then.

She stopped off at Sears to do some shopping; she only had winter clothes with her so she bought some new swimwear and lingerie in a dream that she would win back her husband. "I married, I took vows, and I have an obligation *for better or for worse.*" She had lost weight with the stress of the exams, and she so much wanted to fit into the size 8 dresses that Shelly had worn. That wasn't to be but a size 10 did the job. She bought a beautiful pink dress that had a small neckband and opened into a V shape that showed her endowed breasts. She rubbed them upward to give her an Anne Boleyn look and she did look stunning. That night she went to JFK airport. She cashed in her return flight and bought a flight to San Diego. She had called her father and said, "Don't pick me up at the airport, I am going to San Diego, I have to sort out my marriage." With that she put the phone down and called the apartments to leave a message for Paul. She arrived at the apartment; she still had a key, but she was hesitant to open the door and she had no knowing what to find. The apartment was empty, so she knocked on Taffy's door. "What are you doing here?" He was shocked and surprised to see her. "Oh Paul has gone away on a work weekend. He will be back tomorrow." Taffy had stuttered and Janet knew he was a lousy liar. She didn't care, she went back to the apartment—she was tired. She opened a bottle of wine and downed a glass within five minutes. She pulled open the bed settee and there was a button, green corduroy, the same as the dressing gown she had bought for Shelly. She was so angry she threw everything out of her case. She drank the bottle of wine and fell asleep. Paul arrived early that morning. There was silence as he entered the door. He was moving around like a thief in the night. He stumbled over the suitcase and with that Janet opened her eyes. "Hi, babe," he said as he was not surprised to see her. Taffy must have sounded the alarm bells, and Paul knew he was going to find her in the apartment. "Sorry it was a work's outing and we stayed over at the boss's." Janet knew he was lying, but she did not want to make a scene—it wasn't the right time. Paul didn't want Janet to think there was anything wrong. He crawled into bed with her and they made love. Janet felt used and she did not enjoy sex. She knew it was sex without love. She dressed later that day and they spent the day by the pool in complete silence. She felt sick for the last couple of months and put it down to stress. She and Paul had not made love since the night he left the UK at the beginning of January. It was now mid-February.

Paul went to work as usual the next day. Janet sat by the poolside and met up with Bo; she cried in his arms and he just listened to her. "Tell you what, I will ring my friend and I will arrange for you and Paul to get time together." Bo was so kind. His friend had worked delivering furniture to Warner Brothers Studios. He had a friend who was a manager there. The next morning Bo gave Janet a present, a meal for two in the Beverly Hills Country Club. Janet dressed in her new pink dress and Paul dressed in his suit. They walked around the landscaped areas and entered the restaurant. Each table was perfectly set, the old teak chairs and tables with pink napkins that were the same color as her dress. The silver tableware was placed so perfectly straight and she was too afraid to untidy the tables. The waiter came in his white suit carrying a silver tray of smoked salmon and the best Californian wine was served in crystal glasses. For a few moments she had that princess feeling again. Today was the time to let it be and enjoy the day. The Salmon flavors lingered in Janet's mouth for long after they finished dinner. Paul held Janet's hand and it felt warm. They talked about her trip to New York, how unsafe she felt there and how the police sirens were constant and how the towered buildings blocked the sunshine on the streets. Paul talked about his contract may be ending and how the future was uncertain, he made it clear that he did not want to return to England, and she listened. She didn't say much about that because she knew she would spoil the day.

They drove back to San Diego that evening and Janet felt much more relaxed and at peace, it was if she had been imagining Shelly and everything else. Paul had told her he had stayed the night at Taffy's while Shelly had stayed with her friend in the apartment, hence the dressing gown button in the bed. She wanted to believe him and he was so convincing he had turned her head around into believing all was well. Paul had explained that Shelly had moved up north and that she was no longer in San Diego. Janet spent the next few days at the apartment and so did Paul. They went to the Wranglers Roost and met up with Andy and Randy. She danced again with Paul and he seemed to be paying attention to her.

Paul still claimed to be working late nights, and sometimes he would make excuses that he stayed at the boss's place, Janet was accepting of this. She seemed to have settled down and she apologized to Paul for being so foolish. She knew the days he would be home and the days he would not. Bo took Janet down to Ensenada to continue with the holistic work. Janet enjoyed the trips down there. She had given up her job in England and was dependent upon Paul. She had little money saved as she had spent it to return to San Diego from New York. Paul began to play the game of the caring husband. He would take Janet out for evening meals. The team of friends used to host dinner evenings and Janet would accompany him. They would never chat to her and there was always plenty of whispering at the table. Janet felt uneasy but she just joined in the certain conversations about the next trip. There wasn't to be a next trip.

A week had gone by and Bo had taken Janet over the border to Ensenada. On their return there seemed to be a problem with her passport. She was detained at San Diego Customs; her B12 visa had expired and that brought interrogation to Paul's company. She was twenty-three years old and questioned as if she had been a criminal. She had no idea. Paul's boss came to the Customs and Janet was given a visa for two months. This was only a visitor's visa. Paul had been summoned to the office the next day and he was to leave for England. He had asked Janet to stay and that he would return for her. He left her with a little pocket money and the car; the rent had been paid in the apartments for another month. Paul assured her he would contact her and he would be back for her.

The company had some clause in their working permits, kind of semi legal. Janet never understood that. She was once again alone without Paul. She waited two weeks for his phone call but it never came. The phone rang and she had the news from her father that her grandmother was very sick. She was the good age of 101 years old. Janet could not jump on the airplane as she did not have the money. Her father asked if they were staying in California as Paul has sold the car in England. He had not been to see them but her sister saw Paul removing his things from the house. Janet assumed he was returning to California.

Janet frequented the Wranglers Roost where Andy took care of her. Bo also took care of her. She had good friends that she could rely upon. There was still no phone call from Paul and there was only one week left at the apartment. Janet had not been well—she had been vomiting and she lost weight. She went to the local drugstore and took a pregnancy test. It was positive. She should be happy but she felt so alone and so unsure. She had no health insurance and could not visit the doctor; she had no contact with the boss of Paul's company. She became truly anxious. She would sit in the Jacuzzi at night and laze by the pool during the day with the other women who were still painting their nails and reading the local magazines. One of the women approached her and asked, "Are you okay?" Janet opened up and the woman took her to one side. "I have to tell you this as I can't stand to see you look so frail. You may hate me but I have to let you know that he has been seeing Shelly—there were no late nights." With that Janet jumped up and ran up the steps to the apartment, she tripped and fell down them. The women by the pool had called Bo. He came to help and they carried her up the stairs. They laid her on the bed so she could rest. Janet woke up as she was feeling intense cramps; she was mentally numb with shock. On the bed was a pool of blood. She knew only too well what that was. She had miscarried. She could not go to a hospital, neither a doctor. Bo had brought some things from his apartment—an IV line and he gave her some fluids to replace what she had lost. He stayed by her side for the next twenty-four hours. He had given her a sedative. She had lost two days. She woke, felt weak but she had to make a phone call only three days at the apartment and she would have nowhere to stay. She was devastated. Her friends gave her assurance that she could stay with them. She was so alone, no money, no home, and a million miles away from her family. She showered that night and she walked down to HJ's. With her she took a box of Panadol. Her intentions were to drink a bottle of bourbon and take the Panadol. She thought she had no reason to live. She felt she had let down her own family and her grandmother that she never got a chance to say good-bye to. She could not let her father down, and she knew he would be there for her when she returned home. Then she started to think about how much it would cost her family to get her home in a coffin. The truth was she did not have it in her—there was no way she could top herself. It was as if someone was saying "it is not your time yet." Somehow she lifted from a state of depression into a sense of humor. The two glasses of bourbon gave her a boost of energy. She threw the Panadol in the bin and returned home. She found the courage to call her father who was arranging her ticket home. She felt so good after speaking to him. She felt like Dorothy clicking her heels shouting, "Home, home take me home." She knew she had hit the rock bottom of her life for a few moments, actually about half an hour.

"What am I doing letting everything get me down, I am strong and I was born in the year of the monkey." she thought. Instead of depression, she chose to party. She went to the Wranglers that evening, she downed a few Dirty Mothers, and she danced with Andy. Of course she blurted out how she was feeling how else she was going to get over it. "Who needs a man, and welcome to the league of the divorced and separated!"

"We'll drink to that!" And Andy and Randy raised their glasses. "Hey girl, you've got a lot of catching up to do, we are the experts you know." That night she danced, played pool, and she was free. Free from watching what Paul was doing, free from comparing how she looked against Shelly. "Here is to freedom."

Lanny was playing onstage; he stood up and raised his glass. "To all the boys you're gonna love, to the boys you are going to hurt and to the lucky guy that deserves you!" They sang and raised their glasses to the song "A Bag Full of Avocados and a Bottle of Wine." Janet went to the jukebox and she had a ball playing all of the songs that she knew would boost her energy—Helen Reddy's "I Am Woman," Blondie's "Heart of Glass," Dr. Hook's "Better Love Next Time Baby," Leif Garret's "I Was Made For Dancing," and Patrick Hernandez's "Born to Be Alive." There was not one song that put her to the ground. Andy and Randy supported her all the way.

Janet returned to the bar for the next three nights. On the last night Andy had a surprise in store. "I am going to take you somewhere very different, so get dressed to kill." That she did. She put on the long pink satin dress that showed off her cleavage and the top of her thighs. The last night in San Diego she would never forget—absolutely never forget. Andy got her to put on a blindfold and he led her about two hundred yards down the road. He pushed open doors and she heard the sound of sexy, raunchy music. He removed the blindfolds and before she could say a word, he put his fingers over her mouth. "I thought I would take you to a strip bar so you would never live your life wondering what you missed! Only in America!" he said.

Janet spun around as the groups of men were crowded at the bar, their stage and show seemed to be filled with middle-aged men shoving dollar notes in the high crutch pants. The young men at the bar were oblivious. "Oh I get it, I get it," she said. "You are not angry with me." Andy looked at her.

"No way."

"This is the way I see it." And as her arm slipped from the bar, she stretched forward across the glass bar. She was definitely a boobie girl. She scrunched her boobs, they were uplifting. She had certainly downed a few Dirty Mothers and she wasn't into dirty men and Janet was not going to hold back her humor. "Do you know I have been so polite all of my life, I want to be a real shit and speak the honest truth, so I am going to tell you what I see . . ." She slid her boobie breasts back across the bar. She pointed across the room. "See, the young ones here, they don't notice anything except the drink in their hands and they are so busy catching up with what fishing trip or what car race or baseball game they are going to visit. They have plenty of one night stands. That is, their testosterone levels are satisfied . . .

"Now look at the stage, there is no one there less than fifty. All probably married and have spent their lives running a calendar of events. Kids soccer, kids karaoke, kids, kids, kids. They work nine-five and have their dinner at six thirty, sit in front of the TV, and go to bed early. They don't converse with their wives who are too busy doing the ironing, washing, cleaning after dinner. They have high levels of unused testosterone and they want to taste a little grass that is a bit greener than in their backyard. They go out, try the grass, gets caught out and then they divorce."

Janet couldn't help herself. "It has been that way for centuries. They will say 'I have a wife who dœs not understand me' when really they have never discussed what their wives need. The male selfish ego has been in place for centuries. Don't get me wrong there are women who visit the male strip clubs, or who can't wait for a night out with the girls to escape their boring tedious lives. Men are like cats—they want the sex but when satisfied they drop the litter and walk away." She was rather tipsy. "That's right, isn't it, Andy?"

Andy looked over to Janet he know only too well what she was saying, he had married five times after all. "Wow, getting sarcastic in your young age." They had enough of the noisy bar and "dirty old men." The left and it was around 4:00 a.m. They went to Denny's to celebrate breakfast.

"I could talk to you all night," Andy said to her.

"That's what gets me into trouble," she said as he took her arm and they continued their conversations till 8:00 a.m. Janet returned to Madrid Suites and spent the day sleeping and soaking in the last days of the Californian sunshine. She had packed her bags. Paul had moved his to heaven knows where and she didn't really care. She needed to get back to reality and was looking forward to hearing her father's words.

Andy took Janet to the airport, Janet did not know what she was going to find on her return to England. All she knew was that she was re-energized and Andy had helped her get back on track with her life. She knew she would never see him again, but she would never forget his friendship. She never got the chance to say good-bye to Bo as he was away visiting family.

It was a long flight to England as she fought with her multitude of thoughts of what ifs and what could have been. She found it to be exhausting and there were really no answers. Her bags were full of her San Diego memories and the photographs she had taken without Paul. Andy had taken her to places Paul never did. Balboa Park, Coronado Beach, Sea World, and so many more. The freedom she had felt in those beautiful places and that is how she wanted to remember America. She knew only too well how happy she had been for the last few days; the only person she had needed to please was herself and she had the company of a very dear friend to share it with. "I will come back someday," she said. That she was sure of.

Janet's brother had collected her from the airport. He did that because he wanted to protect his baby sister, who was not a baby anymore; she was well-endowed with her life experiences. She ran toward him and held him so tight. "Be careful, I can hardly breathe," he said.

Janet had told him the whole story; he had never been happy that she married Paul, but he had never told her that. "You were so happy and I didn't want to spoil that, you were so in love with him that you wouldn't have believed me in any case." Janet knew he was speaking the truth. She had been in her fairy tale world, and now the fairy tale was about to end.

Janet's father greeted his daughter with warmth and a huge loving smile; he took her close and said that he would always be there for her no matter what. She couldn't face going to her home that night—she just wasn't ready. "Don't worry the house is safe and I have changed the locks. Here are your new keys and here is to your new life." He handed Janet a glass of vodka and they toasted that. "*Nostrovia!*" They clunked glasses, drank the vodka, and threw the empty glasses over their shoulder. "For luck," Janet replied. She felt so good to be surrounded by family.

Janet rose early the next morning; she sat around the table with her father who helped her make some plans of what to do next. Paul had sold the car and she had no transport other than the bus and train service. She would need to get back to work, and she knew she could not return to the hospital where she had previously worked. She just wasn't ready for that as her nursing colleagues knew so much about her life. She and Paul had attended many of the hospital dances. She just wasn't ready to answer questions about her current situation. Her father took her shopping and bought her a new car, an old triumph Toledo. It was on sale, and she liked the registration PET. She had been her father's pet, it made her smile. At least she could get around easily looking for jobs. She enrolled with a local nursing bureau and took some work working as an industrial nurse. After working a few shifts she decided to move back into the house where she and Paul had lived. It was cold inside but very clean as her sister who lived next door had taken good care of it. The telephone had been disconnected. Paul had stopped paying the bills. There was a huge mess that she had to clean up financially. The mortgage needed to be paid, so she contacted the bank and explained the situation. They gave her two months reprieve from that knowing that she had some work lined up. She tried to contact Paul, but he never answered the phone. His father answered, "He has finished with you and you should not bother him, it is over, do you understand!" She didn't know what Paul had told them, what she did know is that they wanted her out of his life and that she had destroyed their son getting his Green Card for the Land of Golden

Opportunities. She was deeply hurt as she had been rejected. It was clear that she had been labeled as being the thief or the criminal or the wrongdœr. "Just let it be," she used to remind herself. She knew she had to move on with her life and that was not going to be easy as there was so much to sort out. That was there would be lots of legalities around the house and possessions. Her sister had divorced and she knew how painful that experience was.

She drove down to the church where they had married one more time, she sat in front of the altar where she was once married and asked so many questions. She was conversing with God, hoping for answers. She spoke with the priest who comforted her. "You know people make mistakes, they can sometimes be fixed and sometimes they cannot. You took vows for better or for worse and you need to fulfill your obligation, you need to find a way to try and salvage something, then if nothing is salvaged you will go through life knowing you tried." She was very grateful for his words of wisdom. The words were easy enough but putting them into practice was a different story.

Janet went to the nightclub where Paul had worked as DJ. Geoff and Mark and Stephan were the bouncers on the nightclub door; she had always been close to them especially Mark and they used to have lots of laughs when she worked there. "I don't know if I should let you in, we don't want any fights in here." He smiled at her.

"Don't worry, I haven't come to fight."

Paul was there; he was standing by the bar chatting to some young girls. Janet had to find the courage to walk over. She didn't know how she would feel seeing him again. He turned around, took one look at her as if she was a complete stranger, then he walked away. She could not get near to ask just one question. It was as if she had to play some cat and mouse game. She needed answers and she needed to talk about what would happen to the house. They played cat and mouse for two months; she would go out with friends and he would be on some couch groping the different girls. She would dance ensuring some handsome man would be in her arms as she left the club. There were times she would go over and ask, "Just be honest with me." But he would walk away. It was painful in the beginning, painful to see someone she had loved so much reject her. The pain lessened as time went by. She just had to get over it and seeing what a pain in the arse he had been made it so much easier.

Chapter Seven

JANET WALKED TO the nightclub one evening and a young man walked by waving papers. "I am from the league of the divorced and separated. We meet every Saturday afternoon, you can bring something to eat, a packet of chips if that is all you can afford." She took the leaflet and wiped her forehead with it as if she had the word divorced written all over it. "How did he know? Do I resemble a divorcee?" she said. Probably because in that era, one out of three couples were divorcing, but it wasn't so noticeable in the larger city. She knew that was where she preferred to spend her nights because she would never see the same faces.

The following Saturday she thought she would pay a visit to the so-called league of divorced and separated people. She took about three pizzas and ten bags of chips. They met in a small community hall. There were around thirty people, traumatized from separation and divorce, some with children, sharing stories of how they had been badly treated by their ex. Janet listened to their stories, and many were caused by alcohol. It seemed as if they were enjoying being the victims, no one really spoke how they were trying to get out of their trapped circumstances. Many women had little or no education; they had no career to fall back onto. Janet saw just how lucky she had been. She witnessed how they described both mental and physical cruelty. "Bruises heal but mental cruelty can cause destruction permanently." Some of these people had never left their backyard. "At least I got to Disneyland and at least I lived a fairytale," she used to tell herself. She attended for three weeks, but she could not listen to the people who seemed to be self-absorbed with their pain—it is as if they were feeding themselves with the traumas. "I want to be the victor and not victim." She was brave enough to stand up and say that. She never went back and she knew the only way was forward for the rest of her life.

Janet had been working as an industrial nurse, most nurses there were about in the retirement age group. There were queues of young men coming to see who the young nurse was; she had given out a week's supply of panadol. So many came with headaches. *This is unbelievable,* she thought. One young man had taken her phone number from one of the nurses. That weekend she received a phone call.

"Hi, this is June, Tommy's wife."

"Hi, June, haven't heard from you in years," Janet replied thinking it was her old school friend.

"No, this is Tommy's wife from the steelworks. I found your number in his pocket." Janet fell backward speechless and she had to quickly get her thoughts together to say the right words. "I am just going through a divorce and I would never have an affair with a married man. How about we meet and I will help you cut it off!" Janet was so angry. She slammed down the phone. She pulled out a glass of vodka and said, "I needed that." She dare not go to work the next day. She just wasn't good at handling such situations despite managing the phone call perfectly.

There was a knock on the door she opened it. "Divorce papers." the man who delivered it said. Paul had applied for a divorce.

He could have delivered them himself. What a coward, she thought. He wanted the divorce to be settled. "Wait you can take them back and I will not sign them until he meets me face to face." Janet slammed the door closed. She had called her father and told him her reply. "That's the Polish spirit, keep a good strong head on you," he said.

There was a phone call from Paul that week and they agreed to meet. He seemed to be in a rush to get things over with. "These are my terms. We pay my father back the half house he paid for and then we split the rest."

"I will not sign papers without adultery on them and her name on them." Janet knew that would be the only way she could get annulment from the church. "I will not back down." She didn't have to struggle with her anger, it came so naturally. Three weeks later a date had been set in the courts. The divorce was granted and Shelly's name was on the paper. Janet's father accompanied her to the court rooms. Paul was accompanied by his father who looked at Janet with disgust. Janet did not care, she knew it was not over as there were material things to sort out. She was strong enough and she remembered how Andy had forewarned her about the materialistic fights when they had talked in San Diego. Divorce is very bitter and it will ground you if you let it.

Janet did go back to the nightclub; Paul had resumed his duties as DJ. He was living there with another woman, she had two small children. The woman was older than him. Janet was quite puzzled as to why he hadn't returned to Shelly. The woman came over and took Janet by the hand. "His mother wants to know why you keep the name." Janet was angry. "First, tell her to pay me the hundreds of pounds it costs to change my name legally. So tell her that she can call me Smith or Jones or Black or White, it is only a name after all. Secondly I am telling you because I care for your children. He is going to America and he is going to dump you and the kids, and I don't care about you but I don't want to see those kids get hurt." Janet took off her engagement ring and gave it to the woman. "Here, you can sell it for what it's worth and buy something for the kids." With that she left. She was only to see Paul one more time.

Janet had managed to go into the loft and sort out the multitude of presents they had received for their wedding and engagement—many were unopened. "How many roast meat trays do you need, how many candlestick holders, how many picture frames?" There were many and she put them in boxes; she was going to take them to the local Oxfam shop. Then she opened a case with her wedding dress. It was still as if it was brand new. She took it out of the tissue paper and put it on; she went downstairs and looked in the mirror. Slipped into the world of her wedding day and she danced, but the dance was with her father. She waltzed and did polkas in front of the mirror as if it was that day. Then with one turn she returned to the present moment. "Oh my goodness, the best time of my wedding was dancing with my father." Paul never entered her vision. She began to question was she in love or was she in a fantasy world that made her believe she had been in love with love. She felt like she could put her hand through a matrix into the past and the present. One minute she seemed to be in a dream and the next minute she stepped into reality. She looked back in time. "Were we talking with one another or at one another, did we meet eye to eye with conversation? What did we talk about? Because we knew very little and we were inexperienced." She had a multitude of questions. She had no answers, but what she did see is that if the truth be known they were outgrowing one another a long time ago. They had started their journey travelling down the same road and then they were splitting apart at the crossroads. She called it destiny. She couldn't hate Paul and she began to forgive all of the behaviors, the immaturity and the cowardice of not being able to confront the truths.

She had been blinded into thinking that the fairy tale wedding would always have a secure future; the truth is they were too young. How many couples make the same mistake and how many take married life seriously. Her parents had been together for forty years; all in all her marriage was less than three years and courtship around four years. How life looks at relationships and marriage in the early twenties and how much pressure there is to settle down. That one in three couples married before the age of twenty will end in divorce. There was so much about life she had yet to learn. She packed her dress and she took it to the local Oxfam shop. "I hope this brings someone more happiness than it did me," Then she took the words back. "I was happy. I hope the bride will celebrate her wedding day like I did, but I hope that it brings future happiness always." She handed it over to the shop manageress.

"It's beautiful," she said.

"I know," said Janet, and with that she left the shop feeling somewhat relieved yet very tearful.

Families behave strangely about divorce. Janet remembered the words from Bo. "Always treat people with kindness even if they hurt you. Anger will destroy your soul." Paul came to the house with a list of wedding presents that were bought by his family and friends. The list included the sink plunger and the cooling tray. This was the usual sarcastic bit of wit she expected from her mother-in-law. Janet only has expected that. She was never good enough for the only son. The self-ego was inherited and Janet knew it would destroy all of them one day. They could not hurt her anymore, and she was glad of that. She didn't know who bought presents but the boxes intended for Oxfam were handed to Paul—even the top layers to the wedding cake, the sink plunger, and the cooling tray. Truthfully she wanted to smash them to the ground in front of him, but she remembered Bo, and she knew she would hate herself because she didn't have a nasty bone in her body. She felt like she had let Oxfam down so she went to the shop next day and donated £100; she knew she could make that much working overtime. She felt good knowing that she could help someone. She never saw Paul again but she did hear that Shelly was pregnant at the time Paul walked out of Janet's life. She should have been deeply hurt especially the fact that she could never tell Paul that she had been pregnant, and for a brief moment she remembered her miscarriage. Mostly she remembered the kindness of Bo. She knew it was time to *let it be*, and let it go. It was time for her to move on. She had seen the traumas of divorce in her family and she remembered the fights her sister used to have after her husband came home early hours of the morning after a night out with the boys. At least she had never reached the stage of fighting with Paul. She knew only too well that if there had been no America and if there was no Shelly, there would have been a Marie, Angela, Joan—there would have been fights and much more bitterness. The tables may have turned around that she may have found someone else. She had no control of her destiny.

Janet decided to move away from her hometown, she needed to start somewhere where she could let go and where she would not bump into Paul or his friends. It would need to be a place where people would not judge her. "Oh poor you, divorced, not you and Paul, we would never have believed it." It just seemed to be a normal response from everyone. She just wanted to play the tape recording back to everyone. She knew they just didn't know how to handle it. "I'm not a poor girl," Janet would say, "and stop feeling sorry for me, you don't know what I'm feeling. Why don't you ask me how I feel. You all presume that my life is falling through the ground. How about, let's have dinner and let's get on with our lives, let's move on."

She actually knew that the split was more painful for her friends because they didn't know how to deal with her. They thought they were being kind with their sympathy, but their sympathy was nearly killing her. What she needed was tough love and guidance and more so her self-determination could move on; and with that she had decided to move to her parents' home by the sea in Lincolnshire. She knew this was the height of the summer season and there would be many holidaymakers there. She was also reaching her twenty-fourth birthday and what would have been her third wedding anniversary. The local rag was boasting that the Lincolnshire Coastal Resorts had welcomed holidaymakers since the Victorian fashion of "taking the sea air." "You can still enjoy miles of award-winning beaches with tranquil bays and local wildlife found between Mablethorpe and Skegness." Janet knew that these were not the beaches she had been accustomed to in California. La Jolla Beach, Coronado Beach, or Laguna Beach, and Skegness did not boast the Hollywood girls with immaculate figures. Here the girls came in all shapes and sizes and on their heads would be the Kiss-Me-Quick hats. Skegness boasted fish and chip shops, hotdog stands, candy floss, and rock stalls and clubs with stainless steel chairs and plastic benches. The restaurants were dull in comparison to the Beverly Hills Country Club, and there were no waitresses boasting the PPP service, no free refills of coffee, and there seemed to be more spilled coffee in the saucer plates than in the cups. Spirits did not arrive at the table in a long glass with an umbrella and topped with ice and lemon but in a miniature glass that looked like a beerglass filled with a warm softdrink. The fantasy rides could not compare to Disneyland, and the night lights were not the neon lights of Las Vegas, and the penny gaming machines did not give out free Bloody Marys.

Janet felt she had jumped through another matrix—a different world. And as she started to go out at night with her friends, the disco scenes were not for her; she was not ready for dating, and she certainly did not want any men in her life, not at this moment in time. Janet did not know what the future had in store for her, she had never worried about that; she had always been so happy to let destiny take its own course, but this one time she walked through the Skegness Gardens and a gypsy took her by the hand. "Don't worry so much, my dear, you will have luck in your future and there will be many travels." She must have known that is exactly what Janet wanted to hear. She gave the gypsy £5.00 and with that the gypsy gave her a set of beads. "These will bring you luck. Go and face the world with optimism." Janet turned around and the gypsy had disappeared. She returned to the gardens the next day and the same gypsy came forward to her again. "Come with me," she said. Janet had no idea where she was going to and she was intrigued by the lively spirit of this young woman. The woman took her to a caravan where she took Janet by the hand, and placed a crystal ball in the palm of her hand. "You will have a very long life and you will travel many places, you have a strong long headline which means lots of knowledge. You have healing hands and you will help many people. You will have some more heartache and you must watch your heart line and never let your emotions rule your life. The lines on your hands always change and so will your destiny."

"How do you know all of that?" Janet asked the young woman.

"It is a very old gypsy tradition to be able to predict and see into the future," she replied. Janet went to visit the woman every day for a week, she learned so much about the lines on her hands. Although she never took it seriously, she would often look at her hands and wonder what tomorrow would bring.

Janet stayed at her parents' holiday home; she spent a lot of time lazing in the garden soaking in the summer sunshine, and she topped up her tan. The problem was the English sunshine was so much stronger than that in California, and instead of going golden brown immediately, she turned bright red and spent the night applying yoghurt to her skin. She knew to limit her time in the sunshine. She bought the local newspaper and there was a community nursing position advertised from the local hospital. She applied for the post and she got the job and was to start in eight weeks. Meanwhile she was dependent upon her father to give her pocket money and she didn't like that she had lost her independence. She had never applied for benefit and her father would not allow that. "You need to work and earn a living and then you will appreciate the things you buy. Nothing in this world comes for free," he used to tell her. While waiting for her work to start she found a job in the local bar, cleaning bed and breakfast. She used to enjoy watching the holidaymakers sing along to the Goldie's old songs in the local bar. Everyone seemed to have a good old-fashioned fun time and dance. She had made some friends and when not working she would go and see the local talent singers at the nearby caravan clubs. Everyone would enter competitions such as the Lovely Leg Competition or the Glamorous Grandmother Competition. There was always laughter and fun. The compares used to know how to get the best out of everyone. It wasn't California but it was the normal British working-class families having fun.

She spent a day at home and there was a knock on the door, the community nursing manager had turned up at the house. Janet came to the door wearing a headscarf and her foam rollers that used to curl the front of her hair. "They need midwives in Boston, Lincolnshire, and they are desperate, can you help out? And this is the phone number and you need to call the manager." Then he left. Janet had nothing to lose so she made the phone call. "What size dress do you need and can you start work on Monday?" She never stayed in Skegness; she had moved into the nurse's residence at the hospital where she shared with three girls. There was a bathroom, a small kitchen, and three bedrooms; this was to be her home for the next six months. She quickly made friends with the girls, Anna was a local girl and Mary was from Ireland. They were all midwives, and they had a lot in common. That is, they were single. Anna spent her time playing the guitar. The girls would stay up late at night Anna would play The Beatles' hits. They would have a few drinks of Irish whiskey and sing along to The Beatles' melodies. They used to go down to the staff club and meet the young nurses and doctors.

Janet remembered how she used to go to the hospital dances and fancy dress parties in Rotherham where she used to take Paul. This time she was young, free, and single. She rekindled her pool skills and her darts. She made such wonderful friends. It seemed the nurses were still chasing the young doctors, and the young doctors were still skilled at breaking someone's heart as many would only be working at the hospital for a few months then they would move on. Janet did not want to start up a relationship and she knew only too well that she did not want a doctor in her life. Her mother would have loved the idea of her daughter settling down with someone so professional.

The three girls would entertain themselves, and they had all been through some kind of heartache. They were happy with casual friendships. Their life was far from boring, and being so young they could survive the day with only a few hours of sleep. Janet would always remember the night she would hear banging on Anna's window, sometimes at 1:00 a.m. The young doctors used to climb to the third door up the drainpipes so they could escape the young nurses who were chasing them. Anna always slept with her windows open. Jimmy was the anesthetist from Scotland and he played the Scottish bagpipes. Mary used to play the Irish bagpipes, and Anna the guitar. They would play many tunes and they would share Irish and Scottish whisky. Janet used to get a set of spoons from the kitchen as Mary had shown Janet how to play the spoons. The foursome would have a party. They had partied most of the night. Mary was dashing off to work in the morning

"Hey, Mary, you have forgotten something," Anna said as she ran down the stairs.

"What?" Mary asked.

"Only your clothes," Anna replied. They never forgot that night.

They would take trips to the local castle and pretend that they were visiting the sixteenth centuries; Anna and Jimmy would play the bagpipes around the castle gardens and Janet would mimic the sixteenth-century dance jesting with her Ann Boleyn breasts. They had so much fun and they enjoyed their own company. Anna would take Janet to the local pubs where they would drive down the back roads of Boston into the countryside and there they would play in the darts and pool tournaments. They would drive out to the local airforce base and play ten-pin bowls. They all seemed be so good at whatever they did, Janet had forgotten about California—it seemed such a long time ago.

No matter what bar Janet visited, she was invited on dinner dates; she did not want to date and she refused so many times. Anna took her to one side. "You will never find your Prince Charming unless you actually date someone." She would always try to find a perfect partner for Janet. She started to play the guitar—it was the song from *Evita*.

I don't expect my love affairs to last for long
Never fool myself that my dreams will come true
Being used to trouble I anticipate it
But all the same I hate it, wouldn't you?
So what happens now?
Another suitcase in another hall
So what happens now?
Take your picture off another wall
Where am I going to?
You'll get by, you always have before
Where am I going to?
Time and time again I've said that I don't care
That I'm immune to gloom, that I'm hard through and through . . . .

Anna finished singing then she said, "You won't know unless you open the doors." Janet thought maybe she should go on an occasional date. "Okay, the next time we go out I will take the next offer just to prove a point." They had gone to the local bar and there was a young man wearing a Stetson. He hadn't bought it Mexico, it was from Skegness Market. "Nice hat, I used to wear one just like it," Janet said. She flipped the front and walked over to the pool table. Not surprisingly he followed. They played pool. He couldn't take his eyes away from Janet's shapely butt nor could he resist her femininity. She had dressed to kill and that night she did. She even killed him at a game of pool. "Where did you learn to play like that?" he asked.

"Oh, that's another story for another day." She did not want to go into the past.

"I'm Tom and my parents own a farm, would you like to come to a barn dance? We are having one at the weekend. There will be live music and we are having a spit-roasted pig. There will be plenty of food."

"Of course she will, if we are invited too." Anna couldn't help but answer for Janet. "She even has a cowboy hat." Janet knew that was a lie but by the weekend Anna had placed a box on Janet's bed and she had purchased a cowboy hat. "Cinderella to the ball," Anna said as she placed the hat on Janet's head. Tom arrived that Saturday at 12:00 noon. The barn dance was to start at 2:00 p.m. Janet dressed in her Wrangler jeans and she wore a blue sapphire colored silk blouse. The buttons opened just above her silk bra and slightly revealed her cleavage, so it left a little imagination and didn't make her look tarty; she looked like a refined cowgirl. She tucked her jeans into the leather boots she had bought in Mexico. The barn was lit with colored lights, the bar in the corner hosted champagne, and there were crystal glasses.

"My sister is getting engaged and it is her engagement party. Come let's have some fun." Tom said. Janet was so taken back with the country music; the band played many country hits from Jim Reeves, Johnny Cash, and then they played "Blue Moon of Kentucky." Janet remembered her time with Andy at the Wranglers Roost. "Come let me show you something." She took Tom and showed him how to dance the cowboy polka, the country swing. She had never laughed so much and she became a little tipsy from the champagne. "Oh, I'm praying for rain in Boston where the grapes can grow and we can drink more wine," She had changed the words.

"Where did you learn all of this?" Tom asked. One more glass of champagne, and she could not hold back her secrets.

"I don't like to talk about it because I recently divorced, and I don't want to bore you with my past. I learned all of this in California."

"You don't bore me, it excites me, and I only wish I had been there with you."

With that he put his arms around her, and they walked under the stars in the fields around the farmhouse. Tom was taken in by Janet's warmth and openness, the charms of her bubbly personality. She took his hand and opened it and lifted it so she could see the lines on his hands under the moonlight. "You are destined to good things, you will marry, have two children, you will never be short of money and this is your home and you will never leave it." He was a country boy at heart and that is where he would be. He looked at Janet. "How do you know that?" he asked.

"Oh, a gypsy taught me."

Janet dated Tom for three months; he would often visit the rooms where the girls stayed. Anna would always be at home when the bouquets of red roses arrived, and she would always lay them on Janet's bed. Tom took Janet to many restaurants and she drank many bottles of wine with him; they would spend the nights together. Janet never felt her feet lift off the ground like she felt with Paul but she had made a new friend. Tom was in love with her but she was confused. Tom had invited her to meet the family at the farmhouse. They had been very friendly but there was a kind of aloofness. They asked many questions about her life. Where she lived, and she was honest and told them she's at the nurse's accommodation. She never told them that her father owned three homes, or that she had a house for sale in Yorkshire. She did not like the interrogation. It was a very English thing.

"Harry was buying a new Rover car." That was Tom's brother. "It was so materialistic and so sterile." Janet knew she would have no place there and that she did not want to spend her life painting her nails and discussing the latest *Vogue* magazine. She couldn't be herself, and she found that she could not use her sense of humor. She had to show Tom just how she could not fit into his life. "I am divorced you know," she said. Tom had not told his family that and she just had to look at their faces. Every picture tells a story and this photograph told Janet exactly where she should be. With that she said that she must leave. Tom followed her and he took her home. "Why did you only tell them half of the truth? If they knew you had a house and if they knew you background, they would accept you."

"That is exactly the point, they shouldn't judge me for what I have. They shouldn't judge at all and I cannot spend the rest of my life being judged. I am so sorry, Tom, you need to move on and so do I."

With that Janet ran upstairs to her small room; she burst into tears, the first time since the divorce. Anna knocked on the door. She sat by Janet's bed and put her arms around her. Janet cried the tears. "I know he will be hurt but I know what isn't right for me." With that Anna cleared the roses from the room. "There will be plenty more of these."

"I had a friend you know, we grew up together, I used to visit her home and she had lived in rented accommodation. I used to be invited to her home during the day, never at night. I was so blind because they had the electricity bill cut off so many times. Her father used to drink a lot and gamble. She found someone who had a good career, she married him for a better life, not for love and although she did get a better life materialistically, it was one without love. I know that because people have told me so. I have tried to visit her but she isolates herself." Janet put her hands to her head and could not help but show her sadness then she continued, "How many women do that? Gregory taught me that you have to live every day, that life should not be an existence but a celebrated life, and I have to learn what that is." Anna did not know who Gregory was but she knew he was right.

Janet woke early the next day and she worked her shift in the hospital. She would look around at the many women who had given birth; she wondered how many were truly happy. She was confused— she reflected upon her life with Paul and if they had stayed in their home, if she had children, where would it have taken them. She could see he had been cruel to be kind, and she wrote the following words in her diary.

To want to love and the trust is gone, to want to give and the damage is done, visiting new places, meeting new friends, and the broken hearts that they help mend. Cruel to be kind your only way out and now I'm learning what life's about.

Thank you.

Janet had sold the house in Yorkshire and she paid her father back the money he had paid, the rest she split between Paul and herself. Everything had been finalized. Her father came to visit her in Boston. "You need a home and you need your roots." He took her shopping. Most people go shopping for clothes, but he took her shopping for a house. He thought it would give her something to take care of and give her an interest. He knew she couldn't spend forever in the nursing home. Janet found a beautiful cottage with two bedrooms, Georgian windows and a third acre of land. It was set two miles out of town and across the road was a local country pub that she could walk to so she could meet the locals.

They had looked around many homes and that was the first one Janet looked at and the first one she fell in love with. They bought the house, and she moved in to it within a month. She spent her spare time making curtains. Her father had built her a stone fireplace with a pinewood surround. He had sold the old furniture that she had shared with Paul and she had bought everything from scratch. She remembers putting together the bed head; she was practical and her mother and father had taught her to be independent. She could manage a screwdriver very easily. She had decided to put the whole thing together without the instructions. The problem was she had put the cabinet sided back to front, so she spent a few more hours undoing them to put them together again. She learned her lesson to always read the instructions first. Parents would be parents, they worked all day painting and decorating the house; they would leave at 10:00 p.m. Janet wanted to do something to show her parents that she was capable of doing a good job. One night she arranged a painting party. She invited Anna, Mary, and Jimmy. They had waited in the local bar until 10:00 p.m. They took some takeaways of beer to the house; Janet's parents had just left.

The foursome took out the paint and painted the whole house. Janet's father had put up the pine cabinets around the fireplace. Jimmy wanted to fix the handles and after a few Scottish whiskies the young anæsthetist must have thought he was putting someone to sleep because the handles tilted to the right just as if he had used a laryngoscope. Janet never changed them because every time she opened that door she would remember her friend. They spent all night painting the house, Jimmy couldn't help but splash a little paint over Janet's hair. "My, how stunning you will look with grey hair when you become mature." With that, she splashed paint back at him; Anna joined them and they became children having fun, splashing paint and dancing to the music of Village People. Anna pointed her brush at Jimmy and with one hand on her hip she started to sing, *In the navy you can sail the seven seas . . . can't you see we need a hand.* Needless to say it took longer to clean up the mess than it did to paint the house. Janet would always remember that song, the paint, the mess, and her friends.

The threesome had crashed out after the long party, painting, and clean up. Janet was so proud of her beautiful home and her parents arrived the next morning very surprised to see they had little to do. "Amazing, it's just amazing," her father said as he took her into his arms. "I'm so proud and thanks to all of you." He then looked over to Anna and Jimmy. "Sorry I don't have vodka to celebrate." Anna and Jimmy just ran their hands over their heavy heads. That was the last thing they needed after the last night's binge.

The next year they spent most of their time celebrating in Janet's home. It was much more comfortable than the small unit they shared in the hospital. They all contributed to the heating and food bills. They would invite their friends; even the quiet country neighborhood joined them. They brought life to the countryside. Janet used to visit the local bar which was only two minutes' walk away; she would chat to the locals, and she became friends with the owners of the inn. When not working she would help them with bed and breakfast for the tourists. Boston boasted its history of the Pilgrim Fathers when the Mayflower set sail for America in 1620; its last landfall was Plymouth in the south of England, but the core of its Pilgrims came from that quiet corner of England where Lincolnshire, Nottinghamshire, and Yorkshire meet beside the River Trent. Many tourists come to Boston from around the globe, especially from its twin town Boston, Massachusetts. Massachusetts became the largest and best organized, educated, and governed colony in New England. The Boston group dominated the colony for two generations and formed nearly half of the Board of Overseers of the College of Further Education, which was founded in 1636. Renamed Harvard in 1639, it is the oldest university in the

United States. Janet loved meeting the American tourists and listening to stories, she boasted that Boston had something in common with America and she would feel she could relate to them as she had visited the USA. She shared her stories with the tourists and they shared their stories with her.

Janet visited her parents' home by the sea in Skegness; she had visited the Oasis Club in Skegness. Standing on the door front was Stephan the bouncer who used to work at the nightclub in Rotherham. He recognized her straight away. "What are you doing in this neck of the woods?" she asked. He had come to work for the summer season. Stephan had been notorious for dating the girls; there was never a night that Janet could remember where he did not have a beautiful young woman in his arms or a night that he didn't take one to bed. He gave her such a warm hug. "Wow, you look great, and a woman now." Yes, she had changed since her childhood days of seventeen when she danced at the nightclub and partied with the staff at the Rotherham Night Club; six years had passed since the early days. Stephan was more handsome than he used to be. He had that masculine semi-shaved face, where his dark whiskers emphasized his masculinity. "It is so good to see you, I heard about you and Paul. You were too good for him you know." Janet put her hands over his lips and said, "I don't need to go there, and it's better that I don't know everything, that way I remember the good and happy times and I don't want to poison my memories with what I don't know." Stephan was amazed at how much she had matured and as to how wise she was. They spent the whole night dancing and talking, catching up and laughing about the past. Stephan invited her to an all-night disco after the club had closed. "Why not," she said. The club was loud and noisy and they could not hear themselves speak, they had a drink and a dance. Stephan put his arms around her. "Come let's go back to my place." She followed him to the local caravan site where he was staying for the duration of the summer. The caravan was tidy but definitely did not have a woman's touch—it lacked the plants and color. "You need a good woman to take care of you," she said to Stephan, knowing well that he was destined to be a bachelor for life. "And what about you," he said as he poured a glass of champagne. "For the good times," he said as he raised his glass to hers. "To the good times," she answered with a smile. Stephan continued to talk about his work as a bouncer, how you see trouble before it starts, and how you need to be aware of the "too good to be true type."

"Watch out for what seems to be perfection because there is no ultimate perfection in this life, these men are overprotective and jealous and obsessed. That's where the fights start," he told her. "Someone makes a comment about his young woman and then the beer glasses fly."

"I'm beginning to realize that," replied Janet. They two talked for hours. "How would you feel if couples added a menu to what was presented in the dining room?" Janet asked.

"What do you mean?" asked Stephan.

"Well it could be a 'How do you like your sex!'" Stephan nearly choked on the champagne he had just sipped. Janet stood and started to thump him on the back. "Don't choke on me now," she said and then continued, "Well I see it like this, sex is like serving an egg, and well, they all have something to do with reproduction, don't they?" She did her usual nonstop analysis.

"*And but.*" Stephan took another drink because he knew this would be interesting especially with Janet's sense of humor. "Okay," she said, "instead of asking how you like your eggs, say how would you like your *sex*—easy over, sunny-side up on the side, hard or soft, three minutes or five minutes, then they could order their meal as they would know what to expect on their night of passion. Eggs and sex have a lot in common and they both have something to do with reproduction, don't they?" Janet had another sip of champagne; she was so emotionally high with her sexual analysis. Stephan began to choke a little after his next sip of champagne. "There would be a lot of starving people and they would never reach dessert!"

"Oh," said Janet as she rolled her eyes bemused by the expected response from Stephan. "You see this is the way I see it. Have you ever gone to a nightclub and looked at how people react in there. People are standing on the outside looking onto the dance floor, and people are on the dance floor looking on the outside, but they are moving to music around the floor." She kept on talking but Stephan interrupted her

"*And?*" he asked.

"Well it is like the people on the dance floor are like fish in an aquarium, some beautiful, some ugly. The people on the outside represent the Calico colors of a cat, some shady, some black, some white, some bright, and some very dull. They could be feline or tomcats. The fish want to be hooked and the cats want to hook the fish. Then they get hooked and the calico shades of the cats clash with the diversities of the fish, most of them rarely they meet the ideal. Sometimes the cats actually eat the fish because the opposites are attracted, and then they reject one another. That's when everyone goes home, has sex, and then one of them creeps out the door wondering where the hell they are and can't believe they had a disappointment. How many times have you woken up in the morning and can't wait to bolt out of the door?" Stephan could not do anything but burst into laughter. "That is so very true."

"Then why dœs everyone still do it?" she asked. He could not answer that. "I love how you see things but I still love being so single and so love the ladies."

"I know and you will never change, but what about when your testosterone levels fail, you will reach sixty, take Viagra or put an elastic band around it because you can't get an erection and some poor prostitute will be comforting you." Stephan slid of the chair. "Okay, young lady, time for bed."

"Not with you, Stephan, I don't know where you have been!" She laughed but she really meant what she said. She left early hours of the morning it was 4:30 a.m. and she was to help her friends serve breakfast at the inn. She arrived just in time to prepare breakfast as an American couple were sitting at the breakfast table. "How would you like your sex, sir? Oh, I mean eggs . . . so, so sorry." She smiled at the night she had spent with Stephan, and she looked at the couple sitting at the table who were definitely not man and wife. "I would like mine easy over!" he said. Janet smirked."Oh sure." She returned with the eggs on the plate and passed them over to the table.

"I asked for my eggs easy over."

Janet grinned. "I thought you would like them on the side." Looking at the woman next to him, "So sorry," she replied.

"My sister would like hers scrambled." Janet could not help but laugh. "I am so sorry. I thought this lovely lady was your girlfriend." They laughed and Janet sat beside them to tell them a little about Boston. "You know we are the Twin City to Boston, USA. The Pilgrim Fathers set sail from here and that led to the making of your renowned university *Harvard* and come to think of it, I wonder how those intellectual students like their sex, I mean eggs!" She hoped they would have complimented her intellect but the guy finished breakfast and handed Janet £50.00. "That is for your irresistible cheek."

Time moved by so quickly. Anna married, Mary moved back to Ireland, and Jimmy joined the navy as he wanted to travel and gain more experience with his medical profession. Boston was a very small town and soon everyone had become so close. Janet felt she could not breathe. She would walk into town and someone would know her, whether it was a new parent or someone she had met in the local bars. Visits to the local wine bars were usually that of gossip as to which relationships had split, who was having affairs. There was not only a resemblance of the TV series *Coronation Street*. Boston had its own *Coronation Street*. Janet wanted to follow her career. She missed her dear friends and she knew like them she would have to move on. Her parents had bought a home in Boston, a house with one and a half acres of land. Her brother and his family had moved to live just around the corner. Her parents thought they would have a family life together. Janet was struggling with her small income; she was twenty-four years old and she owned a beautiful cottage. She loved the apple trees and the cherry trees that blossomed in the spring. Her income was spent on the mortgage and she could barely afford the petrol for her car, she would often walk two miles to work every day. She would spend time with her family and entertain the children that she loved dearly. She would take them to the local parks and have fun with them yet she felt like she was trapped. She knew it would probably be the ideal if she were married and had children, but she was single and there was so much she still wanted to see. She wanted to travel and experience what she had in California. She knew she could not spend the rest of her life visiting the clubs in Skegness. Neither could she spend the rest of her life cutting the grass and painting the Georgian windows of her home. She did not want to live with strangers

Her nursing friends and midwives were talking about Saudi Arabia; they were attracted to the high salaries offered there and Janet knew this would be a golden opportunity to travel and enhance her midwifery expertise. She walked to the local newspaper store and she bought the Nursing magazines. There she saw three jobs advertised—one with an American company and two with British companies. Free air travel every four months. How could she not be curious? She applied for all three jobs and she had interviews for all three in London on the same day; she had taken two weeks holiday and had booked into a budget hotel in London for three nights, near Regent's Park. She tried to visit the local library but could find little information about Saudi Arabia or about working in hospitals in Saudi Arabia. She could not prepare for the interview but she trusted her monkey attributes—intelligent, smart, curious, observant, and she knew her humor and social skills would win the day. She was not afraid of the new challenges that were ahead of her.

She had taken the train from Peterborough and then taken the tube from King's Cross to Regent's Park. This time she did not have to battle with heavy cases down the escalators at King's Cross. She was dressed casually smart, a knee length skirt and up to the neck shirt. She knew that there were restrictions in Saudi Arabia and she wanted to show the team who were to interview her that she could be quite conservative. The first interview went very well and her previous travel stories helped her selection. She was offered all three jobs on the day. She was asked to produce her travel and hotel chits for reimbursement. She could not tell them that she had other interviews and she was reimbursed three times for the three interviews. "Wow, I can celebrate and stay in London. Maybe I should do this more often," she talked to herself.

That night she went to see the show *Evita* and she was singing,

Don't cry for me Saudi Arabia, the truth is I will always love you through my wild days and my mad existence. She had changed the words slightly. She stopped off at a local bar; she was alone and she wanted to celebrate. On the next table she saw a young man who resembled Omar Sharif. He was very good-looking and very well-dressed. He was sitting with a young English woman, she was very petite and very beautiful. She certainly was not wearing a dress from C&A. The young man came over to the bar where Janet was sitting. He smiled at her. "You look very happy," he said.

"Yes, I am," she said. "I have a choice of three positions working in Saudi Arabia."

"Oh that is my country," he said. "Come join us and we can talk." He was intrigued at Janet's Yorkshire accent and she was taken aback with his kindness. "This is Liz." They didn't talk about the background to their lives and no one asked about Janet's life. "How would you like to taste some good Arabic cuisine?" he asked. Liz was yearning for the company of another woman. "Come to our apartment tomorrow, here is the address."   Janet took the address folded the paper and put it safely in her bag. "I would love to," she replied with a smile. They had arranged to meet at twelve noon.

Janet arrived at the apartment which was directly opposite Harrods. She pressed the intercom button and Liz answered, "Come up to the second floor. I will be waiting for you." She welcomed Janet into the apartment. It was just like the Beverly Hills Country Club, the teak furniture and the crystal chandelier, the old paintings on the wall, and a beautiful white afghan carpet with a Persian rug on the floor. The tables were edged with gold plate. Janet felt so underdressed. She had just taken a seat when, "Time to go shopping," Khalil said. He escorted the ladies across the road to Harrods. There the girls were taken to buy evening dresses. Janet chose a sapphire blue halter neck satin gown and Liz had chosen a black dress. They looked stunning. Then they went to the shoe department. Janet chose a matching Bally shoes and handbag. "We are going to the famous restaurant at the Ritz Club," Liz explained to Janet. The girls returned to the apartment and Liz had loaned Janet a string of pearls and a pair of tiny pearl earrings. That emphasized Janet's tiny ears and her neckline.

They arrived at the Ritz Club around 9:00 p.m. Janet could not believe how beautiful the décor was. The club restaurant boasted a cuisine with fine fusion of flavors and textures, but the décor was certainly designed with a fine fusion of favorable color and textures. She felt she had walked into a palace. This was to be another fairy tale story for the "Disneyland princess."

They were seated at the elegantly décored tables and Khalil ordered champagne. He then took the menu and chose the entrees. Janet could not take her eyes off the colorful platters of tabouleh, moutabal, hummus, and mixed pickles. On a second platter came some kebbeh, falafel, sojok, and fatayer. They raised their glasses and they enjoyed the evening together. Khalil said he visits England around four times a year, and Liz would journey from Scotland to join him. You could see she was totally taken in by this handsome man and his gentleman manners that were a rarity amongst Janet's circle of friends.

Khalil had ordered the main courses He chose the Samak Harrah for Liz, he knew she liked fish and this was baked sea bass fillet served with harrah and tahini sauce. He ordered the Kharouf Mahshi, which was roasted lamb served with rice and mixed nuts for Janet and him. The Lebanese salad added a vibrant color to the dishes. The fusion of flavors lingered in Janet's taste buds until the next day. Khalil left the girls to converse at the bar while he tried his luck in the casino. "I am so glad you are here, I often sit here by myself and it is wonderful to have someone to talk to." Janet sensed that Liz was quite lonely and despite the beautiful dinners and places, Janet took notice that she portrayed a little sadness. "For you, dear Janet, do not be taken aback by this lifestyle, tonight you will feel like a princess because it is all new to you, but when you do this several times a year the novelty wears away." Liz put her arm around Janet. "Be careful when you are overseas and do not become so obsessed with the five-star life\style that you forget who you are." Liz could not explain any more but Janet was not really listening as she was absorbed within her own world.

They arrived to the apartment early hours of the morning. Khalil had ordered the girls a chauffeur and they returned to the apartment. Liz opened a bottle of champagne and they leaned over the small balcony facing Harrods store which glistened and resembled the neon lights in Las Vegas. There were still plenty of taxis and people walking the streets of London at that time.

Liz was feeling the effects of the champagne, and she had tears in her eyes. "I have known Khalil for two years, he was very kind to me and I fell in love with the glitz and the money and then him. We can never marry and he holds many secrets."

"Then why do you stay with him?" Janet asked. She knew Liz was afraid to be alone, she had no career and no independence—she relied on Khalil. "You need to break that you are still young and you should take his generosity and go to college and so something your heart wants to do." Janet raised her glass. "To Liz—to your future and your independence. You should never let that go." She only too well of how she let her independence go in California and she had to get her family to bail her out of there. She explained her life to Liz, Liz felt quite optimistic after her conversation.

The girls never heard Khalil return that next morning. They never saw the next morning as they had slept through it. It was 1:00 p.m. before they dressed. Liz had given Janet two kaftan dresses to take on her trip to Saudi Arabia, and later that day Khalil presented her with a black abaya, the over garment that women in Saudi Arabia wore. It was embroidered with gold and the black actually suited Janet's auburn hair. She had a matching scarf that too was black and embroidered with the same gold edging. They had booked in at the Carlton Hotel for a very late lunch. Janet started to talk to Khalil, "Wouldn't it be wonderful if Liz took up some studies?" Khalil did not answer. "In Saudi Arabia, the women do not work." Janet left the conversation there. She knew she would find the answers as she journeyed on. She never met Liz again and she would not stop wondering how some women could live being very dependent for their whole lives. Janet knew that she would never ever give up being her own person even if she stayed single for the rest of her life.

Janet returned to Lincolnshire she had accepted the position with the American company as she knew how Paul had such good perks with his job over there. She had to break the news to her family. Her father could not understand why she had to leave when she had so much security. She had a good job, a house, and family. He knew how important those three things were, having lost them during the war in Poland. They lost their homes and he had not seen his wife of children for six years. They had no choice but to start life over in a new country and rebuild everything. They had worked very hard to give their children security. Janet felt like she was a disappointment and she openly apologized to her father. "I don't know where I am going to but there is so much I need to learn." With that her father took her into his arms and said that he would support her.

Janet gave in her notice at the hospital, she had rented out her home and before she left, her friends decided to give her a leaving party. They had put a marquis up in the garden and more than 100 people came to say good-bye. The marquis was decorated with balloons and her friends provided live music; they played the hits from the'60s and '70s and some country and western music. She danced all night with friends and neighbors who all wished her well. She hadn't realized just how many people had entered her life for those two years and how many memories she would hold of her time in Boston. Anna presented her with a kaftan dress that was around three sizes too big. "Very nice," she said as she held it against her. "It looks like a tablecloth." Anna smiled and responded with, "It is your tablecloth, you will be wearing memories of your home." With that Janet began to laugh. "Sure, I'll treasure it always."

Janet spent her last few days at Skegness; she visited the bars where she had known many of the landlords and the singers in the pubs. She knew "Mad Barry" on the drums, George singing country and western songs, and finally the Oasis Club. She had taken her friend there to see Jerry and the Pacemakers. The club was booked out and they were not going to let the girls in. Janet called over the manager who had known her for the last two years. She used her monkey charms. "It is my birthday and I am leaving to go overseas tomorrow." With that the girls were brought to the front of the queue and they were given seats at the manager's table. They danced and Jerry Marsden played "You'll Never Walk Alone" especially for Janet. He came to sit at the manager's table. "Oh, my son was born by C-section two years ago." Janet smiled and she knew how the midwife and birth was part of everyone's life. She had met someone famous; she remembered how she had shook hands with the Four Tops in the Fiesta Club many years ago. She felt so alive and was ready for her new adventure.

She had taken the train from Peterborough to London and once again she battled with those escalators at King's Cross. She had the same suitcase as she had taken to America and the same folding trolley that she attached to the case. The same bruises on her legs from carrying the heavy case, and one more time those bag straps caught in the escalator at King's Cross, and her bag toppled down the escalators. She didn't get angry, she just laughed as she would expect this on every journey and she knew she would be using those escalators and cursing them for many years to come.

Chapter Eight

THE FLIGHT FROM London to Riyadh was around seven hours. There was no alcohol on this flight. Janet had brought books and crosswords to keep her occupied. Her friends had packed two bottles of water in her bag. Janet opened a bottle and took a drink. She nearly choked as the water had turned into Vodka. "*Nostrovia,*" she would say as she remembered how her father always celebrated with a glass of vodka. For one moment she forgot she was on a Saudi flight. She suddenly realized and packed away her water bottle. She looked out of the window and she could see the dusty desert haze obscuring the tall buildings on their descent. It looked rather like Las Vegas during the day, very barren and hazy.

Sitting next to her was an older gentleman in a business suit, he travelled to Saudi Arabia three times a year; and although very quiet, he turned to Janet as the plane had started to descend into Riyadh airport. "Hold on tight like this, it is going to be bumpy." He braced his hands over the seat in front. Sure enough the plane bounced up and down four times as it hit the runway. It was not the smooth landing that she had experienced with Pan Am Airlines. "When they don't announce the pilot, it is usually a trainee pilot and then you know to experience a rough landing. I work for Lockheed by the way." Lockheed designed the DC10 airplanes.

Janet had dressed in her tablecloth kaftan dress that Anna had made and she slipped on her abaya and head scarf. She made her way through customs which seemed to take ages. She noticed women in one queue and men dressed in white thobes and red and white headdresses in the other. She followed the women. Once her passport had been stamped, she was directed to baggage claim where she collected her bags. There she had to open them and they had confiscated her magazines which bore pictures of women wearing bikinis. They had scribbled over her breastfeeding and medical books, and literally tore out pages that they felt to be unfitting for Saudi Arabia. She said nothing but moved forward and was very relieved when she saw someone carrying a card with her name. He was standing in front of her and she was so relieved to hear the American accent. He took her to the bus and helped her with her luggage.

She had no idea where they were driving to, but it took an hour and she noticed the Pepsi Cola factory to the left. "This is Pepsi Cola Road." There were no street names at that time other than in the central city. "Soon we will move onto Pylon Road. The road was lined with electricity pylons," the driver explained. It was not clear to see anything as it was around 5:00 p.m. and very dark. They arrived at a compound that was surrounded by a huge wall and at the front was a small guardhouse with a barrier. The barrier lifted and the bus entered the compound. The compound was lined with small barrack style houses as she had seen at the holiday camps in Skegness.

She was shown to her new home where she was greeted by two other women. Jodie was from Australia and Sam from America. The girls had made a welcome tea for Janet. Jodie was around forty years old and Sam was in her thirties. It seemed Janet was the youngest. She unpacked her bags then took a shower. The girls had cooked steak and salad and had set the table beautifully. There were crystal glasses. "Would you like some grape juice?" Jodie asked. Janet replied, "Yes." With that they raised their glasses and Janet had a sip of grape juice and before she could say anything there was a, "Shush, we can turn water into wine, and enjoy." Janet knew exactly what they were trying to tell her. After dinner, the girls took Janet for a walk to another block on the compound; there was someone's birthday party. She was surprised as this was a mixed family compound. There she met the hospital staff including the plumber and electrician. They were to become her new family. She went to the kitchen and took out a bottle of water and poured a cupful of water into the kettle and put it to boil on the stove. The whistling top of the kettle shot up and hit the ceiling and bounced around the room. That got everyone's attention. It was not water but uncut alcohol. "What is it with me and water bottles?" she asked herself. She smiled. "Riyadh was not quite as dry as one would have thought."

Janet was given two days to settle in at the complex and she spent her first day by the swimming pool. The swimming pool was huge—it could have been used for the Olympics. It was very barren though there were no palm trees as she had seen when she stayed in California. The sun loungers were made of wood and they had faded in the desert heat. The floor was so hot that she burnt the soles of her feet walking to the pool. How she so much wanted to learn to swim, but she had never been deep in water where she could not see her feet as she had suffered a jellyfish sting when she was eleven years old in the muddy English seawater.

One of the male nurses had arrived from night duty and he was taking a morning swim. He must have swum twenty lengths of the pool with ease. He approached Janet who was soaking up the sunshine in the dry heat where the temperature was around 38 degrees. He asked Janet why she was not swimming and she explained her fear of the deep waters. "To survive in this country, you need to overcome your fears." He took her by the hand and they entered the pool. "First you need to know how to float in the water." He gently tilted her backward and spread out her hands. "Breathe in and out and you need to feel light." She did that several times and soon she began to float in the water. He then took her to the deep end of the pool and she sat on the edge; he taught her to stretch her arms forward and she managed a gentle dive into the water. She overcame her fears and although she was not a water monkey, she used to swim length of the pool with a backstroke. She was a natural swimmer but she never gave herself the opportunity to take up swimming due to fear. She felt so wonderful and she had conquered another part of her life.

The expatriate life was so friendly, she felt completely at home; everyone shared something whether it was their skills cutting hair or their skills teaching sporting activities or even fixing the cooker or the shower. They became such a close community and they were protective of one another. "If only the whole world could be like this." Janet was soon invited to sporting activities. There were hash runs in the desert where the human hare would set out the trail in the desert and shout, "On, on" to guide the many families and expats around the desert trails. Janet tried to uphill to the top of the sand dunes. The golden color of the sand and the light blue skies used to reflect, giving her an orange glow. She took many pictures standing on the top of sand dunes where she would overlook the desert sands and see the infinite rippled contours of the golden landscape. Sometimes they would dress in fancy dress costumes and Janet turned up as superwoman running through the desert.

Janet wanted to rekindle the games of squash she used to play with her brother. However, there were no squash courts on the complex, and they were usually on the male compounds. One day she was so determined to play squash, she arranged a time with the guys on the compound. She caught the ladies shopping bus nearest to the complex.

She would be wearing a jogging suit and size 12 trainers that she had stuffed with paper. At the corner of the complex she would take off her abaya and put on a baseball cap and with her head down she would jog into the forbidden complex. She knew that to follow you dreams, there would always be a way. She knew that if caught she may be deported but nothing could stop her love for sport. The guards got so used to her jogging through the complex, they used to think it was normal and they would never have known she was a woman.

Actually you could say that behind the high walls of this city there was a California, where people would be very normal. "And who knows what gœs on behind closed doors," she would tell herself. She kept this secret to herself; she did not want to put the other complex at risk as she knew there would be more than one jogger entering the forbidden complex.

Janet became used to her female flatmates. She never needed an alarm clock as Jodie had a passion for classical music and every morning the alarm would play Amadeus. That was enough to wake the whole compound. Sam would give her American description of how she managed the day. "I woke to the sounds of my Smiths alarm clock, I would roll over, turn it off, and then I would pull back my Sheridan satin sheets and step into my Gucci slippers. I would make my way to the bathroom where I would shower in my Lancôme gel. I would apply my Dior makeup carefully and then I would slip into my Armani dress." Janet would reply, "And then . . ."

Jodie would shout, "Don't encourage her!" Janet knew that she could have explained all of that in five minutes with her direct Yorkshire accent and how she could not endure living such a full and descriptive life every day.

Janet received her first month's salary, a check for eighteen thousand Saudi riyals the equivalent of three thousand British pounds. Janet had walked from the hospital to the money changes. There she had to stand in a very long queue, there were no queues for women as Saudi women did not work in Saudi Arabia. The only women that worked there were health care workers and only expatriate women. On the first counter, a very pleasant young man smiled, took the check, and put a stamp on it; then she was directed to the next counter where another young Saudi gentleman would sign it. Then she would have to queue again so another signature could be obtained and finally she would be directed to a long queue where she could cash her check. She then had to queue again to transfer money to England. She had spent more than five hours cash in her check. She realized how she had taken the banks for granted in England, how she could walk to a cash teller and remove money from it. She returned back to the compound that night had dinner with her friends and the girls planned their shopping trip. Janet felt so good that she had money to spend. She wanted to cook dinner for the girls and friends the next evening, so she walked down to the shop on the compound. She had a Polish meal that she loved to cook. She walked into the store. The potatœs were very sandy and did not resemble the King Edward potatœs in Boston. The tomatœs looked burnt on the skins and they were neither rounded nor plum-shaped. The lettuce was covered in dirty orange sand. She decided that she would change the date to cook as she desperately needed to go to the city for a shopping expedition.

The next morning the girls woke to the sounds of Amadeus. Sam did her usual descriptive wake up with the designer slippers and perfumed shower and dressed in her designer clothes. Not that it mattered as no one could see beneath her black abaya. Jodie and Janet dressed in their kaftans as they knew they were to feel the Riyadh heat while walking the shops. The bus had taken them to the souk—the Arabic markets. Janet was overwhelmed by the long narrow alleys. The first stop was Seiko alley. Yes, the alley was full of shops selling watches. They were all names that Janet had never seen before such as Rado, Raymond Weil, Rolex, Gucci, and so on. They were very glitzy trimmed with diamonds that suited the Arabic taste and the European style with leather straps and gold-plated backs. Janet found a beautiful Raymond Weil watch it was black trimmed with a fine gold edging and one tiny diamond that sat at twelve o'clock. She tried it and it looked so classy against her tanned skin. She did not resist and bought something for herself. She earned it and she deserved it. They moved into the next alley—this was lined with gold shops. The whole alley glistened with gold. There was more gold here than what she had seen in the *Argos Magazine* as the 24-carat gold was hanging from the ceiling and down the walls and there was no security vaults to prevent theft as they were not needed. The locals knew that the punishment for theft was to lose a hand, and this would be publically executed in the famous chop-chop square situated in front of the police headquarters in Riyadh.

The three European women were greeted with a smile from the young Arabic men behind the counter; they looked so alike. They were wearing white thobes and the red and white headdress. "Can I help you, luv?" asked this young man. Janet could not believe the accuracy of his Yorkshire accent.

"Have you been to Yorkshire?" she asked.

"Oh no not at all but my English teacher was from Yorkshire."

"Hello, pet," the other young man greeted Sam and Jodie. He had a Jordie accent.

"Don't tell me your teacher was from Newcastle," Janet couldn't help but state the obvious. He nodded his head. It was not uncommon for the young Saudi men to have been educated in the English language by private tuition. It was obvious as in every part of the gold souq, someone would greet them with many different British and American accents. There were no women serving behind the counters. Janet knew she had stepped through another matrix into a different time zone—this time into a world that mimicked the fifteenth century with what she called the primitive rules. She knew you could not turn the fifteenth century into the twenty-first century overnight. They left the shop and the girls were walking down the alley. Janet knew someone was behind, and then she received a heavy blow to the back of her knees. Her head scarf had slipped backward and she was showing her hair. It was the Mutawa—the religious policeman. The little old man had a very long beard, a grubby headdress, and he wore what looked to be a dirty off-white dress he could have resembled Merlin the Magician, but he was not kind. He was very angry and pointed to Janet's head, he pulled her headscarf forward. It was all very frightening. Only then did she begin to appreciate the freedom that she had in Europe. The freedom to be herself, to be educated, and to have the opportunity to hold a profession; the freedom of speech, the freedom to welcome someone with open arms, the freedom to visit her friends—male or female, to dress with fashion openly, and more so the freedom to jump in her car and drive somewhere. Janet would never go shopping alone after that incident. She was so pleased that she had taken up her working contract with the American company because once her feet landed back on that compound; she forgot about the restrictive rules and would join in the dinner parties with the hospital staff.

There was always something to celebrate, be it birthdays, Halloween, or Independence Day on the many compounds. The Europeans knew how to relax and they would throw parties every weekend and Janet soon learned that Riyadh was not quite as dry she had thought as there was always a recipe to turn grape juice into wine. There was always a fancy dress party somewhere, and being a woman outnumbered by men one to ten, there was always an invitation to a party somewhere. The art was getting from one compound to the next because as a single woman she could not be seen in public with a single man, and if they took the risk of being driven by an unmarried man, she would run the risk of deportation as a prostitute. Janet felt that in some way she had returned to her teenage years where she would have been supervised when going to parties. She knew how to break the rules then and she was learning how to make the rules work for her in Saudi Arabia. She knew that by breaking the rules there could be serious consequences because of the virgin ideologies of this religious and fundamentalist country

Janet would always take a bag to work with her, it was an overnight bag. It was her "just-in-case-there-was-a-party bag." There would always be a phone call with a party invite, and the young women would never refuse an invitation from the people they had met and whom they could trust. One day she received a phone call from a senior management consultant. The girls from the hospital had been invited to a dinner party with a ministry official. This was to be her first invitation to a Saudi home. Some twelve girls were taken by bus to a huge villa in the city. The villa was surrounded by high walls and resembled a small mini palace. There was a swimming pool down on the lower floor. They walked up the marble steps into a huge lounge area. It boasted crystal chandeliers and white fabricated furniture that were Georgian style chairs and sofas with high backs and teak accessories and marble gold-trimmed tables. The floors were white afghan carpets and over the carpet were beautiful red Persian rugs. The girls were seated inside and welcomed. Their abayas were collected and the girls wore their evening dresses. A tall slim Saudi gentleman, boasting his white thobe and headdress, welcomed everyone by shaking hands. Janet could help but notice the gold Rolex watch trimmed with a multitude of diamonds. After greeting the girls, he reached over toward a huge oil painting that portrayed an Arabic woman's face wearing a yashmak and headdress. She had stunning eyes and her beautiful face was offset against the Arabian desert dunes at sunset. This certainly resembled a lot of class. He reached to a switch on the wall and there rotated out of the wall a glass bar filled with spirits. "Drinks, ladies?" Janet knew she would only accept a drink if she trusted where she was. And despite taking everyone at face value without prejudice, her father's words echœd in her ears, "Never trust an Arab." She was very intuitive and on this occasion she trusted that instinct. She nudged the other women who were with her, all of which were European and hospital employees. She slid her fingers side to side to warn the girls. "Yes, we would love a lovely cup of tea, wouldn't we, girls?" The girls were astounded. They looked at Janet as they were going to metaphorically kill her. Janet knew it wasn't the first time someone wanted to metaphorically kill her and she knew it would not be the last. "Tea would be wonderful," she replied. She was actually looking for an exit door but with the security she knew there was no way out and she knew that she needed to employ her monkey charms. "Actually we are the night shift and we don't drink and work, it is just not appropriate, is it, girls, and if not tea how about some of your beautiful Arabic coffee with dates. That will keep me awake on the night shift." She had remembered that drink from the time she had spent in London with Khalil. How she wanted to have a vodka toast to the beautiful house but there was an aura of deceit moving through her bones.

With that, a tray of Arabic coffee appeared in a gold jug on a gold tray with the small Arabic cups that resembled an egg cup. They were white porcelain trimmed with gold. Then came a second tray mounted with Arabic dates that were stuffed with almonds. Janet took a few dates and they tasted delicious. The doorbell rang and with that entered another eleven well-dressed Saudi men wearing their immaculate thobes. The girls entered conversations relating to their life experiences overseas. Janet shared many stories about her trips through California, how she enjoyed music. They played some Arabic music. They continued to converse sharing stories for more than two hours. Janet could not help but notice how the men took the Johnnie Walker Blue Label whisky in crystal glasses and topped the whisky with a Vimto fruit drink. "If Johnny Walker was right here he would be wondering how you could destroy the Scottish flavor of whisky with Vimto. It would be like adding soda water to a good French wine and insulting a French man." Janet showed her humor to the hosts and they laughed. As the night moved on, the spills of the reddish-brown fruit drink on the beautiful afghan carpet could not go unnoticed and the intoxicated hosts that were obviously not used to consuming alcohol in a way that her father had taught her. To Janet these adult men were behaving like rowdy teenagers at a party. Janet did not feel safe. She asked Karen her manager if they could leave; it was just around 11:30p.m. She gave the excuse she had to work. With that a driver had been arranged to take Janet to work. She left the other girls behind. She did not want to know what happened after she left. Once dropped off at the hospital, she took the last bus to the compound. That next morning she heard that an administrator who was Saudi had been arrested and Karen was deported from the country. Karen had been accused of being a female consort that took advantage of the hosts and the Saudi administrator was arrested for consuming alcohol. Janet knew that in this city that proclaimed pureness, and yet she knew that there was always going to be someone who defied the rules—be it hosts or guests to the country. Janet could clearly see why people revolt in countries where they are suppressed and dictated to. She had been told stories where both expatriates and locals have been taken in by someone claiming to have a ready-made supply of alcohol. They never thought to inquire who the supplier was and they were hooked as the supplier had something more sinister in mind. They were the victims of the so called Sting Operations as the local police dressed as undercover suppliers of alcohol and they would snare unsuspecting victims. The victims were carted off to prison without downing one shot. That night their stories had become Janet's reality.

Janet stayed awake that evening she opened her diary and wrote,

To visit this country; this foreign land.
This massive building site
Mainly of Sand
Who are we to question integrity?
When in this city we live far from Sincerity
Western women cannot accelerate the highways
For the man, imprisoned as god sets their ways
The whole western society suffering delusions
And an increasing demand for state institutions

Janet knew she would not be sending this note to her father. She had heard stories about the communist suppression in Eastern Europe, but this was different. Europe had a history of well-educated countrymen with strong labor skills and here that education and trade experience was lacking. Not only that, she begun to question the strong tribal influences of the very country that had invited her to share her professional skills. "Were they just brainwashed or were they happy to accept the life they were living?" She just knew that everything was so unpredictable in the country she was staying. She knew she had to take great care and she knew that her ultimate goals were to enhance her profession, pay off her mortgage, travel, and learn more about the lives of the people in this country.

Janet came to learn more and more about Saudi Arabia, she needed to sit on the fence and view the country from all perspectives. She knew she was fortunate to be given that opportunity, but she also knew that she would be walking on shady waters. There was no green grass in this country but she was to find out if the sand was sandier on the other side. How many secrets would she have to keep within her heart, how many times would she have to close her eyes and just *let it be* when she would find the conflicts of the two worlds. How would she survive and retain her sanity?

She remembered arriving at her new post and she was forced to hand over her passport. "You can't take that, it is the property of her Majesty the Queen of England," she would say and when the passport was taken she knew how little influence the Queen had in this country. Her passport would only be returned when she had been given permission to exit the country and on her return they would retain it. "So much for the Queen," Janet used to say every time she returned. She now understood why a portrait of the queen stood in so many compounds in Saudi Arabia.

Janet was taken in with the many phone calls from her distressed expatriate. They knew the only twenty-four-hour helpline was the hospital. She received a phone call on day from a close friend. She was working on the birthing unit and had a woman in labor. "Janet. Phone. Urgent. Now!"

"Don't push, dear, I have an emergency." She smiled as she knew there was a while for the baby to arrive. She picked up the phone. "Hi, it's me, John. I have one minute so just grab a pen and listen." He was so afraid and anxious. "I am in the nick and this is the address." She wrote it down. "Now call this number and tell them who I am and where I am." Then the phone cut off. Janet had to redirect someone to care for her laboring woman. "I have a Country Crisis." The girls on the unit laughed at her. "What, have they run out of oil?"

One of the girls answered with her British wit, "Not quite but anyone going on leave will be delayed."

"That is a crisis," was another reply.

Janet called the number; she was calling the aircraft base. "I need to speak to the director. Manager, CEO, or whatever you call him." It was 1:00 a.m. She had called the airbase. A grumpy tired man answered the phone, "What the hell," in his American accent. "No swearing, I'm from a Catholic family and it is not allowed in Saudi Arabia *but* you telecommunications offer is in the nick." He went through a red light because the Mercedes behind him was travelling at 120 km and definitely not going to stop and this is a crisis because he is the only one on duty this morning and the other is on leave. He wondered how on earth Janet knew so much about the company, and she dare not say it was the compound that she dressed as a man and jogged through it three times a week to play squash. *Thank heavens I broke the rules,* she thought to herself. Thank goodness for an American company, it would have taken the Brits a week of negotiations. John was released that morning. Janet went back to birth her baby. She wiped her forehead. "I think I am in the wrong job, I should be with the CIA." She smiled and continued to work. There were many episodes about the unfortunate expats but they had a sense of humor to get over them. It could only happen in the third world and this was the twentieth century with a third world mentality. She had heard the girls tell a story about one of the husbands who was working for a local engineering company. If you were employed by the armed forces, you were treated at the armed forces hospital. If you were employed by the security forces, you were treated at the security forces hospital. If you had private insurance, you would be treated at the private hospital. Simon had no insurance and he had developed appendicitis (inflammation of his appendix); he was taken to the local public hospital where they performed an emergency appendectomy. He woke up from the general anesthetic still wearing his work clothes. Janet became accustomed to hearing so many stories.

One of the girls received a phone call. "I cannot see you, my wife's waters have broken and I am flying to Europe." With that, she picked up the bunch of red roses he had sent to her and they flew across the room into the incinerator bag. "I wonder how much money Interflora makes from this side of the world?" she asked and Janet replied, "Boys will be boys all over the world and there will be plenty more roses in your life." Janet took her friend by the arm as she knew only too well from her own experience. "Maybe his wife paid him to be out here." Janet could not help but release a little of her life's observational skills as she tried to comfort her friend.

Janet spent the two years mixing with many cultures; she had been to Thai barbeques in the desert where she learned how to cook fish underground and barbeque the largest sea prawns she had ever seen and welcome the clear desert skies at night. They took guitars and music with them and played both modern and cultural music and many were very talented. They would sit around a campfire share stories and eat the Thai-flavored seafood, the herbs, and spices stayed in Janet's taste buds long into the next day. They shared their soft drinks and cuisine gladly. The Thai community had very little and they lived in the poorest of conditions. There was no health system in Thailand and these young Thai people had sacrificed leaving their families to send money home to support them. They were such a happy culture to be with, and they would always give gifts to Janet for her kindness at work. They knew how to celebrate life, and they knew how to be happy and optimistic. She wondered how the western world had become so materialistic and so spoiled, and never satisfied. Janet had never visited Thailand but with this community, Thailand came to her. They shared pictures of family and scenery from Thailand. They accepted Janet as part of their family. She had attended the Thai queen's birthday celebrations in Riyadh and experienced a Thai kickboxing performance and the cultural dances of Thailand, which told stories of love and romance. For those sporadic moments Janet returned to her fairy tale existence and she had forgotten the extreme restrictions being a woman in Saudi Arabia. She would join in with the dancing and celebrate the Thai Queen's birthday even if she didn't have any idea who the Thai queen was. She had learned how the Thai culture was a strong part of their lives. How their roots influenced their views, their values, their humor, their hopes, their loyalties, alongside their worries and fears.

Janet spent a lot of her time with her newfound Thai and Filipino friends, she shared and celebrated their customs and respected them as if they were her own. She felt quite sad that she had not had the opportunity to learn about the Polish traditional customs, and she knew that she had started to hunger for her own heritage in many ways; she became confused and suddenly she felt how despite having a Polish heritage in England, many cultural traditions were never taught in schools and how she felt like she didn't belong to anything. She envied the strong sense of community and how well the Thai community supported one another. She was not aware that she was interrogating her own soul and that was her very own identity. She did not know what she wanted and that was the truth.

Janet was very fortunate to meet the Saudi families; they were Bedouin families and the families that held their traditions close to their heart. Many women were not educated and their culture was based around the Koran. They had never been immersed to the capitalist western world. They were what they knew. They were happy and very gentle, and Janet soon began to learn their language. It was pœtic, romantic, soft, and very gentle; they celebrated the birth of their child and if the first was a son they would give a gold present to Janet. It was not payment for services, but it was a genuine thank you and appreciation—something she rarely experienced while working in England. Janet took the opportunity to visit many homes that were not the modern Saudi Arabia, they were small homes on the outskirts of Riyadh, and they did not bear the palace like features with crystal chandeliers. They did boast floor coverings of the beautiful handwoven carpets. The seats were small mattresses placed around the floors. The coffee cups were not white porcelain but they were small brass cups. The coffeepot was silver and had a high neck and a base that resembled an Aladdin's lamp. The coffee beans were ground with fresh cardamom and had a wonderful aroma. The home cooked meals of fresh lamb biryani cooked with spices especially cardamom and lamb and chicken kebabs, with hummus and salads and dates were spread as a banquet across the floor. The families would sit on the floor and Janet would join them; she would always wear a kaftan dress that covered her arms and legs and she would wear the black scarf that covered her head. These were the genuine families as Janet called them. Their simple life was so simply beautiful and calm. The children would sing songs and the ladies would dance to Arabic music. They would pull Janet up from the ground and teach her to dance. Janet would learn to shake her hips like never before.

The grandmother would tell stories of how they lived their life in the desert before moving to the city. How they lived by the oasis and reared animals including goats, cattle, sheep, horses, and camels. How her father was a hunter. Janet loved listening to the stories that were translated by the younger children who had learned English. It reminded her of her grandmother's tales of the farm the villages of Poland. Janet's grandmother would read the Bible and here this family would read the Koran all sharing the same ideologies and beliefs of the importance of family and putting food on the table. They were no different except where the women would cover in front of strange men. Janet would often wonder how the western invasion and money would change all of this in the future. She attended a local camel race; the family took her into the desert where there were not thousands of camels racing as at the Riyadh City camel races, where more than 2,500 camels would race. There were only twenty camels but the riders were proud of their camels and there was no prize, just a celebration of families eating foods and soft drinks in the desert. Janet was overwhelmed with the hospitality of these families and they would take her shopping to the souks where she would be guided to purchase presents without having to barter. That was such a relief for Janet as she felt safe from the Mutawa.

She loved these opportunities and embraced these times in Saudi Arabia and would take every given opportunity to spend time with the families that invited her; there was one brief moment where the family thought she should marry and they introduced her to a cousin of the family. They actually left the couple to talk and were hoping that she would be a member of the family. Janet knew that she could not be isolated in Saudi Arabia and she valued her freedom far too much for that. She realized just how many beautiful people there were in the world and no one could take these memories away and that her time in Saudi Arabia would stay with her for the rest of her life. When she became cynical of the restrictive laws of the city, she would jump back into her matrix and remember the gentle Bedouin families and that not all people are the same. There are good and bad in every nation.

She accepted invitations by families to take her into the remote places of Saudi Arabia such as Hofuf, which was located in eastern Saudi Arabia. Hofuf lies in the large Al-Hasaoasis. She had visited the old fort and then shopped at the most interesting old souks in Hofuf where she bought many antique brass and silver items. The families would do the buying for her, and they would stop at the number of picturesque villages scattered through its central oasis, Al-Ahsa, which boasted two million date palm trees. She would visit the date plantations and meet the old workers who had long white beards and grubby thobes and headdresses; they would give her a tour as they were proud of their wooden date press. Janet felt she had stepped back in time to the fifteenth century. She was taken to the camel market and would go to the camel races.

Janet would never forget her invitation to a palace. She was accompanied by an obstetrician as they were invited to have dinner there. This was yet another world. Janet had purchased a small bottle of perfume. One of the maids from the palace had delivered a stillborn child and Janet had shown such kindness and respect. She had washed and clothed the child and passed it to the mother and the family prayed around the bed. They were so forgiving and accepted traumas as God's will. Janet had more trouble overcoming the grief than the mother. How they had such a strong belief and how they mourned but they had forgiveness in her hearts.

Janet and the obstetrician were welcomed to the palace. Janet was taken to the maid's quarters where she entered a very large room. The women were wearing head scarves and kaftan dresses that were made of a variety of silk and satin materials and that were finely embroidered. There were twenty maids in the room and all were entertained with the tablet of electronic games. She was welcomed and she had so many kisses on her cheeks from the excited women. Here she was stuck in translation as she had not brought a translator and she had relied on sign language. She had learned enough Arabic for a basic family conversation but the women and their excitement spoke so gently and quickly, Janet could not understand a word. They had shown her a place to sit on the ground and they shared their games with her. There was a clanking of sounds as if it was an amusement arcade at Skegness. These young women were totally amused by the games and Janet was able to mingle and she joined in the fun. She finally shook hands with the maid that she brought the perfume to. She was taken to the bedroom that had a high four-posted bed. There were around a hundred bottles of perfumes standing on the shelves. Janet took out her little present with a flushed red face of embarrassment for her small gift. The maid smiled and presented her with a box that was wrapped in a blue ribbon. Janet could not say anything but *shukran* (Thank you) and neither opened their boxes.

Janet spent the whole of two hours playing games and the servants arrived with a banquet of food. The colorful, articulately filled plates were spread along the floor and they enjoyed the Arabic cuisine. Janet was taken aback that the maids had servants. After dinner they played Arabic music and Janet joined in the dancing. She knew how to move her hips as the Bedouin ladies had taught her to dance. They asked Janet to dance European style and they had changed the music to Michæl Jackson's "Thriller." She had all of the ladies doing the graveyard walk. *Thank goodness they did not understand the words,* Janet thought while dancing. This was another momentous visit to fairy tale land and another memory that she would remember for the rest of her life. The evening passed surprisingly quickly and Janet was escorted to the front entrance. There the obstetrician joined her; she had never met the princesses but she felt like one. They returned to the black Mercedes that drove them to the compound. There the obstetrician handed her an envelope which she did not open until she returned to her room. First, she opened the box and in it was a male and female watch by Raymond Weil. She knew exactly what she was going to do with that—she was going to give it to her brother so that when she wore it and he wore hers they would always be together. She had not found a partner that she thought deserved it and she was not going to keep it just in case she would find someone because she knew in her heart she would be waiting for a long time. She then opened the envelope with six thousand riyals the equivalent of one thousand British pounds. She knew she would have to do something very special with that so she would always remember her trip to the palace.

Chapter Nine

T WAS FEBRUARY 1984, Janet had played her usual game of squash but she had twisted and damaged her tendon. How on earth she managed out of the compound with a strapped leg, she does not know but she had no choice. From there she caught the shopping bus and returned to the hospital. She was told she needed to wear a cast for six weeks. This was just prior to her holidays and she did not look forward to meeting those escalators at King's Cross station with a cast on her leg. She waited in the hospital emergency room and she met a young English woman who was her age. She had very short blonde hair and with a tomboy look and raised, colored cheeks. She was Judy and Judy had only arrived in the kingdom six months previously. She had never put a plaster of Paris cast in place and she was anxious. Janet openly said, "It doesn't matter, you can practice on me, so let's have fun." Judy took out the plaster—it has well expired its shelf life for more than five years. The hospital was initially a hospital some seven years prior, then it became a university and now it was converted to a hospital and the old supplies had been kept. "This can only happen in Saudi Arabia," Janet remarked. Judy placed the cast on Janet's leg; there was so much thick cast, it weighed heavy for Janet's small leg. Judy was very proud of her first attempt. Janet did not want to disappoint her. "Marvelous, the 'Angels' could not have done it better." She was relating to the UK TV series that was based around student midwives in the late 1970s. Judy laughed. They met a few times to check the cast which seemed to be stable. Judy was heading to England at the same time as Janet and she asked Janet if she would fly through Amsterdam with her. Janet did not refuse but she wondered how she would trek around Amsterdam with a cast on her leg. Janet spent four days on the compound before the flight. Getting in and out of the shower was a mission with the huge cast and the only clothes Janet could wear were her kaftan dresses as nothing would fit over the foot of the cast. Judy came to the rescue and had bought some fake Lacoste joggers from the souk. There were large but they slid over Janet's plastered leg. The joggers fell in folds down the leg. "I feel like a Munchkin. You know one of those little fat people from the *Wizard of Oz*." Judy laughed. "As if people will be looking at you, and who cares, you will be on holiday." Judy had put a walking heel on the cast the previous day and that had given her the look of a concrete breezeblock on her foot.

The girls were packed and they were taken to the airport and they were handed their passports at the airport. Janet kissed the front of the passport. "Alas the queen's property has returned." That caused the entire queue in the airport to turn around. "Brain injury," Judy responded pointing to Janet's cast. "Cuckoo, cuckoo," Judy continued. Janet laughed but pushed Judy to one side. She spun around and slipped on the floor. The cast did not take the knock and Janet's foot had shot through the bottom of the cast. With that, Judy asked for a wheelchair and Janet was seated in it. "Thank goodness for travel insurance and health insurance and the first stop to visit Amsterdam's Hospital." The girls had to see the bright side, and although customs were so quiet, the girls sang "Always Look On the Bright Side of Life." They were seated first on the plane as Janet took priority with the wheelchair. They were in first class. The stewardess felt sorry for Janet and said that there were plenty seats as it was winter in Europe and few people were flying to England.

It took around eight hours to fly to Amsterdam and the girls were first off the airplane and first through customs. Judy wheeled Janet to the taxi rank and they took a cab to the hospital. Judy was to get her first lesson in the application of casts and fortunately it was a very modern hospital and the fiberglass casts were in fashion with a choice of colors. Janet being practical chose black as she knew it would be very wet walking through Amsterdam. The cast took all of fifteen minutes to set. "This is a nonslip heel," the nurse explained, "and the cast is waterproof." Janet was relieved now that her swollen ankle was supported. The girls caught a cab to the five-star Grand Krasnapolsky Hotel which was located in the heart of Dam Square. Their stay was free of charge compliments of the airline. It was very common in those days as the airlines touted for business. They had a luxury twin room that had a charming and old bathtub with lions' feet on it. Janet could not wait to hop into the bath and she filled it with shower foam and sat with the black-casted foot hanging over the bath. Judy opened a bottle of champagne, and Janet drank half of it while having her soak in the bubbles. Judy had already planned the trip. "Canal boat trip today, the clog shœ factory tomorrow, and finally the Red Light area." It was a twenty-minute walk to the canal. Janet was in love with Amsterdam. It was busy with people walking the streets. Bands and groups were playing during the day, jugglers and jesters were on the main stretch of road.

They arrived at the boat booth and as Janet walked down the nonslip slope with her nonslip cast. Unfortunately, Janet went for a landslide, landing on her buttocks; the man at the booth reached over laughing at her only to reply, "Sorry wrong booth, you need number 4 and this is number 10." With that, Judy pulled Janet upward only for her to slip again, pulling Judy on top of her. The young man at the booth stepped down to help the girls up and with that he said, "I am Andre and I will take you to see Amsterdam if you wish." Judy wiped the mud from her trousers and accepted the invitation and arranged to meet the young man that evening at the Cherry Tree Pub which was situated around the ice skating rink. "At least falling on our butts attracted someone's attention." Janet smiled.

Janet and Judy made their way down to the Cherry Tree Pub in the square; they sat at the bar casually dressed with jeans and winter jackets. They were enjoying their great escape from Riyadh. Janet ordered the long-awaited vodka shot, not only to toast to their freedom, but to warm the cold air running through their body. There was a small live band playing most of the hits from the seventies. Janet had requested them to sing The Beatles' "Let It Be" as a tribute to their freedom and the slippery slope fall earlier in the day. Andre had arrived to meet them. They shared stories for about an hour or so. Janet ordered three vodka shots. "To life," she said as she looked at Andre and Judy and she could see there were some romantic sparks flying in the air. Andre's friends were playing ice hockey on the central ice rink. The whole ice hockey team entered the bar still wearing their skis and carrying their hockey sticks. Andre leaned over and whispered into Judy's ear, "I have arranged a surprise." No sooner had he said that when this hulk of a blond-haired hockey player thrust Janet into the air and carried her out onto the ice. He was skating at such a speed that the whole Amsterdam square was spinning around her. The vodka was also spinning her head a little. *Carried off by a prince on ice,* she thought to herself as she felt the cold air brush against her face. She felt alive, happy, and excited as the surrounding lights flickered as if they were a continuous display of colorful Catherine wheels.

She returned to the bar and once on the ground she was still spinning. "See how much you can do with a cast on your leg, anything is possible!" And with that she bought a bottle of vodka for the whole hockey team.

They left the bar that evening around twelve midnight and Andre escorted the girls down to the Red-light area. They felt safe with their escort as they walked down the canal front that boasted the pinkish-red display of windows. Janet was really into looking at the girls in the window, but she couldn't help but laugh at the silicone breasts and facial expressions of the girls. She remembered Las Vegas and the XXX-rated movies on the ceiling where she would have the occasional peep through her fingers. She was repeating the peeps at the local display of buttocks and boobs. "I wonder if all the Dutch men here respect women in this country. It's disempowering women really, makes all of us look really cheap and stupid as if we don't have anything more than boobs, buttocks, and a hole called a vagina." Andre laughed.

"Have you always analyzed everything?" Judy asked.

"Since the day I was born," Janet replied. "Take it this way. We work in a country that suppresses the male animal instinct. Lust is a good enough word for that, and then all of these suppressed lusty men with their unused testosterone levels come to Europe and have all of the wham-bang-thank-you-ma'am's. They return to their so called Virgin Land and then they think that all women are walking prostitutes. That leads to all of the groping that ends with the women like us punching them in the face." And with that Janet needed to catch her breath. "Come on let's get out of here." Andre and Judy walked Janet back to the hotel. Janet was ready to drop but Judy and Andre were still ready to party. Andre insisted they went to the local hotel where the young musicians strummed their guitars and everyone would join in with the singing. Janet forgot about being tired. She wanted to party long after Andre and Judy. "Why don't you go to the hotel and I will meet you here for brunch. I will book in here for the night. Go off and have fun." In her own way she wanted to encourage the relationship between the couple—that they did—and Janet spent the whole night dancing and singing with the artists. She crashed into a bed around 7:00 a.m. Judy and Andre turned up around midday. "Change of plans," Judy said as she looked passionately at Andre. "Really," Janet replied as she knew Judy's life was about to head in a brand-new direction.

Judy never returned to Saudi Arabia, she stayed with Andre. Janet knew that lightning can strike in the most unexpected places. How Maggs met her Paul when they collided on the football field many years ago. How she met with her first wet kiss on the heathery hills of Scotland. How she had met her Paul in the kitchen of her own home and how Judy had landed on her butt with Andre at the boat booth. Janet just smiled as she wanted everyone to be happy. Inside she wanted them to live their own fairy tale, it didn't matter if it lasted forever or for a few sporadic moments—at least they were living it. Janet gave the hotel keys to Judy and said, "Enjoy," and with that Janet took an earlier flight to London. She would always remember being carried onto the ice with her prince even though she would never meet that man again, and in her imaginative world he would always be a prince.

Janet had called her father who was to collect her from the train station; she was as excited as she had not seen them for a year. She did not take the underground in London with her heavy bags; she took a cab from Heathrow because this time she had money and could afford many things.

Her father was waiting at the train station, it was snowing and how the cold crisp air of the Lincolnshire countryside felt so good and clean but she didn't rush forward to hug him or kiss him. She froze.

Her father asked if there was anything wrong, Janet had remembered that she was no longer in Saudi Arabia where she could not hug anyone in public especially a male. She knew that the cultural restraints were affecting her whole being and her freedom of expression. She knew that it was time to move on before she would need to visit a behavioral therapist. Janet looked at this as being a reality check and she did not want to suffer from suppressed emotions. Her parents had moved into their new home and Janet walked in with the Christmas tree was still standing. Her parents had brought the whole family together and they celebrated Christmas in February. "It should be Christmas every day," her father said as the entire family raised their vodka glass to wish health and happiness to the whole family. How she loved all of them and how she wished every day could be like this one.

Her family exchanged presents and Janet gave a watch to everyone and the special one to her brother. "This came from a palace and it is identical to mine and when we wear them every time we look at the time, we will remember each other." She had a new niece that she had never seen. She was now one-year-old and taking her first steps. Her choice to travel missed watching them grow and she was a stranger in their life. She knew exactly what her Thai and Filipino friends were giving up to provide financially for their families. Some of those girls were married and had their own children at home, and they would not see them for after a year. *To not see your own child grow,* Janet thought, *I could not even comprehend it.* She looked over at her mother and two sisters who had been separated from her father for six years after the war. Yet they were living in the present and celebrated life like it never happened. "You just have to *let it be.* and you have two choices in this life—you sink or you swim and we always choose to swim through it with optimism," her parents would always remind her and they would always remind her to be kind, careful, and nonjudgmental. "There are a lot of snakes in many countries but there are a lot of dolphins too!" Janet knew exactly what he was talking about after her last year and a half in Saudi Arabia. He would then continue, "When you have seen one palm tree, you will have seen them all." Janet did not know what he was trying to tell her but she was sure that one day she would find out.

Chapter Ten

JANET RETURNED TO Riyadh feeling very refreshed. She continued to live her Saudi life and it was coming to the last few months of her contract. One of her girlfriends, Sally, had invited her to Kenya for a holiday. They had recently returned from Bahrain and they had met a tour operator from Kenya. Janet was so excited and could not wait to join her. They were going on safari. There was a small problem—the other girls going were from Australia and just before they left they had told Sally that they were not going to entertain a Pom. Sally felt hurt and she did not want to let Janet down as they had purchased the tickets. "Well, I will go by myself, it doesn't matter. I don't care if this pomegranate travels alone. I have done it so many times." Sally loved Janet's sense of humor and she really wanted to spend time with her. Sally was not as adventurous as Janet and often lived a life of routine. "Come on, Sally, we slaves love to have fun. We love to polka and drink vodka. I can't give you a vodka here but we can polka." Janet knew Sally needed cheering and it definitely was not the end of the world. "It's just a woman's clique thing. If you don't fit, we will click you out. Actually it's like the behavior of school teenagers that some women never outgrow, let it be and get over it, you don't need friends who want to control your life." She played a polka and she started to dance with Sally. Sally was not a dancer or a mover. "Gosh you are so stiff, if you want to survive this world you have just got to loosen up, gal," Janet continued to dance with Sally until Sally took Janet to polka. They had fun that afternoon that is for sure.

Bags were packed and the girls were heading to Nairobi. Janet was very excited. "The only animals, other than some men of course, that I have ever seen have been in the zoo. Well actually that is not true because we have seen camels and goats here and my grandmother raised pigs, geese, and chickens in the backyard. But to see a lion and a rhino and an alligator and the elephants in the wild—I just can't wait."

They arrived at Nairobi airport. Janet had been accustomed to travelling through the flash airports of Amsterdam, Riyadh, and London. She found Nairobi so dull and it felt kind of scary as they passed through customs. The dark security guards looked very sad despite looking very official. The atmosphere was as dark as he was. Then she remembered Bo's words, "don't let first impressions spoil your day." They cleared customs and they were collected by the hotel guide and were taken to the Hilton Hotel in Nairobi. The Hilton was much more like the hotels she was accustomed to with the grand marble and granite floor entry. The bellboys were wearing neat maroon gold-buttoned jackets. They actually looked like they were part of a big brass band. The girls walked to the counter with their passports.

"Sorry but the hotel is overbooked. We have no room for you as it is the twenty-fourth Parliamentary Commonwealth Conference here in Nairobi and the hotel has been booked for the officials."

"But we have a booking." Sally was waving her papers at the very young boy behind the desk. That did not make any difference as there was definitely no room at the inn. Sally was very upset and she was getting angry. "Anger will just spoil your holiday, just chill and we will sort it, will all be all right on the night, gal."

Janet took the booking tickets and she found a phone number to call. She called the tour operator and asked for the address and they took a cab to that address. Sally could not calm down. "He promised us that it would be okay," she was talking about the tour operator that she had met in Bahrain. Janet couldn't help but laugh. Sally looked back and Janet continued to say, "Sod the bloody politicians. They don't do well at changing the world with all their meetings that are done at high levels with a lot of roaring and screaming and it takes a long time to get results. Just like mating elephants, they are in the right country for that, but they sure can take over a hotel when they want to. We are the small fires that have been thrown out, but we will survive on, on," Janet finished.

The tour operator had been very genuine and they had been booked into the Hilton but he had no control over the government. He offered the girls alternative accommodation not far from the Hilton. At least they had a bed for the night or so they thought until they arrived there. It was dirty and very hot. The air conditioning did not work. Janet pulled back the bedsheets. Not only are the bed sheets stitched together, but so are the beds. The beds actually dipped in the center. They had no choice and they slept with their butts well down and their feet up in the air. Needless to say they had a restless night.

The tour guide came to see them the next morning and he was totally embarrassed. He therefore handed them free tickets to spend on Mombasa Beach for five days. "This is a new hotel on the beach front and you will love it there."

The girls were given their travel itinerary. They were to spend ten days on safari and five days on Mombasa Beach. Despite Kenya being a poor country, safari, and accommodation was very expensive and a totally out of the question trip for the average traveler at that time. They were allocated a driver—his name was George and he was a native of Nairobi. He was going to be their guide for the entire safari tours. There were twelve on the bus and Janet had taken the front seat. Sally was sitting behind her and woe and behold, the Australian girls joined in the trip; they chose to sit on the rear seats. They had totally ignored Sally and there was certainly a personal rift on the bus between the front and backseat passengers. Janet was her usual chirpy self. She had her Walkman in her ears and was listening to the sounds of the seventies and she did not realize that she was singing out loudly. George the driver looked at Janet and he was more interested in her Walkman.

With bags packed on the bus, they set off on their journey into the wilds of Africa. They drove to a small shantytown near to Nairobi which took them for a walk down a street where there was an equator sign. George took photographs of the girls and then he took them to a small area where the African villagers were selling their handicrafts. Janet bought a few animal carvings and she bought soap and red sandstone chess set for her brother. There were other stalls and Janet picked up two bookstands that were carved buffalo. The stall owner took an admiration to Janet's trainers and he kept pointing to them and would not let Janet leave. He was pushing lots of carvings into Janet's hands. George the driver came to the rescue. He explained that European shoes were very expensive in Kenya and people wearing European clothes were looked upon as being important. He explained that the normal villager could not afford such luxuries. Janet felt so touched by this and she knew she had other shoes in her case. She returned to the bus with no shoes and no socks. She was not going to give up her jeans. Sally could not help but laugh when she looked down at Janet's bare feet. They returned to the bus with lots of handmade goodies. They opened the bus trunk to get Janet's case so she could take out another set of shoes when another man tugged at her trousers and placed more carvings on the floor. George laughed as Janet actually blushed. Then right there in the midst of the tourists, Janet dropped her trousers and handed them to the young man. "It's a good thing we are not in Riyadh," she smirked. She jumped onto the bus with a new set of clothes, but she was reluctant to put them on until they had left the town. George had never seen someone as kind as Janet, nor had anyone stripped off on his bus before. Janet tuned into her Walkman and as they were clear of the town she turned to George. "Is it safe to dress now?" she asked. George nodded his head. "May the holiday start." Janet had purchased a bottle of papaya wine and she shared it with the other tourists. "Okay, George, where to now?" she asked. They had already completed 120 km to reach the equator line and then they headed northeast to the Samburu National Park. The scenery was very dry and bland and the dusty roads reminded Janet of the movie *Born Free*. Just as Janet had been thinking that, George replied, "This is the famous park where they filmed the movie *Born Free* and I will be driving very slowly you can see the lions here." It was difficult to see anything as the wildlife was well camouflaged amongst the bush and the rocks. George knew exactly where to find them and he did. He drove maybe 10 meters from a large lion resembling Elsa. The lion was lazing on the rocks under the heat of the sun. Janet was expecting to see lots of lions but there were only one or two to be seen. They were close enough to take photographs. The lion never moved, gave the largest yawn, and seemed to be looking at the bus as if to say, "Oh no, not again." He must have been used to the frequent trail of travelers visiting every day. The Arabian desert had more color from its orange sand and clear blue skies. Here in Kenya there seemed to be a constant haze surrounding the barren land and bush. They had stopped to take many photographs of the wildlife. The lions, cheetahs, elephants, rhinos, and the buffalos—all were lazing in the afternoon heat. George would not stop to take photographs unless Janet sat in the front seat of the bus, and to make him more accommodating for the rest of the tour, Janet gave her Walkman to George to keep him happy so the tourists could keep snapping their shots of the wildlife. The most colorful and exciting time was when they arrived at the Samburu Lodge. It was situated on the banks of the Uaso Nyrio River. Janet saw more wildlife than she had ever seen while relaxing here. Janet and Sally would sit enjoying her glass of papaya wine. The crocodiles would climb up the riverbank and would feast on the food in front of them. She could not get over how wide their jaws opened and when she saw the 60–70 teeth, she could help but say, "I wonder if that is the one that swallowed the clock." Sally laughed knowing full well Janet loved her fairy tale movies. "We only need to look out for the pirates," Sally answered looking at the young male residents in the next hut. The girls dined surrounded with décor that resembled the 1920s and the beautifully teak carved furniture made by hand.

The lodge was surrounded by cultivated greenery, and the bright colors of the trees and plants gave a much more cheerful atmosphere than the barren wildlife areas. The sleeping accommodation was set in rows of thatched roof cottages with small veranda balconies so they could watch the wildlife. Janet and Sally were sitting on the deck and she had just placed a glass of Bacardi and Coke on the sill. Then along came a baboon and ran away with the glass in hand. "One monkey stealing from another. How cute." Sally laughed and raised her glass to Janet, "To Kenya."

The next morning they set out to the Maasai Mara reserve. There they took endless photographs and snapshots of the wildebeest, giraffe, impala, lions, cheetahs, and the occasional leopard if you could spot one because of their ability to hide amongst the trees as their spotted coats blended with the trees. Here the girls took a hot air balloon flight where they could absorb the miles and miles of the Maasai Mara Wildlife Park. Following that they visited a local Maasai village. They were directed to a small hut and for a small fee they were invited inside. Janet was definitely going to hold onto her shoes. The Maasai people very friendly and they were not interested in Janet's clothing but she was interested to learn about their life. She paid some extra shillings so she could sit down and learn about the people. How they respected the wildlife and they did not consume the wildlife or birds. They were conservationists and they lived to protect the wildlife. They evaded slavery and they stood their ground with governments to stay and maintain village life. Janet could have stayed there for the whole duration of the safari. She could not get enough of their stories; they gave her food and drinks. George had to personally escort her to the bus as it was getting late. "Shoo, shoo! Bus, bus!" George pushed her from behind.

They continued their journey to the Mount Kenya Safari Club where they spent two days lazing around and enjoying both a glass of wine and the surrounding greenery and Janet could not help admire the multitude of peacocks elegantly boasting their colorful spray of majestic feathers.

George rounded up the girls and once again on the bus. "We are going to the Shimba National Reserve which is home of Kenya's last remaining habitat of the Rare 'Sable Antelope' and where we will stay at Treetops Hotel. It is in the heart of the Kenya forest and is renowned as the place where on the sixth of February 1952, Princess Elizabeth first heard the news that her father had died and that she was to be queen." George had learned that speech off by heart and he was proud to associate the Queen with Kenya. "However that is not the true story, George," Janet began to tell the tale. "She certainly was at Treetops the night her father died but she was told the next day when she had returned to a fishing lodge called Sagana which is twenty miles away. Apparently she was standing beside a trout stream in the foothills of Mount Kenya when Prince Philip broke the news." Janet had remembered reading the story some years ago. Sally nudged Janet, "You have spoilt his day, George did so well to learn his topic." Janet felt embarrassed that she could be seen to belittle George. She moved to the front seat to apologize but then she saw he was wearing earplugs and listening to music from the Walkman that Janet had given to him. She was so relieved.

Treetops looked like a very old hut with a walkway high around the building so the visitors could view the animals coming to the waterhole at night. The room was a basic wooden bed and with white sheets, the restaurant walls had a wooden surround, and the seats and tables were made of dark wood. There were white tablecloths on the tables set with silver dinnerware and serviettes and small candles. It was very dark but kind of quaint. Dinner was served and the waiter came to the table, and before asking the girls what they would like to eat, he pulled the tablecloth away quickly and that left the dinnerware standing in exactly the same place. The girls looked up as the waiter was so happy with his skilled trick. The girls began to clap and urged the other guests to do the same. Janet noticed that the group visitors were dressed in designer safari suits and were well into their fifties. They definitely spoke the Queen's English with very haughty tones of voice as they complained about the food and they had the young waiters running up and down after them. Janet did not appreciate the rudeness shown by these tourists. Sally looked at Janet. "Let it be," Janet remembered Bo's words and let out a deep breath. "If you don't like the food send it over here because we think it is delicious, don't we?" Actually there was nothing wrong with the food or the service. The ladies at the next table managed to rest their vocal chords for the evening. "Nicely done," said Sally. The waiters brought the girls a complimentary bottle of papaya wine and thanked them. After dinner they walked onto the outside decks to see the animals come to the waterhole. A herd of elephants were making a lot of noise and screaming. They were mating. "Look it's a political meeting," Sally said. Janet could see that Sally was developing a sense of humor.

They raised their glasses as they stood below the small wooden board that commemorated the Queen. Janet pulled out her British passport saying, "To the Queen"

It was about a three-hour drive from Tree Tops to Nairobi. The girls were pretty exhausted and they slept for almost the whole journey. They were dropped off in Nairobi. They were actually booked into the Hilton Hotel for the day. They were too exhausted to walk around the city, so they spent the day in their hotel room where they bathed, dined, and slept until the evening. George came to collect them around 6:00 p.m.; the train was due to depart at 7:30p.m.

He handed over the train tickets and meal tickets. They were booked into first class that included an evening meal and breakfast. The girls had no idea what to expect and they asked George, he had never taken the train himself as it was out of his price range. What he did say was, "People call it the Lunatic Train, they have described it to be a little shaky." They arrived at the station on time. The train looked very old. The front boasted bright colors that resembled a jester's coat and was followed by carriages which were painted maroon and cream. The line of uneven carriages certainly resembled the bygone colonial Kenya. "Are you sure it is going to stay on the rails?' Sally asked. "Of course it is silly, it is the Jumbo Deluxe Train." Janet waved the tickets in front of Sally. "You just worry too much, you need to live life to the fullest and not be so fearful of everything. You can't help the inevitable and if the inevitable happens you just have to cope with it." Janet looked at Sally as she tried to comfort her anxieties.

They boarded the train and were shown to their compartment—it was very basic and very dull. There was a small washbasin in the room and two bunk beds one above the other, with hardly enough room to put their cases in. Beds were made as if it were a camping bed with grey blankets and starched white sheets and one pillow. There was a seating for two against the wall opposite their bunks. The guards asked which dinner they would like to attend and they chose the first sitting at 8:30p.m. They made their way down to the restaurant. The seats were high back seats of a maroon color which matched the exterior of the train and the tables were set with starched white cloths and silver cutlery. There were small candle lamps at the side of the tables nearest to the windows. There were special soups, different types of fried and steam roasts, many varieties of chicken or beef dishes, and a large range of delicious sauces, which was presented with fried spicy potatœs and boiled rice; steamy fruit nourished salad, coffee, and tea.

The soup had arrived it was a spicy cream of tomato soup in a flat-plated soup bowl. The train was swaying from side to side while in motion, and so did the table and the soup. Janet lifted the soup spoon but she would sway in a different direction from the soup. "Maybe we need a bottle of papaya wine that will help us move with the soup." Sally laughed and with that she ordered two bottles of wine. The waiter arrived wearing a white jacket and carried starched towels in over his arm. He presented the bottle of wine and as soon as he poured it, the train swerved to the side and he missed the glass. He was truly embarrassed. The girls laughed as they were still struggling with the soup. "Maybe we should drink it from the bottle?"

"I don't think that would be a very good idea," he said, looking at the other guests who were much older than the girls and they were dressed in evening wear. The meal was not like what they were used to eating in the five-star hotels. It was tasty and filled their stomachs for the evening. There were plenty of spare seats in the restaurant. The dimmed lights gave rather a romantic feel to the journey, not that the girls were going to have an affair. The older couples finished their food early and returned to their cabins. Janet encouraged Sally to go to the bar with her.

There were only a few people in the bar; the many tourists had returned to their rooms as their intentions were to retire early so they could view scenic Africa from sunrise through their cabin windows. Janet knew that she would only have five days before returning to Saudi Arabia and she wanted to make the most of their freedom. Sitting by the bar were two European guys in their thirties and with them three Kenyan girls who were well-dressed in European jeans and very sexy satin pink blouses that revealed their cleavage. The high heeled shoes and tight fitting jeans showed their shapely long legs and shapely butts. They were dancing to music and drinking wine. Escorting them were two very tall Kenyan men in their midthirties and they were very well dressed in tailored trousers and you could not help but notice the Cartier belts. "There is money in Kenya," Sally commented as she looked over how well-dressed these people were. They seemed to be enjoying their time drinking wine and the Tusker beers. One played a guitar and they were singing to The Beatles' hits and to some African music that was unfamiliar to Janet. The girls walked down toward the bar and they were asked to join the party. Janet was well into the swing of things and enjoyed the dancing and singing. She never asked any questions and they never exchanged names. They just partied danced and sang a few songs. Sally left as she felt uncomfortable, but Janet stayed until early hours of the morning. She must have taken at least forty pictures of her party friends posing and dancing. She would post her memories to her friends in England from the hotel in Mombasa. She was somewhat merry when she left the party. She arrived at the cabin and Sally had tucked into the lower bunk. This actually became a little problematic for Janet as her small five feet stature could not reach to the top bunk and she could not find any steps to reach the top, so she found herself merrily swinging to and fro as she tried to throw up one leg to reach the bunk. Sally was fast asleep and had not stirred despite Janet brushing her swinging legs above Sally's head. Janet was quite hysterical as she saw the situation to be very comical. She realized that she needed to put on her night clothes but could not find them. She fell onto the floor and made a large thud. That woke Sally. "Where is the cupboard?" Janet asked and Sally pointed to a bolt on the door. Janet had undressed and she pulled open the bolt. With that the train had swerved around a bend and the door spun open. Janet found herself thrust into the neighbors honeymoon bed in the next cabin. "Congratulations, all the best to you both, and oops, so sorry. Have a good night." She quickly retreated backward covering what she could of her slender body. "That was so embarrassing!" Janet laughed with her embarrassment. "How many people could that happen to?" Sally could not help but laugh at Janet. "It could only happen to a monkey and you could have at least offered them breakfast in bed."

The girls slept for a few hours and the guards knocked on the doors for first breakfast. Janet woke up with a bit of a hangover and she had remembered her visit to the next doors cabin during the night. "Can you knock on the door and see if they are going to first breakfast?" Janet asked Sally as for all of her outgoing personality, she was not looking forward to the embarrassment of saying hello in the breakfast cabin. As a matter of fact, she couldn't remember what the couple looked like. Sally declined and she rushed Janet to the restaurant for breakfast. Janet had all eyes looking at her and she was almost dying with embarrassment. A young man stood up and looked at her. "You shared our bed, would you care to share breakfast?" They all laughed together. "We have to thank you because we will never forget our honeymoon as you will always be part of it."

"Thanks for the invitation but we have eaten." Janet knew she was lying as this was the first sitting, and Sally turned around. "Of course we will join you and we have not eaten." She pushed Janet into the seats opposite the young couple. "And you will remember eating breakfast with the couple you shared a bed with." Everyone began to laugh and they began to exchange stories over breakfast. The thirteen hours on the train had passed by very quickly. Janet still had the music and dancing session spinning around in her head and she chuckled to her night of dance and embarrassment. That was another story she could tell the folks back home.

The hotel bus was waiting to greet them and they were taken to the Bamburi Beach Hotel. The hotel was in the final stages of being renovated, and apart from the occasional piles of sand and dust, Janet could not believe how beautifully it was set with its Arab style architecture. "Home from Home," Janet commented as they walked through the entrance—she was referring to Riyadh. They were greeted by warm welcoming smiles of the staff and a fruity cocktail. They arrived at their third floor room and relaxed overlooking the sea and the heart-shaped pool that was decked with palm trees and Janet could breathe the fresh salty sea air. "A hair of the dog." Janet opened a bottle of Bacardi and toasted the impressive view of the palm trees offset against the ocean and clear blue skies. "To paradise," she said as she clunked her glass against Sally's.

The girls spent a lazy day relaxing around the swimming pool and then they took the hotel bus to go shopping in Mombasa. For the first two days they remained in what they understood to be the safe zones, and they spent the evenings watching the Maasai dances at the hotel and devouring the charcoal-fired fish. The locals used to climb the palm trees and drop down a few coconuts for the girls. On day three one of the coconuts fell onto a nearby older gentleman who was lazing by the pool. Janet moved to retrieve the coconut and apologized to the gentleman. He answered her in German. She had not spoken that language for many years and she remembered how her grandmother taught her the language. "Ich Heisse Janet un wie heist zie." She knew her grammar was not correct and the gentleman laughed. He replied in English. That was easier. He was Hugo and he was one of the many German tourists staying at the resort. He visited Mombasa every year. He was so fatherly. Hugo was gay and he had no hesitation saying that to the girls and Janet did not care. The three became friends and Hugo escorted Janet and Sally everywhere. They felt safe with him as the ventured into the small alleys of Mombasa. They had eaten dinner at the hotel and the two waiters had invited the girls to the local discotheque where it was not known to all of the tourists. Janet wanted to see the real Mombasa and Hugo said he would go with them—that way they would feel safe. Janet was to find that despite the palms, the sunshine, and the happy languor, all is not bliss in Mombasa and it is far from perfection.

They had taken the hotel taxi to the African Bush Disco which was around two kilometers from the hotel. It was only two kilometers but it seemed as it was called the Bush Disco. It was no more than a wooden hut bar surrounded by bush. It was very dark and smoky inside with wooden stools and high bar stands. They were drinking Tusker beers and they were very cheap to buy. The music played was African and the songs were the drumming sounds of Mombasa and the song "Jambo Jambo." The girls and the waiters started dancing; Hugo got a firm eye on the girls. It was midnight but still early for the Bush Disco. Around 2:00 a.m. the bar started to fill with locals. Some of the girls were sitting around the bar, and to Janet's surprise, so were the girls and men she had been partying with on the train. There were young girls maybe just sixteen wearing high heeled shœs and very short skirts, all of which were bright colors and were designed to catch the eye of the male onlookers. A group of Europeans entered the bar—all male. Janet realized her friends on the train were prostitutes that were seduced by the fast cash of the European men, some sailors off the boats and the men were clearly showing that they were there to have a cheap good time.

Janet glanced across the bar and there were some of the guys she knew from Riyadh. Guys that earned plenty money and guys she knew who were married. They were making it with the girls. "Hi, Carl, hi, Jo, small world, isn't it?" Janet could not help but be rather rude with her remarks. Sally tried to stop Janet from being her usual outspoken self. Carl and Jo left without a girl. "That's a couple of marriages we might have saved," Janet said as she raised her glass. Hugo smiled at her. "Maybe, who knows?" he replied. The waiters and the girls finished their drinks and they danced the night away. At the end of the night the waiters sat around the table and introduced them to the workers at the bar. Janet was to receive a message that she would never forget. "Mombasa is a mainly Muslim city and many girls are lured to the city at a very young age with promises of a better life, but they get duped and trapped into a sophisticated web of the sex trade and for many there is no way out and a night of sex with a one thousand shilling payment for their services. That means sex for the price of a pint of beer in Europe. They are the twilight girls." The waiters bought Janet a beer and all she could think of was "sex for this" as she looked at her bottle of beer. "Something in this world needs to change, there is a difference between choosing to do something and being forced to do something."

Janet had made a new friend in Mombasa. Hugo remained a good friend for twenty years until he passed away; she used to visit him many times in Germany where he and his partner would take her to bars and spoil her with German cuisine. They would walk through the forests and parks where they would celebrate life with coffee and cakes.

Janet returned and settled into her life in Saudi Arabia; her contract was coming to an end and she knew she could not stay any longer. She learned so much about the life of the gentle Saudi families that had welcomed her. She also learned that the Virgin Land that boasted money from oil was far cry away from virginity. She witnessed how human beings will always find a way to break the tight rules that suppress them from freedom. Janet knew she had choices around her life and many people around the world did not. She knew just how lucky she was to have that freedom. Despite her fun times she was learning more about herself and how she began to perceive the world for what it was. She returned to England to spend time with family and friends.

Chapter Eleven

SHE RETURNED TO England in the height of summer. How she loved being amidst the greenery of the English countryside after the barren dry existence in the desert. As she walked through the old town of Boston, the old buildings came to life especially St. Botolph's Church (The Stump) that boasted a history from around the thirteenth century with its cascade of summer flowers which surrounded the gardens. She had taken for granted the beautiful country in which she had been born. She had never really noticed how beautiful England was until she returned from Riyadh.

She had settled into meeting her family who all seemed to have a calendar of events. They seemed to be doing exactly the same things as when she had left the country two years ago. The routine supermarket shopping, visiting the market stalls, cooking dinner at home, and the occasional dinner out in town. Her nieces and nephews were toddlers now and they barely knew her. Skegness had not changed with the young girls portraying their Kiss-Me-Quick Hats, the clubs and pubs hosting talent competitions, and the penny slot machines did not excite her anymore. The sandy beaches of Skegness could not compare with the palm trees of Mombasa. Everyone seemed to be talking about the TV soaps such as *Coronation Street* and *Neighbours*. They would talk about JR and Sue Ellen in the *Dallas* TV series. Janet had not seen the TV for more than two years. Her life had been fulfilled with the real life stories and adventures; she no longer needed the make-believe world that was portrayed on the television.

Janet arranged to meet her friends for dinner at the local Chinese restaurant. There were few choices of restaurants—English, Chinese, Cantonese, and Indian. They were not the five-star hotels that she had become familiar with in the Middle East and on her travels. She had taken with her photographs of Kenya and wanted to boast of her time away but actually no one was really interested. She pulled put her pictures taken on the train in Kenya, where she was sitting at a table with friends. "What will people think about you having photographs with black men?" Janet slid back into her seat. For the first time in her life she had been exposed to prejudice and this coming home was to be another new learning in her life. She told anyone and she needed to show what wonderful people she had met on her travels and share her stories freely. "I thought I had no freedom in Saudi Arabia, but I was wrong as I had the freedom to mix with many cultures, and here you do not get the opportunity and you all criticize so openly about what you know nothing about." She did not like was she was hearing, and she did not like what she had to say. She had met with the kindness of the Kenyan waiters in Mombasa and George the driver on the bus from Nairobi, the Filipino and Thai nurses, and the gentle Arabic families in Saudi Arabia. She realized just how sheltered her friends and family had been. The words of "Let It Be" echœd in her ears but this time she could not let it be. She needed to stand up for her friends, the people she had met overseas. She did not want to create discord between them and she wondered, did she every truly know her friends at home? She needed to express exactly how she felt. "How would Bo do this without battling for the rights of everyone?" she muttered to herself. "Why does life have to be so complex?" This time she knew that it could not be Bo's words—it would have to come from Janet. She was a woman now and she would have to stand up for herself as Janet. Janet left her friends at the dinner table as she made an excuse to visit the bathroom. She paced the floors of the bathroom in the restaurant. She paced up and down so many times. "Let me think, let me think." She took a deep breath in and out, and in and out, and in and out. She was pointing her fingers and shaking them; a woman came out of the toilet and looked at her as if she definitely needed admission to the local institution. "I'm manic," Janet said to her as she rushed out of the doors.

Eventually she returned to the table. Her friends had forgotten the conversation and were planning their holidays. However Janet did not forget. She leaned over the table and called their attention as she raised her glass. "A toast to my friends." She was meaning the ones she met overseas. "Very kind of you to think of us," her friends replied as they raised their glasses and started to toast. Janet raced into breaking the toast, "Imagine the whole of Europe being black and Kenya white, would you have said what is a black person doing with a white person on this picture?" She pointed to everyone. "Answer me then and just think about it as you can't be prejudice without reason." They had totally ignored her vision and they were not going to change from their comfortable unexposed life. "Cocked that up then, didn't I?" She toasted herself, and with that she had let go of her friends. She had previously lost her friends over boys and relationships and now she was losing her friends because she had developed a voice.

She was sitting alone at the table with her hands over her face trying to make sense of everything. She had so much more to learn about life. A small hand touched her shoulders and placed a glass of wine in front of her. The Chinese waitress comforted her. "You should be very proud that you are able to see people for who they are and you need to love the people for whom they are and accept them." That night she returned home and sorted out her old music and spent a nostalgic musical night at home. She listened to the records she had danced to over the years and she would look back at the happy times, and for a brief few moments she reminisced and relived those times through her mind. She would remember Maggi May and Maggs and her first kiss in Scotland. The mariachis in Tijuana, Lanny, Andy, and Randy with the cowboy polkas in California, MacArthur Park and her trip to Las Vegas, The Village People, Anna, Mary and Jimmy and the painting party at her home in Lincolnshire. She would show tears of laughter. She would also reflect upon her most painful times. The Chi-Lites reminded her of how she had hurt her first boyfriend Dave and she would play all of the songs she had remembered from her wedding night and how she had remembered the hurt from Paul. She was experiencing the highs and lows of her life through music and as the tears of sadness overwhelmed her she had remembered the stories of Gregory and her parents and how they had suffered so much more in life than she had. With that she poured out a glass of red wine and started singing, *Red, red wine, go to my head, make me forget.* She began to cry. She had never really cried like that before, even after the breakup from Paul. She knew that she was not lonely from life but lonely within her heart. Her eyes became so red and swollen but after a while she felt better for releasing the tears. She played her favorite song "Let It Be" then curled up in her bed. She knew only too well she had to let it be and she needed to stay strong enough to be the victor of her life and never the victim. She fell into a deep sleep.

The next month Janet spent visiting her hometown and family. She returned to the clubs that she used to frequent. Everything had remained almost the same as when she had left four years earlier. Some of the nightclubs had closed and some had been renovated. Her sisters had taken her for a girl's night out and they visited Josephine's Nightclub in Sheffield. Janet remembered how she had perceived it as being a good nightclub and while the two bob millionaires frequented the wine bar and restaurant dressed in their suits, there were plenty of normal people in the rest of the club. After her five-star travels, Janet felt she could easily sort out the two bob millionaires but she still wondered what she used to think the normal was. She was dancing on the floor; she was not in the present world but in her own world of music. She was oblivious to the surroundings as she moved around the dance floor moving to the beat of the drums. A young man had joined in to dance with her and was certainly not going to leave her side. The music stopped and she had not even noticed him. She returned to the bar to buy a drink and he followed her. Not that he was going to put his hand in his pocket and buy her one. He waited until she had been served and then he moved in to talk to her. "Good choice of drink." She had asked the barmaid to make her a Dirty Mother, and she sipped it with a small straw. Janet was tired of the guys asking her out and she was tired of the hundreds of conversations that start with "do you come here often" or "I haven't seen you here before." This conversation started with all of those. Janet did not want to spend the evening with anyone—she was there to enjoy the music and dance. The young man would not leave so Janet put on her charms. "Do men believe everything women say?" she asked the barmaid. The barmaid nodded. "Usually." Janet told the barmaid to stand nearby and listen. The young man had obviously devoured quite a few drinks. "What do you do for a living?" he asked.

"You would never believe," replied Janet.

"Go on then, tell me," he insisted.

"Actually my name is Agatha but my friends at the factory call me Aggie for short." She began to make up a story and she did not know where it was going to end. "Are you a manager?" He was looking at Janet's elegantly padded blouse which looked rather dynasty style and it fell into a beautiful V shape that showed a little of her cleavage. She was dressed to be fashionable but the padded shoulders gave her flat breasts. "Oh no," she said, "I borrowed this blouse from my sister." She knew he was looking at her cleavage. "Have you ever eaten a hairy gooseberry?" Janet asked.

"No," he replied.

"You don't know what you have missed. I actually work at the local canning factory and we have a special conveyor belt. It holds the best of Sheffield's stainless steel blades and the gooseberries. Hundreds of them are washed down the belt where they are sorted and shaved. Then they go into the cans were people eat them for desert or put them into pies." She could hardly keep a straight face and the barmaid was laughing. The young man believed every word and Janet thought she might put him off but there was no chance of that. "Can I see you tomorrow? My name is Tom by the way," he asked Janet. The barmaid poured Janet another drink. "This one is on me and now I know they will believe anything so you win." The young man would not leave her side. Janet made an excuse to go to the ladies' room and he was still waiting at the bar. She approached a good-looking gentleman. "Will you pretend to be my husband and I will buy you a drink." This man escorted her to the bar and spoke to Tom. "I hope you enjoyed the dance with my wife?" With that Tom left rather quickly. Janet thanked her quick lived husband and bought him a drink. With that she left the club and returned home. She felt alone on her nostalgic night but she was just not ready to play the dating game. The more clubs she visited, the more she did not want to stay in England. She needed someone who was grounded and knowledgeable and someone that would hold a two way conversation with her.

The following week she visited the local working men's club where she had visited many years with her brother. There were some old flames and people she used to dance with before she met Paul. Here the snooker room still held the majority of men discussing fishing trips and planning their next holidays. The same old boys were sitting in the same seats and they would get very annoyed if someone sat in their seat. On one visit she would recollect Stu; he had been sitting in the same seat for twenty years. Janet made a Reserved sign and wrote Reserved on it with her best Lancôme lipstick—the Brightest Red. She posted that sign above the seat. Stu came into the room and sat unknowingly beneath the sign. Janet called the boys over and yelled, "Family photo!" They took a snapshot of Stu and the boys beneath the Reserved sign. That photograph still stands in the snooker room and the boys would talk about that for years to come. Janet brought laughter into the room that night. Bingo nights were held in the large hall and live bands continued to play music from the '60s, '70s, and '80s. Janet remembered how she used to join in their fun she remembered winning the Easter turkey twice in one day on the local raffle. She would always remember the younger years of her life, but on this visit, she didn't feel any kind of buzz around what she used to do. Everyone seemed to be so happy in their comfortable world, and they welcomed Janet as if she had never been away.   She would join the boys who she had grown up with and she would shout them all a pint of beer and sit around the table with them. She had learned to use her pool skills on the snooker table and once again became one of the boys. She would share stories of her travels, and she would bring more laughter and fun into the room. She knew deep within her heart that she enjoyed being with everyone, but she had changed, and she knew that this is not what her future would be. She could have easily resembled Rita in the movie *Educating Rita.* Rita wanted to understand the world through literature and Janet wanted to learn through experiencing life. Rita had a passion for books and Janet had a passion for life. She just needed more in her life than what the boys and the club here could offer. She was not referring to the finer materialistic life that she had become accustomed to, she could take that or leave that as easily as she could mingle with everyone. She had developed her passion for life and people and sadly she knew that she would not find what she was looking for in her hometown.

Janet had made her decision to move on and she applied for a senior position in Bahrain. She had visited the small island with her expatriate friends as a great escape from Saudi Arabia. It was a country where she could drive a car and enjoy a drink at the bar as well as soaking in the sunshine at the five-star hotels.

It was not easy breaking the news to her parents and family who had enjoyed her stay. Her parents were hoping that she would settle down close by. She made a lot of effort to stay with them for two weeks before flying overseas. Many evenings she would spend with her parents and she would talk to her father who was her best friend. "You obviously haven't seen enough palm trees then." Her father would put his arms around her. They would spend an evening with vodka to celebrate Janet's future, whatever it may have in store for her.

"Come tell me about your life in Saudi Arabia." He knew Janet had not portrayed the whole truths in her letters.

"It's very confusing really, that is I mean the segregation and all of that. Men wear white dresses and they can walk hand in hand and kiss on the streets. Women can walk hand in hand, their heads and faces covered, yet young male and female couples cannot."

"Sounds like a country full of lesbian and gay relationships to me," her father replied. "I just think that people should have freedom and that comes when people choose to do the things they want to do—they feel fulfilled and satisfied and when people are forced into things, conflict and war is inevitable, as they say, enough is enough," he continued to say. Janet did not want to go there but she knew what he was talking about. He was forced in the war to do things he never wanted to do and there was an uprising. She felt his sadness so she shared her good stories with him. She told him how she had met so many different cultures, how she had tasted the different cuisines, how they shared stories and how they turned sadness to laughter with music and kindness, and how she enjoyed her work. She never told him how she had dressed as a man to play sports. If he knew the whole truth, she would not be travelling again and he would not sleep at night. Her father turned on his cassette player and played his favorite music, *Que sera sera, whatever will be.* And they danced and turned their sadness into laughter. She would sit on her father's knees. "It dœsn't matter how old you are, you will always be my baby and I will always be three steps behind you."

Janet had a good sleep that night and spent the next few days catching up with family and the children. She would take the kids to the local parks, play games, and have fun with them; she was their favorite aunt and she knew how to play make-believe games with them—pirates and fairies and so on. She would spoil them with shopping, and of course, the occasional lollies. She would let them get so messed up that when they walked home she would have to go through the front door of her parent's home and give them a bath party, wash their clothes, and dry them. Then they would walk out of the back door of her father's home and walk into the front door of their home as if nothing had ever happened. They were dressed as beautiful and clean as they had walked out of her brother's home. She and the kids had so much fun as they would roll down the hills in the local park. They would hold their fairy tale secrets within their hearts always.

It was July 13, 1985 and Janet was glued to the television watching the *Live Aid Concert.* All the stars were there. Madonna, Dire Straits, Queen, and Paul McCartney had a small mishap with the piano sounds just before he sang "Let It Be." Live Aid eventually raised $127,000,000 toward famine relief for African nations, and the publicity it generated encouraged Western nations to make available enough surplus grain to end the immediate hunger crisis in Africa. Bob Geldof was later knighted by Queen Elizabeth II for his efforts. Janet felt so overwhelmed at the generosity of the world because she knew only too well what she witnessed in Africa. Janet was uplifted knowing so many people in the world cared and so many people were generous and this kept her spirit alive. She was tired of the self-centered, egotistical people she had met in the bars and clubs. She needed to feel the warmth of people around her and she certainly developed a hunger to understand so much more about life and the people in it.

Chapter Twelve

JANET HAD PACKED her cases and she set off to fulfill her two-year contract in Bahrain. Once again she had said good-bye to her father at the train station. The flight to Bahrain took around seven hours. This time she had taken a British Airways flight and she would frequent visiting the air hostesses at the rear of the plane where she would top up her wine. She would join in the conversations with the young girls who were immaculately dressed. They were all very beautiful as their hair was well-groomed, their makeup flawless, and they wore classical suits which were fitted to embrace their slim, trim figures. In other words, they were everything she wanted to be. Actually she was just as beautiful but she never realized that, and somehow with her breakup from Paul, she had lost some confidence. She met a girl called Maria who came from her hometown. Maria gave Janet a telephone number of the hotel where they used to stay and wrote down their scheduled flights to Bahrain. "Call us and join in the fun." Maria passed Janet the paper with contact details. She had already made friends. Janet had noticed just how hard the girls worked on the airline and how they had to put up with the somewhat drunken expatriates on the airplane. Smoking was allowed on the airplane at that time, and although Janet had the occasional cigarette, the fumes on the plane were overwhelming. Many were returning to Saudi Arabia via Bahrain and taking the opportunity to down a few good whiskeys and beers.

Travelling through customs in Bahrain was a breeze compared to Saudi Arabia, it was much more relaxed and there was no segregated queue for male or female. She did not have to wear an abaya and for that she was so relieved. This time she was not greeted at the airport; she had a list of directions of how to get to the hospital and the manager would greet her there. She was to take a cab and there were plenty of yellow cabs in Bahrain. It took around thirty minutes to arrive at Al Awali and Janet felt she was on holiday with the clear blue skies and palm trees. She was greeted at the small hospital and taken to her new home. This time she had a telephone in her home, she could walk to the hospital, and there were no security barriers on the complex as in Riyadh. She had a small wooden bungalow that resembled 1950s still with wooden floors and very old kitchen units. There was a small garden and Janet was surprised to see the green grass. She had a huge lounge area and dining area with a small entrance porch. She had a large double bed. It was basic but it was to be her new home for two years, and not like rental properties, she was free to decorate and make it her home. She was given two days to unpack her bags and then she would start hospital duties. The complex had around a thousand small bungalows and a central swimming pool with tennis courts. Janet spent many days lazing around the pool and topping up her tan.

The other nurses at the hospital made her feel welcomed and they all seemed to be a family who worked and socialized together. The girls took her to a local garage where she bought a small secondhand car— she bought a small white Mazda 1200cc hatchback. She had wheels and she was free to come and go as she pleased; it was wonderful to feel free. She knew the minute she had stepped off that airplane, when her feet touched the ground, her past was so far behind her and all she could think about was the present being with her new friends, a warm country, and a new job.

Bahrain was like a breath of fresh air to escape the pressured life of so called normality. Paying bills, a mortgage, home rental, etc. were taken care of and she had a tax-free salary. She needed to escape the tribal influences of life that surrounded her. That was what her family expected of her, what the system expected of her. She just needed to be able to breathe and have some fun so she could think with clarity and she knew she could only do that by moving away. She sometimes thought she had been a little selfish to think only of herself, but she knew that she had only one person to please and that was herself. Janet was coping with the trauma in her life and the only way she could do that was to find her own Never Land. J. M Barrie described Never Land as being a magical place where people never grow up. He said that if people stay there, they will never turn a second older than they were when they got there; and Janet was soon to realize that everyone needed a Never Land in their life.

She found that in Bahrain as she made new friends who were also at the crossroads of their lives, she would name that very small island as the Island of Lost Souls. Here everyone was looking for that special something that would make them feel alive and it was a place where they could leave the past behind them and where they could bring out their long-lost youthfulness. She knew only too well the women she had cared for in the community in England. They were financially deprived and life was far from easy but she would often find them reading a book that would take them into a fantasy world so they could escape reality for a short time. Books do just that and authors have a special gift in bringing escapism to many. Janet felt she was so privileged to have an opportunity escape into her real life adventures and embrace the world.

The many expatriates in Bahrain were professional people and that led to very stimulating and challenging conversations with the people who were not only well travelled in their physical life, but they were creative in their mind. Bahrain was a place where you could eat, sleep, work, and play.

It didn't take Janet long to meet friends and the expatriates were just one magnificent family. They would support one another in any way that they could and they would entertain everyone and welcome them at any hour of the day. Everyone would just walk in to a home on an off chance visit and they would make everyone welcome. This was the upbringing she had encountered from her parents—the Slav heart that was so open and flexible. That is, they would never plan or arrange the week. If you wanted to do something or visit someone, you would do just that on impulse. If you threw a party, it would happen with a few hours of notice. This was much more exciting than the arranged meetings and calendar events in what she called her colonial life back home, where in many homes, you would call first to see if the visit was to be convenient and then arrange how many would come for dinner and plan for that set amount of people. In her expatriate life there was always food in the house and a drink in the bar for the unexpected guests. The guests would bring a bottle or some food to share or a small gift. They would never turn up empty-handed. "Are you ok, can we do anything for you?" they would often ask. And not only that, they never asked questions about the past. The people shared their stories openly and freely and here she did not feel alone.

Janet had called into the Londoner Bar in Bahrain where they had gone for happy hour, and leaning on the bar post was a familiar face with whom she had secretly partied in Saudi Arabia. "Hi," she said as she looked at Pete who was enjoying his beer. "What are you doing in this neck of the woods?" she asked. He looked so relaxed; he put his arms around her and gave her a huge hug. That's something that would never have happened in Saudi Arabia. Not in public places.

She had known Pete for the two years in Saudi Arabia but she had never really known him at all because in Saudi Arabia the expatriates were different, they would party but never openly share stories, probably because the suppressed climate led to some tension. Yet in this small island where there was much more freedom, everyone was much more relaxed and there was a lot more trust. Janet realized that her life in Saudi Arabia was that of fun but with lots of caution as to who was invited where because if you turned grape juice to wine there, you had to be careful who got invited to the home to share it. Here in Bahrain it did not matter because expatriates could buy alcohol freely and share it freely. She did not have to sneak into complexes dressed as a man.

Pete was originally from Liverpool and he was a great fan of Gerry Marsden; that is, Gerry and the Pacemakers. Pete always played that music when Janet had secretly visited him in Saudi Arabia where they shared a little of their transformed grape juice and used to dance to all of the hits especially "You Will Never Walk Alone." Pete was an engineer working on a construction site on a two-year contract. "You look much more relaxed over here and you look younger," Janet could not help but notice that.

"Oh, it's the magic of Bahrain." He smiled. And they began to talk. Pete was suffering from a mistake he made many years ago. He was once very happily married. Then when on an overseas contract he had visited Bangkok with some of the expatriate boys. He blacked out at a bar and found himself one morning waking up in bed with a Thai girl. The girl stole his ID, found his address, and would blackmail him with threats of telling his wife. He used to make payments but then stopped. The Thai girl sent photographs to Pete's wife and that resulted in divorce. "All for one lousy mistake," he said. "I had to pay the price, I don't see my kids anymore and I just have to carry that with me always." Janet knew Pete did not have a bad bone in his body and he would never hurt anyone and the years she had known him he was always the gentleman taking care of everyone especially when she was in Saudi Arabia. She noticed the sadness in his eyes and she wondered if there was such a thing as forgiveness. "You are only human and you deserve some forgiveness." She raised her glass, "Now you have to learn to let it be as the clock moves forward, not backward, and I know you'll find happiness." Janet would talk about Paul and her early marriage, she had not done that openly for many years yet this time in Bahrain talking to Pete it seemed okay and comfortable. "I know you will meet someone wonderful when you least expect it." Janet gave Pete another hug. They had developed a sister-brother relationship.

Janet decided to throw her birthday party at her home. "I need a favor. I need some floodlights in the garden and a bar building in my entrance." Pete knew how much Janet liked to meet people and how she spent most of her time making sure everyone was enjoying themselves. "Your wish is my command." Janet felt like she had just rubbed Aladdin's magic lamp and there was Pete the Genie. He did as she asked. He actually closed the construction site for the day and took all the workers to Janet's home where they built a bar and put floodlights in the garden.

"Where else in the world could this happen?" Janet asked.

"And only you could make it happen." Pete replied.

Janet wanted to welcome her friends so she made out party invitations you can swing along to Janet's birthday party or sit at home reading your favorite Mills and Boon novel. There was no need to add bring a bottle or bring a plate because the generous expats always did just that.

The night of the party arrived. Their garden was well lit and the entrance bar could have been the local pub. To Janet's surprise, nearly half of Bahrain turned up. Someone had copied the invites and shared them around the island. She had some Bahraini friends and they had managed to get a copy of the invite. The Mercedes car pulled up with food on the top. Half a sheep was on a bed of rice and a birthday cake as large as her dining table with her name on it.

Music played from every era and everyone danced, mingled, and had fun. Everyone had something to say sharing their stories. You would never see silent bodies sitting in a corner and anyone that was new to Bahrain was welcomed with open arms. Janet introduced Pete to her best friend Faye. They were alike and Janet knew they would be good company for one another. Pete married Faye later that year. "Yet another happy ending," Janet would say with a smile.

Time was of no importance to Janet and she rarely spent time alone. The weekends would be spent socializing with her expatriate friends. There was not one week where she did not put on a fancy dress outfit— she had found Never Land. She would dress as a white witch, a pirate, a fairy, or a film star, run through the desert and attend so many parties. It was as if she could wear any mask and fit into any social event. She would visit the rugby club, play tennis, squash, and go ten-pin bowling. She would join in the boat trip camping events and camp out on the small islands to the northeast of Bahrain. She attempted water skiing but she could not hold the strength in her legs. Her expatriate friends tried to help her, they even had her balancing on the sand wearing skis and they pulled her into the water with a speedboat. She would end up somersaulting and in the end would return with a very sore and painful crutch and her skin was chaffed from the salty water. She was determined to succeed, but she never managed to water ski. Her friends never gave up trying to help her, and she would never give up trying to take up that challenge. Her friends had taken photographs of her attempts at waterskiing and she used to laugh at the memories, and one day they had posted her pictures in the local magazine. That was of her catastrophic attempts to ski alongside a skiing dog, standing with paws on the handles and doing a professional job. She had developed a sense of humor, and she was able to laugh about what she could not do. Little did they know it but her supporting expatriate family was teaching her to survive the challenges of the world.

She was lazing by the swimming pool and someone very familiar was swimming in it. "I don't believe this," she walked over to a middle-aged man who was somewhat wet and drying of his middle-aged abdominal spread. "Hi, Gerry, I remember you. How is your son born by cæsarean section, I believe some six years ago." Gerry looked at her as if she was some psychopath. "How did you know that?" he asked.

"A little bird told me in Skegness." He laughed and he obviously did not recognize her and Janet knew he must have met millions of fans in his life. He was playing in Bahrain that weekend.

Janet was invited as a guest and she arranged for Pete and Faye to come to the concert; she had invited her friend Liz and a few others. There must have been a thousand people at that concert. The guests were at a benched table at the front. Gerry played "Ferry Cross the Mersey" and all thought the words were about Liverpool—they resembled her life in Bahrain. Pete was in his elements singing about his own city of Liverpool. Janet had made some banners in her best Lancôme lipstick, "You'll never walk alone." Gerry played that song as a request to Janet. They had a few beers and stood up waving those banners, "Walk on, walk on with hope in your hearts and you'll never walk alone." There was peace and fun in the air and people in Bahrain knew how to enjoy themselves without drunken brawls. They could enjoy a drink and respect the entertainment. Janet thought about the sterile concerts in the UK where drinks were not allowed due to the careless drinking bouts of fans. "My, how people have driven the fun out of life by being stupid back home and how sensible people have to suffer," she whispered to Pete.

"Let it be this is not the time for your analysis of life now," Pete answered. "I feel like I am home and that is the most amazing feeling in the world." Janet knew just how that felt as if they were in a different matrix. It was one of nostalgia. They continued to dance and Lizzy started to dance as they played "Dizzy Miss Lizzy." Janet and Faye had an old-fashioned jive and Janet's memories of Dave and the dancing school in Rotherham came to the forefront. How she had disappointed Dave but how she had learned to dance. She looked over as to how Pete and Faye were very happy and how Lizzy of all people was on the dance floor as Lizzy would spend most of her time at home reading romance novels. "To life and the memories that brought us here," they all toasted to that.

At this concert Janet met an older couple. They had lived in Bahrain for more than thirty years and they were coming to retirement. It was so wonderful to see the older couples moving back in time and dancing. They invited Janet to their home. They had a small bar and a dartboard in the entrance of their wooden home. It was beautifully decorated with memorabilia that the couple had collected over the years—Persian rugs, brass lamps, brass vases standing from the floor, and a crystal chandelier hanging from the ceiling. Standing by the bar was an old Bahraini gentleman; he was at least seventy years of age and he had been friends with the couple for the past thirty years. He wore an immaculate white thobe that was tailored to western style with side and breast pockets, a collar, and French cuffs. The cuffs were neatly folded back with solid gold and diamond cufflinks. Janet couldn't help but notice his gold Rolex watch that was edged with a multitude of diamonds that were sparkling from the rays of the spotlights over the bar and the pyramid of colors reflected across the walls of the room.

Mustafa was definitely westernized. He did not drink alcohol but he enjoyed the company of Jean, Eddie, and friends and he had no objection to them drinking alcohol in their presence. He had brought a bottle of Johnnie Walker Blue Label as a gift. "Hi, I am Mustafa and I live in Riffa, just a few minutes down the road." He had an excellent command of the Queen's English; he spoke better English than Janet. Jean and Eddie were from Yorkshire and despite having lived in this Never Land for over thirty years, they would still dance and entertain everyone and they had so much youthfulness about them. The couple may have been older in their appearance but in their hearts they were still teenagers enjoying life. "I just want to feel like you when I get older," Janet remarked. Mustafa was also very young at heart—he was modernized and very intellectual; he owned his own business and he was certainly well-travelled. Standing next to him was another well-dressed young man wearing a white thobe, he originated from Kuwait and he was a pilot. "This is Abdullah," the gentleman shook hands with Janet. "This is my first Arabic handshake." Janet could not get over how polite they were and how comfortable and safe she felt in their presence. She remembered the party she had been to in Riyadh where she had declined to drink alcohol, yet here Mustafa and Abdullah were devout Muslims. "Have a drink, you will not be arrested in Bahrain." Mustafa poured a drink for Janet. "But you must never drink and drive because that is an offense and there is a very hefty fine of a sum of one thousand dinars and imprisonment. You would not want to be in a prison cell where seventeen prisoners are crammed in one cell that could not accommodate more than four beds. Those prisoners are kept in the cell for at least twenty hours a day where they have only one health facility for shower, toilet, and washing. And the room itself is being used to eat, sleep, rest, and worship so you need to obey the rules of Bahrain. Drunkenness and disorderly behavior in public is forbidden and punishable."

"It is a pity we don't have those prisons in England then we might have people behaving sensibly," Eddie remarked. "I am not looking forward to returning to my home country because I am embarrassed at the behavior in our bars and clubs in England." Janet knew only too well what Eddie was talking about.

Mustafa had brought a plate of sandwiches and offered one to Janet. They were ham sandwiches. "Just because we do not eat pork in our culture dœs not mean that you cannot eat it, so please enjoy." He passed the plate to Janet. "This would never happen in Saudi Arabia as they are very strict over there." Janet took a sandwich. "Yes, Saudi Arabia is very strict and Islam is taken very seriously, but here in Bahrain we take our religion seriously but we also respect everyone as we are all God's children."

The five some played darts until early hours of the morning. Janet had rekindled her skills from when she used to play as a teenager in England. She was as amused as to how the men in thobes had to bend over and pick up the fallen darts from the floor and how they had to brush their gutra backward so they could see the board. She was clearly beginning to understand that kindness presented in all cultures and she adored her multicultural existence. Mustafa invited Janet and her friends to the Sheraton Hotel New Year's party. Jean and Eddie accompanied her. The discothèque looked like a grand ballroom with beautiful balloons and décor. Jean, Eddie, and Janet sat at the table with Mustafa and Abdullah, both dressed in their immaculate white western thobes and gutra. They placed party hats on their heads and they all began to enjoy the evening and dance. There was a power cut just before midnight and the room was dark except for the small candle lamps on the tables. Everything went quiet. Jean looked at Eddie. They stood up, took Janet by the hand, and walked on the dance floor. Jean and Eddie started dancing and singing, Janet joined in as she had remembered the song from the sing-along parties in Skegness.

Bye bye Blackbird by
Pack up all my care and wœ,
Here I go,
Singing low,
Bye bye blackbird,
Where somebody waits for me,
Sugar's sweet, so is she,
Bye bye
Blackbird!

No one here can love or understand me,
Oh, what hard luck stories they all hand me,
Make my bed and light the light,
I'll be home late tonight,
Blackbird bye bye

Everyone in the nightclub began to clap to the song. The audience swayed to the music from side to side. Janet would remember the party hats on top of the gutras swaying from side to side. They were having fun and Jean and Eddie walked back into their youthful memories. "We lived through the war and we knew how to entertain and we knew how to make the best out of everything." They had entertained in the forces and they could sing. It was her first New Year's party where "Bye Bye Blackbird" brought in the New Year. Janet would remember that year for the rest of her life.

Janet wanted to move away from her comfortable European expatriate existence. She decided to call Maria, the airhostess she met on the airplane. Maria was in Bahrain and had invited her to the hotel. They were going dancing. They arranged to meet around six in the evening at the Diplomat Hotel and then they were going to the Sheraton Hotel discothèque. She took a taxi to the Diplomat Hotel and arrived about thirty minutes early; she was never late as she never liked to rush. She sat alone at the bar and ordered a Bacardi and Coke. She was sitting alone at the bar when an Arabic gentleman sat next to her. Janet was being polite, his command of English was very poor but she had learned some Arabic in Saudi Arabia. She was trying to be polite but this young man was far from that. He leaned over and grabbed her breasts. Janet was not the polite young woman anymore—she retaliated, swung at the man, and he fell from his stool to the floor. With that came a rush of waiters, the bar manager, and security. She was shaking somewhat but she remained in control. "Do you have a tissue? I am sweating from the exercise." The young man was sitting on the floor. She got down off her stool and she helped him up from the ground. Another young Arabic man in his thobe and red and white gutra came to talk to Janet. "I am so very sorry, this is my cousin he came across the causeway from Kuwait and he is not used to European women or women at all." Janet could see that a lesson had been learned and she thought of the Bahrain prison and she did not want to be accountable for putting anyone in there. She had remembered Bo's words, "treat everyone with kindness and let it be." She took a deep breath in and she replied, "No problem everyone, my glass slipped in my hand. Can you take this gentleman to his seat, I think he needs to rest for a while." The security came and asked Janet to make a complaint but she did not want to spoil her evening and she could see the young man was very embarrassed. "No harm done. I am all intact and my mistake', she looked over at the dazed young man. "Is he okay?" The cousin had disappeared and the dazed young man was almost hiding beneath the table. "Can you play some music?" Janet asked the band. "We need to enjoy the evening." The young cousin returned to the bar with a beautiful blue gift wrapped box. He handed it to Janet. "I am so sorry for my cousin's behavior, he has never behaved like this." Janet knew that he had never taken alcohol before and she could see that he didn't know how to handle it. "Do you have any eggs?" she asked the bartender. She whisked up an eggnog and asked the young man to drink it. "What is his name?" she asked.

"Ahmed," his cousin replied.

"And yours?" she asked.

"Ayman," he replied.

"Can you get Ahmed to drink this? He will feel better." Janet passed the glass over and started to do her nursing duties. "Put his head between his knees." That was easier said than done because the thobe sat tight across his knees. "Poor Ahmed." They comforted Ahmed and Ayman asked that Janet opened the box. She did and in it was a 24-carat gold crucifix—it was beautiful and bought from the gold shop in the hotel. "My mother would adore this, it is beautiful and you shouldn't—I can't take this," she handed the box back but Ayman insisted she take it. "Is there anything else I can do for you? We are so very sorry." Janet smiled and her sense of humor returned. "Is there anyone else I can knock off a stool because my sister would like one just like it?" Ayman laughed. "Tell Ahmed it's okay and let's move on."

Just as she said that a group of expatriates entered the bar; they were leaving Saudi Arabia and decided to have a bar binge but they already had too much. "What do you call an Arab with a lump of pork on his head? Ham-ed. What do you call an Arab with a lump of pork and beef on his head? Moo-ham-ed." Janet could not believe that in half an hour there were Arabs behaving badly and expatriates behaving badly and she was in the line of fire. "Okay, that is enough," she actually took charge. "This is Ham Ed, I mean Ahmed, and he is a neat guy and you lot are just escaping a life that was suppressed so take it back and apologize." The expats suddenly sobered up and she took the expat's hands and Ahmed's hand and said, "We need to create world peace, so let's enjoy the evening and stop all of this nonsense." She asked the band to play some music, she took Ahmed to dance and she let Ayman make peace with the expatriate group. The young expatriate introduced himself. "Hi, my name is Sam."

Janet looked at him—he had long hair tied back. "If you were Samson and I was Delilah and if I cut your hair, this hotel would fall upon all of you and this world would be a much better place." Security arrived and the expatriates and Ayman and Ahmed left. Janet was sitting alone by the bar. Maria and her friends arrived late. They came to the bar saying, "I, sorry we are late, were you bored waiting for us?" Janet sighed deeply. "Not really I have been well entertained." She laughed within.

The girls had a drink and left for the Sheraton Hotel. The girls arrived at the Sheraton Hotel—it was so refined with its marble and granite entrance. They made their way into the discotheque which was rather like the Fiesta Club at Sheffield except the tables were not in a line but in a circle around the dance floor and the small orange lamps on the tables. They found a table next to the dance floor and no sooner had they sat down a bottle of Moët & Chandon champagne arrived. Janet was just calming herself down from the Diplomat Hotel and she did not want to be bought, so she sent the bottle back and Maria and her friends wanted to metaphorically kill her. *Not again,* Janet uttered to herself. Maria explained that they were used to this. "Just enjoy the drink, you are not paying for it." Janet knew there was a price to be paid and nothing comes for free. The champagne returned and Janet sent it back. "Will you please stop doing that?" Maria was already getting annoyed. "If I want a drink, I will get my own," Janet replied. She left the girls and went to the bar. She looked back and the girls already had company. Janet was sitting alone at the bar; for once she felt she had made a mistake, but she was going to hold on to her Polish pride and she knew that something would turn out okay. Maria had met her boyfriend, he was well dressed in Arabic costume and they seemed to be having fun. Janet just wanted to listen to the music and dance. She did not feel in place as everyone was dressed in their designer dresses. She had put on her long blue dress that she purchased from Harrods in England two years ago. She looked stunning but she was not in fashion with the clothes that the air stewardesses wore and their refined makeup. Janet could be ready for a date in five minutes, the air hostesses would take hours to get ready. Janet was more natural and down to earth. She began to think she had made a mistake and was about to call a taxi and leave. Then this well-dressed gentleman sat next to her. He was wearing beautifully cut trousers and silk blue shirt. It was the blue and the reflection of his brown eyes and long eyelashes that caught her eye. It was as if he was trying to escape his company and he asked the bartender for a drink very politely. "May I have a Blue Lagoon?"

"What is that?" Janet asked.

"Oh, it is vodka and blue curacao with lemonade and ice." He was well spoken and he was not afraid to speak. "Would you like to taste this one?" Janet took a sip and then she kind of accidentally spit it out. "It is far too sweet for me," she said.

"My name is Khaleel and it means beautiful good friend."

"Are you a beautiful good friend?" Janet asked. "My name is Janet."

"Most of my friends think so and I have many," he answered.

"If you have many friends then you must be, "she replied.

"Would you like to dance?" he asked. Janet could not say no. They were playing "Rhythm of the Night" by De Barge and she just loved to dance to that song. Khaleel took her to the dance floor. He could certainly move better than the stiff-boarded Brits in Sheffield. He moved so naturally. They danced for many records. They played Bob Marley's "No Woman No Cry.""I adore Bob Marley." Khaleel took her by the arms. He felt so warm and her feet lifted off the ground. She did not know him and yet she had been smitten by his looks and his personality. She had not felt like this since she had met Paul in her home. Khaleel was mature in his thirties and he was so gentle.

He did not make a pass at her but he could not stop looking into her brown eyes. "You have Persian eyes and they are very warm," he said. Janet knew very little about Persia but she knew she would soon learn more. "Tell me about your name." Khaleel wanted to know so much more about Janet and she wanted to know more about him. "My middle name is Irena and it is the Greek goddess of peace." Khaleel laughed. "What is so funny?" Janet asked.

"In Arabic it means two penises."

"Oh my goodness," Janet blushed but she thought it to be funny. "Best I don't spend the rest of my life in an Arabic country," she replied and then she could not stop laughing about the translations of the expats in the diplomat and then her name in Arabic. She knew then that they were lost in translation and she was sure she could hold her own comedy show solely upon the translation of names. Khaleel adored her sense of humor and how she could laugh at most things even herself.

The night moved by very quickly and he said he was having a party at his home and he invited her. "I don't know," she said. "I have so much to learn and I just need to be sure when I go to places that I don't know. I just landed myself in bother at the Diplomat." She explained her story to Khaleel and he was amused. "How hilarious, you encountered expats and Arabs behaving badly, that goes to show you can't trust either." Janet didn't like that he was accusing her of mistrust. "Actually people are the same. The world over it, doesn't matter what race you are, testosterone is in all of you and it's all about how you manage its levels." Khaleel laughed. "Please come, you will be very safe with me."

They took a taxi to his central apartment. It was on the fifth floor and security guards were at the entrance. There inside she couldn't help but notice a designer fish tank that took the whole length of the apartment wall. It had beautiful colors of coral and fish. She remembered her description of the dance floor and onlookers in the British night clubs. "Are you expecting any cats?" Janet asked. He had no idea what she was talking about as she was referring to expected arrivals to the party.

Everything was in black leather and silver. It was much more modern than the apartments she had seen in Saudi Arabia where there everything seemed to be red, white, and gold. "It's very cozy." But she noticed it was missing the woman's touch as it lacked color and lacked plants.

To Janet's surprise, the party people were young couples, mainly Bahraini men with young European air hostess girls. They were very young and extremely well dressed in their designer dresses that were classic and followed the Princess Di trend with matching handbags and shœs. The young Bahraini men wore European clothes—they wore designer pants and shirts like Hugo Boss, Calvin Klein, and so on. The girls would mingle and the conversations revolved around.

"Lovely outfit, where did you get that dress?"

"Love the earrings and the watch."

"Where did you get the shœs?" And so on. It seemed as if these well-dressed girls spent their whole life shopping and painting their faces and not to forget the sunbathing.

They were mixed group of youths wanting to have fun. Janet could see that they were not the expats whom would bring a bottle or a plate, they came to the party to enjoy the free everything. She could see Khaleel was too soft and that many were using his generosity. He was rich and they knew he could afford it. It was the first time she had been invited and she was already getting to know Khaleel; he was certainly more than a beautiful good friend to all of these people. He was more of a barman's free lottery ticket.

Janet mingled for a while but she found the conversations to be rather tedious and she spent the whole evening absorbed by how the girls fixed their lipsticks or sprayed on a little more perfume, then they would flick back their long hair. She had moved over to Khaleel. "I'm not being rude but this could be the Hollywood wives as portrayed on the movies." She sat beside the fish tank and started to converse with the fish. "My, how elegant you look and I love your stripes. I bet you didn't buy those stripes at Harrods." Khaleel looked at her. "What are you doing?' he asked.

"I am admiring your fish and we are having a conversation." She began to move her lips in the same way the fish did. "You can't sit there all night." Janet knew that she was being rather anti-social but she was finding it difficult to converse. A young woman came up to her and they started talking about the last trip. She had been dating her boyfriend for only two weeks and she was head over heels in love. "Let me look at your hands." Janet stretched out the young woman's hands and started to read her lines. "You have a strong head line but you don't use it enough. The line stops halfway across your hand and it should extend across your hand. You will marry in a few years and you will have two children very close together."

"Where did you learn that?" the young woman asked. "Oh, a gypsy taught me." Janet smiled as she remembered the young gypsy in Skegness. With that there was a whole line of couples waiting to have their palms read. Janet could not understand how insecure everyone was and they just wanted to wish their lives away. "You should enjoy today and let tomorrow come naturally," Janet would tell them. She spent the whole night reading palms and they spent the whole night opening up and sharing life stories. She also made up some stories and everyone was entertained. Khaleel could not get near to her; he was amazed how the night went and that everyone mingled and danced together. "How do you do that?" he asked. "You just seem to bring out the best in people."

"Bahrain magic," she replied.

Khaleel had been such a gentleman and he did not entice her to stay the evening. They exchanged telephone numbers, and they never made plans to meet again. Janet had returned to work and had finished a relief shift at the refinery. There she had been performing hearing tests and vision tests on the oil tanker drivers. Haji Ali was sixty years old and he had failed both tests. She had to break the news as he could no longer drive and he actually cried. "I have eight children and a wife and I have to feed them." Janet did not know that he did not receive a pension. Her soft heart reached out to him and she asked for his address. He invited her to his home. Janet found herself on a mission to help Ali and she met with one her expatriate colleagues, Annie, and she had asked Annie to accompany her into the village. They arrived at a very barren stone house—it was somewhat elevated on a hill. Their children were running in the streets, playing and having fun. The young boys wearing shorts and no shoes and the young girls would be wearing long simple cotton dresses. Ali invited them into his home. There was very little furniture, just a few mats scattered around the floor. There was an old wardrobe that he must have picked up from an old expatriate house and a small old television. Ali's clothes were old and grey and he wore his gutra as if it was a turban. When he smiled he was missing most of his front teeth, he obviously had no money to visit a dentist.

Ali's wife placed papers on the floor and they shared some lunch, she had made a lamb biryani dish but it was more rice than meat. With that came some desert. The family did not eat, they fed the guests first. Annie and Janet sat on the floor. Janet did not want to eat without the family. The truth was this was all the food they had and they did not want to be embarrassed. Janet could see straight through this. She invited the children to join them and she made sure the children ate something with them. Ali gave the Annie and Janet some ice cream.

Janet noticed the children looking and she knew just how much they would have wanted that ice cream. She remembered that as a child her parents would take her to other families and they were never allowed to eat in someone else's home. It was a pride thing. She remembers how she used to yearn for just a small piece of chocolate cake and just how she felt when she could not have it. Janet shared her ice cream with the children. This was a life far from the Sheraton restaurant buffet. She looked in the garden, and there were live electricity wires running down there. She had worked in the emergency department where a small boy was admitted; he had been electrocuted from such wires and his short life ended. Janet could only see why. The locals used to tap into the street supply as they could not pay the bills. Was this real? How could this be in a land that boasts oil, in a land that had so many Rolex, Lamborghinis, and Mercedes? Janet and Annie could not understand how this could be. Janet knew she was lucky, she remembered the poverty in Nairobi and Kenya, but she would never have expected this in Bahrain.

Ali could speak fairly good English and his son who was eleven years of age began to translate. Janet invited Ali to her home. "I have some work for you, can you come and cut my grass and fix my garden?" Annie replied, "You must come and fix mine too." Ali did fix Janet's garden beautifully; he would come every day and if she was out, he would leave fruit and dates at the front door. She knew when he had been as there was always something at the door. The girls found Ali lots of gardens and homes to clean in the expatriate community. He had some income as long as there would be expatriates there. The expatriates donated some furniture. Annie and Janet took the family for a picnic at the local amusement park. The family never had money to take them there. The eight children would run around and Janet was so happy to see them enjoy a kind of Disneyland in Bahrain. Janet felt so fulfilled and Ali never forgot her kindness. Janet would visit Ali's home every week and the children would teach her some Arabic. She learned how to cook biryani and they learned some English. She had bought a sewing machine for Ali's wife and they had fun sewing together. Janet was not a seamstress but she could sew curtains. Janet was thankful that her mother had taught her the needlework skills as a child. The family here had nothing but they were full of optimism and their family values were so rich that they put the materialistic western world to shame. She had never seen such generosity from such a poor but happy family.

Janet had been invited to the palace where she was to attend a first birthday party of a small princess. The party was held in a large marquis on the palace grounds; the birthday cake was seven layers from floor to ceiling—it boasted Snow White and the seven dwarfs. Every layer was a different flavor. The fruits would be stacked from the floor to the ceiling and the silver platter dishes of Arabic cuisine scattered a table larger than her lounge. The presents were astounding for such a small girl, and she ran around in a beautiful party dress that was definitely purchased from Harrods and fairy shœs. The family was polite and entertaining and they shook hands and welcomed the expatriate guests. This was their life one, they had grown into and a life where they knew no difference. It was a life of splendor. Janet could not fault the generosity or the hospitality shown to her but she could only vision Ali, his garden, his home, and the children. She asked if she could take some food away, "It is so tasty could I please take some for later? I would like eight pieces of cake." The maids packed a banquet and Janet took a large box home with her. She knew exactly where she would take that package. That afternoon she took the package to Ali and the children. Janet would have thought they would have opened it. Ali took it to a deep freezer that he had been given. There was not much in it. "Treats are for special occasions." He would use the frozen foods for the children's birthday. Ali was so thankful and his wife kissed Janet. Janet's soul lifted that day. She had never been exposed to the lush life in England as she was from a refugee family and a normal working-class family and she knew how hard her parents had to work to give her a reasonable lifestyle. She didn't hate the fact that the little princess had everything; she just couldn't understand how they had never been exposed to poverty. She knew in the Western world the divide between rich and poor was widening and that day she returned home and played "Let It Be," hoping that the world would change and that there would be much more equality and generosity in the world. She was learning that money did not bring happiness and that family values were the richest possession anyone could have.

Janet was working at the hospital and a bouquet of red roses arrived—there must have been three dozen. They were from Khaleel. One of her working colleagues passed them to her but had obviously read the message. "I will call you this evening, Khaleel." She was soon to learn that it was not appreciated that she mixed outside the expatriate community. Janet was beginning to see that she could not live in Never Land forever and she wondered what happened to freedom. She felt that the tribal influences were beginning to affect her freedom and she didn't need a fortune teller to forecast that there is no freedom without pain. Wars evolve as people fight for freedom, those was her father's words. "Sometimes you just need to comply," he used to tell her. Janet would never do that as she valued her freedom far too much. She would shrug off the comments from her colleagues. Khaleel invited her for lunch; they met at the Diplomat Hotel where they sipped champagne and ate by the poolside. Khaleel enjoyed listening to her stories and she enjoyed listening to his stories.

They would spend many hours sharing their worlds and they would learn from one another. Khaleel took Janet shopping; his family owned a gold store—it was very modern and had some beautiful Italian designed jewelry. He wanted to buy her something. Janet did not want that, she told him that if she loved something so much she would buy it herself and that way she would appreciate it and remember how hard she had worked for it. That was something her father taught her and she adored his philosophy. She found it difficult to accept gifts. She had seen a beautiful shield. It held seventy-two diamonds and they were very small, but when she held it against her tanned skin, she fell in love with it. Khaleel wanted to buy it for her and she declined and insisted she would buy it. "I will buy this and I will remember my life. I will wear my memories around my neck and this will be my shield." Janet did buy it but Khaleel gave it at cost price. "I remember when I was small, I remember reading the story of 'The Tower of Babylon' and the seventy-two languages, about how the strong should not harm the weak, and did not Persia take over Babylon in 478BC? This shield will remind me of a world where all people will live together and respect who they are that they will mix and integrate in a much kinder world. Seventy-two Fahrenheit is also body temperature and I hope that I will always maintain my life's temperature and support peace." Khaleel was smitten by her words and he was impressed with her knowledge. She knew so much more than he did. "You are not just a person with a pretty face." He passed her the box which was much larger than the pendant.

They dated for three months and Khaleel asked Janet to move in with him. She cared for him deeply and she grew to love his kindness. She was still unsettled in her mind about the meaning of love. She had thought she loved Paul, that was a different time and the love was about different reasons. Love then was when she was so naive, and now she was more educated, more travelled, and much more experienced. "I don't know what love is," she said to Khaleel. He put his arms around her and said, "Neither do I. But we can try."

Janet had thought a little about it and she had moved some of her things into the apartment. Khaleel was sorting out his business. She lay on the bed in the apartment and thousands of questions and thoughts passed through her head. These were the tribal issues and conflict from her own family, her expatriate friends; if this was going somewhere, she would she need to change religion. That would mean giving up her freedom; just how much would she need to sacrifice and how much would Khaleel need to sacrifice in this world that was far from free. She could see many people getting hurt and she could see bitterness between Khaleel and herself because of all the tribal conflicts. Just how strong were they to fight a war. She knew she wasn't ready, and after just four hours of arriving, she moved her belongings out. She took them to her small house. She looked into the mirror and she wept a few tears. "Why does life have to be so complicated?" She could see the two of them in the Garden of Eden having tasted the forbidden fruit and they would both suffer the consequences. She couldn't do that to Khaleel or herself. She returned to Khaleel's apartment and she waited for him to return. He arrived looking so excited; there were more red roses for Janet and he looked so incredibly happy.

He passed the roses to Janet and he put his arms around her. She felt his warmth and every time he did that her feet would lift from the ground and a warm flash of heat would rise through her body. How could she not be with him? She thought to herself. Khaleel told her that he was taking a few days away from the business and he was taking her out on the boat for a few days. "Where are your things?" he asked.

"I haven't sorted them out yet." She did not tell him that she had moved them in and then back out again. Khaleel drove her to her house. She had never invited him there. He had the latest white Mercedes and he parked it in front of her house. Janet ran in to collect her things and she bumped into Faye who couldn't help but notice the car. "I'm going away for a few days," Janet told Faye. "Will you feed the cat?" Faye nodded but Janet could already see that there was some disappointment in Faye's face. Janet just wanted to get away and spend some time with Khaleel so she could decide for herself. Janet was already feeling the pains of the forbidden fruit.

Khaleel took her to the islands northwest of Bahrain. They were small islands and there were few expatriates there on weekdays as everyone was working. The sea was so green and calm and the skies were so blue. It was so peaceful and they could only hear the waves flapping against the boat. It was still daylight and Khaleel had prepared the food for a barbeque. "This is a special island, this is where the two seas meet. When the tides come in the island disappears." Khaleel anchored the boat and they took a smaller boat to the small island. There they barbequed quail and sat on the small strip of sand watching the two seas on either side. Janet lazed in the sunshine and Khaleel would help her with the tan lotion. They played some music and danced alone on the small strip of sand. The tide was coming in and Khaleel wanted Janet to see both seas meet. Janet was amazed how the water waves wrapped around one another and embraced one another. "This is like you and I as we are the two tribes that meet and share our life, and when together we wrap our ideas together into a sandwich and enjoy the food. Then as the tide leaves we are the parting tribes that must leave because of the tribal influences that cause us to part. Then that leaves a barren, dry island of sand that is empty. That is our empty hearts when we are apart." Janet leaned over to Khaleel as the two seas swept over their feet. "It is good to be out here away from everyone, we have our togetherness." They returned to the boat and they toasted to their lives with a little champagne as they danced and watched the sun set over the sea. It was so beautiful just the two of them and the reflections of the sunset turning their skin golden orange.

There was a new moon that night; Janet called it the upside-down moon as it was upside down compared to the moon in England. This was so bright and reflected above the gentle sea. And the star filled skies were just breathtaking. Janet played her Beatles songs and she and Khaleel sat back to back supporting one another and enjoying their togetherness. John Lennon was singing "Imagine" and Janet joined in with the words. As she sang the words she felt John and Yoko's presence, and for that moment while she was leaning against Khaleel, she knew exactly what John meant with his words. "Did you know that *Yoko Ono* name means 'ocean child?'" Khaleel did not know and he was once again mesmerized by Janet's knowledge. "The song had a lot of controversy you know. That is, I think people misinterpreted what he was trying to say. He didn't mean no heaven, he didn't mean any religion. I know now as I am sitting with you." Khaleel sat closer to her. "I know," he replied. "It is a song about escaping all the things in life that bring conflict—the tribal influences and the rules that keep you and I apart."

"Yes," Janet replied as she fell back into his arms. "This place, here under the stars, where the two seas meet—this is freedom. People should not need to escape to be free, they should feel free always." Janet snug closely to Khaleel. "This is John Lennon's 'Imagine.'. It is as we are in it right now. Please play it again." Khaleel pressed the remote control and they fell asleep under the stars listening to the very words of the song. Khaleel had brought Janet's box and there were two packets.

The first she opened was her shield and he placed it around her neck. It sparkled with the moon's rays. "It looks so beautiful against your skin and now you have your shield to protect you when I am away." Janet opened the second packet and it was a diamond ring trimmed with the lightest blue amethysts. It fitted her delicate finger and he looked at her. "This will be our friendship ring and we will always be close." How could two people care for one another so much and yet they knew they could never be together. Neither would hurt their families and they knew that this was not the right time for them in this unforgiving world. They spent their three days together and Khaleel treated her like a princess and she treated him like a prince. This was their fairy tale.

Janet had to break her relationship with Khaleel. Faye had written to Janet's parents telling them she was scared for Janet as she had an Arabic boyfriend. Janet lost friendship with Faye. She felt let down that she was not the one to share stories with her parents and that Faye had no understanding of how Janet was much grounded and that hurt Janet. There were remarks about Khaleel and the Mercedes visiting Janet's home—tea room gossip adding to Janet's affairs. Women at their worst.

Janet was working night duty and Khaleel carried thee bunches of roses; he had a bit too much champagne and he could have easily resembled Dudley Moor playing Arthur. "But I love you and I miss you, Janet." Janet got the girls to cover and she drove Khaleel to her home and the Mercedes. She made him rest there until he was in fit state to drive. That was another problem for Janet as the gossip around the Mercedes being there overnight. Suddenly her Never Land had ended and she was faced with reality. She made sure Khaleel arrived home and she made him promise that if he cared for her, they would need to split. "You will marry someone wonderful and so will I and we will remember one another always." They both shed tears.

Janet told her colleagues that her friendship had ended and she had no hesitation to tell them how inconsiderate and prejudice they were being. That they were deciding what was appropriate for her. "This is my life and I will live it," she reminded them. Time moves very quickly and Janet tried to get her life back once again; she knew she could not turn back the clock but there was one thing for sure, she had learned to stand up for herself and she knew she was capable of loving someone again.

Janet had visited the Sheraton one last time; it was a celebration of foods from around the world and there was to be a discothèque. There were tables of food from China, India, Mediterranean, Europe, Japan, and Thailand. The cuisine was certainly out of this world. The function was attended by many. Janet went with her girlfriends and she took to the dance floor. She danced the night away with her European and some Arabic and Bahraini friends; she was dancing the conga, the row boat song where everyone sat on the floor and swayed forward and backward and side to side. She was amused at the red and white gutras moving backward and forward, and the designer shoes and socks and bare-skinned Bahraini legs as the thobes crept up their thigh. She was having a wonderful time as she was trying to move on with her life. She was full of wit and laughter. She was sitting at the table telling stories and Khaleel had walked up to her. He was with another girl but he did not look happy. She greeted him. She wanted to hug him but she knew what her party of friends would think and there were enough rumors to sink Bahrain. She wished him well. He returned two hours later.

"Where is your girlfriend?" she asked,

"I sent her off in a taxi because I miss you and she was very boring. You are meant to be with me." Janet's eyes filled with tears but she knew that if she gave in for one brief moment the happiness they had would be turned into misery by everyone that surrounded them. She walked to the bar with him and they shared a last drink. "Don't you see? I am trying to save you. I cannot be with you, I don't love you enough to give up my freedom." She knew she never meant to say those words, and she never meant to be so harsh. She had thrust out so much pain in her words that she may as well have thrown a spear through his heart. She knew she would have to leave Bahrain before the two of them would break down. The gossip grew and actually her contract was not renewed. She did not need to ask why, she could see the reasons on everyone's face. She was beginning to understand humans and how unjust their assumptions could be. She had been humanly sensible in making her decision.

She received a phone call from Maria, the air hostess. Maria had changed her religion and had married in Bahrain. Maria was crying on the telephone. She had not heard from Maria since earlier that year. Maria was settled in a home in Bahrain and she had given up her freedom. Her days were spent with the Bahraini women and families. She was very unhappy. "I did not think it would be so difficult. I love my husband but I rarely see him, only in the evenings. The women do not welcome me as I am very different and I do not have anything in common. I cannot leave the house when I want to. He never takes me to all of the places we used to go to and I don't see my friends. My life changed the day I married." Janet's hear sank as she heard those words and she realized her parting words to Khaleel were not as speared as she thought because she knew she could have been wearing Maria's shœs and crying out those same words. Janet became very confused and she wanted to understand the truths around her life. She would always remember Bahrain and the two seas, how they would meet and entwine their waves and how they would part. Maria's words made Janet's parting from Khaleel so much easier yet the parting was painful. Maria's phone call to Janet was timely and Janet's wounds healed quickly. Janet remembered her words and that she was not going to be the victim of life but the victor. She drove to visit Ali and his family and she gave Khaleel's ring to Ali's wife hoping that they would do something with it. She said good-bye to the family she knew so well and that Ali had some secure work and she saw just how happy Ali and his family were. They had the simple family life and that is all they needed. She knew that all the money in the world could not buy happiness. She left Bahrain knowing that she had the most important gift and that was her freedom and even love would never take that away from her. She was to learn that Khaleel married one year later; he had an arranged marriage and he conformed to his tribal ways and Janet learned to let it be.

Chapter Thirteen

ANET ARRIVED IN England the summer of 1987; "Let It Be" was in the hit charts. It was released by Ferry Aid to raise money for the Belgian ferry disaster. The song was playing in the taxi cab as Janet left the airport. She had lost contact with what was happening in England. She had spent two years without seeing the television while in Bahrain. All she could think of on her journey home was her family that she had seen little of. She had arrived at another crossroads in her life. It was to be another turning point for Janet. She was more confused now than she had been when she left California some seven years ago. She sang the words to the song which gave her a new hope and that she was to remain positive and optimistic about life.

Her brother met her at Peterborough station where she had taken the train from King's Cross. Johnny welcomed her with open arms. He was expecting his baby sister to be bouncing with fun and laughter but this time she was unusually quiet. He stopped over at a small country pub so they could talk and have lunch. She loved her big brother and they could always be so open with one another. Her big brother was happily married and she was happy for him. "I envied you for many years as you have travelled through so many places." He put his arms around Janet. "Why would you envy me as you have everything, wonderful kids, wife, and family? You are far richer than I have ever been," Janet replied and she was referring to the happiness of Haji Ali and his family in Bahrain. "I don't envy anyone," Janet said. "I just love to see people happy."

"And are you happy?" Johnny asked her.

"No one ever asked me that before," she snugly leant against her brother. "I am just tired," she replied. "Of course my life has been full of travel and excitement and I am happy with all of my experiences."

Her brother looked at her. "But . . ." he said.

"Yes, there is always a *but* in life, isn't there?" she continued. "I guess at the moment I am just confused." She told him the story of Khaleel and Bahrain. "Well didn't you venture through stormy waters?" He passed her a glass of beer. "I ventured into Never Land and lived a high and exciting life, but I learned that we can't live in a fantasy world forever but it's good to know that we all have the inner child within us. I could have stayed in a fantasy but I chose to step out of it when I met Khaleel. I thought I was stepping from one fantasy to another when actually the fantasy became reality." She was referring to the place where the two seas met. She tried to explain it to her brother but he just didn't understand that. "Why do I have to be such an analyst?"

"I don't know but we love you for it and we wouldn't want you to change at all."

For one moment Janet stepped out into another matrix; she was back in Bahrain on the boat at night listening to "Imagine" and she was leaning back toward Khaleel. She smiled and she seemed to metaphorically lift from her seat. "You know that when I split from Paul I thought my fairytale had ended, but I found another one and for a few months I was swept off my feet and it was wonderful. And I know that someday I will find that love again and I know it will last forever, but it just isn't my time yet."

"I know you will, sis," her brother said as he hugged her. "There's a right somebody for everybody out there." He hugged her once more and said, "Come, Dad is waiting for you and Mum has put up the Christmas tree."

Janet arrived home and it was Christmas all over again. The family was waiting and so was the vodka. "Alas! My prodigal daughter has arrived." Her father smiled and they sat around their turkey feast. Janet's father could see his daughter needed some family TLC. "Come let me show you something." He took her for a walk around the garden. He sky was so blue and in the distance she could see the Boston stump across the field. He took her for a walk around the garden that was full of summer flowers. It was very colorful and beautiful, and with that, her father had shown her his small greenhouse that he had built. "Come and taste these." He pulled the most amazing red tomato from the vine and he gave it to Janet. "Taste this one." She did and it was so sweet. Then he pulled off another one and said, "Now taste this one." And it was very sour. "You see they all come from the same family and yet they are different. If I take the seeds from the sour one and grow it, some of its offspring will be sweet. Sometimes your life will be very sweet and beautiful and sometimes it will be sour, you just learn to love and adore the sweet times and you learn from the sour times so you can make them sweet again for you and those around you, and that is what makes you who you are." He put his arms around his daughter and he knew how to make her feel better. "I am so proud of you. So come, let's go back inside and you can tell me about your journey." They toasted to life with the usual vodka and Janet shared her stories about Bahrain and how she had learned that money would never bring total happiness. How she had entered her Never Land and how eventually that became a reality. He smiled. "Now, my daughter, you are learning about the fruits of life." He passed her another tomato and that one was very sweet. "I just want you to settle and be happy."

"Easier said than done," Janet replied.

Janet spent a month visiting some old friends and family who were still doing the same routines with their life but this time she noticed how many of them were very happy with what little they had. She was very happy for them, and they always made her welcome. She visited Skegness, this time she did not need to find a gypsy because she was happy to let her destiny take its course. Her friends had bought a bed and breakfast place in Skegness and she stayed with them for a while; she helped them for a couple of weeks and she listened to the stories of the holidaymakers. She spent a month in Skegness and she and her father used to go for long walks. There was a small field and her father stopped by a gate. He whistled and bolting to the gate was a gypsy horse. The horse put his nose through the gate and rubbed it against her father's pocket. He knew there was something in there and her father took out two apples. He fed one to the horse and gave the other to Janet. The horse ate the apple from her hand. "This reminds me of the farm we had in Poland and how I loved the animals. The horse is very clever and if he does not trust you, he will not feed from your hand. He knows who is good and bad."

"How long have you had this friend?" she asked her father.

"Seven years," he said.

"But you never brought me with you."

"You never had time," he said. "You were growing and finding out who you were." Janet realized how the time had flown by. She remembers as a child they had many pet animals in the back of their home and she used to feed them with her grandmother and she had forgotten. "You never lose those memories, they always return at the right time." She smiled and he took her by the arm. "You are not a child anymore but you are a beautiful young woman with a big heart and the horse knows that." He took her by the arm and they walked across a field where he stopped to pick up some mushrooms. Janet thought that they were poisonous. "English people do not know what good mushrooms are. We used to pick mushrooms from the forests in Poland. They make a beautiful soup." He collected a bucketful. "My friend the horse showed me where they were and I have been collecting them here ever since. The ground needs to be full of morning dew and then there are plenty of mushrooms here." Janet realized she had been through the world but she did not understand nature like her father. They were growing closer together and she spent more time with her parents. Her mother would cook with her in the kitchen. He would remember how she would fight with her mother in the kitchen as a teenager but this time they were the best of friends. They loved cooking together, and Janet was happier to do things the way her mother liked to do things. She remembered how as a teenager she had been very stubborn and wanted to do things her way. She didn't like her attitude then and she realized that her life's experiences had turned her into a more open and caring person. Janet was rekindling her family ties and she loved every minute she spent with her parents. She could easily stay at home with them. "I wish it could be like this forever." She hugged her mother.

Janet's father did not want her to spend every evening at home, and one night he dressed in his suit and he had chosen a bright red halter neck dress from her wardrobe. "I remember when you used to dance in this dress he," said. "Put it on, we will go out and have some fun." To Janet's surprise he turned on her music and played Bruce Springsteen's "Out in the Street." *Put on your best dress baby . . .*

He actually knew the words and he knew that this song was so apt for Janet. He knew she would walk the way she wanted to walk and she would always talk the way she wanted to talk and he was proud that he had taught her just that—to be proud of herself. And they danced out on to the street. They walked from bar to bar, had a few vodkas, and they danced together on every floor. He was so proud to be escorting his daughter and she was so proud to be with him.

They were in one bar and Janet went to get her father a drink. "What would you and your husband like?" Janet's father was standing next to her. "Two vodkas please and he is not my husband, I am his bit on the side. What do people think when they look around, they seem to think everyone belongs to one another." The barmaid looked rather shocked. "Only kidding," Janet said to her. "He is my father and he is my best friend." With that they left for home. They were quite tipsy and on the way home it started to rain. Janet sang and danced to the song "Singing in the Rain." Her father joined her and her mother came to the door as they were both dancing and singing at the front door. "What will the neighbors say, come in right now you two." They were full of laughter. "And if you think you are getting into this bed with that alcohol on your breath, you can forget it." Janet's mother closed her bedroom door. "Don't worry, we have been together for fifty-nine years and we still love one another." Her father smiled at Janet and with that he toasted with another shot of vodka. "How did you survive the war and build your home and feed all of us?" He went to the music center and played Frank Sinatra's "I Did It My Way." They sang and danced together. "Life should have some fun and there is no life without music and memories," he said.

"I'll drink to that," Janet said. Janet felt so uplifted and happy she felt like she could conquer the world after that night.

Janet had to think about what she wanted to do next. She was still single and she did not want to come back to simply living an existence of life—she wanted to keep it alive. She knew that despite the heartache of Bahrain she had learned so much about life and she loved her work over there. She was looking through the papers and she found a position in Oman. She had an interview in London and she was accepted for the senior position. She knew she could not settle in Skegness or Boston; she knew she had outgrown the country where she was born, and when she visiting the town at night, she did not like seeing the drunken youths and the rowdy clubs. She did appreciate Bahrain because the people there were her own age group and she had so much more in common with them. She had changed so much in that she needed stimulating conversations and she loved the multicultural society that did not exist in her neighborhood.

By August she was to set off on a new adventure a new country and another chapter in her life.

Chapter Fourteen

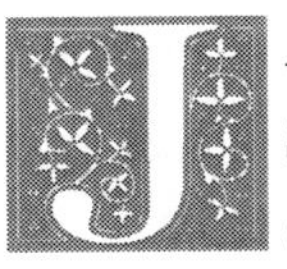JANET ARRIVED IN Oman at the end of August of 1987. She had taken a senior position at the new hospital and although her salary was half of that she earned in Bahrain, it seemed that the more freedom in the Gulf states, the less the salary as it was deemed that the expatriate should be honored to be invited into the country. Janet did feel honored to be able to spend time in this exotic and wildly beautiful country. She was soon to find out that this was the Jewel of the Gulf and a jewel that glittered in the sun. She was fortunate to have her own apartment in the hospital grounds that boasted the latest IKEA furniture and the finest Johnston Pottery. The marble floors shone as the sun filled the room and she could not have wished for a more beautiful place.

Three days after her arrival she had purchased a green Subaru four-wheel drive, and she ventured alone into the city of Muscat. She was impressed with its gorgeous landscaping and the overall cleanliness of the city. The white villa-styled buildings contrasted with the abundance of flowers, palm trees, and green grass. It was the most colorful city she had seen in the Middle East. The Omani shopkeepers were very warm and hospitable and only too willing to help. Although Janet had to barter for the items she purchased, it was very gentle and the agreed price always came with a warm smile. As she walked through the city she found it to be full of children playing in the streets and the occasional wadi dog crossing the road in front of her. The sunbirds would fly across the bluest of skies and she could not help notice the abundantly colorful flowering trees on the roadside. The city was calm and there was not the hustle and bustle on the streets that she had seen in Riyadh or Bahrain. She felt like she was on a long exotic vacation and with that she did feel honored and blessed to be amongst such beauty. She had driven down to the port where the Portuguese forts turned orange with the sun's rays, and she would lean over the walls and look at the turquoise sea and watch the waves in the water brush up to the cliffs. The humid sea air would brush against her face and she felt that the cobwebs were being swept away. She felt she had some clarity and peace within her mind. She knew she could enter the expatriate party scene at any time but she enjoyed being alone in her own tranquil world.

Janet was sitting at the hospital restaurant and a very tall fair-haired gentleman came over. "Do you mind if I join you?" He had a French accent and the most adorable smile. "Of course not," Janet replied.

"I have only been in Oman for three months and my family is in Jordan."

"I have never been to Jordan," Janet said as she looked at him through his gold-rimmed spectacles. "It is very beautiful," he said. "I am Maurice."

"I'm sure I may get there sometime and I am Janet," she answered. He invited her to take a trip into the mountains to visit the Omani Village. Janet felt safe with the medical consultant and she accepted his invitation. They drove for about two hours into the hills and passed through the small village. The homes seem to be cut out into the mountains and were of stone. It reminded her of Haji Ali's house in Bahrain except here it was very orange and very dry despite there being a few palm trees. There were children playing in the street and she couldn't help but notice the bright colored clothes that the young women wore and the bright kaftan style thobes that the young men wore. Their clothing brought to the small village to life. They were invited to a home. They stepped inside. Maurice was so tall he had to bend his head below the entrance. The stone walls inside were painted bright blue. They sat crossed legged on the floor mats and they were served Arabic coffee and dates. Maurice could speak fluent Arabic and he conversed freely and openly with the Omani family. "How did you know to come here?" Janet asked.

"This is one of my patients and they invited me." After coffee they walked to a flat area that was covered with thatched roof. And there was an Omani wedding. Janet did not feel dressed for an Omani wedding as she had a pair of Lacoste red trousers and a bright yellow T-shirt. Her colors were fitting for the occasion and she knew the villagers did not care about her dress. The women and men wore the brightest of green and oranges. They were dancing and the men were riding dressed grey horses that were also dressed in bright colors. The couple was invited to dance where Janet managed her Arabic dance. "You can move your hips," Maurice looked at her. "You need a little more practice," she said to him and smiled.

After the dance they were taken to look at the camels, these were a wedding gift and the Omani's took pride in their camels. There was no camel race here but the family gave the couple a beautifully woven camel blanket. "It is so nice to see everyone so happy," Janet remarked. They joined in the Arabic feast of taboule and biryanis and barbequed quail. They watched the sunset over the mountain's light and the reflections which lit up the wedding festivities. Janet felt so relaxed and turned to thank Maurice who put his arm around her. "No sex please, I'm British." He laughed and he knew what she meant and she was not going to have an affair with a happily married man. He withdrew as a

French gentleman should. "Speaking of that, there is a play showing at the Sheraton. British Airways flew in the whole cast from London. They were playing *No Sex Please We Are British.* I have two tickets and would like you to be my guest." Janet accepted. They talked the evening and for the whole of the trip back to Muscat. Maurice stopped off at the white sandy beach where they walked under the stars. He stopped by the water. "Watch this." He splashed the water and the phosphorous sparkled as stars falling. "How beautiful." Janet sat by the water and splashed the star-filled water. "It's magic," she said, and he replied, "Oman is the natural Disneyland of the Gulf states."

"I can see that," she replied. They arrived home late that evening. Janet felt so much at peace and she slept without analyzing her life.

Maurice collected her the following evening and he took her to dinner at the Al Bustan Palace Hotel which was set in the backdrop of the rugged mountains of Oman and had more breathtaking views. Janet could not get over its grandness with the marble and granite floors and in the entrance a portrait of the Sultan of Oman set above a gold edged marble table. Maurice had given her a red rose and she posed for a portrait picture with the sultan. "Now I have a picture of royalty," she said. The hotel boasted three restaurants and had the most scenic views. It was so relaxing and very grand. "This is a palace," Janet remarked. Maurice escorted her to the French restaurant where the carpets were red and the seats were black. The tables were decorated with white tablecloths, napkins, and the finest silverware. There was a grand piano that sat on a platform so it was raised just above the dining area. Janet was wearing a black halter neck dress and she wore her diamond shield, dangling diamond earrings which sparkled from the crystal reflections of the chandelier. Her hair was pinned into a French plait and she looked beautiful. "You look stunning and beautiful."

Maurice was playing the romantic French gentlemen that she had seen in the movies.

The pianist started to play Chopin's "Polonaise As Dur.""I love this music, my father used to play this when I was young, Chopin was Polish and his girlfriend was French. Her name George Sand but you must know all of that." Janet looked at Maurice and he was impressed by her taste in music. Maurice had taken the opportunity to order the meal as a surprise for Janet. The waiter arrived with a gold-covered terrine and he opened it, lit a match, and flames rose above the lobster thermidor. The salad arrived in another gold bowl but this time it was not tossed with his hands.

"Thank you for this romantic evening, just what I needed."

"My pleasure, young lady."

They had champagne with dinner and afterward they strolled outside to take in the nostalgic scenery. "I will find my Prince Charming one day," she said.

"I am sure you will and lightening will strike when you least expect it," he replied.

Maurice escorted Janet home safely and once again she the most peaceful sleep. How she enjoyed being in Oman. Maurice returned to Jordan and Janet would never forget his kindness.

Janet had decided to drive down to the expats' beach so she could meet some more friends away from the hospital. There were many lazing around the sands, and many had their small boats. It was such a relaxing and peaceful place to be. She was lying on the beach when a few of the young men had been playing volleyball. The ball had rolled over toward her and a fair-haired man who resembled Harrison Ford leaned over and she passed him the ball. He smiled at her and took the ball and returned to his game. The ball came back over and he collected it again. "Hi, my name is Pete, pleased to meet you." Janet handed over the ball. "No problem," she replied. She was listening to her favorite music with her Walkman Janet knew that there was nothing better than listening to Whitney Houston when watching the sea waves and blue skies. She was listening to "I Want to Dance With Somebody." Pete came over and he removed her earphones and started to dance with the music. *I want to dance with somebody*, he sang as he was fooling around and he certainly was going to capture her attention and with that he did. He had been in the Air Force and was working as a civilian in Oman. "Can I take you for dinner?" he asked. Janet was not dressed for dinner but she said, "Why not?" She was hungry. He did not have transport as his friends had brought him to the beach but he drove Janet back to the "mess." Pete lived in the barracks and they had a restaurant. They never needed to cook food and Janet was taken into the mess bar and restaurant. It was certainly a mess and it resembled the old barracks at Butlins Holiday Camp at Skegness. Skegness Holiday Camp had more color than this mess, but it was home to the boys that had served England. She met with a crowd of friendly guys who were having fun at work. Pete introduced her to Andy, Chris, John, Tom, and so on. She could not remember their names. They sat and ate their very British cooked roast and then walked into the bar. There was a dart board and Janet could not resist challenging the boys at darts. She won a few games and lost a few games.

"Where did you learn to play?"

"I had a good teacher, he was my brother and I grew up with the boys." She was much older but she felt like she had never changed that part of her life where she was able to socialize with the boys. These boys were mature physically but they were just young at heart. She actually enjoyed their company and they enjoyed hers.

Pete would send her red roses and he would not give up until he had charmed her, wooed her. He would call her every day, take her to restaurants, and he finally succeeded. They would go camping to the white beaches in the isolated coves. They would swim in the turquoise warm sea and they would mix and party with everyone. The guys at the mess were so generous. One evening they held an auction as one of the guys had an accident, he was killed in a car crash and his wife was left widowed. They were raising money to send to her. They would auction anything—Tommy auctioned his suit and then bought it back again. Then someone paid a thousand riyals for a Rangers shirt, brought in a bin and set it alight because he was a Celtic fan. They raised some ten thousand Dinars that night. Janet could not help but be swarmed in to the kindness that they had shown. Pete would fly to England on holiday and telephone her every day, he would send more roses. Janet had no time to think as their relationship snowballed. They were good together and they understood one another. She didn't stop to think if she was doing the right thing. Her family would love her to settle down in England.

Janet remembers that one evening her car had refused to start. Pete had arranged a towing truck to the garage. Pete was towing the truck and Janet was in the car. They had travelled ten kilometers and had almost arrived at the garage when a Mercedes travelling behind was speeding and came so close to Janet she panicked and put her foot on the break and skidded into the back of the truck. Not only did she have a broken down car, it no longer had a bonnet. The car was fixed without problems but the boys used to tease her. The car was returned and this time it failed to start; she opened the bonnet and someone had replaced her new battery. The garage owner would not admit to it but she was accustomed to the shady deals from the garages over there. They sent someone out to replace the battery. "You Brits are very silly, you teach everything you know and then your contracts end because you are replaced for cheaper labor. We only teach half of what we know so we stay much longer." This young Indian man smiled. "You are not silly," Janet replied. She had spent the night over at the mess barracks and left her car parked against the wall and she woke up the next morning to see her bonnet had been smashed. There was a note stuck to the front of it, "Oops, sorry GED." He must have had a drink and reversed into it. That green car had visited the garage twice in one week.

Janet started a ladies' darts team in Oman and teaching the girls was not an easy task. They held a fancy dress party and Janet and the girls wore their fishnet stocking and miniskirts. This was a definite distraction and they won the game. Pete would not say goodnight to Janet that evening and she could not understand why he was being so angry. She left the party that night rather confused. He turned up the next day with red roses and an apology. He was very good at wooing her back and he did as she forgave him.

Pete and Janet decided to return to England and settle down. There were no marriage plans yet they had planned to start a small business. Pete didn't have much and Janet had just sold her house in Lincolnshire. She fetched $40,000. The house prices doubled within a month and she could not afford to buy a property in Lincolnshire so she decided to move north and catch the house price blast before it took over the whole of England. While they were on holiday from Oman, she and Pete visited Newcastle and they found a small corner shop and liquor store. Janet was paying for the shop and she had been through her split with Paul. She said she would only do that but she would keep the building in her name. That had been her father's advice to her. She knew that she would need to retain her independence she had worked so hard to pay off her mortgage and she knew she was taking a chance with Pete.

They returned to Oman and had a final farewell party—an *Out of Africa* theme and the blues brothers turned up. "What are the blues brothers doing here?" Janet asked. "We thought Chicago was as far out of Africa as you could get." Janet knew she was going to miss the sense of humor but she knew that she was now ready to return home. Janet left four months before Pete.

Chapter Fifteen

JANET RETURNED TO England in September 1988; her parents and her niece had moved to Newcastle to help with the new business. This was to be very new for Janet that was to run a shop. She had never done anything like that before and although she had managed hospitals, this was to be very different. She had remembered her ledger skills from her office job as a teenager and she had no problem managing stock controls as she had done that when commissioning the hospitals. She was excited but a little scared. Her father pulled down the old shelves in the shop and replaced them. He had replaced the window at the front of the shop and Janet had painted the outside a rich red maroon color. Janet's niece had retail experience and was helping keep the shop functioning while the renovations were complete. Her father had replaced the old bathroom and Janet and her mother had decorated the upstairs flat. She had managed to find a good accountant and within three months the shop had trebled its income. Janet was learning how hard it was to manage a shop. She would get out of bed at 6:00 a.m., go to the Cash and Carry, fill the car with stock, and then she would have to unload it and put it on the shelves. The shop would close at 11:00 p.m. and she would crawl into bed after midnight. She had purchased new fridges and freezers and the corner shop lifted the street atmosphere. She was exhausted but proud and she was proud of her family for their help. Pete arrived back for Christmas and there was nothing for him to do but manage the shop. Janet had returned to a midwifery post at the nearby hospital. She started at junior level as her overseas experience had not been acknowledged. She did not mind relinquishing the management positions she had previously held.

She would work seven twelve-hour night shifts and take seven days off. That way she could help Pete. Her career was her independence and she knew how she had given that up many years ago for Paul. She was much older and she hoped she was much wiser. The shop had gone up in value and she made back the money that she had lost selling her home in Lincolnshire, and she knew if things did not work out, she could sell the shop and move back home.

Returning to England was quite a shock to the system as she now had to organize and pay bills and there was little money left to play around with as she had invested it into the business. Paul settled in with her and he seemed to work pretty hard. The business thrived for the next five years. Janet and Pete would get family to look over the shop while they took holidays; they had visited Paris and the island of Jersey, south of England. Every year their expatriate friends would come and visit and they would visit the more classy nightclubs in Newcastle.

Their friends were getting married in Ireland and she and Pete flew over for the wedding. They had a reunion with many of their expatriate friends. They visited the small town of Donaghadee eighteen miles east of Belfast, about six thousand people live there. Janet had never visited Ireland before but she knew how warm and welcoming the people were with the Irish expatriate friends she had made overseas. Janet knew Simon from Oman where they had partied together but she had never met his future wife Mary. Apparently he had returned to Ireland for a holiday and while walking the dogs, Mary was riding her bike and took a fancy to the handsome young man so she decided to ride into him. That's how they met one another and as Janet would say, "No one knows where lightning strikes." They spent a lot of time in the Irish pubs; Simon would play the guitar and sing and the girls would play the spoons and join in the songs. Janet would remember lifting up her pint pot of Guinness with him and drinking it as they sang,

> *Her eyes they shown like diamonds.*
> *I thought her the queen of the land*
> *and her hair, it hung over her shoulder*
> *tied up with a black velvet band.*

How Janet fell in love with Ireland was because of the optimistic people who lived there. The night before the wedding the girls carried with them a jug and a pot. They went to every bar for a fill and someone would throw money in the pot. She was very tipsy as she arrived back at Mary's house. Pete had been out with the boys and they all continued to party on through the night, dancing to the Irish music. Janet knew how much she missed dancing and for one moment she felt she had returned to Bahrain. It was a quiet wedding ceremony with a few friends and family. Most of the friends were expatriates. Simon introduced Janet to his old buddies and especially Alistair whom he used to go walking with. Sunday after the wedding the group partied in the sixteenth century Grace Neill's bar. The bar closed at 2:00 p.m. and everyone left through the front door only to return by climbing in through the back window. Now that was Irish hospitality. Janet was introduced to Mat; he was from New Zealand and he was married to a beautiful Irish girl. He had decided to treat everyone to a *Maori Hangi(H□ngi* is a traditional New Zealand Maori method of cooking food using heated rocks buried in a pit oven still used for special occasions). Mat had decided to dig a hole in his backyard and cook the food under the ground. The problem was he had never done that in Ireland before and the damp ground of Donaghadee threw black thick smog over the whole of the town. Janet laughed. "That's what happens when you mix a Kiwi with the Irish—a volcanic eruption." She would remember that day always.

They returned to Newcastle and they felt refreshed after their youthful time in Ireland. She would receive postcards from her expatriate friends addressed to Arkwright's *Open All Hours* after the UK TV series. They would laugh and tease Janet as being similar to Gladys the nurse. Janet enjoyed the times in the shop; she had made some good friends and she began to learn about the community. She would have some chairs for the pensioners that used to visit and she would always have the kettle on the boil to make them a cup of tea. There were two women, they were sisters in their eighties, and they were very active. They would go for French lessons, go swimming, travel to Europe, and call into the shop every day. They would share their stories. They had lost their husbands during the war but they never lost their optimism. "I want to be just like you when I get to be as young as you are." Janet used to tell them. Janet would help the students who were struggling with money; they never had any so she would chat to them and offer them tea. She was interested at what they were studying and one young man was studying politics. "I never wanted to be a politician, but I will remember you when you become prime minister," she would always joke with them. The hardest time for Janet was when she tried to employ a Saturday girl or boy; she must have hired and fired at least fifteen before she found someone who could do the job. She had asked a young boy to clean the shelves around the potato scales.

"Why should I do that, potatoes are mucky, aren't they?"

"Not much hope for the future of this country with that attitude," she would say.

Janet met a dear woman in her fifties, she had not had an easy life—her husband was an alcoholic and she worked very hard. Janet gave her a job cleaning the shop and flat upstairs. She would invite Gwen around for dinners and share stories. Gwen would visit Janet; they would have a glass of wine together and share stories. Gwen's younger daughter passed away in her sleep—she was twenty years of age. Gwen had a broken heart and Janet would try to help her get through life. It was too much for Gwen, and at fifty-nine, she went to bed and never woke up she died of a broken heart. Janet lost a dear friend with Gwen's passing. Janet would hear lots of these stories whilst working in the shop and she would remember just how fortunate she was. She would remember the sunny days when everyone would come in smiling and then the dark winter days when everyone would complain if she didn't have a particular brand of tea, coffee, biscuits, and wine and so on.

Janet had made some leaflets for the shop and she had decided to meet the community and post them door to door. Most people were out and older people were afraid to answer the doors as the crime rates were escalating in the north. Janet remembers pushing the brochures through the letterboxes in the doors. She was wearing gloves and one day she posted a brochure and the little terrier dog took her glove. There would be bristles to push the papers through the doors and it would scrape her hands. She knew she would never apply for a job with the Royal Mail as a postman and she shook hands with every postman that came into the shop. "How I admire your work," she would say, "and what would England do without you?"

Pete would get his family to mind the shop and he would tell Janet he was going to meet Alistair and go trekking through the countryside. Janet would not mind as she did not want to stop his freedom. He would phone her at the hospital while he was away. Janet would go and visit her parents and Pete encouraged her to do that. Janet's niece would come and help in the shop. Janet's sister came to visit. "He is away a lot, do you trust him?"

"Of course, why shouldn't I?" Janet replied.

It was 1993 and Pete was acting very strangely; he was having temper tantrums. He would throw things down and get angry. She did not understand why, and the following day he would bring her flowers and apologize. Janet would forget it she had learned to let it be. The business was not doing well and Pete had blamed it on the recession and the opening of a new supermarket. Janet would take it as being the truth and she would use her money to top up the shop. Then at New Year they had been invited to a fancy dress party at the sailing club. Janet went dressed as a baby and Pete had dressed as her mother. He had been out and came back wearing flawless makeup. "Who did that good job?" She smiled and thought it looked great. "I have a friend who works at the TV studio," he replied. He had hired an evening dress and wore fishnet stockings. He certainly looked the part and her friends could not stop commenting about how well he looked. He danced with everyone at that party and that was very unusual for him. Janet just put it down to him having a good time. She wanted to leave soon after New Year had set in. Pete had not bothered to look for her to wish her happy new year. He gave her a drink of punch from the bar and twenty minutes later she remembered her head spinning and how she spent that New Year with her head in the toilet. Someone had spiked her drink. She was ill and almost unconscious; her nursing friends came to the rescue and took care of her. She did not remember getting home that night and when she woke in the morning her night was very blurry. That year her car had been broken into four times as if someone was watching her travel to and from the Cash and Carry. Then there was a brick thrown through the shop window. There was glass everywhere, her new fridges damaged and all for a packet of cigarettes. She and Pete had been upstairs when they heard the glass smash and the alarms. They called the police but they were too busy. Janet walked over the broken glass on the shop floor and the thief had urinated on the way out. There were blood stains from where he must have cut his finger. Janet had much more to cope with as they had to repair the damages and buy electric shutters for the windows. What profits they made in the shop were used to employ further security.

The night of the break-in Janet cried and then she took out a bottle of Baileys and put on some music as she knew her father would do. *We shall not be moved,* she sang and she drank a couple of glasses of Baileys so she fell asleep. Pete had boarded up the window. The next morning she went downstairs to clean up the mess. "I really don't understand it and all for a packet of cigarettes. If they would have knocked on the door, I would have given them twenty packets if they were so desperate."

She refused to be the victim and she needed to move on. The window was bricked up and painted white and she had a sign made, "The Corner Shop." The shutters arrived and she was ten thousand pounds out of pocket. The council workers came the next day and they put concrete bollards in front of the windows. "Why are you doing that," Janet asked.

"To stop the ram raiders," he said. "Thugs were driving cars through shop windows, you know, like the *Blues Brothers* movie. That's the American movies of today and is there any wonder the teenagers grow up behaving badly."

This was the time Janet knew she could not stay in England and she had applied to move to New Zealand. She had been accepted for residency and Pete as her partner could go with her. They were to go there the following July.

Janet woke up one morning and she could not find her shield pendant. She had asked Pete if he had seen it. He had not. She thought it must have fallen by the back of the settee so she unpicked the threads underneath each piece of furniture and she did not find it. "I can lose anything but not that," she said to Pete. He watched her turn everything upside down. She knew she had left it on the book cabinet in the lounge. She would never misplace that.

Janet looked for the shield pendant for over a week. She was cleaning all of the drawers in the house and she found a pawn ticket. She read it and that was her pendant. How stupid had she been? She needed to know what else was happening around her. Her trust had been betrayed and she was trapped with the shop and Pete. She never said a word to Pete but she spent three days in bed in a much darkened room; she was sinking into the depth of depression. She did not want to open the curtains and she did not want to see the light of day. She made excuses to Pete that she was ill. For seventy-two hours she could not think—her mind, her body, and her will was numb. She did not have the strength to question anything. She had lost a lot of weight over those few days. Pete had brought her breakfast in bed and there was a nursing magazine, it had fallen to the floor and it had opened to a page looking for a locum midwife in Saudi Arabia. She needed to escape and return to Never Land. She needed to go somewhere where she could think.

She dressed that morning and she had applied for the job; it was managed by a phone call and she was to leave at the beginning of

January. She had four months in which to sort out the business. She needed to think and use her monkey ways as she needed to be a lot smarter than Pete had been.

Janet retrieved her diamond shield pendent from the pawn shop and she packed it in a small box where Pete would not find it. She returned home that evening and she had cooked dinner. "I have an idea," she said to Pete over the dinner table. "How about we rent the shop out and I can go to Jeddah for a locum so we will have money for New Zealand. That way the rent will support you while I am away." Pete looked at her. "What a great idea," he answered. Janet knew he had other things on his mind; she did not know anything about him and she truly would not believe anything he said. "I am going to visit my parents for a few days so can you find someone to rent the shop out." She knew that by giving him some responsibility he would not know her motives. Janet went to visit her parents and she left the shield pendant with her father. She said nothing to her parents as she did not want to give them any stress, they were getting older and they did not need her problems at this time of their lives. She knew her father would support her if she asked but this was something she needed to do by herself. She had applied to retrieve her superannuation monies which would be around ten thousand pounds and that would help her in New Zealand.

Pete had returned home one evening and he seemed rather nervous. Janet tried to comfort him but he was too angry. She was in the bathroom and he walked in shouting at her. She asked him to calm down, he picked up the glass vase from the window and he threw it toward her; it cut the corner of her eyebrow and smashed against the tiles and fell into the bath. Janet mopped the blood from her eye. "What is wrong with you?" He would not answer her she went to bed early and she could not sleep. He was fumbling around the drawers where she had found the pawn ticket. She knew what he was looking for and she knew he had a deadline to return the ticket for the pendant but she had already done that. She watched him go through every drawer as he had watched her unstitch the furniture to find the pendant. *Now you know what it feels like* were her thoughts. She turned over and slept knowing she had delivered some of his own medicine back to him. She watched in silence yet there was some gratification seeing him anxiously emptying the drawers to find nothing. That next morning he had brought Janet some red roses. "I am so sorry." Janet took the roses and gave him a kiss on the cheek. This was not a kiss that say I forgive you, that kiss was to say I will not put up with your mental cruelty anymore and I am stronger than you think and you should never underestimate my capabilities for I am woman and I am strong. Pete had left the house, he promised to find a tenant. Janet moved over to the mirror and looked at the cut and the bruise around her eye. She turned on her music as she remembered how Randy, Andy, and Lanny played the music to lift her spirits when she had to confront her separation from Paul. This time she had tears and this time there were bruises. "Bruises and wounds heal but I wonder if my head will ever heal this time," she was talking to herself. She played Helen Reddy.

I am woman, hear me roar
In numbers too big to ignore
And I know too much to go back an' pretend
'cause I've heard it all before
And I've been down there on the floor
No one's ever gonna keep me down again

Oh yes I am wise
But it's wisdom born of pain
Yes, I've paid the price
But look how much I gained
If I have to, I can do anything
I am strong (strong)
I am invincible (invincible)
I am woman
You can bend but never break me
'cause it only serves to make me
More determined to achieve my final goal
And I come back even stronger
Not a novice any longer
'cause you've deepened the conviction in my soul

Janet played that song three times, and the more she played it, the stronger she felt from within. She wanted to tell Pete to walk out of the door but she had remembered Bo's words, "Do not let your emotions rule your head 'cause you need to think on your feet, gal." She felt Bo's presence and she knew when the time came she would be strong and she would be safe. She played "Let It Be" three times over and once she felt strong enough and once she had repaired her face with makeup, she had some details to resolve. Janet called her father and she asked if he would take over her power of attorney, she certainly did not want to leave that with Pete. Her father came to visit and he spent a day with her. Janet was so glad to see him and yet she felt she couldn't be honest with him. He was getting older and she did not want him to worry, and his Polish temper would get the better of him. She told him of her plans to go to Jeddah for three months and of her plans to go to New Zealand. He thought going to New Zealand was a good move as the crime in England was rising and so was a recession. However going back to Saudi Arabia he did not like, he did not want his daughter to go back there. He even offered to buy her a new car so she would not leave. She could not tell him her reasons. "I'll be fine, I have done it all before," she said. "I will be careful." They had taken an appointment at the solicitors. Janet knew the solicitor well as he had helped when she bought the shop and the flat and he recognized her father too. "What can I do for you?" he asked. Janet explained that she was going away and that she wanted to give the power of attorney to her father. "Oh, but Pete came here six months ago and he brought signed papers to put him as power of attorney. That was just after New Year." Janet remembered the New Year's party and how she had blacked out and how she did not remember anything. "Here let me show you." The signature definitely looked like hers. She did not remember signing that. She did not want her father to know anything. "Sorry, I forgot. I have changed my mind and I want my father to be in charge when I am away, is that okay?" The new documents were prepared and Janet and her father signed them and the old documents were cancelled. Janet felt so much better that she had changed the papers, but she was more resentful toward Pete for deceiving her.

Pete had found a Muslim family from Pakistan to rent the shop. She met with Ismail and his family. They were very kind, they liked Janet and she liked them. Janet entertained their children while they looked around the shop and they decided to take up renting the property providing they would have an option to buy it. Pete was to live in the flat until Janet returned from Jeddah. They were to start taking over the shop in November. Meanwhile Janet continued to work at the hospital and she would work in the shop on her days off. Janet took sick in November and was admitted to hospital where she had part of her bowel removed—the stress had been far too much for Janet. She spent one month in hospital. Pete would visit and bring flowers. Ismail came to visit her in hospital and he brought some flowers and a gift box. "I am no fool," Ismail said to her. "Pete is not truthful to you and you need to know my family will support and help you." Janet gave Ismail her brother's address and telephone number in Boston. "If you need anything you call him and I promise you will be able to buy the shop in installments when I return from Jeddah, but this is our secret and I promise I will keep my word." They did not need papers for their promise and Ismail shook hands with her and that was enough for Janet. Janet opened her present—he had bought her a black headscarf and abaya for her journey to Jeddah.

Janet left her job at the hospital and went to spend two weeks with her parents to recover from her surgery. She spent Christmas and New Year at home with them. Pete stayed in Newcastle and joined Janet for Christmas. Janet made sure that she enjoyed the holiday season with her family. She would play with the children and they would open presents. She would dance and sing with her father and toast with a little vodka. She knew that she had to keep some things secret and that caused her so much pain inside but she was strong enough not to show how much she was hurting inside.

<h1 style="text-align:center">Chapter Sixteen</h1>

ETE TOOK JANET to the airport; she left for Jeddah on the second of January 1995. He gave her a hug and they said their good-byes. Janet could not wait to get on that plane, she did not know what was in store for her in Jeddah and she certainly had no idea what she would find on her return. She did know she would have the time to think and that she would have time to spend in Never Land and have fun with her expatriate friends. It was a Saudia flight and there was no alcohol. She opened her bag and there was a small bottle of water, she had not put it there but there was a small card from her father. "May you never get thirsty." She took a drink and nearly spit it out—her father had put some of the famous Polish vodka, Wabrowka, in the bottle. "This seems all so familiar." The plane was packed full of Muslim men going to Mecca. They were to change into clean clothing for their trip to Mecca and there were not enough toilets for them to change. She had never been surrounded by so many hairy chested bodies and white sheets. She adored them for their faith and family values but she knew they were the same tribal values that prevented her from being with Khaleel. For a moment she was sitting on the boat in Bahrain where the two seas met. She looked down at her pendant and counted seventy-two, the languages set in Babylon; she understood that they were the tribes that would challenge freedom for the whole world and how she was seen to taste the forbidden fruits and how she suffered the pain of the tribal conflicts. She wept for a while. *If only the world could be different, if only everyone learned to live together, value cultures, and share them . . . if only,* she thought to herself.

Sitting next to her was a very young girl. Janet was now thirty-seven. It was hard to believe that thirteen years had passed since her first trip to Saudi Arabia. Jules was only twenty-six, she was two years older than Janet had been. She was pretty and had a very lively personality. How she reminded Janet so much of herself in her younger years. Jules would listen to Janet's stories. Janet gave Jules a list of things to do and things not to do in Saudi Arabia. It was much more than anyone gave Janet the first time she visited the Middle East. Jules was eleven years younger and Janet was already feeling like a mother. They were to work at the same hospital and they had the same residential address. That was a very old hotel that had been converted to residence for women. Janet had dressed in long sleeves and a long skirt ready for arrival. Jules was wearing a low cut T-shirt with no sleeves. She gave Jules her abaya as she didn't want the young woman to have any hassle arriving in Jeddah. Janet was not afraid of country that claimed virginity because she knew it was far from that and she was not afraid of the challenges. The worst thing that could happen is that they would send her home and that wouldn't be a bad thing, she thought, and she knew that would never happen as she had her feet firmly on the ground.

She took Jules under her arm and guided her through passport control though the ladies section. It took some time as the security scrambled through their bags to find anything that was haram to the Islamic culture. There was nothing to be found. Actually Janet respected Ismail and she remembered the kindness of Mustafa and Haji Ali, and she remembered Khaleel and how open they were and how kind they were. "It dœsn't matter where you go in the world, there are good and bad people in every country," she told Jules. She warned Jules to be patient as they entered into another time zone and that although everything surrounding them would seem the twenty-first century, the evolution frame and thinking was around the fifteenth century. "You will understand in time," Janet said to Jules.

They were greeted at the airport and they arrived at the old hotel. It reminded Janet of the old hotel rooms where she had spent her time many years ago. The teak wardrobes and the paintings were the same as she had seen in the hotels in the '80s. Janet knew she was a guest in this country and that she needed to respect that, she also knew that it was not always reciprocal as the young Saudis visited other countries. She knew only too well the act of human nature. She was older and she had certainly viewed the world with experience.

Janet met at the hospital where she was taken to human relations and they tried to take her passport away. "You cannot take this, it is the property of her Majesty the Queen and I am keeping it this time." They could not contest that and she knew they were desperate for her to work there. She was already in a win-win situation. It did not matter that she could not leave without an exit visa but it mattered to her that she kept her passport. She kept her passport. She was in the second largest city of Saudi Arabia with a population of around three million people. Jeddah was much freer than Riyadh in that she did not need to wear her abaya in public. She would wear a long-sleeved kaftan dress and that she had no objection to as it was very loose and comfortable in the humid heat of Jeddah. It was still a time where women could not drive and Janet used to take a taxi everywhere she visited except that she caught a bus to work. If she missed the bus, she would have to pay for her own transport to get there. She had to pay for her own food which had been provided for her some thirteen years ago. Her tax-free salary did not equate to its value thirteen years previously and the cost of living in Saudi Arabia had escalated. Janet knew that her reason for being there was to save money to take to New Zealand, and she did not make any extravagant shopping trips.

Janet had made some new friends in the hospital and she would go to the beach on her days off, she would laze and swim by the salty Red Sea; it was so salty she could almost float in it. She would enjoy the warm humid air and the views of the beautiful green sea. She would go snorkeling and enjoy seeking out the colorful red coral and fish. The colors in the coral reefs ranged from purples to blues and greens and reds and oranges and yellows. The fish were equally as colorful in stripes, dots, two-tones, shiny metallics, and many fish appeared to have a mesmerizing neon glow to them. Janet would think of Khaleel's fish tank and she would remember conversing with them about their clothing; she would remember the good times and return feeling very happy and would smile as she returned to the beach. She would join in the games of volleyball at the beach.

Janet was lazing on the beach and the volleyball landed by her sun lounger; this was not the first time as this is how she had met Pete. A dark-haired Scottish gentleman came to collect the ball. Janet passed it over. "Thank you, madam, would you care to join in?" She did join them as she did not want to be completely alone as she knew she would be analyzing her life too deeply and she needed some fun. She had always been very good at sports and the guys welcomed that. They were all married and they were on a short contract. With that Janet felt very safe and she would accept their invitations to the married quarters at their villa. Here she met James, he was very polite and there was some sadness to his life. They would go to a place where the grape juice had turned into wine and they would dance and sing along to the music. Janet had fallen asleep on the couch as she had stayed there overnight. She would never travel in Saudi if she had consumed the converted juice.

James had fallen asleep on the other sofa. They woke up early hours of the morning and he prepared breakfast for everyone. He openly started to talk to Janet, he was finding it hard with his relationship at home, the children had grown and he was at a crossroads with his wife. Janet told her story about Pete, she felt so relieved that someone had a listening ear. "He sounds too good to be true," James said in a very sincere tone.

"I know," Janet replied. "I don't know what will happen when I get home and actually I don't want to think about it."

"Me neither," replied James referring to his relationship back home.

"Well, aren't we a pair of lost souls" Janet remarked. James took Janet out to dinner and they would go to the many expatriate functions. They became really good friends sharing their stories and they were actually healing one another. James was very structured and a little selfish when it came to making arrangements and he would let people down. "There is no wonder your life is in turmoil as you are far too structured and set in your ways. If I was your wife, I'd be terribly fed up with you and I hope you don't mind me telling you that," Janet looked over at him. "You don't have any interests that inspire yourself so every day you get up doing the same things and feeling bored." She told him directly that was one thing she was not afraid of and when she connected with her intuitive self, she was usually right. James could clearly see his failings and he appreciated Janet's honesty. "You were not clearly intuitive when you met Pete," James replied.

"Ouch that was painful," Janet responded, but she knew it to be true as she was wooed and things happened so quickly, she never stopped to think. "I am woman, not a princess, I have an attitude, opinions, and a very loud voice. I am independent, intelligent, and strong," Janet replied and he did not know that she had quoted the words from Helen Reddy. She then continued to say, *"But* I was stupid and I made the second mistake in my life and I will never do that again and I realize how the strong can fall very easily in this challenging world." James took her hand. "I know everything will be fine and you deserve so much more." He kissed her hand as if she were a princess. She responded by kissing his hand as if he were a prince. "Did that feel good?" she asked him. "No one has ever kissed me on the hand like that before," he responded laughing as they entered their fantasy world. They would meet when she was not working and they would walk along the beach in the evenings under the clear dark blue skies watching the moon's reflection on the still water. They would look up at the stars and they would make a silent wish then they would spend the whole evening trying to guess what they secretly wished for. James would put his arm around her and they would cuddle up close. "You are one of the few men that has not made any pass at me, are you gay?" she asked. James burst into laughter. "No silly. I would love to make love to you. You are beautiful and all of those things that you quoted but we both know it would not be right, not at this time." Janet confessed that the words were not her own and that they were quoted by Helen Reddy at the time she sang "I Am Woman.""Oh, you are not that bright then," James would tease her as her brother Johnny would have done.

Janet spent two months in James's company and for those two months they nurtured one another. "You remind me so much of my good friend Bo who helped me when I was at my lowest in California, he was so kind and he was wise," Janet would tell James. "Kind, yes but wise, well I don't know about that." James would reflect upon the things that Janet had told him and in her company he lost the starchiness from his character. She found that she could trust someone and that was just what she needed to do, to be able to trust again.

James returned to his wife and family and Janet had played a part in helping him find his youthful self. He rekindled his life and stayed friends with Janet. Janet made many more friends in Jeddah; she would go running in the desert, join in fancy dress parties, and she found the youthfulness in herself.

Janet would always be there to help her friends. This one time she was dressed in a ball gown to go to a function at the French embassy when she received a telephone call from one of her girlfriends, Gina. Gina had been dating one of the many guys who could not overcome his lust for sex and women. Gina was an ex-model, she was beautiful, blond, and had the shapeliest figure. She had fallen for Kenny. Kenny had given Gina the keys to his apartment and they had been staying together; he had made the excuse he was going to Egypt with a friend. Gina had turned up at his apartment to find her clothes hidden and another woman's clothes hanging in the wardrobe. Gina was angry and she had consumed a little too much of the vine juice. "It's me Gina and I am at Kenny's. I need you." The two men driving Janet to the embassy were dressed in dinner suits and they were both wearing their Gucci gold-rimmed glasses. Ian was young twenty-nine years old, a sales rep from Canada, and George was in his fifties, an executive in some firm. Janet and the two men turned up at Kenny's apartment dressed in their evening wear. Janet opened the door and Marilyn Monroe may have just as well been standing there in front of them. Gina was wearing red Marni laced underwear. Her long beautiful legs and flawless body took up the whole doorway. Janet could not help but notice the sweat on both Ian and George's forehead and their glasses were totally steamed up. "Gina, go back inside before you give George a heart attack." Janet followed inside and she had aftermath of an irate, angry, and deceived woman. Gina had artistically decorated the walls with her best Lancôme red nail polish. "You f— —ing ba— —d!" She had cut up Kenny's clothes and more so she had dumped the fermenting vine juice down the bath tub. Janet dressed Gina in one of the few remaining of Kenny's shirts and joggers. She had pulled Gina into the car and they delivered Gina to her residence. That was the only ball Janet was going to attend in Jeddah. She spent the night comforting Gina as good friends would do. "You just have a bad taste in men," Janet said to Gina and Gina replied, "Speak for yourself." Janet knew what she was talking about and for a brief moment those words pierced Janet's heart. "Then we need to change that," Janet replied and laughed.

Two days later, Kenny had returned from his lustful holiday in Egypt. Janet was working on the unit. "Urgent phone call for Janet."

"Hold the birth we have an emergency." Janet had been in this situation thirteen years before. She picked up the phone and a distraught Kenny was on the phone. "My clothes have disappeared, and so have my car keys," he was extremely upset. "Really," replied Janet, "play with fire and you will get your fingers burnt and she is just too good for you." And with that she put the telephone down and returned to the job she does so well with a smile on her face.

Through Gina, Janet met Mike. Mike was a would be millionaire living in Saudi Arabia, he always boasted at how well he was doing with his business and how much land he owned; he would throw banquets for the guests and there would be servants serving the food. Janet could see straight through Mike, he had the same birth sign as Pete—Libra at his worst. His wife and family had come to visit from Melbourne and he boasted the new clothes he had bought for his daughters. He introduced his wife as Margaret. Janet took one look at Margaret, she was not vibrant or happy despite being very beautiful for her age, she was almost the same age as Janet but she looked much younger. Janet said nothing she spoke to Margaret who gave a telephone number of her family in Melbourne and Mike had given a number of his so-called very rich friend in Melbourne. Janet had family over there and she knew she would be visiting at some time. Mike threw a leaving party for Janet. Janet had sent her money to England and unbeknownst to her Pete had already spent it. That night Janet's bags were packed to leave, she was at the airport when the administrator arrived. "Please do not get on that plane, we have had an emergency and someone has had to go on compassionate leave. She will take your flight and if you leave we will have to close the hospital." Janet's intuition told her that something like this does not happen out of the blue, and she knew someone was watching over her. "We will pay you three times your salary if you stay for one more month," the administrator was begging her to stay. Janet was a much stronger person than when she had left Pete and she was not looking forward to going back. She had nothing to lose so she stayed. She called Pete and told him not to collect her at the airport. "I will bring more money for New Zealand." She knew he would not object to that.

She stayed one more month, and this time she collected the cash and she put it in her pocket. She was ready to face whatever was waiting for her as she knew she would never return to Saudi Arabia again. Her friends saw her off at the airport and they gave her a small jug. "This is holy water from Mecca." Janet knew exactly what was in that jug. She smiled and put the small jug in her bag and said good-bye to everyone. She knew they would never meet again but she was thankful of the time she had spent with James and Gina; she would remember the moonlight walks along the beach and the Marilyn Monrœ propping up the doorway to Kenny's apartment, let alone the steamed up glasses of George and Ian. She was strong and she could face up to anything now.

Chapter Seventeen

JANET RETURNED TO England feeling very refreshed and golden brown from the desert sun. She brought with her more memories, and she had little time to think what was waiting for her in England. She had kept her money in her pocket some five thousand Pounds for her trip to New Zealand. Pete met her at Heathrow Airport. He was waiting with red roses and he was his charming self. Janet was very tired and could not wait to arrive home. They were going to stay in Lincolnshire with her family. Pete insisted that they travel through London and pick up their documents from the New Zealand Immigration Service. Janet could not understand why he was in such a hurry as they had some two months before they were to arrive in New Zealand. "Let's just go home." He would not have any of that; he drove into London and they visited the immigration service where they collected their papers. "Good and tomorrow I will buy our tickets." He was so keen to leave England.

The four-hour drive to Lincolnshire was a long drive as Pete hardly said a word and Janet slept the whole journey north. They arrived at her father's home in the afternoon. It was spring; the garden was full of daffodils and blue irises. There was a clear blue sky and the sun was shining over Boston. It was not shining over her parent's home. Janet's brother had taken Pete to his house at the back and Janet stayed with her father. She gave them all a hug but the atmosphere was as cold as ice "Has someone died?" Janet asked. Her sister-in-law had come to greet her. Janet's mother looked very tearful. "You need to come with us," her sister-in-law said. She took Janet's hand. "One moment," her father poured her a shot of vodka, "you will be needing this."

Janet ran out from the back of the house and down the driveway. She was terrified and no one would explain what was happening. There were many photographs scattered across the kitchen table. Janet did not recognize any of them. "He has been cheating on you and more so a double life." Janet's sister in law picked up the photographs. "Here is Pete at your parent's sixtieth birthday."

"I remember that," said Janet. "We had a wonderful time."

"But . . ." That was the strongest but she had ever heard. "Here is Pete at another sixtieth birthday party," her sister in law continued. "This is Shelly, the other woman in his life." Janet looked at the photograph, she knew there had been something but not two Shelly's coming to destroy her life. How she hated that name. "Here is Pete in his cashmere coat, there was no walking with Alistair, he was in New York living a high life and buying cashmere coats. Here he is with Shelly in New York and wearing the cashmere coat." Janet looked at the photographs and she could not believe the double pictures and the double life and New York—the place she disliked the most. Her sister-in-law continued. "And here is Pete dressed in women's clothing, he is a transvestite, and here is Shelly." She brought the real Shelly out of the room. She was much older than Janet, at least ten years older; she was blonde and she was very rounded and she certainly had a bad taste in clothes. "I love him." Shelly looked at Janet. Janet did not know what she was expecting on her return, she knew Pete had been disloyal but Janet was speechless. Pete walked into the room, he was nervous and shaking and he looked like as very small boy who was pushed into a corner for misbehaving. "But I love you both," he said looking at Janet and Shelly. "What has love got to do with anything and what is love?" Janet picked up the photographs and pushed them into Shelly's hand. "You deserve him and you win, you can have him." Pete walked over to Shelly. "But what about new Zealand?" Janet could not believe what she was hearing, she knew in her heart she was going to finish her relationship with Pete, but he finished it nicely—as a matter of fact he did it in such an astonishing way. It was climatic and Janet was still speechless. She remembered what Gina had done to Kenny's things and how she wrecked his belongings and his apartment. Janet just wished she had the strength to do all of that but once again she felt Bo's strong presence. "Seal everything with kindness otherwise the only hear to be broken will be yours."

Janet left the house and returned to her father's. "I am so so sorry for not letting you know, I never wanted to cause you any pain, but do not worry, I am strong and I can handle this." She went to the bathroom and she put on some makeup with her red lipstick, she tidied her hair and she put on her red halter neck dress and her high heel shœs. She looked like she was going to a ball. Her father looked at her. "First I need to make a phone call." She called Pete's parents who she knew so well and she did not want them to be hurt but she had no choice. "Hi, this is Janet. I am sending your son home to you, he has been cheating on me and our relationship has ended." She did not tell them that he had cross-dressed or that he had embezzled money from her or that he had pawned her pendant. She wanted to save them from that and they did not deserve that. "I am going to New Zealand alone and don't worry about me. He needs you and will be arriving this evening." Pete had just entered her father's home. She posed. "Is this who you want to be?" She posed very sexily and started to blow kisses at him as she pursed her red hot lips. "Is this why you were jealous while I wore fishnet stockings in Oman and is this why you fixed my drink at the sailing club and is this why you pawned my shield?" Her father needed to take a seat and the whole family and Shelly were standing in the room. "I feel so sorry for you because you have been living a lie with yourself, at least I know who I am and I like who I am." With that she took Shelly's hand. "You can keep him." And then she placed forty-five pounds in Pete's hand. "And that is more than you had when you first met me and that is your train ticket to your mother." She picked up a glass of vodka and drank it. "Dad, Johnny, will you escort this man and his cases to the train station *and*"—she pointed to Shelly—"will you get out of this house and my life." Shelly ran out of the house as if a tornado carried her through the doors.

Pete and Shelly were out of her life and Janet wasn't gutted, she felt free and she would never give up her freedom for love. "Here's a cup of tea, luv," her mother said in her Yorkshire-Polish accent. Janet burst into laughter. "It's a midwife's privilege to have a lovely cup of tea before she starts the day, I mean, new life." Janet took the tea and gave her mother her hug. There were no tears yet, there was a sense of relief. Janet was exhausted. "Give me a few minutes." She was shivering and she felt chilled in her red dress. She changed into her jeans and put on her father's jumper as she had no time to unpack her bags. Her brother Johnny and her father had returned from the train station. "Well that's done," her father said. The family sat around the kitchen table and they shared their story of events. This was another page of Janet's life history.

Pete had dumped Shelly and Shelly had gone to the shop where she had spoken to Ismail. Ismail gave her Janet's brothers address. Ismail had called Johnny to explain that he had been concerned as Pete was selling furniture and behaving mysteriously. He had described Shelly visiting Pete at the shop and staying overnight. That there were many parties and men dressed as women partying at the shop. The whole neighborhood knew about it. Janet made a phone call to Ismail. "Thank you so much, you promised me you would look after me and you did the right thing for me, and I promise you will have the shop. I will come next week to sort it out."

Janet's family was expecting her to breakdown but she knew she was not going to do that. "I am woman, not a princess, I have an attitude, opinions, and a very loud voice. And I am independent, intelligent, and strong. I have quoted those words so many times in the last months and I know exactly who I am." Janet's father put his arms around her, "I am so very proud of you and you are my princess and always will be."

Janet asked her father to take her to the bank. Pete had spent her superannuation money and the money she had sent from Saudi Arabia. She pulled out her five thousand pounds from her pocket and she opened a new account in her name. "That is for New Zealand." Her father nodded. "You have travelled the world and you need to start again in a new world. Your family is in Melbourne and I am sending you there to stay with them for two months, then you will go to New Zealand." Her father went to the counter and withdrew another five thousand pounds and he gave it to Janet. "You will need a car and some pocket money." She threw her arms around him in front of the teller. "I love you so much." The teller and the bank queue looked at them "He's my bit on the side," she said and they laughed.

The next week Janet's father took her to Newcastle where they drew up a plan for Ismail to rent the shop and he could buy it for installments from July. Janet gave him the furniture to the flat. "I definitely don't want that bed." She had packed what Pete had not sold in her memorabilia from her life and she sent it to New Zealand. It was to arrive there two weeks after her arrival. It was a very traumatic time as she went to the solicitor's. She was told that Pete managed to put some stop on her selling the property on the council deeds. He claimed he had worked in the shop and that he was entitled to part of it and he wanted ten thousand pounds. "I would rather give that money to charity than to give it to him," Janet told the solicitor. She knew she had to think very quickly as she did not have much time to waste and she did not want to leave her father carrying any more problems. She had the accounts from the shop in her car and she went to the Cash and Carry and had them print out every invoice over the last five years. She took her father back to Ismail's and Ismail invited them upstairs. Janet sat with the accounts and tallied up the invoices with what had been put through the books. She found sixty thousand pounds that had been purchased and not put through the books. She took the invoices and the books to the solicitor. "You can write to Pete and tell him if he does not back off I will take him to the courts for fraud." The solicitor did just that and Janet signed the papers so Ismail could purchase the shop over the next three years. "You are smarter than I thought," her father said to her. "You taught me well," she replied.

They returned to Lincolnshire and Janet spent her last week preparing for her trip to "the other side of the world." Her father had bought the airline tickets for her. She had one more thing to do. She called the New Zealand Immigration Service to cancel Pete's permit. She did not want to think he would be there and New Zealand did not need a cheat, liar, or a thief.

Chapter Eighteen

IT WAS ANOTHER farewell and good-byes were becoming more difficult. Janet's father was getting older and she did not know when she would come home again. He wished her luck and he knew that she would be fine. He had arranged that her family collect her at the airport. Flying on an airplane was no more than taking a bus for Janet, she had done it so many times before and she had no problem meeting new friends. "Just think before you leap next time," her father whispered in her ears. "Next time I'll get it right," she whispered back.

The flight was twenty-four hours and it seemed much less as Janet ventured back in time through her life. Her life had been both full of joy and sadness, fairy tales and "monsters" and it was certainly experiential. She thought of the tower of Babel and the seventy-two languages (610BC) and she knew that there were more than 2,700 languages spoken and with over 7,000 dialects. She had experienced that where the different cultures would meet and mix, new languages would be developed. She remembered reading that in the world there were 195 countries and more than four thousand religions. *I wonder if there will ever be peace in the world with all this diversity of belief systems* she questioned silently and wondered if her analytical mind would ever rest.

She had experienced the tribal influence and control that segregates the world and how she had experienced that in her relationship with Khaleel. How Mustafa held his Islamic beliefs but respected the guests to his country and how he offered that plate of ham sandwiches to his guests, and even if it was haram for him to eat them, he would enjoy watching his guests enjoy them. "If only the world could be different and if it could learn to celebrate its individuality and yet learn to integrate with kindness and compassion that comes with every religion. If they could remove the power and replace it with love for one another, it would be a wonderful world if only." Janet was becoming very analytical again, and with that analysis of life, she turned on the music and played the Disney song she remembered as a child.

> *It's a world of laughter, a world of tears*
> *It's a world of hopes and a world of fears*
> *There's so much that we share that it's time we're aware*
> *It's a small world after all*
>
> *There is just one moon and one golden sun*
> *and a smile means friendship to everyone.*
> *Though the mountains divide*
> *And the oceans are wide*
> *It's a small, small world.*

She had not seen her auntie or her cousin for fifteen years. She had never grown up to be around them. She only met her grandmother and she never knew her father's parents, her family had been split during the war and she remembered the stories of Gregory and her mother. They had lost their loved ones and their homes and their country. It was these stories that kept Janet strong as though she had been through traumas in her life, it was nothing compared to the stories they shared with her. Janet fell asleep with the few emotional tears strolling down her cheeks and she danced with the people of the world in her dreams.

Her family came to collect her at the airport, they were so excited to see her and they recognized one another immediately. The family genetics were very strong. They all shared a vibrant lively sense of humor. There were so much of their life stories to catch up on. Her cousin was so much like her sister and she became Janet's sister. In those two months they took her to the beautiful parks and places in Victoria. They shared cultural evenings together. Janet could understand what they were saying but she could not speak their language. It did not matter, she felt at home. She rekindled time with her auntie and she had left Pete well behind her, for Janet kept the clock moving forward and her family was surprised at her optimism. She did not hold any bitterness but brought joy from what she had learned on her adventurous life.

She had to make a visit in Melbourne to visit Tom, the friend of Mike, and to meet Margaret, Mike's wife as she had promised. Tom was in his seventies and he came to collect her from her family's home. He lived in a very large house that was decorated with expensive antique furniture and there were original oil paintings on the wall he had bought from Sotheby's Fine Art Auctions in London. He was well-spoken and he seemed to be a gentleman. Janet's sister was visiting Tom's home as there was to be some bad news for Janet. Margaret had been admitted to the hospital with a brain hemorrhage—she had suffered a stroke. Mike had embezzled her money and she had lost her farm. Margaret had developed high blood pressure that caused the stroke. Janet nearly sank through Tom's antique armchair. Tom took Janet to the hospital to visit Margaret; she was lying in intensive care and was semi-conscious. Janet leaned over and tears fell onto Margaret's face. Margaret had recognized her but she could not speak. The family left Janet with Margaret as they went to eat some lunch. Janet held Margaret's hand knowing that could have been Janet and how Janet had been spared. Janet leaned over and sang silently, *I am woman I am strong.* Margaret gave a small smile and Janet noticed Margaret's face light up. "You have to get well, your daughters need you, you can do this don't give up, please don't give up." Janet once again faced reality of how deceitful humans could be. Janet had been looking forward to Margaret's friendship because they had spoken so closely and openly in Jeddah, and this was not to be as Margaret was not as strong as Janet and she gave up that night.

Janet returned to Tom's home; it was late and she was going to sleep on the couch. Tom was to drive her back in the morning. She had a nightcap and curled up on the settee. It was dark in the room and she felt something move on the settee. Tom had decided to try his unused testosterone levels. Janet was shocked; she had some drink in her glass and she threw it over Tom. "You might be able to buy furniture from Harrods and paintings from Sotheby's but you cannot buy me, so take your disgusting self out of here. You are just as bad as Mike and you deserve one another." With that she went to the phone and called her cousin who came to collect her. "How many more surprises?"

Janet knew that her Muslim friend Ismail had saved her and that she was very lucky to have such friends in her life. It seemed as if Janet always had an angel on her shoulder taking good care of her. When she split up from Khaleel, Marie had called her and warned her about could have been; and now after Pete, Margaret was a warning at what could have been. Somehow Margaret gave more strength to Janet and Janet was more determined to stay positive and she would share her stories to help others. As for Tom, she learned to let it be and she actually felt sorry for that very lonely and very rich man and it was another lesson to remind her that money would not bring happiness.

The family vacation in Melbourne came to an end. Janet had promised her family she would take to learning the Polish language once she had settled in New Zealand. She arrived in New Zealand on the fourth of July 1995 and she fell in love with that country the day it was the bluest of skies, the green sea, the greenery, and the little houses on the hilltops. She was at the end of the world but for her it was just the beginning. She had found somewhere to live, bought a car, and started work within a week. She was not on the salary she was accustomed to in the Middle East but she was happy. She made new friends very easily and she would spend a lot of time walking along the sea front. She would play her favorite music and watch the sea waves brush against the volcanic rocks. She was not in a rush to go anywhere and she needed some time alone. She had made contact with the Polish priest although she was not Catholic and he invited her to the church with open arms. After church she went to the Polish house. Standing by the bar was a very tall gentleman, he was several years older than she was; he had long hair and looked very much like an artist. She went to the bar to buy a drink but he insisted he would like to buy her one. That he did. He turned around and started speaking in German. "How are you and what is your name?" She wondered how he knew she could speak German, He was Polish, and he felt very familiar as though she had known him from somewhere but she did not. He introduced himself as Marian, the same name as her father and he came from the same part of Poland as her parents. Janet was very curious about all of their familiarities. They spoke for several hours and he told her more about the hometown of her father than her father did. She felt so at home with his Polish accent and she wanted to know more. She left that evening and she felt so uplifted after his company. She called him the next day after work. "I hope you don't mind but I would like to learn more about Poland." He invited her to his home; it was a small unit but very homely; he had pictures of Picasso on the walls. He took her out to dinner as he lived in the city and they shared stories about their lives. He had suffered similar traumas to Janet and he had lived an adventurous life.

He was extremely well educated and knowledgeable. They went to the Thai restaurant and they looked at the menu. They ordered the same seafood dish and the same wine. He was very generous and he paid for dinner. They walked back to his home and they shared more stories and the more they shared, the more alike they seemed to be. Marian escorted her to many restaurants over the next weeks. They had the same birthdays in July; they were both the same birth sign. He sent her peach roses, many of them. He would not call her but she would call him. He would share stories about his artist friends in Poland and in Prague. She would share stories about her life's experiences. They were growing closer together. He took her to Fiji in the November where they stayed at the Fijian Sheraton Resort. They would celebrate breakfast together. The maids would place peach hibiscus flowers on the beds. They would sit outside looking into the dark blue skies and admire the stars. They spent the whole night looking at the silhouettes in the trees using their creativity visualizing the Disneyland characters in the trees and they would enter their own world of make-believe. They would share their Fijian beer and Janet felt so calm in his presence.

Janet soon became introduced to his many close friends and they made her very welcome. They must have dined in every restaurant in Auckland, and one day Janet decided she had eaten out too often and she missed the home cooked food. She called Marian one evening after work and she invited herself around. She cooked dinner for two and they drank a bottle of wine. They spent the whole evening playing music; he would play the classical music of Chopin and Janet would reminisce her childhood with her father. They would play music from the '60s and '70s and they would dance at home together. Marian would take her to dances and they would waltz, polka, and swing together. When she would get emotional about her work, he would calm her down. There was a balance of energies and calmness about the two of them.

Marian was kind and generous and his heart would reach out to anyone in need, he was no different than Janet. Together they healed their wounds and celebrated their life's experiences and reached the hearts of many people. In fact, they were made for each other and Janet was becoming closer and closer. He did not woo her or try to charm her; he would send her flowers but never red roses; it was as if he had known she had seen too many red roses. He could read her and he knew exactly what she wanted.

Valentine's Day arrived in February 1996 and it was a leap year. "Would you like to be old-fashioned?" Janet asked. She couldn't believe she actually said that. "Why not?" he replied. He had been secretly saving just in case the inevitable happened and so had she. They had enough money for a city apartment. He had no idea she had money in England, he never asked and when she told him he refused to use any of it. "That would be yours, we will make our life together." She stayed with him and they bought an apartment overlooking the sea. They planned to marry in August 1997. Marian supported Janet with her career, with her education, with her friends, and she supported him. They had an adopted family of friends in New Zealand and it was growing with them. He had been married before and he had a daughter whom he lost contact with and Janet encouraged him to rekindle the contact. She invited Ella to their home and Janet loved her as if she were her own daughter. They invited Ella to the wedding.

Janet called her father to break the news. "He's wonderful, he has your name and he is from the same part of Poland," she said to her father. Marian supported Janet in whatever she chose to do and she suggested that they married in England so they could have a family wedding and Ella could be there. She did not want anything fancy and she would actually be happy to marry wearing jeans, but that was not going to happen. Janet had called her friends in Oman and she ordered wedding rings; she sent over the ring sizes.

"What style?" her best friend asked.

"Oh, five diamonds and you can choose the design. That way my best friends will always be with me on my finger and you must bring them over to the wedding." Janet sent the necessary papers to her sister-in-law and the completed the documents. Sadly they could not marry in the church because they were divorced and Marian was Catholic and she was protestant and she had seen enough of tribal warfare to last a lifetime. They opted to marry in a small register office. Janet asked her brother to organize the venue, nothing fancy so they chose the sports center, walking distance from the home of her father. Her brother was to dress up his Volvo car.

Marian invited his best friend from Poland to be best man and Janet took her best friend from New Zealand to be maid of honor. They had flown through Singapore and luckily the sales were in full swing. The girls left Marian enjoying a beer and they went shopping. Janet found a beautiful dark blue cut suit for Marian with shirt, shœs, and tie. She knew his exact size. The girls enjoyed their shopping and they had not intentionally been trying to find a dress, but they were walking through a small mall and there was dress for sale in the window exactly Janet's size. It had a beautiful A-line skirt that swirled as she spun around and it had a beautiful bodice that had hand embroidered sequins and pearls. It fitted perfectly and Janet felt like a princess. They had taken the train from London to Peterborough where the family came to greet them. Janet's father was so happy to see his daughter smiling radiantly and Janet introduced them. "Marian, meet Marian." The two of them spoke in Polish on the journey home. They seemed to joke and laugh together. They spent two days in Boston where Janet's sister-in-law had taken Janet shopping and to get her shœs and small headdress. Janet had her nails done and she had ordered the fresh flowers that were peach roses. The night before the wedding was a family gathering in her father's home and Marian had bought some flowers in pots. They were toasting with their Polish Wabrowka vodka. "Only the best," her father said. Marian got down on his knees in front of Janet's father and made a speech in Polish. He asked her father for Janet's hand in marriage and he promised to take care of her always. Janet had not expected that and her father felt appreciated and respected in the Polish tradition that meant so much to him. They all walked into Boston that evening and celebrated a prewedding night in the gardens of the local pub. They would sing songs and they were all so very happy to be together. They made Marian's daughter very welcome.

The morning of the wedding everyone made the buffet and took it to the dance hall. The cake was not elegant, just two layers from Marks & Spencer. Janet bought a porcelain bride and groom for the top of her cake and her niece made the flowers to decorate the tables. Janet's niece perfected Janet's hair and she actually cut Marian's hair. Then haircut made him look even more handsome.

Janet's brother had taken Marian to the pub for a premarital drink and Janet looked so beautiful in her off-white dress. It was a perfect day with blue skies. There was not a cloud in the sky. Johnny had decorated the car with white ribbons and peach flowers and there were white silk sheets on the inside. Janet's father sat in the car beside her and she looked over to her. "You are not coming back again," he said and smiled and then gave her father to daughter kiss. "I love you baby."

"I know," she said. "This time is the last and I have found my prince, I am so happy." She returned a kiss to her father. "Cut it out you two, the car is steaming up." Her brother smiled as he proudly drove her to the register office. Her father proudly walked into the celebrant's office and handed her to Marian. He looked so handsome and he was proudly waiting for her. "My princess," he said as he took her hand. They said the magic words, kissed, and they all left the registry office which was situated next to St. Bartolph's Church. The gardens were in full bloom of summer flowers. They stopped there and the family had paid for a professional photographer as a gift. The confetti filled the air and seventy-two family and friends posed for photographs. Marian took Janet to the bench under the old oak tree where she raised her dress and the traditional garter fitted perfectly around her thigh showing off her slender legs. "Kiss kiss!" everyone shouted and that they did—they hadn't noticed the photographer take the pictures. Marian and Janet gave a passionate kiss and they both felt themselves lift from the ground. This was for real and this was her day.

They returned to the reception where her father greeted them with a Polish vodka shot and they threw the glasses to the ground for luck and tradition. Janet and Marian danced the first dance. "I'll never find another you." Marian was such a good dancer and they danced so beautifully together. The family and friends applauded them and Janet was to dance with her father and Marian dance with her mother then played the Polish song, "Mariana." They all danced perfectly around the floor. Janet took her brother to the dance floor and Marian danced with her sister-in-law. The dancing never stopped. They played a Polish polka and Janet and her father danced again. Shenk had dressed as a clown and he played some German music, where everyone danced again and then he entertained the children.

Johnny started the speeches. "To my baby sister who would never leave my side and who would win me over so many times and I'm not going to talk about your adventures because that would take me a lifetime, and I wish you and Marian another lifetime of adventures."

Janet's father gave his speech. "To my baby daughter who I have said good-bye too many times and this time it is not snowing. But I know Marian will take good care of you and I welcome our new son." With that they had another vodka toast.

They spent the next night at the holiday home in Skegness where they toasted again and celebrated dinner outside while Shenk played his guitar, Ella and her boyfriend shared stories with the family, and they danced in the garden.

Marian and Janet left the next morning for their honeymoon; he was taking her to Acapulco as he knew she wanted to see the mariachis and Mexico one more time.

Chapter Nineteen

THEY ARRIVED IN Los Angeles and went through customs. "How long do you plan to stay?" The customs officer asked Janet. "Not too long as California would be much safer without me." Janet smiled as it was almost seventeen years since she was last asked that question.

They stopped for a drink in Los Angeles airport—it was not so shiny and new as she had remembered it. "Nothing stays new forever," Janet said to Marian. They had taken the bus to Disneyland. Janet wanted to show Marian the magical land and she wanted to see it once again. Although the skies were blue and the streets were colorful, it did not have the magic she remembered on her first trip. The Guinness was even flatter than the second time she had visited and was served in plastic cups. There were no "people pleasing people" as she had remembered; the service was plastic and so were the plates and cups and full of fast foods. It was not pleasurable to sit down and relax; the queues were twice as long to take any ride. Marian could see her disappointment. "Walt Disney would have a fit if he saw Disneyland today. He built it for everyone and how could every child visit it like this."

"That's capitalism. It's all about money and they have lost the magic and humanity of life." They had a walk around but it was far too crowded so they left and went to a nearby Mexican restaurant. Janet thought she would try another tossed salad. But there was no music and no mariachis and no friendly service. "My, everything has changed so much," she said to Marian. They waited for their bus to return and they set off to the real Mexico.

Janet had chosen a small villa in the old town of Caleta. It was a ten-minute walk up a hill from the beach. She wanted somewhere away from the tourists where she could meet the Mexican people—the real people of the world. The villa had eight bedrooms, a very large lounge, and a moon-shaped swimming pool outside with a large mango tree. There was no glass in the windows but they were quaint wrought iron designs. The floors were of marble and the kitchen had an old gas cooker.

They had arrived in the afternoon and there to greet them was the neighbor. On the table was a welcoming bottle of Tequila. Marian shook hands with the neighbor who was an architect and he had two daughters. Marian began to speak a little Spanish but not enough to have a conversation. The architect's daughter, Ingrid, came to say hello and she had a wonderful command of English; she was very well-educated and she was around fourteen years of age. She was very beautiful and had the longest, waviest Mexican black hair and very olive skin. She did not need any makeup—she was naturally beautiful. She introduced Maria who was cleaning the villa and she would do the washing. Janet was told if they needed anything they were to simply ask. Janet explained that she did not want to go to the typical tourist attractions and that she wanted to enjoy the company of the Mexican people. Janet had seen far too many hotels in her life. Ingrid said she would help and Marian invited Ingrid and her family to join them for dinner. Not that they had bought any food to cook. Janet asked if Ingrid knew someone who would cook for them. That was not a problem and Maria came to cook dinner. The Guerra family came to dinner that evening. They all sat outside and enjoyed the sea air. The moon shone over the villa and reflected over the swimming pool.

"You speak very good English," Janet told Ingrid,

"Yes, I am very fortunate. I go to a private school."

"I was in Mexico for a very small time, I was in Tijuana many years ago. I know some people do not see Tijuana, the real Mexico."

"We are all Mexican—different cities—but we are very Mexican," Ingrid replied.

"I love the bright colors of Mexico and I adore the mariachis and their music. Do you know where we can find a good band?" Ingrid knew of many places and she said she would ask if her father would take them some places. "That would be wonderful," Janet replied, "thank you so much." Maria had prepared a dinner of enchiladas and salad that was just perfect for the evening. Marian had brought some Corona beers and he had brought some Polish vodka with him. They would toast the Polish way and then the Mexican way. The Slav heart and the Mexican heart were very similar in that they were alive and they knew how to enjoy life and share life with their family and friends. The family would enjoy the conversation and Ingrid would translate the whole evening. Ingrid had brought some mariachi music and they danced all night. Ingrid's father would teach Janet to dance, Ingrid and her mother would teach Marian to dance the Mexican way. They were one night in Mexico and the couple had bonded with the Mexican family. Marian and Janet were so much in love and they were dancing together; Janet knew she would never be lonely and her life would always be full of magic.

Ingrid's father offered to take them out to the sailing club in Caleta. The next morning, they walked down the hill to the bakery, they passed many villas and the beautiful colors of the hanging flowers fell down the walls of every villa. "Hola," they would say to the people of the small town. "Hola, gringos!" A small boy would follow them down the road and Marian would give the small boy a few pesetas. The smell of the fresh bread was something Janet had not encountered for many years. It was a sweet smell as it mingled with the Mexican sea air. They arrived at the sailing club where they were served a lunch of tacos and it blended beautifully with the Corona beer which was served with a slice of lemon and salt. They made their way to the boat, it was very large and the blue and white colors of the boat contrasted beautifully with the green sea. On board they sailed through the bay of Acapulco, the high-rise hotels and the white sands and palm trees looked brilliantly crisp and clean as they sailed around the Pacific Ocean. The sea was not as calm as the glass turquoise seas of Oman, and it was rather wild, and the boat sprays were much whiter as it foamed the boat's trail behind them. They sailed a few hours out from Acapulco until there was nothing but blue skies and the wild seas of the Pacific. Janet was sitting over the front of the boat and beside her came a pod of oceanic dolphins—she counted them—there were twelve and from the other side came another pod of oceanic dolphins. They joined at the front of the boat. This super pod of dolphins performed in front of them. The dolphins would take turns two at a time and would jump out of the ocean about fifteen feet into the air. They would splash back into the water. Janet must have taken a hundred snapshots with her camera. "There are not only snakes in the world, there are dolphins too," she had remembered her father's words that had given her gave her optimism. Her Mexican family was her dolphins. They were surrounded by dolphins both on and off the boat.

Janet, Marian, and the family returned back to Caleta and Janet could not thank the family for their kindness and showing her a world where not only the pods of dolphins came together but how people from around the world could be so beautiful and happy together. They spent another happy evening with the family by the poolside.

The next morning Janet woke very early; she could hear the birds in the trees and there was a very loud sound as if it was an alarm clock. Janet walked out to the poolside and there was this beautiful colored parrot standing on the wall. He was making random noises as if to say, "Look at me, I am here." Janet smiled at the parrot and wondered if it was descendent to Taffy's parrot from when she had stayed in California. She was not going to feed this parrot the tequila worm. The parrot would wake them every morning. Janet would laze under the sun, floating in the pool until late afternoon as it was too hot to go to the beach. Marian would sit in his own world drinking a Corona beer under the mango tree and Maria would bring them a cooked breakfast every morning.

They had taken the small bus at the bottom of the hill to the main stretch of Acapulco. The bus was alive—it had disco lights and music, everything was dressed in bright and happy colors and although the people had very little, they knew how to great everyone with "Hola." They would stop and help the old ladies off the bus. They would carry the heavy bags onto the bus. They were very caring. Marian and Janet were followed down the streets as small children were selling their chicolata gum. Marian would give the children a few pesetas and he would tell them to keep the gum. There was a whole line of children behind them. Janet would turn around and sing "La Cucaracha," the children would clap. They would sing too. "If I won the lottery, I would throw it all in the air right here." Janet had remembered the fun she had in Tijuana. Marian threw a few dollars for the children. "I would do that too," he smiled at Janet. "I have worked in many places and I have lived the grand life but nothing could replace this. Money is just a vehicle and as long as you pay the bills, you will be blessed if you share what you have with the less fortunate." Marian had taken the words right out of her mouth and she loved him for that. They walked a little further and on the roadside was a beautiful grey horse attached to a carriage and the cart was trimmed with bright pink balloons. The horse's coat was steaming. He looked to be tired and so did the small Mexican man wearing his sombrero and bright Mexican blanket. Janet felt sorry for the two of them, the horse and the young man. They must have been worn out from the tourists taking romantic rides from the previous night. Marian gave the man ten dollars. "For you and the horse." They did not want to ride as they knew the horse needed food so they walked along the roadside, Marian on one side of the horse and Janet on the other. The man came back with apples, and he passed one to Janet. He had left them minding the horse. "That was trust," Janet said to Marian. She took an apple in her hand, she twisted it so it became two halves and she held it out to the horse who fed from her. "He likes you, señorita," said the young Mexican man. "Horses are no fools, they know who to trust and they will only take food if they trust you." She once again had remembered her father's words. They gave the man another ten dollars. "This is for your children." The left and they stopped at one of the small cantinas that sat over the beach. Marian and Janet enjoyed a Corona beer as they watched over the ocean they sat until the sun set over the horizon. The mariachis played romantic music; Marian gave them a generous tip and the mariachis stayed there the whole evening. They knew that the tip was from the heart. They dined there that evening. They chose the same seafood dish and they listened to the Mexican music. Various Mexicans would arrive carrying blankets for sale and other goods. Janet already had kept her collection from Tijuana but she would always buy something. Marian and Janet had such big hearts and they were not very good at bartering but it was not about what they paid, it was seeing the happiness on the face of the locals as they knew they had money to take home and feed their children.

Ingrid and her family took the couple to a Mexican restaurant overlooking the sea, it was private and there were no tourists to be seen there. The mariachis were there dressed in their white suits and wore hats (sombreros). One played a violin; another, a guitar; two lifted muted trumpets, and the smallest of them held tightly to his guitarrón, an oversized, bass version of the guitar. They were mariachis. Janet wondered if they were the same mariachis from Tijuana as she remembered her time in Tijuana and the cantina there. This time was very different as she was with Marian. They played "La Cucaracha" and Janet stood up and danced with the waiters. She ordered a tossed salad and Ingrid tried to warn her, "I know they throw in spices and eggs and they throw it in the air with their hands." She looked at Ingrid. "I trust them and the salad is so beautiful and he has probably been doing this job for a very long time."

"Oh, since I was little," Ingrid replied. Janet felt so much at home in Mexico and she just could not get enough of its hospitality.

Marian and Janet hired a car and a driver and they travelled ten kilometers to the Pie de la Cuesta Coyuca lagoon from Acapulco. There they hired a small boat and a boatman. The boat was made of very old wood and had a small motor and two posts on each side of the boat carried a thatched roof to protect them from the sun. They took a three-hour trip around the lagoon where they enjoyed seeking out the wildlife. Janet was wearing a straw hat to protect her from the sun and a blue cotton dress. It was on this very lagoon where the *African Queen* was filmed in the 1950s. Janet sat close to Marian as they sailed around the lagoon which was some 10.5 miles long and around 5 miles wide. The hills of the Sierra Madre were a spectacular site in the backdrop of the lagoon. Janet felt like a queen as they had a personal tour around the lagoon. They had paid the young Mexican extra money to take them to the Parador Del Sol resort which sits between the lagoon and the Pacific Ocean. The young man dropped them off at what looked to be a resort and he helped them onto the sandy embankment and then he had disappeared. Marian and Janet were stranded on the sandy beach and they walked toward what they thought to be the resort. There was a swimming pool but it was still under construction and as they walked toward the building they were approached by what appeared to be a young Mexican soldier. He was wearing a dark green uniform and he carried a shotgun. They had been left stranded at a private hacienda which was closed to the locals and the public. Janet and Marian were escorted to the roadside via the plantation by a very serious Mexican and he was holding the shotgun as if the couple were a pair of convicts. Once on the very barren road the soldier disappeared and the couple where alone in the middle of nowhere. *I'm on the road to nowhere and I'm feeling okay this morning, and you know, we're on the road to paradise here we go, here we go,* she began to sing and dance in the middle of nowhere. Marian joined in the fun. They just kept walking in the direction that would hopefully take them to the Parador Del Sol. They had been walking for more than one hour on the desolate road; Janet was very dry as they had not any refreshments with them. Fortunately the local bus stopped to pick them up. The driver held out his hand and he helped Janet onto the bus. It was very dusty and all of the windows were cracked; it was very hot and there was no air conditioning. For one peseta he dropped them off at the resort they had been looking for. There they lazed in hammocks drinking the Coco Locos as they enjoyed watching the high waves of the Pacific crash against the sandy beach. They had the whole beach to themselves. The hotel waiters brought them the most beautifully grilled seafood and they enjoyed the afternoon under the sun.

The couple arrived home late that evening where Ingrid's family were waiting to great them; Janet had just a few minutes to change as they were taking them to a nightclub where they could enjoy Mexican dancing. Ingrid had a small package and she gave Marian a collection of music from the mariachis and the Mexican dance music. Marian was overwhelmed with their kindness. That night the salsa club was full of Mexican people enjoying the music. There was a large dance floor and above it were four coves lined with colored satin curtains and the floodlights brought out the bright colors of the tight fitting salsa dresses. The young dancing couples danced elegantly and romantically in the coves and Ingrid's family and friends taught Janet and Marian to dance Mexican style.

The honeymoon was coming to an end; Janet and Marian spent most of their time with their Mexican family who took them around Mexico. They drove them up into the hills where Janet could see how some of the poorer Mexican people were living. They were living in huts with corrugated roofing. Empty Coca-Cola bottles would sometimes cover their homes. There were live wire cables on the roadsides as they tapped into the energy for their homes. The hillsides of Mexico were something that Marian and Janet would never forget and they would realize just how lucky they were every time they took a shower or turned on the electric light. This only strengthened their kindness to help those in need.

They spent their last night at the villa with Ingrid and her family who brought many of their friends, they drank tequila and danced until early hours of the morning. There was a celebration in the town of Caleta that night and the fireworks filled the skies, the rainbows of colors cascaded down upon them. "Disneyland did come to Mexico," Janet looked at Marian and he said, "Yes, and the prince will take Sleeping Beauty to bed."

Chapter Twenty

T WAS WET, windy, and raining when they arrived back in New Zealand. It was normal for that time of year. They were sitting comfortably in their new home sharing a glass of wine and looking at their wedding photographs. Marian turned on the television and the news said that Princess Diana was killed in a car crash; it was August 31ˑ 1997. Janet's heart sank and she wept. "Diana was four years younger than me. She was the same birth sign and she was the caring Cancer princess. I remembered crying at her wedding. She was having the fairy tale and mine was coming to an end. She had the bulimia when I had overcome mine, she had to fight for her prince as I had to fight for mine. She divorced when I found you. She found love again where the two seas met and entwined and the tribal forces tried to pull them apart and I know only too well how that felt. I truly hope the world will change through this and that cultures learn to accept differences and love one another and learn to live together because only when the world learns to integrate there will be peace. God bless you, Diana." Marian put his arms around Janet and comforted her as she wept and fell asleep in his arms. "Sleep well, my princess, I will never leave you," he whispered to her.

They were happy to be in their new home and they lived happily there for fifteen years. They opened doors to many new migrants and would help those in need. Marian supported her with her career and her life. They would make frequent trips to Europe to visit family. They travelled through Thailand, Kuala Lumpur, Hong Kong, Korea and had many wonderful romantic adventures together. They had gained an extended family in New Zealand and they had so many friends surrounding them. They would look back and paint pictures of their life. Janet had been welcomed into the homes of many families from all around the world, many new migrants, and many refugees. They would share stories and heal their wounds together. They had made friends from all around the world: Maori, Pacific Islanders, Australia, New Zealanders, Afghanistan, Pakistan, Iran, Iraq, Kurdistan, Serbia, India, Sri Lanka, Thailand, the Philippines, China, Japan, South Africa, Germany, Poland. Czechoslovakia, Croatia, Russia, Peru, Brazil, Cuba and many more. They were living in Aotearoa, New Zealand—the Land of the Big White Cloud where culture is celebrated in an integrated New Zealand.

It was the evening of their fifteenth wedding anniversary and their closest friends had gathered around their home. They had taken Janet's photographs from her adventures and they had put them on a disc. Her whole life was flashing on the screen in front of her. She would relive the stories as the pictures reflected her past. Family and friends would laugh and cry with her. "I have had a wonderful journey, it has been full of laughter and tears and I have lived my fairy tale. I have loved and lost love and I have found love again. More so, I have learnt from the heartache and that has made me a more compassionate person. I want all of you to live a fairy tale but with a lot less pain." She turned to her music and she played Judith Durham singing the old Seekers hit, *Join in the journey to every corner of your dreams, yours and mine and all mankind.* The whole family of friends danced and sang with her. The song had finished and the children were playing in the garden. "Tell her she can't play with me," Janet heard the little voices as she recollected the times with her brother. She opened the window and she yelled, "LET IT BE!"

CPSIA information can be obtained at www.ICGtesting.com
Printed in the USA
LVOW06s1620030614

388433LV00004B/491/P